The Promise We Didn't Plan

THE PEOPLE OF CEDAR RIDGE, BOOK 1

Written by Diane Kann

Brought to you by Volans Galaxy Press

Published by Kannceptual Creations LLC

An imprint of Volans Galaxy Press

ISBN: 978-1-971356-48-8

Printed in the United States of America

First Edition, January 2026

Contents

Dedication

To those who returned home carrying more than memories.
To the ones who learned that love doesn't always arrive on schedule,
and that the promises that change us most
are often the ones we never meant to make.

This story is for the hearts that have known loss,
the souls brave enough to begin again,
and anyone who has discovered that healing sometimes comes quietly—
through shared silences, unexpected hands held,
and love that grows not from perfection,
but from choosing to stay.

May these pages remind you
that even when life unravels your plans,
it can still offer something tender, lasting,
and beautifully unplanned.

— *Diane Kann*

Author's Biography

Diane Kann writes sweet romance stories that celebrate love, second chances, and the quiet moments that change everything. Her stories focus on emotional connection, gentle healing, and relationships built on trust, hope, and heart.

When she's not writing, Diane enjoys spending time in nature with her family and dogs, finding inspiration in peaceful landscapes and everyday moments, and dreaming up tender stories rooted in compassion.

Chapter 1 The Return to Cedar Ridge

The crunch of gravel under Clara Bennett's tires was a sound both alien and achingly familiar. It was the soundtrack to her arrival, a dusty fanfare announcing her return to Cedar Ridge after a decade's absence. The car, a sensible sedan that had seen better days, coughed and sputtered its way down the unpaved lane leading to her childhood home, kicking up a plume of red earth that hung in the still, late-afternoon air. Main Street, when she finally reached it, was a postcard from her past, stubbornly resisting the march of time. The same faded awning of Miller's General Store, the same slightly crooked sign for "The Daily Grind" coffee shop, the same weathered brick façade of the library. Yet, the stillness, the quiet hum of a town that seemed to operate on its own rhythm, was a stark contrast to the ceaseless thrum of the city she had fled.

A decade. Ten years had etched themselves onto the landscape of her memory, transforming youthful impressions into something more complex, tinged with both fondness and a lingering unease. She'd come seeking solace, a quiet antidote to the city's incessant demands and the gnawing echoes of a life that had recently imploded. The concrete jungle had become too loud, too demanding, its artificial lights unable to penetrate the shadows that had begun to gather around her. Cedar Ridge, in its unassuming way, promised a different kind of light, a gentler illumination.

She rolled down the window, allowing the air to flood the car. It was a scent she'd nearly forgotten, a potent blend of pine needles and damp earth, the subtle perfume of an impending rain shower. It was a scent that spoke of roots, of stability, of a world that moved at a pace dictated by seasons rather than deadlines. It was a balm to her frayed nerves, a silent whisper of comfort that seeped into her very bones. The city had offered only exhaust fumes and the sterile scent of recycled air. This, this was real.

Her childhood home stood at the edge of town, a sentinel on a slight rise overlooking the sprawling pines. It was as she remembered it, and yet, profoundly different. The porch swing, once a vibrant splash of robin's egg blue, was now chipped and faded. The paint on the clapboard siding, a soft butter yellow in her memory, was peeling in places, revealing the weathered wood beneath. It was a house that had seen better days, a house that bore the marks of time and, perhaps, a certain neglect. But it was still standing. It was solid. And in that solidity, Clara found a flicker of the stability she so desperately craved. Her life had felt like a house of cards, easily toppled by the slightest gust of wind. This house, this weathered, quiet structure, felt like an anchor, a tangible link to a past that, for all its complexities, had offered a sense of permanence.

She parked the car, the engine falling silent with a sigh that seemed to mirror her own exhaustion. Stepping out, she felt a strange sensation, as if the very ground beneath her feet was acknowledging her return. It was a grounding, a sense of belonging that had eluded her for years. The city had offered anonymity, a cloak she had worn with a mixture of relief and a growing sense of isolation. Here, she suspected, anonymity would be a luxury she couldn't afford. Cedar Ridge was a town where everyone knew everyone, a place where lives were intertwined like the intricate patterns of a well-worn quilt. It was this very intimacy that both drew her in and sent a ripple of apprehension through her. She was returning with ghosts, and she wasn't sure if this small town, so steeped in its own history, was ready to welcome hers.

She walked towards the house, the overgrown path crunching underfoot. The porch creaked in protest as she stepped onto it, a familiar, mournful sound. The front door, a solid oak, was unlocked, just as she'd left it a decade ago, a testament to a simpler time, a time before locks felt necessary. Pushing it open, she was met by the scent of dust and disuse, a faint aroma of lemon polish long since faded. The furniture, draped in white sheets, loomed like pale specters in the dim light filtering through the lace-curtained windows. It was a tableau frozen in time, a museum of her childhood, each object holding a story, a memory waiting to be resurrected.

She made her way to the living room, her footsteps echoing in the quiet space. The grand piano, a cherished heirloom, sat in the corner, its lid closed, a silent monument to hours of practice and whispered melodies. She ran a hand over the dusty surface, a faint tremor in her fingers. Music had always been her solace, a language she understood when words failed her. But lately, even the keys had felt cold, unresponsive to the turmoil within her.

Her gaze drifted to the mantelpiece, where a framed photograph sat, slightly askew. It was her and her aunt, taken years ago, both of them smiling, younger, carefree. Her aunt, a woman of robust laughter and an even more robust appetite for life, had been the heart of this house, and, in many ways, the heart of Cedar Ridge's Community Hall and Pantry. The thought of her aunt brought a fresh wave of grief, a sharp ache in Clara's chest. Her aunt's passing had been the catalyst for this return, a duty call she couldn't ignore, a final request that had pulled her back from the life she'd built, or perhaps, more accurately, the life that had been dismantled around her.

She moved through the house, opening windows, letting the fresh, pine-scented air chase away the mustiness. Each room held a memory, a ghost of a past self. The kitchen, with its checkered linoleum floor and the worn butcher block counter, where her aunt had taught her to bake. The small study, filled with overflowing bookshelves, where her aunt had kept the records for the Hall, a place of quiet industry and endless cups of tea. And her childhood bedroom, with its floral wallpaper and the window overlooking the sprawling oak in the backyard, a tree she had climbed countless times, a silent witness to her youthful dreams and adolescent angst.

As she stood in the center of her old bedroom, a profound sense of weariness washed over her. It was more than physical exhaustion; it was the heavy cloak of responsibility, the weight of a past she couldn't outrun, and the daunting uncertainty of a future she hadn't yet begun to sketch. The city had offered escape, but it had also stripped her bare, leaving her vulnerable and adrift. Cedar Ridge, with its familiar embrace, offered a chance to rebuild, but the foundations felt shaky, uncertain. She was a solitary figure in a town that thrived on connection, a woman carrying a burden she was determined to bear alone. The thought of asking for help, of admitting her need, felt like a betrayal of the self-reliance she had so painstakingly cultivated in the harsh crucible of her recent past.

The scent of pine and rain, once a welcome balm, now seemed to carry a subtle undertone of obligation. The house, her childhood sanctuary, had become a stark reminder of what was at stake, not just for her, but for the town she had left behind. The Community Hall and Pantry, a place woven into the very fabric of her memories, was in peril. Her aunt, in her final days, had entrusted its care to Clara, a responsibility Clara felt woefully unprepared to handle. The weight of her aunt's legacy, coupled with the echoes of her own past failures, settled upon Clara's shoulders, a burden she was determined not to share. She would face this challenge alone, just as she had faced so many other challenges, a solitary warrior against the tide of circumstance.

The late afternoon sun cast long shadows across the room, painting the familiar landscape in hues of gold and amber. It was a beautiful, bittersweet light, a fitting accompaniment to her homecoming. As the shadows deepened, Clara knew she couldn't simply unpack her belongings. She had to unpack her past, confront the ghosts that still lingered, and somehow, find a way to build a future in the quiet embrace of Cedar Ridge.

The path ahead was uncertain, shrouded in the same twilight that was now enveloping the small town, but for the first time in a long time, it felt like a path she could walk, even if it was a solitary one. She closed her eyes, taking a deep breath, and let the scent of pine and rain fill her lungs, a reminder of the promise, and the peril, of this unexpected return. The dust, still swirling outside, felt like a metaphor for her own unsettled life, a tangible representation of the disruption her arrival had brought, a disruption that was only just beginning.

She was home, but the journey was far from over; in many ways, it was just beginning to unfold, with all its unexpected turns and hidden challenges. The house stood silent, waiting. And Clara, standing in its quiet embrace, knew she had a great deal of work to do, not just on the house, but on herself. The echoes of the past were here, in every creaking floorboard, in every shaft of dusty light, and she would have to learn to live with them, perhaps even learn from them, if she were to find any semblance of peace in this place she once called home. The weight of it all pressed down, a familiar, almost comforting pressure. She was ready to begin, even if "alone" was the only word she could truly grasp.

The afternoon light, which had initially held a soft, welcoming glow, began to deepen, painting the familiar landscape of Cedar Ridge in long, melancholic shadows. Clara stood in the quietude of her aunt's study, a room that still held the faint, comforting scent of old paper and Earl Grey tea. It was a scent that spoke of her aunt's life, a life dedicated to the community, to the well-being of this small town she had loved so fiercely. But now, that life was extinguished, leaving behind not just memories, but a complex legacy that had landed squarely in Clara's lap.

She had spent the last hour sifting through stacks of papers, her aunt's meticulous handwriting a constant companion. Bills, invoices, donation requests, ledgers filled with rows and columns of numbers that told a story of dwindling resources and increasing expenses. It was a story Clara had braced herself for, but the reality of it was far more stark than she had anticipated. Her aunt, bless her generous heart, had poured everything she had into the Community Hall and Pantry, her own finances seemingly secondary to the needs of others. The building, a beloved landmark that had hosted countless town events, bake sales, and holiday gatherings, was clearly in a state of disrepair. Leaky pipes, a sputtering furnace, and a roof that had seen better decades were just a few of the issues Clara's initial assessment had revealed.

But it wasn't just the physical structure that was ailing. The pantry shelves, once overflowing with canned goods, fresh produce, and non-perishables, were now sparsely populated. A quick inventory confirmed Clara's worst fears: the donations had slowed to a trickle, and the demand, predictably, had continued to rise. Children who had once brought their mothers to the pantry with hopeful eyes were now coming alone, their small faces etched with a worry far beyond their years. This wasn't just a building in need of renovation; it was a lifeline fraying at the edges.

Then there were the numbers. The debt. It wasn't just a few overdue notices; it was a substantial sum, accumulated over months, perhaps even years, as her aunt had struggled to keep the doors open, to continue providing for those who relied on the pantry. Clara's fingers traced the figures on a particularly damning invoice, her breath catching in her throat. It was a weight, a crushing, suffocating weight, that settled deep within her chest. This was more than a financial burden; it was an emotional one, a tangible manifestation of her aunt's final, desperate struggle.

A sigh escaped Clara's lips, a sound heavy with the unspoken. She had come back to Cedar Ridge seeking refuge, a quiet place to lick her wounds and figure out what came next. She had envisioned days spent tending to the house, reconnecting with the familiar rhythms of small-town life, and slowly, tentatively, rebuilding herself. She hadn't envisioned inheriting a crumbling institution, a community's well-being resting on her shoulders, a mountain of debt threatening to swallow her whole.

The instinct to retreat, to turn tail and flee back to the anonymous embrace of the city, was a powerful one. It whispered temptations of escape, of a life unburdened by the needs of others. But the image of her aunt, her kind eyes and her unwavering dedication, flashed in Clara's mind. Her aunt wouldn't have wanted this. She wouldn't have wanted the pantry to close, the Hall to fall into disuse, the community to suffer. She had poured her life into this place, and now, in her absence, it was falling apart.

Clara's gaze drifted to a framed photograph on the desk. It was a picture of her aunt, beaming, standing in front of the Community Hall, a banner proclaiming "Cedar Ridge Community Hall – Est. 1952" draped across the entrance. The Hall looked vibrant in the photo, alive with the energy of a community united. It was a stark contrast to the worn, faded reality Clara had witnessed earlier that day.

A familiar knot of anxiety tightened in Clara's stomach. She had always struggled with relying on others. As a child, she had been fiercely independent, a trait her aunt had often praised, but also subtly cautioned against. "There's strength in numbers, Clara-bug," she'd say, her voice warm and reassuring. "No one has to carry the world on their own shoulders." But Clara had never truly learned to share that load. The city had only amplified this tendency. The fast-paced, competitive environment had demanded self-reliance, a constant striving for individual success. Asking for help was often perceived as a weakness, a sign of inadequacy.

And now, here she was, faced with a situation that demanded collaboration, a willingness to lean on the very community she had so long avoided. The thought of asking for donations, for volunteers, for financial assistance, sent a fresh wave of dread through her. It meant exposing her own vulnerabilities, admitting that she couldn't do it all on her own. It meant facing the possibility of rejection, of seeing the same pitying glances she had so often tried to avoid.

She picked up a small, worn ledger from the desk, its pages brittle with age. Inside, her aunt had recorded every single donation, every single person who had benefited from the pantry's services. There were names Clara recognized from her childhood, families she knew had fallen on hard times. There were also names of people she didn't know, individuals whose struggles were a testament to the ongoing needs of the community. Each entry was a testament to her aunt's compassion, her unwavering belief in the inherent goodness of people, and her commitment to helping those less fortunate.

Clara ran a finger down a column of figures, her mind racing. Her aunt had been a master at stretching a dollar, at making do with whatever she had. But even her ingenuity had its limits. The current deficit was simply too large to overcome with her aunt's usual methods. It would require a significant influx of resources, a concerted effort from the entire town.

She closed her eyes, picturing the faces of the people she had seen on Main Street that afternoon. The baker, his hands dusted with flour, who always had a warm smile and a free sample. The librarian, her spectacles perched on the end of her nose, who had lent Clara countless books when she was a lonely child. The elderly gentleman who ran the hardware store, his gruff exterior hiding a surprisingly kind heart. These were the people who made up Cedar Ridge, the people her aunt had served with such dedication.

Could she ask them for help? Could she, Clara Bennett, the city dweller who had fled this town ten years ago, now expect them to rally around her, to trust her with the legacy her aunt had so carefully nurtured? The fear of being a burden, a reliance, clawed at her. It was a deeply ingrained fear, a residue of past experiences that had taught her that independence was the safest path.

She remembered a time, years ago, when a project at work had gone disastrously wrong. She had been so proud of her initial concept, so confident in her abilities, that she had refused to delegate, to ask for input from her colleagues. The result had been a spectacular failure, a public embarrassment that had cost her dearly. The sting of that failure had never quite faded, serving as a constant reminder of her perceived inability to collaborate effectively.

And then there were the more personal failures, the relationships that had crumbled under the weight of her own emotional reticence. She had always kept people at arm's length, afraid of what might happen if they got too close, if they saw the cracks in her carefully constructed façade.

The weight of the inheritance felt heavier now, not just in terms of financial responsibility, but in the challenge it posed to her ingrained patterns of behavior. This wasn't just about saving a building; it was about confronting her own deeply held fears, about learning to trust and to accept help.

She walked over to the window, looking out at the darkening sky. The first stars were beginning to prick through the twilight, tiny points of light in the vast expanse. They seemed so distant, so unreachable, much like the sense of peace and stability she craved.

Her aunt had left her a monumental task, a legacy of service that Clara felt utterly unqualified to uphold. But as she stood there, surrounded by the tangible evidence of her aunt's devotion, a flicker of something akin to resolve began to stir within her. It wasn't the fierce, unyielding independence she had always relied on, but something softer, something more vulnerable. It was the dawning realization that perhaps, just perhaps, she didn't have to carry this burden entirely alone.

The path ahead was daunting, shrouded in uncertainty, but for the first time since arriving back in Cedar Ridge, Clara felt a stirring of possibility, a faint hope that she might, with help, find a way to honor her aunt's memory and rebuild not just the Community Hall and Pantry, but a part of herself that had long been neglected. The challenge was immense, the fear palpable, but the quiet determination to try, to at least attempt to shoulder this inherited burden, was slowly, steadily, taking root. She took a deep, steadying breath, the scent of pine and damp earth filling her lungs, a reminder of the roots that, for better or worse, still held her here.

The late afternoon sun, a tired, golden hue, slanted through the grimy windows of the Cedar Ridge Community Hall, illuminating the dust motes dancing in the air like tiny, forgotten spirits. Clara pushed open the heavy oak door, its hinges groaning a mournful protest that echoed in the cavernous space. The air inside was thick with the scent of disuse – a musty combination of stale air, old wood, and something faintly metallic, like forgotten tools left to rust. This was it, the heart of her aunt's final endeavors, the place that had consumed so much of Eleanor's energy and, Clara now knew, her finances.

She'd anticipated wear and tear; the invoice mentioned a roof needing repair. But the reality was a stark, gut-wrenching testament to years of neglect, a slow decay that had crept in like a silent thief. Peeling paint curled away from the walls like sunburnt skin, revealing the drab plaster beneath. In the main hall, a large, irregular stain bloomed across the acoustic tiles of the ceiling, a dark map of a persistent leak.

Clara traced its edges with her eyes, imagining the water damage seeping into the floorboards below, into the very structure of the building. She could almost hear the drip, drip, drip, a relentless rhythm that spoke of rot and ruin. The once-vibrant parquet floor, where generations of Cedar Ridge residents had danced at holiday parties and wedding receptions, was now scuffed and worn, gouged in places by furniture that had clearly been dragged rather than lifted.

She stepped further into the hall, her footsteps unnervingly loud in the silence. This space, she remembered, was the lifeblood of Cedar Ridge. It was where the annual chili cook-off was held, the bake sales that funded the local Little League, the Christmas tree lighting ceremony that drew every soul in town. She pictured it filled with laughter, with the murmur of excited chatter, with the joyous cacophony of children's squeals. Now, it was an empty shell, its former vibrancy a distant memory, a ghost haunting its decaying frame.

Her gaze drifted to the stage at the far end of the hall. It was a simple platform, draped with a faded, moth-eaten velvet curtain that hung in limp, sad folds. She remembered seeing local school plays performed here, amateur theatricals that were more charm than polish, but always filled with heart. The backdrop, a painted panorama of a quaint village scene, was cracked and peeling, the colors muted by time and exposure. Even the stage lights, hanging limply from their fixtures, seemed weary, as if they too had given up the ghost.

Clara walked towards the stage, her hand trailing along a chipped wooden pillar. She imagined her aunt, Eleanor, standing here, her voice ringing out with encouragement as she welcomed newcomers, thanked volunteers, or announced the winner of the pie-eating contest. Eleanor had a way of making everyone feel seen, valued. She'd built this place, not just brick by brick, but through a tireless dedication to fostering connection, to nurturing the bonds that held this small town together. And now, it was crumbling.

A chill, unrelated to the building's draftiness, snaked down Clara's spine. This wasn't just about a leaky roof or peeling paint. This was about the erosion of a community's anchor, the slow dissolution of a vital hub that had served as Cedar Ridge's living room for decades. She'd always been a city person, comfortable in the anonymity of crowds, in the constant hum of urban life. Cedar Ridge had always felt like a postcard, charming but somewhat static. But seeing the Hall like this, seeing the tangible evidence of her aunt's final, desperate fight, stirred something within her. It was more than just a building; it was a repository of shared memories, a testament to a legacy of service that felt too precious to let wither and die.

She moved towards a side room, likely the former kitchen, envisioning the countless volunteers who had slaved over hot stoves here, preparing meals for town events, organizing food drives. The counters were stained, the linoleum cracked. A rusted-out sink stood as a monument to neglect. Even the shelves, which should have been stocked with supplies for the pantry, were bare, save for a few cobwebs and a forgotten, dust-covered can of beans. It was a stark visual representation of the dwindling resources her aunt had battled.

The sheer scale of the task ahead began to press down on Clara. It wasn't just financial; it was the sheer physical labor, the organization, the rallying of a community that, from her brief observations, seemed to be more accustomed to looking after its own problems than to rallying behind a single, grand cause. She remembered her aunt's pleas in her letters, her subtle hints about the Hall's struggles. Clara, in her self-imposed exile, had dismissed them as the worries of an aging woman, perhaps a touch too sentimental about a building. Now, she saw the truth in her aunt's words, the quiet desperation that had underpinned them.

She walked back into the main hall, the emptiness of the space amplifying the weight of her responsibility. The silence was no longer just an absence of noise; it felt like a heavy shroud, muffling the echoes of past celebrations. But as she stood there, the fading light casting long shadows that seemed to swallow the room, a different feeling began to emerge. It wasn't the panic she had expected, or the overwhelming urge to flee. Instead, it was a quiet, determined resolve. Her aunt had poured her life into this place, into this community. To let it crumble into dust would be to betray not just Eleanor, but the spirit of Cedar Ridge itself.

She imagined the doors of the pantry being permanently closed, the shelves remaining bare. She pictured the elderly struggling to find affordable food, the single mothers unable to stretch their meager budgets further, the children's faces falling as they were told there was nothing left. The thought was unbearable. Her aunt, in her final years, had been a bulwark against such hardship for so many. Clara couldn't, wouldn't, let that bulwark fall.

A tiny spark ignited within her, a flicker of defiance against the encroaching decay. It was the same spark that had driven her to succeed in the city, the same tenacity she'd applied to her career. But this time, it wasn't about personal ambition. It was about stewardship, about honoring a legacy. The Hall was more than just a building; it was a symbol. It represented generosity, community spirit, and the quiet strength of a small town. And it deserved to be saved.

She looked around the hall again, her gaze sharper now, less filled with despair and more with a critical assessment. She noticed the sturdy beams supporting the ceiling, the solid construction of the walls. It was damaged, yes, but it wasn't beyond repair. It was a project, a monumental one, but a project nonetheless. And projects, Clara knew, could be tackled, bit by bit, with planning, and with help.

The thought of asking for help, however, still sent a tremor of apprehension through her. It was a deeply ingrained aversion, a vulnerability she had learned to mask. But here, in the ghost of her aunt's cherished Community Hall, that aversion began to feel... less important. The needs of this place, of the people it served, outweighed her own discomfort.

She walked over to a dusty bulletin board, still adorned with faded flyers advertising events from years past. A photograph, tacked crookedly, showed a younger Eleanor beaming, surrounded by a crowd of smiling faces at a summer picnic. Clara recognized some of them – Mrs. Gable from the bakery, Mr. Henderson from the hardware store, even a younger, less weathered version of Sheriff Brody. They looked happy, connected, a community united. A faint smile touched Clara's lips. Perhaps, just perhaps, these were the people who could help her bring the Hall back to life.

Perhaps Cedar Ridge, despite its faded glow, still held enough warmth to rekindle its heart. The path ahead was daunting, the challenges immense, but for the first time since stepping back onto the soil of her childhood town, Clara felt a nascent sense of purpose, a quiet determination to try and reignite the fading glow of the Hall. It was a daunting prospect, but one that felt, in its own way, like coming home. She took a deep breath, the musty air filling her lungs, and knew, with a certainty that surprised her, that she wouldn't let this place fall. She owed it to Eleanor, and she owed it to Cedar Ridge. The task was immense, the fear palpable, but the dawning realization that she might not have to face it entirely alone, was a flicker of hope in the deepening twilight.

The late afternoon sun, a tired, golden hue, slanted through the grimy windows of the Cedar Ridge Community Hall, illuminating the dust motes dancing in the air like tiny, forgotten spirits. Clara pushed open the heavy oak door, its hinges groaning a mournful protest that echoed in the cavernous space. The air inside was thick with the scent of disuse – a musty combination of stale air, old wood, and something faintly metallic, like forgotten tools left to rust. This was it, the heart of her aunt's final endeavors, the place that had consumed so much of Eleanor's energy and, Clara now knew, her finances.

She'd anticipated wear and tear; the invoice mentioned a roof needing repair. But the reality was a stark, gut-wrenching testament to years of neglect, a slow decay that had crept in like a silent thief. Peeling paint curled away from the walls like sunburnt skin, revealing the drab plaster beneath. In the main hall, a large, irregular stain bloomed across the acoustic tiles of the ceiling, a dark map of a persistent leak. Clara traced its edges with her eyes, imagining the water damage seeping into the floorboards below, into the very structure of the building. She could almost hear the drip, drip, drip, a relentless rhythm that spoke of rot and ruin. The once-vibrant parquet floor, where generations of Cedar Ridge residents had danced at holiday parties and wedding receptions, was now scuffed and worn, gouged in places by furniture that had clearly been dragged rather than lifted.

She stepped further into the hall, her footsteps unnervingly loud in the silence. This space, she remembered, was the lifeblood of Cedar Ridge. It was where the annual chili cook-off was held, the bake sales that funded the local Little League, the Christmas tree lighting ceremony that drew every soul in town. She pictured it filled with laughter, with the murmur of excited chatter, with the joyous cacophony of children's squeals. Now, it was an empty shell, its former vibrancy a distant memory, a ghost haunting its decaying frame.

Her gaze drifted to the stage at the far end of the hall. It was a simple platform, draped with a faded, moth-eaten velvet curtain that hung in limp, sad folds. She remembered seeing local school plays performed here, amateur theatricals that were more charm than polish, but always filled with heart. The backdrop, a painted panorama of a quaint village scene, was cracked and peeling, the colors muted by time and exposure. Even the stage lights, hanging limply from their fixtures, seemed weary, as if they too had given up the ghost.

Clara walked towards the stage, her hand trailing along a chipped wooden pillar. She imagined her aunt, Eleanor, standing here, her voice ringing out with encouragement as she welcomed newcomers, thanked volunteers, or announced the winner of the pie-eating contest. Eleanor had a way of making everyone feel seen, valued. She'd built this place, not just brick by brick, but through a tireless dedication to fostering connection, to nurturing the bonds that held this small town together. And now, it was crumbling.

A chill, unrelated to the building's draftiness, snaked down Clara's spine. This wasn't just about a leaky roof or peeling paint. This was about the erosion of a community's anchor, the slow dissolution of a vital hub that had served as Cedar Ridge's living room for decades. She'd always been a city person, comfortable in the anonymity of crowds, in the constant hum of urban life. Cedar Ridge had always felt like a postcard, charming but somewhat static. But seeing the Hall like this, seeing the tangible evidence of her aunt's final, desperate fight, stirred something within her. It was more than just a building; it was a repository of shared memories, a testament to a legacy of service that felt too precious to let wither and die.

She moved towards a side room, likely the former kitchen, envisioning the countless volunteers who had slaved over hot stoves here, preparing meals for town events, organizing food drives. The counters were stained, the linoleum cracked. A rusted-out sink stood as a monument to neglect. Even the shelves, which should have been stocked with supplies for the pantry, were bare, save for a few cobwebs and a forgotten, dust-covered can of beans. It was a stark visual representation of the dwindling resources her aunt had battled.

The sheer scale of the task ahead began to press down on Clara. It wasn't just financial; it was the sheer physical labor, the organization, the rallying of a community that, from her brief observations, seemed to be more accustomed to looking after its own problems than to rallying behind a single, grand cause. She remembered her aunt's pleas in her letters, her subtle hints about the Hall's struggles. Clara, in her self-imposed exile, had dismissed them as the worries of an aging woman, perhaps a touch too sentimental about a building. Now, she saw the truth in her aunt's words, the quiet desperation that had underpinned them.

She walked back into the main hall, the emptiness of the space amplifying the weight of her responsibility. The silence was no longer just an absence of noise; it felt like a heavy shroud, muffling the echoes of past celebrations. But as she stood there, the fading light casting long shadows that seemed to swallow the room, a different feeling began to emerge. It wasn't the panic she had expected, or the overwhelming urge to flee. Instead, it was a quiet, determined resolve. Her aunt had poured her life into this place, into this community. To let it crumble into dust would be to betray not just Eleanor, but the spirit of Cedar Ridge itself.

She imagined the doors of the pantry being permanently closed, the shelves remaining bare. She pictured the elderly struggling to find affordable food, the single mothers unable to stretch their meager budgets further, the children's faces falling as they were told there was nothing left. The thought was unbearable. Her aunt, in her final years, had been a bulwark against such hardship for so many. Clara couldn't, wouldn't, let that bulwark fall.

A tiny spark ignited within her, a flicker of defiance against the encroaching decay. It was the same spark that had driven her to succeed in the city, the same tenacity she'd applied to her career. But this time, it wasn't about personal ambition. It was about stewardship, about honoring a legacy. The Hall was more than just a building; it was a symbol. It represented generosity, community spirit, and the quiet strength of a small town. And it deserved to be saved.

She looked around the hall again, her gaze sharper now, less filled with despair and more with a critical assessment. She noticed the sturdy beams supporting the ceiling, the solid construction of the walls. It was damaged, yes, but it wasn't beyond repair. It was a project, a monumental one, but a project nonetheless. And projects, Clara knew, could be tackled, bit by bit, with planning, and with help.

The thought of asking for help, however, still sent a tremor of apprehension through her. It was a deeply ingrained aversion, a vulnerability she had learned to mask. But here, in the ghost of her aunt's cherished Community Hall, that aversion began to feel... less important. The needs of this place, of the people it served, outweighed her own discomfort.

She walked over to a dusty bulletin board, still adorned with faded flyers advertising events from years past. A photograph, tacked crookedly, showed a younger Eleanor beaming, surrounded by a crowd of smiling faces at a summer picnic. Clara recognized some of them – Mrs. Gable from the bakery, Mr. Henderson from the hardware store, even a younger, less weathered version of Sheriff Brody. They looked happy, connected, a community united. A faint smile touched Clara's lips. Perhaps, just perhaps, these were the people who could help her bring the Hall back to life.

Perhaps Cedar Ridge, despite its faded glow, still held enough warmth to rekindle its heart. The path ahead was daunting, the challenges immense, but for the first time since stepping back onto the soil of her childhood town, Clara felt a nascent sense of purpose, a quiet determination to try and reignite the fading glow of the Hall. It was a daunting prospect, but one that felt, in its own way, like coming home. She took a deep breath, the musty air filling her lungs, and knew, with a certainty that surprised her, that she wouldn't let this place fall. She owed it to Eleanor, and she owed it to Cedar Ridge. The task was immense, the fear palpable, but the dawning realization that she might not have to face it entirely alone, was a flicker of hope in the deepening twilight.

Clara emerged from the Community Hall, blinking against the softened light of the late afternoon. The silence of the interior had been oppressive, but the quiet of the late afternoon outside was a different kind of stillness, one that held a promise of evening peace. She'd spent far longer than she'd intended inside, the weight of the building's decay settling heavily on her shoulders. The task ahead felt monumental, a mountain of repairs and renovations that seemed insurmountable. Her city-honed pragmatism warred with a burgeoning sense of obligation, a feeling that she couldn't simply turn her back on her aunt's legacy, on this cornerstone of the community.

As she stood on the worn steps, a faint creak of a nearby gate drew her attention. Across the narrow, unpaved lane that separated the Hall from the next property, a figure emerged from the shadow of a large, gnarled oak tree. Clara's gaze sharpened, a flicker of recognition stirring within her. It was a man, tall and broad-shouldered, his movements unhurried and deliberate. There was a steadiness about him, an air of quiet competence that was instantly recognizable, even after all these years.

Jonah Reed.

The name surfaced in her mind with a surprising clarity. She remembered him from her childhood, a presence as constant and reliable as the sturdy barns that dotted the surrounding landscape. He'd been a few years older than her, always seemed to be around, helping out at community events, his hands rough with the work of the land, his gaze steady and observant. He was the kind of person who didn't demand attention but commanded respect through his quiet capability. He was deeply, irrevocably Cedar Ridge.

He paused for a moment, his eyes – a warm, earthy brown, she recalled – falling on Clara. There was no overt curiosity in his look, no intrusive stare. Instead, it was a knowing glance, a subtle acknowledgment of her presence, and, she suspected, an astute observation of her inner turmoil. He saw the dust on her clothes, the faint lines of worry etched around her eyes, the almost palpable weight of the crumbling building behind her. He didn't need to ask. He understood.

He offered a slight, almost imperceptible nod, a gesture that was both a greeting and a quiet acknowledgement of the shared space, the shared history, even the shared potential for struggle. It wasn't a pitying look, but rather one that conveyed a silent understanding of the immense undertaking Clara had just stepped into. It was the look of someone who had faced his own share of challenges, who understood the quiet resilience required to navigate them.

Clara found herself returning the nod, a little uncertainly. The years had blurred many faces and names, but Jonah Reed's had remained surprisingly vivid. He looked much as she remembered, perhaps a little older, the lines around his eyes a testament to sun and wind, but the fundamental essence of him, that quiet strength, was unchanged. He was leaning against the rough-hewn fence that bordered his property, a silent sentinel observing the scene.

His proximity felt… grounding. It was a stark contrast to the overwhelming emptiness and decay she had just been immersed in. Here was a tangible sign of life, of continuity, a quiet anchor in the sea of her apprehension. His presence was a subtle, unspoken offering of proximity, a quiet declaration that she wasn't entirely alone in this moment, even if he hadn't uttered a single word. He wasn't intruding, not pushing his way in, but simply *being* there, a steady presence on the edge of her newly inherited burden.

She wondered what he was thinking. Did he remember her? Of course he did, she reasoned. Cedar Ridge wasn't a place where people easily forgot faces, especially those of former residents who had returned. Did he know about Eleanor's passing? It was highly likely. News traveled fast in a town this size. And he surely knew about the Hall's state of disrepair. Eleanor had been vocal about her struggles, even if Clara had been too distracted to truly hear her.

Jonah's gaze lingered for another moment, not in an uncomfortable way, but with a thoughtful, assessing air. He seemed to be taking in the entirety of the scene – Clara, the dilapidated Hall, the fading light. Then, with that same unhurried grace, he straightened from the fence and turned back towards his property, a small, well-maintained farmhouse visible beyond the oak. He didn't wave, didn't call out. He simply disappeared back into the landscape, leaving Clara with the lingering impression of his quiet strength, his unspoken understanding.

The brief encounter, no more than thirty seconds, had a surprisingly profound effect. It was a reminder that Cedar Ridge wasn't just a place of memories and decay, but also of people, of lives lived and continuing. Jonah Reed's presence, however fleeting, was a subtle affirmation that life went on, that resilience was a part of the town's fabric. It was a subtle hint that perhaps, just perhaps, the daunting task ahead might be navigable, not just with hard work and planning, but with the quiet, steady support of neighbors who understood the landscape, both literal and emotional.

Clara watched the spot where he had stood, a faint smile touching her lips. He hadn't offered solutions, hadn't pledged assistance, but his quiet acknowledgment of her presence, his silent understanding of the weight she carried, was more valuable than any grand pronouncement. It was a simple, human connection, a moment of shared awareness that cut through her sense of isolation. The Hall was still in dire straits, the challenges still immense, but the unexpected encounter with Jonah Reed had, in a small but significant way, eased the crushing pressure.

It was a subtle reminder that Cedar Ridge, despite its outward signs of decline, still possessed a quiet, inherent strength, a network of lives interwoven, and perhaps, just perhaps, a willingness to lend a hand when needed. She took another deep breath, the air feeling a little less heavy now, a little more breathable. The path forward was still unclear, but for the first time since arriving, Clara felt a faint glimmer of hope, a whisper that she might not have to walk it entirely alone. The sun dipped lower, casting long, gentle shadows across the lane, and Clara turned, ready to face the immediate tasks, her mind now holding a quiet, steady image of a familiar, reliable presence on the other side of the lane.

The familiar scent of lemon polish and old paper greeted Clara as she stepped into the small, sun-drenched bedroom. It was her room, exactly as she'd left it over a decade ago, a perfectly preserved time capsule of her teenage years. Posters of bands long disbanded still adorned the walls, a faint outline where a beloved, well-worn tapestry had once hung. Her desk, a sturdy oak piece scarred with countless ink marks and the accidental gouges of youthful restlessness, was still there, its surface dusted but otherwise undisturbed. It felt both comforting and disorienting, like stepping into a dream where everything was the same, yet everything had changed.

She ran a hand over the smooth, cool surface of her childhood dresser. Each item she touched, each object she saw, tugged at a memory, a forgotten emotion. The worn teddy bear propped against the pillows, the stack of paperback novels on her bedside table, the tiny, chipped porcelain music box her grandmother had given her – they were all tangible pieces of a life she had intentionally left behind. It was a life she had deemed too small, too predictable, for the ambitions that burned within her. And yet, seeing it all laid out before her now, a profound wave of nostalgia washed over her, tinged with a surprising melancholy.

The past few hours had been a whirlwind of emotions. The stark reality of the Community Hall's disrepair had shaken her to her core, stirring a reluctant sense of duty she hadn't anticipated. It wasn't just a building; it was Eleanor's final, tangible gift to Cedar Ridge, a beacon of community that was now flickering precariously. The thought of it closing, of its doors remaining shut, of the services it provided vanishing, was a heavy burden. It felt like a betrayal, not just of her aunt's memory, but of the very essence of what made Cedar Ridge, Cedar Ridge.

She began to unpack, the rhythmic folding of clothes a grounding activity. Each sweater, each pair of jeans, was a silent testament to the life she had built for herself away from this quiet town. She had carved out a successful career, navigated the complexities of city living, and established a sense of independence that was fiercely guarded. She had proven to herself, and perhaps to the ghosts of her past, that she was capable, resourceful, and driven.

But as she placed her neatly folded clothes into the dresser drawers, the image of the decaying Hall kept intruding. She saw the water stains blooming on the ceiling, the peeling paint, the empty shelves in the pantry. She remembered the warmth in Eleanor's letters, the subtle undertones of worry that Clara had, in her youthful arrogance, dismissed. Eleanor had poured her heart and soul into that Hall, into this town, and now it was falling apart.

A quiet resolve began to form within her, a steadfast determination that settled deep in her bones. It wasn't a loud, defiant declaration, but a silent, internal shift. She wouldn't let it happen. She wouldn't let that vibrant center of the community crumble into dust. The thought of failure, of not being able to salvage the Hall, was a bitter prospect, but the thought of not even trying, of walking away from Eleanor's legacy, was infinitely worse.

It was more than just a sense of obligation to her aunt. It was a deeply personal need to prove something, to herself. She had always felt the need to exceed expectations, to shine brightly, to outmaneuver any perceived limitations. This was an opportunity, a daunting one, but an opportunity nonetheless, to demonstrate her resilience, her capacity for leadership, her ability to not just survive, but to *thrive* in the face of adversity. The city had been her proving ground, but Cedar Ridge, with its ingrained familiarity and its unspoken history, presented a different kind of challenge, a more intimate one.

She closed the dresser drawer with a soft click, the sound echoing in the quiet room. She walked over to the window, looking out at the familiar landscape. The sun was beginning its descent, casting a warm, golden glow over the rolling hills and the clusters of houses that dotted the valley. It was a peaceful scene, a stark contrast to the inner turmoil she had been wrestling with.

Her mind was already working, piecing together possibilities. She envisioned the Hall bustling with life again, filled with the sounds of laughter and conversation, the aroma of baking and coffee. She saw the pantry stocked, the stage ready for a performance, the dance floor clean and inviting. It was a beautiful vision, a powerful motivator.

She knew it wouldn't be easy. The financial hurdles alone were significant, not to mention the physical labor and the sheer organizational effort required. But as she stood there, the weight of the challenge settling upon her, it didn't feel insurmountable. It felt... manageable. Not in a naive sense, but in a way that acknowledged the immense effort required, yet held onto the possibility of success.

She thought of Jonah Reed, the man she had seen across the lane from the Hall. His quiet nod, his steady gaze, had conveyed a silent understanding that had resonated deeply. He represented the kind of quiet strength and continuity that Cedar Ridge embodied. He was a part of this place, deeply rooted, and his presence, however brief, had offered a subtle counterpoint to the overwhelming sense of decay she had felt. It was a reminder that even in the face of decline, life and resilience persisted.

A small smile touched her lips. She had always been a planner, a strategist. Now, she would apply those skills to this new, unexpected project. She would need to assess the full extent of the damage, to create a detailed budget, to explore potential funding sources. But first, she needed to commit herself fully, to make this her priority, not just a temporary distraction.

The resolve solidified, hardening into a silent vow. She would not let Eleanor's legacy fade. She would not let the heart of Cedar Ridge be extinguished. She would pour her energy, her resources, and her determination into saving the Community Hall. It was a commitment made not for applause or recognition, but for the quiet satisfaction of knowing she had honored her aunt, preserved a vital piece of her own past, and contributed to the enduring spirit of the town she had once longed to escape. This was her home, in more ways than one, and it deserved to be nurtured. She turned away from the window, her gaze now firm and focused, the scattered remnants of her childhood room fading into the background as her mind began to map out the formidable, yet undeniably meaningful, path ahead. The challenge was immense, the road uncertain, but the quiet hum of determination within her was a steady, unwavering force, a promise whispered in the twilight: she would try. She would give it her all.

CHAPTER TWO

The Weight of Solitude

The scent of damp plaster and aged wood clung to the air, a more potent perfume than any city fragrance Clara had ever encountered. Armed with a flashlight and an almost militant sense of purpose, she began her survey of the Community Hall. The task was immense, a mountainous undertaking that threatened to dwarf her carefully constructed composure. But Clara had always been a builder, a strategist. Give her a problem, and she'd dissect it, analyze it, and meticulously plan its eradication. This was no different, just... bigger. And considerably more personal.

She started in the main hall, its vast emptiness amplifying the silence. Sunlight, filtering through grimy windows, illuminated dust motes dancing in lazy circles. Her flashlight beam, a sharp, intrusive finger of light, probed the shadowy corners. She unfolded a crisp, rolled-up document – a set of original blueprints for the Hall, unearthed from a dusty filing cabinet in the back office. They were brittle with age, the ink faded in places, but they were her roadmap. She smoothed them out on a sturdy, though cobweb-laden, table, anchoring the corners with a few weighty volumes she found scattered nearby.

Her approach was strictly analytical. She needed to quantify the damage, to break down the overwhelming behemoth of a project into manageable chunks. This wasn't about sentimentality; it was about logistics. It was about cold, hard facts. Each crack in the plaster, each warped floorboard, each rusted fixture was meticulously noted. She ran her fingers along a damp patch on the far wall, a bloom of mildew spreading like an unwelcome stain. Her pen scratched across a notepad, a relentless rhythm against the backdrop of the Hall's quiet decay. "Water damage, north wall, east wing," she murmured, her voice a low rumble that seemed to swallow itself in the cavernous space. "Suspect roof leak."

She moved methodically through the building, her flashlight beam a steady beacon in the gloom. The old kitchen was next. The once-gleaming stainless steel was now dull and scarred, the ancient stove a relic of a bygone era. A faint, lingering scent of burnt sugar and something vaguely metallic hung in the air. She opened cupboard doors, their hinges groaning in protest, revealing empty shelves and the occasional forgotten jar of preserves, their contents long since solidified into an unidentifiable mass. She noted the peeling paint on the cabinets, the corroded pipes beneath the sink. "Kitchen: extensive renovation required. Appliances obsolete. Possible mold growth." Her lists grew longer, more detailed, each entry a small victory against the encroaching chaos.

Upstairs, the smaller rooms – the meeting rooms, the former library – presented their own unique challenges. In what had once been Eleanor's office, a single, bare lightbulb dangled precariously from the ceiling. Clara nudged it gently with her finger, a flicker of light briefly chasing away the shadows before dying again. She found stacks of old ledgers, their pages filled with elegant, looping script detailing decades of bake sales, town meetings, and fundraising drives. The sheer volume of activity, the dedication poured into this place, was staggering. It was a tangible testament to a community that had once been vibrant, a stark contrast to the quiet desolation that now reigned.

She was acutely aware of the silence. It wasn't a peaceful quiet, but a heavy, pregnant silence, filled with the echoes of what used to be. It pressed in on her, threatening to unravel the carefully constructed dam she had built around her emotions. Each creak of the floorboards, each gust of wind rattling the windowpanes, seemed to whisper Eleanor's name, a gentle reminder of the legacy that now rested, precariously, in her hands. She pushed those thoughts away, focusing on the tangible. She needed to get the building up to code, to ensure it was safe, functional. She dug out a thick binder of local building codes, its pages dense with regulations and requirements. She cross-referenced the Hall's original blueprints with the current standards, her brow furrowed in concentration.

This meticulous attention to detail, this immersion in the minutiae of renovation and repair, was more than just a practical approach; it was a form of self-preservation. By focusing on the structural integrity of the building, on the quantifiable problems, she could keep the more complex, more painful issues at bay. The fear of failure, a cold knot in her stomach, was a constant companion. What if she couldn't do it? What if the cost was too high, the damage too extensive? What if she let Eleanor down? These were questions she couldn't afford to answer, not yet. Not while she was still in the assessment phase.

She spent hours there, the sunlight shifting, lengthening, and finally fading, painting the Hall in hues of orange and purple. Her back ached, her fingers were smudged with dust and grime, and a dull headache had begun to throb behind her eyes. Yet, she pressed on. She meticulously documented everything, her to-do lists growing to an almost absurd length. She sketched out a rough timeline, assigning priorities, even starting to mentally allocate resources. It was an exercise in control, a way to impose order on a situation that felt profoundly out of her hands.

The silence of the Hall had become a strange sort of companion. It was a quiet that allowed her to think, to strategize, to push the emotional tide back. It was a void that she was determined to fill, not with the ghosts of the past, but with the vibrant energy of the future. She imagined the Hall alive again, the echo of laughter replacing the creaks and groans, the scent of fresh coffee and baking bread overwhelming the musty odor of disrepair. She saw children's drawings taped to the walls, heard the murmur of book clubs, the strumming of guitars during impromptu jam sessions. This vision, this possibility, fueled her, even as the daunting reality of the work ahead weighed heavily on her shoulders.

As dusk settled, casting long, distorted shadows across the floor, Clara finally packed away her notes and blueprints. She stood in the center of the main hall, the flashlight beam illuminating a single, dust-covered chair. The silence felt different now, less oppressive, more expectant. It was the quiet of a battlefield after the initial skirmish, a pause before the real fight began. She took a deep, steadying breath, the cool, still air filling her lungs. The fear was still there, a persistent tremor beneath the surface, but it was no longer paralyzing. It was a reminder of what was at stake, a catalyst for the fierce determination that had begun to take root within her. She was here, she was assessing, she was planning. And she was not going to back down. The Hall might be in disrepair, but her resolve was solid. She would face this challenge, one meticulously planned step at a time. The weight of solitude was heavy, but in the quiet, shadowed expanse of the Community Hall, she was finding a strange kind of strength in its embrace.

The door to the Community Hall's pantry creaked open, a reluctant sigh from its long-dormant hinges. Clara braced herself, flashlight beam cutting a swathe through the gloom. If the rest of the Hall was a monument to neglect, the pantry felt like its skeletal remains. The air was thick with the phantom scent of spices and preserved goods, now overlaid with the musty aroma of disuse. Unlike the main hall, which still held a certain grandeur in its decay, the pantry was a space stripped bare, a testament to the emptying out of more than just supplies.

Her beam swept across the shelves, and a hollow ache began to settle in her chest. What she'd expected, she wasn't entirely sure. Perhaps a few forgotten tins, some ancient jars of jam. What she found was a stark, almost brutal, emptiness. A handful of cans, their labels faded into illegibility, sat like lonely sentinels on the top shelf. She reached for one, her fingers brushing against the cool, dusty metal. "Peaches," she murmured, the word tasting foreign in the silence. Below them, a couple of plastic bags, their seams splitting, held what looked like petrified remnants of flour, clumping together in dense, unappetite-making masses. They were past their prime, past any notion of sustenance, mere shadows of the provisions they once held.

She moved further in, the narrow space confining her. The shelves themselves, constructed of sturdy but unvarnished wood, bore the gouges and scrapes of countless years of use. In places, the wood had warped, hinting at past dampness, a silent warning of the Hall's ongoing battles with the elements. It wasn't just the lack of food that struck her; it was the profound implication of what that emptiness represented. This wasn't a forgotten larder in a private home. This was the Community Pantry of Cedar Ridge. This was the repository for those who struggled, the safety net for families who found themselves on the precipice of need.

Clara had always been a planner, a woman who believed in the power of meticulous organization and foresight. She'd approached the Hall's renovation with a strategist's mindset, breaking down the monumental task into actionable steps. But standing here, in this barren space, she felt the chilling realization dawn that this was not solely about structural repairs and aesthetic improvements. This was about lives. This was about ensuring that no one in Cedar Ridge went hungry, that no child had to face the gnawing emptiness of an insufficient meal. The weight of that responsibility, added to the already considerable burden of saving the Hall, pressed down on her, a physical ache in her shoulders.

Her gaze drifted to a small, tarnished brass plaque screwed into the wall near the door. Wiping away a film of dust with her sleeve, she managed to decipher the embossed words: "Cedar Ridge Community Pantry – Established 1958. Nourishing Our Neighbors." Established 1958. More than sixty years of service. Sixty years of shared abundance, of collective care. The silence of the room seemed to amplify the echo of those sixty years, of all the hands that had stocked these shelves, all the families that had found solace and sustenance within these walls. And now, it was empty.

She took out her notepad, her pen poised, but the usual analytical impulse felt muted. What could she possibly list? "Shelves: empty. Contents: negligible." It felt like a gross understatement, a clinical description of a deeply emotional deficit. She tried to picture it as it must have been: shelves groaning under the weight of canned goods, bags of rice and beans, fresh produce when donations allowed, perhaps even homemade treats from the town's more generous bakers. She envisioned volunteers bustling, sorting, organizing, their faces alight with purpose. The contrast with the present reality was stark, almost painful.

The sheer scale of restocking and managing the pantry, alongside the Herculean task of repairing the Hall itself, began to sink in. It wasn't just about finding the money for new supplies; it was about establishing a reliable system, about finding volunteers again, about rebuilding the trust and community spirit that had evidently waned to the point of near extinction. How could she possibly tackle all of this? The building repairs alone felt overwhelming, a constant drain on her energy and dwindling resources. Now, this added layer of a fundamental human need, unmet, threatened to pull her under.

She remembered snippets of conversations from her initial arrival in Cedar Ridge, hushed mentions of people struggling, of families making difficult choices. She'd dismissed them, in her city-dweller's pragmatism, as common economic realities. But standing here, in the physical embodiment of that struggle, the reality hit her with the force of a physical blow. This was not just a building to be renovated; it was a lifeline that needed to be re-established.

Her isolation, a constant companion since she'd arrived, deepened in the small, bare space. In the main hall, she could lose herself in the blueprints, in the practicalities of plaster and wiring. It was a solitary, albeit daunting, task. But the pantry spoke of collective effort, of a shared purpose that was now fragmented. Her inability to immediately conjure a solution, to magically refill these empty shelves, felt like a personal failing. It amplified the feeling that she was out of her depth, that the expectations placed upon her – by herself, by the memory of Eleanor, and perhaps by the town itself – were too immense to bear.

She ran a hand along the smooth, cool wood of a shelf, her touch almost reverent. Each empty space was a question mark, a silent plea. Who needed these supplies? What were their circumstances? How long had the pantry been in this state of disrepair? Had it been a gradual decline, or a sudden cessation of donations? The questions swirled, unanswered, in the quiet confines of the room. There were no records here, no ledgers detailing past distributions, no sign of recent activity. It was as if the heart of this vital community resource had simply stopped beating.

Clara forced herself to breathe, to push back the rising tide of despair. She couldn't afford to be paralyzed by the magnitude of the problem. She was a problem-solver, wasn't she? She'd always prided herself on her ability to find solutions, even in the most challenging circumstances. But this was different. This required not just logistical prowess, but a deep understanding of a community she barely knew, and a level of emotional resilience she wasn't sure she possessed.

She continued her methodical inventory, not just of what was missing, but of what remained. The few cans, the bags of flour – they were symbolic. They represented the last vestiges, the bare minimum of what had once been a thriving resource. She noted the sturdy construction of the shelves, the basic but functional layout of the room. The infrastructure was sound, at least. That was something. The walls were solid, the floor intact. It was the contents, the very purpose of the space, that was lacking.

She imagined the energy it would take to bring this place back to life. It would involve outreach, persuasion, a rebuilding of goodwill. It would require donations of food, of money, of time. It would necessitate finding a new generation of volunteers, individuals who understood the importance of this pantry, who were willing to dedicate themselves to its mission. And all of this, she reminded herself, was on top of the physical restoration of the Hall itself. The sheer logistical complexity was staggering.

Her flashlight beam lingered on a small, faded notice pinned to a corkboard that was itself peeling away from the wall. It was a flyer, undoubtedly old, announcing a "Pantry Appreciation Luncheon." The date was smudged, impossible to read, but the sentiment was clear. There had been a time when this pantry was celebrated, when its existence was a source of pride for Cedar Ridge. Clara felt a pang of sadness for that lost appreciation, for the community that had once recognized and valued this essential service.

She tried to envision the process of rebuilding. First, she would need to assess the true extent of the need. Were there specific demographics in Cedar Ridge that were particularly vulnerable? Were there existing social services she could partner with, or learn from? Then, she would need to start the fundraising, perhaps a "Restock the Pantry" campaign. It would require more than just appeals; it would need to be a narrative, a story that reminded people of the pantry's history and its vital role.

And the volunteers. Where would she find them? In a town that felt so quiet, so diminished, how could she possibly mobilize enough people to run this place effectively? She thought of the few friendly faces she'd encountered so far, the initial cautious optimism of some of the older residents. Could they be convinced to lend their time and energy? It seemed like a long shot, a mountain to climb even before she'd figured out how to get the Hall's plumbing fixed.

The sheer weight of the task began to feel crushing. It wasn't just about repairing a building; it was about healing a community. It was about restoring a sense of hope, of mutual support, of shared responsibility. And she, Clara, a relative newcomer, felt utterly unqualified for such a monumental undertaking. The silence of the pantry seemed to mock her, to emphasize her own inadequacy. She was alone in this, facing a problem that was deeply rooted in the town's social fabric, a problem that required more than just a hammer and nails. It required a reawakening of civic spirit, a rekindling of the very essence of community.

The empty shelves were a stark, visual representation of a deeper void, a void that felt far more daunting to fill than any structural damage the Hall might present. Her initial methodical approach, her comfort in quantifiable problems, felt woefully insufficient here. This was a realm of intangible needs, of human connection, of a collective spirit that had, for reasons she couldn't yet fathom, faded into silence. And in that silence, Clara's own sense of isolation grew, heavy and palpable, a stark counterpoint to the vibrant life this pantry was meant to sustain.

Jonah Reed's workshop, a cozy haven of sawdust and aged wood, overlooked the back of the Community Hall. From his vantage point, a quiet observer accustomed to the rhythm of Cedar Ridge, he'd watched Clara's arrival with a mixture of curiosity and a familiar sense of weary recognition. He'd seen the ambitious glint in her eyes when she first toured the dilapidated building, the way she'd unfurled blueprints with a decisiveness that spoke of a seasoned professional. But as weeks bled into months, and the initial fervor began to ebb, a different aspect of her presence emerged, one that resonated deeply within him.

He saw her in the late hours, the glow of a single lamp spilling from the Hall's windows, long after the rest of the town had settled into slumber. He saw the determined set of her shoulders as she wrestled with boxes of salvaged materials, her brow furrowed in concentration. There were days when the sheer weight of the task seemed to press down on her, not just physically, but on a deeper, more profound level. He'd witnessed her standing on the porch, staring out at the quiet street, a look of profound solitude etched onto her face, a silent testament to the immense burden she carried. He understood that look. He knew the feeling of trying to shoulder too much, of believing that the responsibility for a task, a place, a community, rested solely on one's own weary back.

He'd seen her in the pantry, her flashlight beam sweeping across the empty shelves, a small gasp escaping her lips. He'd heard the subtle click of the door, the sigh of hinges that had gone so long without use. He couldn't hear her words, but he could read the slump of her shoulders, the way she ran a hand through her hair, a gesture of pure, unadulterated frustration. It was clear she'd stumbled upon something that had shaken her, a tangible representation of the decay that went beyond mere plaster and peeling paint. He imagined her wrestling with the implications, with the sheer, daunting void that represented so much more than a lack of canned goods.

Jonah wasn't a man of grand gestures. His life had been one of quiet competence, of creating beauty from raw materials, of finding order in the chaos of wood and metal. He understood the power of small, consistent acts. He'd watched Clara, a stranger to their town, pour her heart and soul into this project, a project that many had long since given up on. He saw her unwavering dedication, her refusal to be deterred by the overwhelming odds. And he recognized a kindred spirit, albeit one wrestling with a very different kind of craft.

One particularly cold evening, as the first hint of frost began to paint the windows of the Hall, he'd found himself standing by his own workshop door, a forgotten thermos in his hand. He remembered Clara's tired posture that afternoon, the way she'd shivered slightly as she'd locked up. He'd filled the thermos with strong, dark coffee, the kind that chased away the chill and sharpened the mind. He walked the short distance to the Hall, the crunch of fallen leaves under his boots the only sound in the stillness. He placed the thermos on the worn wooden steps, next to a wilting potted plant that Clara had somehow managed to salvage. He didn't knock. He didn't announce his presence. He simply left it there, a silent offering. He pictured her finding it later, a small surprise in the midst of her relentless work, a subtle acknowledgment that someone saw her, truly saw her, and appreciated the immense effort she was making.

Another time, he'd been working on a particularly intricate carving when he saw her emerge from the Hall, her face smudged with dust, her eyes bright with exhaustion and a hint of triumph. She'd been carrying a stack of old framed photographs, clearly unearthed from a forgotten corner. He'd watched her pause, taking a moment to breathe in the cool evening air, her gaze sweeping across the quiet, tree-lined street. He'd walked out of his workshop, wiping his hands on his apron, and simply offered a slow, deliberate nod. It was a gesture that conveyed respect, encouragement, and an unspoken understanding. He saw the flicker of surprise in her eyes, then a small, genuine smile that seemed to lift the weariness from her face. It was a fleeting moment, but it was a connection, a silent acknowledgment of their shared existence in this quiet corner of the world.

He continued to observe, always from a respectful distance. He saw the way she meticulously sorted through old documents, her brow furrowed in concentration as she tried to decipher faded ink and cryptic notes. He saw her late nights, the solitary glow of her lamp a beacon in the darkness, a silent testament to her unwavering commitment. He understood the weight of responsibility, the feeling of being the sole custodian of a dream that others had let fade. He knew the quiet determination that fueled such endeavors, the stubborn refusal to let something important crumble into dust.

He admired her resilience. Cedar Ridge, for all its charm, could be a challenging place for an outsider. He'd seen how some of the older residents, set in their ways, viewed her with a mixture of suspicion and cautious hope. He recognized the subtle barriers she had to overcome, the need to earn trust in a town that held its secrets close. He saw her navigate these social complexities with a quiet grace, her focus always on the task at hand, on the restoration of the Hall itself.

He'd once found a loose board on the path leading to the Hall's back entrance, a tripping hazard that had been there for months. He'd taken it upon himself to fix it, a simple task that required only a few minutes and a handful of nails. He did it anonymously, a small repair that would hopefully prevent a tumble. He didn't do it for recognition; he did it because he believed in the importance of maintaining the small details, the quiet acts of care that made a place feel lived-in and cared for. He saw Clara's efforts as a grander version of that same philosophy, a determined attempt to bring life and purpose back to a forgotten space.

He also saw the toll it was taking. There were days when her shoulders seemed to sag under an invisible load, days when her smile didn't quite reach her eyes. He saw the moments of quiet contemplation, the way she'd pause, gazing at the imposing structure, as if seeking answers from its weathered facade. He understood that building a dream was often a solitary journey, punctuated by moments of doubt and overwhelming fatigue. He recognized the hunger in her eyes, not for food, but for progress, for a sign that her immense efforts were making a tangible difference.

Jonah found himself making excuses to walk past the Hall, to linger near his workshop, to catch a glimpse of her tireless work. He saw the stacks of books she'd brought in, the way she'd meticulously organized them, as if trying to bring order to the chaos of the past. He saw her poring over historical records, her face illuminated by the desk lamp, a silhouette against the darkening sky. He imagined her piecing together the story of Cedar Ridge, of the Hall's place within it, trying to understand the roots of its decline.

He knew that Clara was more than just a woman renovating a building. She was a force of nature, a determined spirit who refused to let a piece of history fade into oblivion. He admired her tenacity, her quiet strength. He understood the invisible battles she was fighting, the internal struggles that were as real as any structural flaw in the Hall. He saw the solitary nature of her mission, the way she seemed to embrace it, even as it clearly weighed on her.

One afternoon, as Clara was struggling to move a particularly heavy wooden cabinet out of the Hall, her movements awkward and strained, Jonah found himself walking towards her. He didn't call out, didn't want to startle her or make her feel like she was being watched. He simply approached, his presence a silent offering of assistance. He saw the surprised look on her face as he reached her side. Without a word, he placed his hands on the cabinet, his movements sure and practiced. Together, with a combined effort, they managed to maneuver the heavy piece of furniture to its new location.

Clara looked at him, her chest heaving slightly, her eyes holding a mixture of gratitude and surprise. "Thank you," she managed, her voice a little breathless. "I... I didn't want to bother you." Jonah offered a small, almost imperceptible smile. "No bother," he said, his voice a low rumble. "Just helping out where I can. This old place has a lot of weight to it, doesn't it?" He met her gaze, a flicker of understanding passing between them. He saw the immense effort she was putting in, the sheer willpower she possessed. He also saw the loneliness that clung to her, a shadow that even her determination couldn't entirely dispel.

He knew that his small gestures, the quiet acts of support, were perhaps the only things he could offer without overstepping the boundaries of her self-imposed solitude. He was an observer, yes, but he was also a witness, and sometimes, witnessing was an act of support in itself. He continued to watch, his presence a quiet, constant hum in the background of her endeavors, a silent acknowledgment that she was not entirely alone in her monumental task.

He offered no grand pronouncements, no unsolicited advice, just the quiet assurance that someone saw her, someone understood the weight she carried, and someone offered a silent, steady hope for her success. He was a craftsman, and he recognized the meticulous, painstaking work of creation, whether it was in wood and metal, or in the delicate art of resurrecting a forgotten community spirit. And he saw in Clara Reed, a fellow artist, wrestling with a canvas far larger and more complex than any he had ever encountered.

The afternoon had been deceptively bright, a fleeting promise of spring that coaxed Clara out of her persistent winter shell. She'd spent the morning meticulously cataloging the salvaged furniture, each piece a testament to a bygone era, and now, armed with a thermos of lukewarm tea and a renewed sense of purpose, she'd ventured back into the main hall. The air inside was still and heavy, carrying the faint, sweet scent of decay and damp plaster. Sunlight, fractured by the grimy windows, illuminated dust motes dancing in ethereal columns, creating an almost sacred atmosphere.

She'd been sketching out potential layouts for the main floor, envisioning rows of chairs, a small refreshment stand, maybe even a designated space for local artisans to display their wares. The stage, a hulking, shadowed entity at the far end of the hall, remained her biggest obstacle. It sagged precariously, its once-proud facade marred by water stains and the insidious creep of mold. Still, she'd refused to let it defeat her. She'd spent hours the previous day carefully assessing its structural integrity, her mind already racing with solutions for reinforcing the floorboards and patching the gaping holes.

She was just about to begin tracing the outline of a potential seating arrangement onto the dusty floorboards with a piece of chalk when the first heavy drops began to fall. It started as a soft patter against the roof, a gentle rhythm that lulled the senses. Then, with alarming speed, the rain intensified, transforming into a furious drumming that echoed through the cavernous space. Clara paused, her chalk hovering inches above the floor. The sound grew louder, more insistent, and a prickle of unease began to crawl up her spine. It wasn't just the sound of rain anymore; it was the sound of *too much* rain, of a deluge that was testing the limits of the old building's defenses.

A soft drip, then another, began to punctuate the drumming. Clara's head snapped up, her gaze instinctively drawn to the ceiling. A dark, wet stain was spreading, almost imperceptibly at first, directly above the stage. Her heart gave a lurch. She'd checked the roof herself, of course, had patched a few minor leaks near the eaves with sealant, but the main structure, especially over the stage, had seemed solid. Or so she'd thought. The drips became more frequent, more distinct, forming small, glistening puddles on the warped wooden planks of the stage. The dry, dusty air began to take on a distinctly musty, damp odor.

Clara walked cautiously towards the stage, her boots crunching on fallen debris. The puddles were growing, reflecting the dim light in distorted, shimmering patches. It was more than just a few drips; it was a steady, unwavering flow, a miniature waterfall cascading from what she'd assumed was a sound seam in the roofline. Her carefully drawn chalk lines, her nascent plans for renovation, felt suddenly, absurdly, fragile. This wasn't a cosmetic issue; this was a fundamental structural problem. The very heart of the hall, the focal point of so many potential gatherings, was succumbing to the relentless assault of the weather.

A wave of something cold and heavy washed over her, a visceral reaction that threatened to drown out any semblance of optimism. She stood there, a solitary figure in the vast, echoing hall, the sound of the falling rain and the dripping water a deafening symphony of failure. Her plans, meticulously crafted over countless sleepless nights, her vision of a vibrant community hub, felt like sand castles being washed away by an unstoppable tide. The blueprints, tucked away safely in her office, suddenly seemed like childish doodles, woefully inadequate against the raw, untamed power of nature.

She remembered the reassuring words of Mr. Henderson, the town's unofficial historian, who had assured her that the hall's frame was exceptionally sound. "Built to last, Clara," he'd said, his voice raspy with age, his eyes twinkling with nostalgia. "Survived a few storms in its day, that old girl." But this storm felt different. It wasn't just a strong wind or a dusting of snow; it was a relentless, drenching downpour, and it was exposing a weakness she hadn't anticipated, a vulnerability that felt far more significant than a few cracked tiles.

The water pooling on the stage floor was more than just water; it was a tangible manifestation of her fears, a liquid symbol of the overwhelming challenges that lay ahead. It represented the hidden decay, the structural compromises that even her most thorough inspections had failed to uncover. It was a reminder that some problems couldn't be fixed with a bit of elbow grease and a positive attitude. Some problems required expertise, resources, and a level of foresight that she was beginning to doubt she possessed.

A knot of anxiety tightened in her chest. She'd poured so much of herself into this project, so much of her savings, so much of her hope. She had envisioned this hall as a fresh start, a way to rebuild not only a building but also a sense of purpose within herself. She had convinced herself that she could do this, that she had the grit and determination to see it through. But standing there, watching the water relentlessly soak the stage, those convictions began to crumble. The weight of the task, which she had been determined to carry alone, suddenly felt impossibly heavy.

She ran a hand through her hair, the strands already feeling slightly damp from the humid air. A tremor ran through her, a mixture of frustration and a dawning fear. Was she out of her depth? Had she overestimated her abilities? The thought of admitting defeat, of facing the town with this new, significant setback, was almost unbearable. She could already hear the whispers, the knowing glances, the "I told you so's" that were sure to follow. They had already been hesitant, these people of Cedar Ridge, their initial reactions a delicate dance between polite curiosity and reserved skepticism. This latest disaster would only serve to confirm their doubts.

She looked around the vast, echoing space, the water continuing its steady descent, creating a growing, shimmering pool on the stage. It felt like a cruel joke, a mocking testament to her efforts. All her meticulous planning, her late-night research, her hopeful brainstorming sessions – what were they worth against the simple, overwhelming force of a leaky roof? The very foundation of her project, the stage, the place where performances would happen, where memories would be made, was now literally crumbling under the weight of the rain.

Clara felt a prickling behind her eyes. She blinked furiously, trying to hold back the tide of emotion that threatened to overwhelm her. She didn't want to cry. Crying wouldn't fix the leak. Crying wouldn't dry the floor.

Crying would only make her feel weaker, more vulnerable, more exposed. She had to be strong. She had to find a solution. But the sheer scale of the problem, so starkly revealed by the cascading water, felt paralyzing. It was a problem that went beyond patching and painting; it suggested deeper structural issues, perhaps compromised beams, weakened supports, or an entirely inadequate drainage system.

She imagined the conversations that would follow. The hushed tones, the worried frowns, the inevitable pronouncements that the hall was beyond repair. She pictured herself standing before the town council, her voice faltering as she tried to explain the extent of the damage, the unforeseen costs, the daunting reality of what lay ahead. The image was so vivid, so painful, that it made her physically flinch.

She walked over to a sturdy, albeit dusty, wooden chair that had been salvaged and placed it near the entrance, its surface still dry. She sat down, the worn wood cool against her thighs, and stared at the stage. The water was now spreading beyond the confines of the stage itself, creeping onto the main floor, small rivulets forming in the grooves of the old floorboards. It was a slow, insidious invasion, a silent enemy that was undermining everything she had worked so hard to build.

Her mind raced, trying to find a practical solution, a quick fix. Could she buy tarps? Could she somehow rig up a temporary drainage system? But even as these thoughts formed, she knew they were insufficient. This wasn't a temporary inconvenience; it was a fundamental flaw that needed to be addressed with proper engineering, with skilled labor, with a significant financial outlay she hadn't budgeted for. The dream of a quick renovation, a swift transformation into a bustling community center, was rapidly dissolving, replaced by the grim reality of costly, complex repairs.

She felt a profound sense of isolation settle over her. She was used to handling things herself, to relying on her own resourcefulness. But this... this felt different. This felt like a challenge that required more than just her own two hands. It required collaboration, expertise, and a level of support that she hadn't yet managed to secure. She had been so focused on the physical act of renovation, on the tangible progress of cleaning, repairing, and rebuilding, that she had perhaps neglected the crucial aspect of building a network of support, of sharing the burden before it became too heavy to bear.

She closed her eyes, the sound of the relentless rain a dull roar in her ears. The sheer magnitude of the task ahead, revealed so dramatically by the flooding stage, felt crushing. It wasn't just about fixing a leak; it was about confronting the possibility that her ambition had outstripped her capabilities, that she had bitten off more than she could chew. The fear that had been lurking beneath the surface, the quiet whisper of doubt, now grew into a deafening roar, echoing the storm raging outside. She had always prided herself on her independence, on her ability to stand on her own two feet. But in this moment, surrounded by the evidence of her limitations, that independence felt more like a heavy chain, binding her to a burden she was beginning to suspect was too great for her to carry alone. The solitude she had embraced, the self-reliance she had cultivated, now felt like a cruel irony, leaving her utterly exposed to the harsh realities of a project that was proving to be far more demanding than she had ever imagined.

Clara found herself adrift in a sea of paperwork, each official-looking document a tiny island of potential reprieve in the vast ocean of her overwhelming challenges. The rain had finally subsided, leaving behind a damp, bruised sky and the lingering scent of wet earth, but the deluge inside the community hall was far from over. The stage, still slick and glistening with residual moisture, served as a constant, accusing reminder of the morning's disquieting discovery.

She had retreated to the small, dusty office she'd carved out for herself at the back of the hall, a space furnished with a secondhand desk and a surprisingly comfortable, if faded, armchair. The grant applications, procured from the county office, lay spread before her, a daunting array of forms demanding details she wasn't sure she possessed. Figures for material costs, labor estimates, timelines for completion – it all felt like a foreign language she was struggling to decipher.

She traced the intricate lines of a required budget projection with a fingertip, a frown etching itself deeper into her brow. The sheer volume of information needed, the meticulous detail, felt like an insurmountable hurdle. How could she accurately estimate the cost of structural repairs when she wasn't even sure of the extent of the damage? The roof over the stage was a prime example – a gaping maw that had wept its way onto the floorboards, exposing a vulnerability that demanded more than just a quick fix. Her instinct was to dive into research, to find answers buried within obscure architectural forums and DIY repair guides. She'd always been a problem-solver, a doer, someone who tackled issues head-on with determination and a healthy dose of grit. Asking for help, however, felt like admitting defeat before the battle had truly begun.

It was this deeply ingrained habit of self-reliance that now acted as a silent, invisible barrier. It had served her well in the past, a shield against disappointment and a testament to her own capabilities. But here, in the echoing silence of the deserted hall, with the weight of its future pressing down on her, that same self-reliance felt more like a prison.

The day before, Mrs. Gable, a woman whose kindly eyes held a perpetual sparkle of neighborly concern, had stopped by. She'd found Clara surveying the damage, her expression a mixture of dismay and steely resolve. "Oh, my dear," she'd said, her voice soft with sympathy, "that looks like a frightful mess. We were thinking, you know, the Ladies' Auxiliary is planning their annual spring potluck next month. It's always a lovely affair, brings everyone out. Perhaps... perhaps you could tell us all about your plans for the hall then? We could all chip in, maybe even organize a bake sale to help with some of the initial costs."

The offer, brimming with genuine warmth and a desire to help, had settled in Clara's chest like a stone. She'd managed a polite smile, her mind already conjuring a thousand reasons to decline. "That's so thoughtful of you, Mrs. Gable," she'd replied, her voice carefully modulated to convey gratitude without inviting further entanglement. "But I'm still in the assessment phase. I wouldn't want to make any promises or ask for support until I have a clearer picture of what's needed. I'm just... trying to get a handle on things myself first." She'd quickly changed the subject, steering the conversation towards the weather and the general state of Cedar Ridge, her heart beating a little faster with the effort of maintaining her carefully constructed facade.

The truth was, the thought of standing before the entire town, explaining the extent of the damage, and then *asking* for their hard-earned money, filled her with a gnawing anxiety. It felt like a public confession of her own inadequacy. She'd been so confident, so sure that she could resurrect this forgotten landmark through sheer willpower and a few well-placed repairs. Admitting that she needed help, that she was out of her depth, felt like admitting a fundamental flaw in her character, a betrayal of the strong, independent woman she'd always strived to be.

So, instead of accepting Mrs. Gable's kind offer, Clara had spent the rest of the day buried in the grant applications. She wrestled with their jargon, deciphered their cryptic instructions, and filled in sections with educated guesses, each stroke of her pen a small act of defiance against the urge to reach out. She imagined the grant reviewers, their stern faces scrutinizing her application, looking for any hint of wavering confidence, any sign that she wasn't fully prepared. This was her opportunity to prove her competence, to show them that she was capable of handling this project, and by extension, that she was capable of handling anything.

The grant writing process was a lonely endeavor. She poured over manuals, cross-referenced data, and consulted online resources, piecing together a narrative of need and potential. Each successful submission felt like a small victory, a testament to her ability to navigate complex bureaucratic systems. But it was also an isolating process. She was a one-woman show, her own administrator, researcher, and project manager. The solitude, once a comforting balm, now felt like a vast, empty space that amplified her anxieties.

She remembered a conversation with her father, a man who had built his own successful business from the ground up. He'd always preached the gospel of hard work and self-sufficiency. "Never depend on anyone else, Clara," he'd told her countless times, his voice firm. "Your own two hands, your own sharp mind – that's all you truly need." Those words, meant to empower her, now echoed in her mind with a disquieting resonance. Was she failing him by even considering the possibility of needing help? Was her struggle a sign of weakness, a deviation from the path he'd so carefully laid out for her?

She pushed the thought away, focusing on the task at hand. She needed to secure funding, and grant applications, however daunting, were the most direct route. She'd meticulously researched various grants – historical preservation grants, community development grants, even grants for rural revitalization. Each one had its own set of criteria, its own peculiar demands. She spent hours poring over eligibility requirements, her brow furrowed in concentration. Some required extensive community support documentation, a testament to widespread local enthusiasm. Others demanded detailed architectural plans and engineering reports, a financial hurdle she hadn't yet overcome.

The applications themselves were intricate puzzles. She had to quantify intangible assets like "community spirit" and "historical significance." She had to project future economic benefits and demonstrate a clear return on investment for the town. It felt like she was trying to sell a dream, and the grant reviewers were the skeptical investors. The pressure to present a flawless, compelling case was immense. Any perceived weakness, any hint of disorganization, could be the very thing that led to rejection.

She found herself meticulously crafting justifications for every line item. The cost of hiring a structural engineer to assess the stage roof? Justified by the "urgent need to ensure public safety and preserve historical integrity." The expense of professional design consultations? Explained as "essential for developing a sustainable and accessible community space." She was building a fortress of data and justification, hoping to shield herself from the potential arrows of criticism.

The process was a mental marathon. She'd spend hours at the desk, her back aching, her eyes strained from the dim light of the desk lamp. She'd pause, cup her hands over her eyes, and take deep, fortifying breaths, trying to ward off the encroaching fatigue. She knew she should take a break, perhaps walk around the hall, clear her head. But the fear of losing momentum, of allowing the doubts to creep back in, kept her tethered to her chair. Every unanswered question, every blank space on a form, felt like a personal failing.

She recalled her childhood, always playing alone in the backyard, constructing elaborate forts from cardboard boxes and old blankets. Her mother, a kind but often preoccupied woman, had encouraged her independence. "You're such a self-sufficient little thing, Clara," she'd often say with a sigh that Clara now understood was laced with a touch of weary resignation. Clara had taken it as a compliment, a badge of honor. She didn't need anyone else to entertain her or to build her world. She could do it all herself.

This self-reliance, so deeply ingrained, was now manifesting as a protective shell. When a stray dog had wandered onto the property a few days ago, thin and timid, Clara had found herself hesitating to call animal control. She'd debated whether she could somehow manage to care for it herself, just for a few days, before admitting she couldn't. It was a small, insignificant incident, yet it highlighted her pattern of deflection. She'd rather shoulder a burden herself, however burdensome, than ask for assistance.

The grant applications were a perfect illustration of this internal struggle. Each form was a silent plea for help, a request for external funding, but Clara was framing it as a demonstration of her own resourcefulness. She was proving her worthiness by her ability to navigate the system, to present a compelling case for financial aid. It wasn't about asking for charity; it was about earning support through her own diligent efforts.

She felt a pang of longing for the ease of connection she'd observed in other small towns. She'd seen neighbors spontaneously helping each other, lending tools, sharing meals, offering childcare without a second thought. Cedar Ridge, she knew, had its own unique rhythm, its own unspoken rules of engagement. She hadn't yet found her place within that rhythm, and her own reticence was a significant factor. She was an outsider, a newcomer, and her efforts to remain entirely self-sufficient only served to reinforce that perception.

Clara sighed, leaning back in her chair. The grant applications were still spread out before her, a formidable stack of paper that represented both hope and a stark reminder of her isolation. She had chosen this path, the path of solitary endeavor. It was a path that promised strength, resilience, and the quiet satisfaction of accomplishment. But as she looked out the window at the vast, empty sky, she couldn't help but wonder if it was also a path that would ultimately leave her utterly alone, surrounded by the fruits of her labor, but lacking the warmth of shared experience. The fortress of her self-reliance was strong, undeniably so, but it was also a place with very few windows, and she was beginning to feel the chill of its isolation seeping into her very bones. The weight of solitude, she was learning, was not just in the tasks she undertook, but in the very act of undertaking them alone. She pressed on, however, meticulously filling out another section, her determination a stubborn flame flickering against the encroaching shadows of doubt.

CHAPTER THREE

An Unsolicited Offer

The afternoon sun, a pale wash of diluted gold, finally managed to pierce through the lingering remnants of the morning's storm clouds, casting long, spectral shadows across the worn floorboards of the community hall. Clara, her shoulders hunched in a posture of determined weariness, was locked in a silent battle with a particularly obstinate window frame. The old wood, warped and swollen by years of exposure and recent drenching, refused to yield.

Dust motes danced in the slivers of light that managed to penetrate the grimy glass, each microscopic particle a tiny testament to the hall's long neglect. She'd been at it for nearly an hour, her fingers raw and stinging, a small, insistent ache blooming in her forearms. She'd tried prying, jiggling, even a bit of brute force, but the stubborn metal of the hinges and the swollen wood seemed to have fused into an unyielding single entity. It was more than just a window; it was another symbol of the overwhelming task that lay before her, another stubborn obstacle in the path of her carefully constructed plans.

Her internal monologue, a constant companion these past few days, was a cacophony of self-recrimination and doubt.

Why can't you just get this open? It's just a window, Clara. You're making a mountain out of a molehill. What will people think if they see you struggling with something so simple? They'll know you're out of your depth. They'll know you can't do this. She pushed a stray strand of hair from her forehead, smudging a streak of grime across her temple. The grant applications were still waiting, a formidable stack on the desk in the back office, each page a silent challenge. But this window, this tangible, physical problem, felt more immediate, more pressing. If she couldn't even conquer this small, recalcitrant piece of the hall, how could she possibly hope to tackle the larger, more complex issues?

Just as she was contemplating a more drastic, potentially damaging approach – perhaps a strategically placed hammer – a voice, calm and unhurried, cut through her internal turmoil.

"That looks like it's seen better days."

Clara startled, her muscles tensing. She hadn't heard anyone approach. She turned, her heart giving a surprised little leap, to see Jonah standing a few feet away, his hands tucked loosely into the pockets of his worn denim jeans. He wasn't lurking; he was simply standing there, observing, his gaze steady and unreadable. There was no judgment in his eyes, no hint of impatience, just a quiet, almost detached interest in the struggle unfolding before him. He was a familiar fixture in Cedar Ridge, the owner of the local hardware store, a man known for his quiet competence and his understated presence. He'd been one of the few people she'd encountered since arriving who hadn't immediately launched into a barrage of questions or offers of unsolicited advice. He simply existed, a steady presence in the often-turbulent waters of small-town life.

She straightened up, trying to smooth the tension from her shoulders, to regain some semblance of control. "It's being a bit stubborn," she admitted, forcing a smile that felt tight and unnatural. She gestured vaguely at the window with her smudged hand. "The damp weather hasn't helped, I think."

Jonah took a step closer, his eyes still fixed on the window frame. He didn't immediately offer solutions or dismiss her efforts. He simply took in the situation, his expression thoughtful. "Metal hinges like that," he began, his voice a low rumble that seemed to vibrate with a quiet understanding of the material world, "they tend to seize up when they get wet and then dry out repeatedly. Especially if there's a bit of rust involved." He paused, as if considering his next words carefully. "There's a particular kind of penetrating oil I keep in the back of the shop. It's designed specifically for old, corroded metal. It works its way into the smallest crevices and loosens things up without damaging the surrounding material."

He didn't offer to fetch it. He didn't suggest she go to his store. He simply stated a fact, a piece of knowledge, a potential tool for her arsenal. It was a subtle offering, a seed of an idea planted without any pressure to accept. Clara found herself surprised by the lack of immediate expectation. She was so accustomed to the immediate push and pull of requests and offers, the dance of asking and receiving, that Jonah's quiet, observational approach felt almost... disarming.

"I've been trying to... persuade it," she said, her voice a little softer now, the defensiveness starting to recede. She met his gaze for a fleeting moment. "I was worried about damaging the frame, but I also really need to get this open." The words tumbled out, a small confession of her frustration and her underlying goal.

Jonah nodded, his expression unchanging. "I understand. Sometimes you need the right tool for the job. Brute force can do more harm than good, especially with these old buildings. They have a certain... resilience, but they also require a delicate touch." He gestured towards the back of the hall. "I've got a can of that oil in my workshop. It's a bit of a drive, but if you think it would be helpful, I could swing by and grab it for you. No charge, of course. Consider it a contribution to the hall's restoration."

The offer hung in the air, simple and direct. It wasn't a grand gesture, not a public declaration of support for her project. It was a practical, everyday act of kindness, rooted in his own expertise and his connection to the community. And it came at a time when Clara was feeling most alone, most burdened by the weight of her self-imposed isolation. The thought of the grant applications, the endless paperwork, the daunting financial figures, momentarily receded. Here was a concrete problem, a tangible solution, offered without fanfare.

Clara hesitated, her mind instinctively reaching for the well-worn scripts of refusal.

No, thank you, I can manage. It's not a big deal. I don't want to put you out. But the weariness was a heavy cloak, and the prospect of another hour wrestling with that stubborn window frame, another failed attempt, felt almost unbearable. And Jonah's offer wasn't an imposition. It was a genuine offer of help, delivered with the quiet sincerity of a man who understood the value of tools and the importance of fixing things.

"That's... that's very kind of you, Jonah," she said, her voice gaining a fraction more warmth. "I... I would appreciate that. Very much." The admission felt like a small victory in itself, a crack in the meticulously constructed wall of her independence. She watched as he turned, his movements fluid and unhurried, and walked towards the exit. As he passed her, he offered a small, almost imperceptible nod, a silent acknowledgment of their shared endeavor.

Left alone again, the silence of the hall seemed to press in on her, but it was a different kind of silence now. It was no longer solely an echo of her own isolation, but a space that held the promise of a solution, a brief respite from her internal struggles. She looked back at the window, no longer a symbol of her inadequacy, but simply a problem waiting to be solved. She ran her finger along the edge of the frame, feeling the rough texture of the wood, the faint ridges of rust. She wondered about Jonah. He was a man who dealt in practicalities, in nuts and bolts and lengths of pipe. What did he truly think of her grand plans for the hall? Did he see her as someone capable, or as another well-meaning outsider destined to fail?

She shook her head, dismissing the thought. It was too early to speculate, too soon to gauge reactions. For now, she would accept the help offered. It was a small step, but it felt significant. She walked back to the office, the grant applications still spread out before her, but her focus had shifted. She found herself rereading the section on community engagement, on the importance of local support. Perhaps, she mused, accepting Jonah's help wasn't a sign of weakness, but a demonstration of her willingness to work *with* the community, rather than solely *for* it. It was a subtle distinction, but one that felt important.

She picked up one of the forms, a grant specifically for historical preservation. It required a detailed assessment of the building's current condition and a comprehensive plan for its restoration. She'd spent days on the condition assessment, painstakingly documenting every crack, every leak, every sign of decay. But the plan... the plan was where her confidence wavered. It required technical expertise, architectural drawings, detailed costings that she was still struggling to formulate. She'd managed to get some preliminary estimates from a local contractor, Mr. Henderson, a man whose gruff exterior hid a surprising tenderness for the town's aging structures. But even those estimates felt... incomplete. They were based on general assumptions, not on the kind of detailed analysis that would be required for a grant application of this magnitude.

She traced the lines of a budget projection, her brow furrowed. The cost of materials alone was staggering. And then there was labor, skilled labor, which was always at a premium. She'd tried to be realistic, to account for unforeseen expenses, but the numbers still seemed to balloon with an alarming speed. She'd researched online suppliers, compared prices, and even looked into bulk purchasing options, but the sheer scale of the project was overwhelming. It was a good thing she was waiting for the grant funding, she told herself, otherwise she'd be bankrupt before she even started.

She recalled a conversation with her mother, who had once observed Clara meticulously cleaning a tarnished silver locket, her brow furrowed in concentration. "You always want to fix everything yourself, don't you, sweetie?" her mother had said, her voice tinged with a familiar blend of pride and gentle concern. At the time, Clara had seen it as a compliment. Now, she wondered if it was also a subtle critique, a recognition of a pattern that might, in the long run, be more of a hindrance than a help.

A faint clinking sound from the front of the hall announced Jonah's return. Clara rose from her chair, a renewed sense of purpose propelling her forward. She walked towards the entrance, and there he was, holding a small, aerosol can with a long, thin nozzle. He offered it to her with a slight tilt of his head.

"Here you go," he said, his voice quiet. "This should do the trick. Just a few good sprays around the hinges, let it sit for a few minutes, then try easing it open. If it's still being difficult, don't force it. Give it another application. Patience is key with these old windows." He didn't linger, didn't demand an explanation of her progress or an update on her grant-writing woes. He simply offered the tool and his quiet counsel, a gesture of neighborly support that felt more potent than any grand pronouncement.

"Thank you, Jonah. Really," Clara said, her voice sincere. She held the can, the cool metal a reassuring weight in her hand. "I... I really appreciate this."

He gave her a small, almost imperceptible smile, the corners of his eyes crinkling slightly. "Glad I could help. The hall means a lot to this town. We'll all be cheering you on." And with that, he turned and walked out, leaving Clara standing in the entryway, the can of penetrating oil a tangible symbol of a connection made, a small crack in her self-imposed isolation.

She returned to the window, a different kind of energy coursing through her. She carefully applied the oil to the rusted hinges, the thin straw reaching into the narrow gaps. The faint, chemical scent filled the air, mingling with the earthy aroma of damp wood. She waited, counting the seconds, her gaze fixed on the stubborn frame. She thought about Jonah's words, about the hall meaning a lot to the town. It was a sentiment she'd heard echoed by Mrs. Gable, by a few other residents she'd spoken to in passing. But it was one thing to hear it, and another to truly feel it, to believe in it.

After a few minutes, she tentatively reached for the window sash. She pulled gently, then a little more firmly. There was a faint creak, a protesting groan, but then, with a sudden, satisfying release, the window swung inward, a cascade of dust and dried leaves falling onto the floor. A gust of fresh, cool air rushed into the hall, carrying with it the scent of pine and damp earth. Clara leaned against the frame, breathing in the clean air, a wave of relief washing over her. It wasn't a monumental victory, but it was a victory nonetheless. A stubborn window, a symbol of neglect and decay, had yielded.

She looked out the open window, the view of the rolling hills now unobstructed. The sun, stronger now, painted the landscape in hues of gold and green. It was beautiful, a quiet, enduring beauty that had been there all along, waiting to be appreciated. She knew this was just the beginning. There were so many more windows to open, so many more rooms to coax back to life. The grant applications were still a daunting prospect, the financial challenges immense. But for the first time in days, a sliver of genuine optimism, as pale and tentative as the morning sun, began to dawn within her.

She had accepted help, and it had made a difference. It was a lesson, hard-won and quietly profound, in the delicate balance between self-reliance and the strength found in community. The fortress of her independence, she realized, didn't need to be impenetrable. It could, in fact, be a gateway, a place where shared effort could begin to mend what had been broken. And in that realization, there was a quiet, unexpected comfort. She closed the newly opened window, the movement smooth and easy now, and turned back to the paperwork, a renewed sense of determination settling over her. The path ahead was still long, but she was no longer entirely alone on it.

Clara's mind immediately recoiled, a defensive instinct ingrained by years of striving to be self-sufficient, to be the one who *had* the answers, not the one seeking them. Her first impulse was to politely decline, to murmur a practiced reassurance that she could, indeed, manage. Admitting she needed help felt akin to admitting failure, to confirming the whispered doubts that had been dogging her since she'd first stepped foot in Cedar Ridge. The image of herself, standing defeated before a recalcitrant window, was a bitter pill to swallow. Her gaze, a battlefield of conflicting emotions, darted from the stubbornly warped wood of the frame to Jonah's calm, observant face. His eyes, a clear, unwavering blue, held no hint of pity or condescension, only a quiet understanding that, paradoxically, made her resistance feel even more pronounced.

The very notion of owing someone, of being indebted, felt like a physical weight settling onto her shoulders. It was a chain, invisible but potent, that bound her autonomy. Her carefully constructed facade of capable competence would crumble, revealing the uncertainty and sheer, overwhelming scope of the task she had undertaken. She pictured the grant applications, the intricate financial projections, the sheer architectural knowledge that felt light-years beyond her grasp. If she couldn't even conquer a single, stubborn window, how could she possibly convince a panel of experts that she was the right person to restore a historic community hall? The silence stretched, taut with her internal debate. Each tick of her wristwatch seemed to echo the relentless march of time, and the growing urgency of her need.

Yet, the window frame remained resolutely in place, a silent, unyielding testament to her current limitations. It was a small obstacle, perhaps, in the grand scheme of the hall's restoration, but it was a tangible, immediate one. And Jonah's quiet patience, his unhurried presence, was a gentle, persistent pressure against her ingrained need for independence. He wasn't pushing, wasn't demanding an answer. He was simply there, offering a potential solution, a tool, a bit of practical wisdom. His offer was like a lifeline tossed into a churning sea, and her mind, though reluctant, was beginning to acknowledge the overwhelming pull of the tide.

She took a slow, steadying breath, the scent of old wood and damp plaster filling her lungs. "It's just that... well, I'm not used to asking for help," she admitted, the words a confession whispered into the cavernous space of the hall. Her voice, though low, held a tremor of vulnerability. "I've always prided myself on being able to handle things myself. It feels... like admitting I'm not capable." She gestured vaguely at the window, a self-deprecating smile touching her lips. "This window, for example. It's just a window, and I can't even get it open without feeling like I'm going to break it. If I can't manage something so simple, how can I possibly lead a project of this magnitude?" The thought was a familiar refrain, a persistent echo of her deepest anxieties.

Jonah remained still, his gaze unwavering. He didn't rush to reassure her, didn't offer platitudes about her strength or her capabilities. Instead, he spoke with a quiet pragmatism that, surprisingly, felt more effective than any effusive praise. "Clara," he began, his voice a low, steady rumble, "nobody can do everything alone. Not really. Especially not with something as complex as restoring an old building. These places... they have their own personalities, their own stubborn streaks. They demand respect, and sometimes, they demand a different kind of approach than you might expect." He paused, his eyes drifting back to the window. "That frame is old, probably oak. It's seen a lot of weather, a lot of years. It's not a sign of weakness that it's resisting you. It's just... what old wood does."

He took a small step closer, his presence a comforting anchor in her sea of doubt. "Think of it this way," he continued, "if you had a leaky roof, and you knew a roofer who was the best in the county, would you try to patch it yourself with duct tape, or would you call him?" He didn't wait for an answer. "It's not about admitting defeat. It's about recognizing that there are people who have skills and knowledge that can help you achieve your goal more effectively, and with less damage in the long run." He picked up a small piece of fallen plaster from the floor, turning it over in his fingers. "This hall... it's a big undertaking. A really big one. And frankly, I'd be more impressed if you *weren't* trying to do it all by yourself. That would be the truly worrying thing."

His words, simple and direct, began to chip away at the carefully constructed walls she had erected around her heart. He wasn't asking her to admit defeat; he was reframing her need for help as a sign of wisdom, of practicality. He was suggesting that her project, the very thing that felt so daunting, was precisely the kind of undertaking that *required* collaboration, not solitary struggle. The weight on her shoulders didn't vanish entirely, but it shifted, becoming less of a burden and more of a shared responsibility. She looked at the spray can in his hand, the utilitarian design a stark contrast to the romanticized vision she often held of her endeavor. This was real. This was practical. This was a step towards making the hall whole again.

"But... the oil," she began, still hesitant, "it's for your shop. I don't want to put you out. And I can't afford to pay you for it." The ingrained politeness, the deeply embedded script of social interaction, kicked in. She was acutely aware of the transactional nature of most human exchanges, and the prospect of receiving something for nothing, especially from a virtual stranger, made her deeply uncomfortable.

Jonah gave a small, almost imperceptible shake of his head. "Clara, the shop is my business. Helping out the community hall is... well, it's community. And frankly," he gave a wry, fleeting smile, "that can of oil costs me next to nothing. It's a few dollars of product. What it can *do* for this hall, and for your peace of mind, is worth a lot more than that." He stepped forward and gently placed the can of penetrating oil into her outstretched hand. The metal was cool against her skin, a tangible symbol of his offer. "Besides," he added, his gaze meeting hers, steady and reassuring, "a community hall isn't just a building. It's a gathering place. It's where people come together. And right now, this building needs people to come together to help it. I'm just one of them."

His words resonated with a profound truth. She had been so focused on the bricks and mortar, the grant proposals and the financial ledgers, that she had, perhaps, lost sight of the hall's true purpose. It wasn't just about preserving history; it was about nurturing the present and the future, about creating a space where the community could thrive. And to do that, she couldn't afford to remain an island. She had to learn to be a part of the ebb and flow of Cedar Ridge, to accept the currents of connection that ran through the town.

"Thank you, Jonah," she said again, her voice softer now, the resistance in her tone replaced by a genuine, heartfelt gratitude. She looked down at the can, tracing the embossed lettering with her fingertip. "I... I truly appreciate this. More than you know." The admission felt like a small, but significant, step forward. It was an acknowledgment that her own efforts, while diligent, were not always sufficient, and that accepting assistance was not a sign of failure, but a strategic choice, a move towards greater success.

He offered a faint, almost imperceptible nod. "Just let me know if you run into any other... stubborn personalities in this building," he said, a hint of amusement in his voice. "I've got a workshop full of solutions, and a healthy respect for things that have stood the test of time, even when they're being difficult." He turned then, his movements fluid and unhurried, and walked towards the main entrance, the echo of his footsteps fading into the vastness of the hall.

Clara stood for a moment, the can of penetrating oil a solid weight in her hand. The silence that settled after Jonah's departure was different now. It was no longer the isolating, oppressive silence of her own struggle, but a quiet hum of possibility. The window, moments ago a symbol of her limitations, now seemed to represent an opportunity. An opportunity to learn, to adapt, and to connect.

She turned back to the window, a renewed sense of purpose guiding her actions. The worn metal hinges, coated in a fine layer of rust, seemed less daunting now. She carefully examined the can, noting the long, slender nozzle designed for precise application. This wasn't brute force; this was targeted intervention. She sprayed a generous amount of the oil directly onto the hinges, the faint, chemical scent mingling with the musty aroma of the old hall. She let it sit, as Jonah had advised, her gaze fixed on the obstinate frame. She imagined the oil seeping into the minuscule cracks and crevices, loosening the corroded metal, whispering a gentle promise of movement.

As she waited, her thoughts drifted. She wondered what other "stubborn personalities" resided within these walls. Were there other windows that refused to budge, doors that stuck, floorboards that creaked in protest? And more importantly, were there other people in Cedar Ridge, like Jonah, who possessed the knowledge and willingness to help her coax them back to life? The idea of a network of support, built not on grand pronouncements or overt demands, but on quiet acts of neighborly assistance, began to take root in her mind. It was a far cry from the solitary, heroic narrative she had envisioned for herself, but it felt more real, more sustainable.

She remembered a conversation with Mrs. Gable, the energetic woman who ran the local bakery, whose hands were perpetually dusted with flour. Mrs. Gable had spoken with such passion about the history of the hall, about the dances and the town meetings that had taken place within its walls. "It's the heart of our town, dear," she had said, her eyes shining, "or at least, it used to be. We need to get it beating again." At the time, Clara had nodded, taking mental notes for her grant applications. But now, Jonah's words echoed Mrs. Gable's sentiment. It wasn't just about restoring a building; it was about reviving the heart of the community. And a heart, by its very nature, required connection, flow, and the contributions of many.

With a deep breath, Clara gently pulled on the window sash. There was a hesitant groan, a protest from the aged wood and metal, but then, with a surprising ease, the window swung inward. A rush of cool, crisp air filled the hall, carrying with it the fresh scent of pine and damp earth. Dust motes, disturbed by the sudden influx of air, swirled in the sunlight that now streamed through the opening. Clara leaned against the frame, her shoulders relaxing, a wave of relief washing over her. It wasn't a dramatic, thunderous victory, but a quiet, satisfying release. A stubborn problem, solved not by her own solitary will, but by accepting a helping hand.

She looked out at the landscape, the rolling hills bathed in the warm glow of the afternoon sun. The view, previously obscured by grimy glass, was now clear and unobstructed. It was a simple thing, this open window, but it felt like a profound shift. It was a tangible representation of progress, a small crack in the fortress of her independence that allowed the light, and the fresh air, to enter.

The grant applications still loomed, a daunting pile of paperwork waiting patiently in the back office. The financial challenges remained immense, the restoration a monumental undertaking. But for the first time since she had arrived in Cedar Ridge, Clara felt a genuine flicker of hope, as clear and bright as the newly revealed vista. She had accepted help, and it had made all the difference. It was a lesson, hard-won and quietly profound, in the delicate balance between self-reliance and the strength that could be found in community.

The fortress of her independence, she realized, didn't need to be impenetrable. It could, in fact, be a gateway, a place where shared effort could begin to mend what had been broken. And in that realization, there was a quiet, unexpected comfort. She closed the window, the movement smooth and easy now, and turned back towards the office, a renewed sense of determination settling over her. The path ahead was still long, but she was no longer entirely alone on it.

Jonah's words, delivered with a quiet sincerity that seemed to emanate from the very timbers of the old hall, began to weave a different narrative in Clara's mind. He spoke not of transactions or debts, but of an intrinsic bond that tied the residents of Cedar Ridge together, a tapestry woven from countless small acts of mutual support. "In Cedar Ridge," he explained, his gaze earnest, "we look out for each other. It's just how things are. This Hall," he gestured around the cavernous space, the afternoon sun illuminating the dust motes dancing in its beams, "it's for all of us. It's not about what you owe, it's about what we build together."

The concept of "building together" felt alien to Clara, a foreign language she was only just beginning to decipher. Her upbringing, marked by a fierce independence instilled by a mother who had shouldered every burden alone, had taught her that reliance on others was a vulnerability, a weakness to be concealed at all costs. She had arrived in Cedar Ridge with the weight of expectation on her shoulders, determined to prove her competence, to single-handedly resurrect this forgotten landmark. The idea that the hall's restoration was not solely her responsibility, but a shared endeavor, was a revelation that simultaneously unnerved and intrigued her.

"I... I'm not sure I understand," she admitted, her voice barely a whisper. She traced the rim of the oil can in her hand, the cool metal a grounding sensation against her restless fingers. "I've always believed that if you start something, you should be able to finish it yourself. It feels... wrong, somehow, to rely on others for something I've taken on." Her confession hung in the air, a testament to the deeply ingrained beliefs that had shaped her identity.

Jonah offered a small, knowing smile. "That's a noble sentiment, Clara. And I'm sure you *can* finish it yourself. But the question is, why should you have to? Why carry that burden alone when there are hands, and skills, and even just a little bit of elbow grease, willing to help lift it?" He leaned against a sturdy support beam, his posture relaxed but his gaze unwavering. "Think about it," he continued, his voice taking on a more storytelling cadence. "When Mrs. Gable's oven broke down right before the harvest festival, did she try to fix it herself with a hairpin and a prayer? No. She called down to the hardware store, and young Billy, who's got a knack for engines, came right over. He didn't charge her a dime. He just... helped. Because he knew that if her oven was working, the whole town would have pies."

He paused, letting the analogy settle. "And then, when Billy's roof started leaking during that big storm last spring, who do you think was up there, handing him shingles and holding the ladder steady? Mrs. Gable. That's the way it works here. It's not about a formal ledger of favors. It's about recognizing that we're all in this together. The more we support each other, the stronger this town becomes. And this Hall," he swept his hand around again, "is a symbol of that strength. It's where our history is, and where our future can be, if we all pitch in."

His words painted a picture of Cedar Ridge that was both charming and, to Clara, surprisingly profound. She had seen the town as a collection of individuals, each pursuing their own path, with the hall as her solitary project. Jonah, however, presented it as a living, breathing entity, a collective of people bound by a shared sense of belonging and a mutual responsibility to one another. His offer of oil, she now realized, was not a charitable act, but an act of participation. He wasn't giving her a handout; he was investing in a shared future, a stake in the very heart of their community.

"So, you're not... you're not doing this out of pity?" she ventured, the question laced with a vulnerability she rarely allowed herself to express. The thought of being pitied was almost as difficult to bear as the thought of failure.

Jonah's brow furrowed slightly, a genuine surprise flickering in his eyes. "Pity? Clara, why would I pity you? You're taking on something that most people would shy away from. That takes guts. What I'm offering is not pity, it's partnership. It's saying, 'I see what you're trying to do, and I believe in it, and I want to be a part of making it happen.'" He pushed off the beam and took a step closer, his presence a warm, steady force. "This isn't about your personal struggle, Clara. It's about our shared history and our shared future. This hall belongs to everyone in Cedar Ridge. And when something that belongs to everyone needs a little attention, then everyone contributes in whatever way they can."

He reached out and gently touched the worn wood of the window frame, his fingers tracing the grain. "This wood," he said softly, "it's seen generations of Cedar Ridge residents. It's been part of birthday parties, town meetings, wedding receptions, and countless conversations. It's a living piece of our town's story. To see it restored, to see this building buzzing with life again… that's something that benefits all of us. So, when I offer you this oil, or my time, or even just a word of advice, it's not charity. It's me investing in my own community. It's me doing my part to ensure that the heart of Cedar Ridge beats strong for years to come."

His perspective was a radical departure from her own deeply entrenched beliefs about self-reliance. She had always viewed help as a sign of weakness, a testament to her own shortcomings. But Jonah was reframing it as a sign of strength, a collective power that could achieve far more than any individual could alone. He wasn't just offering her a can of oil; he was offering her a glimpse into the soul of Cedar Ridge, a community that thrived on connection and shared purpose.

"But… the grant money," she faltered, the financial aspect of her project a constant source of anxiety. "I'm supposed to be managing this all on a tight budget. Accepting help, even something as small as this… it feels like I'm not being a good steward of the funds." The grant application had been meticulously crafted, detailing her plan for efficient resource management. Any deviation, any perceived overspending or reliance on external resources, felt like a betrayal of that trust.

Jonah chuckled, a low, rumbling sound that eased some of the tension in her shoulders. "Clara, that grant money is for the big things, the structural repairs, the materials that cost a pretty penny. This oil? It's a few dollars. The real cost of this project isn't just the money. It's the time, the effort, the knowledge. And sometimes, the most valuable resources aren't the ones you can buy with a check." He gave her a thoughtful look. "Think about it this way: If a carpenter is building a house, and they have a special tool that will make the job faster and better, but it's too expensive for them to buy outright, would it be smarter to struggle along with a less effective tool, or to borrow the right one from a neighbor?"

He continued before she could respond, his logic undeniable. "Cedar Ridge is your neighbor, Clara. And I'm one of its residents. We have tools, in the form of skills and resources, that we're willing to share. It's not about cutting corners on the grant. It's about being smart. It's about using all the assets available to you, human and otherwise, to achieve the best possible outcome for this hall. In fact," he added, a slight grin playing on his lips, "I'd wager that the grant committee would be more impressed with a project that shows collaboration and community involvement than one that portrays a lone wolf trying to conquer a mountain single-handedly. They want to see this hall thrive, and that means seeing the community thrive around it."

The idea that community involvement could be a positive, even a requirement, in her grant proposal was a paradigm shift. She had approached the project with the mindset of a solitary engineer, meticulously planning every step, every material, every cost. But Jonah was suggesting that the 'human element,' the intangible threads of connection that bound people together, were just as crucial as the bricks and mortar.

"It's just... I'm used to being the one who *provides* the solutions," she confessed, her voice low and earnest. "It's hard for me to be the one who needs them." She looked down at the oil can, a symbol of her newfound reliance. It was a small thing, but it represented a crack in the carefully constructed edifice of her independence.

"And that's what makes you so valuable to this project, Clara," Jonah said, his tone gentle but firm. "You have the vision, the drive, the determination to see this through. You're the architect of this dream. But an architect doesn't build the house alone, do they? They need a crew. They need skilled hands to lay the foundation, raise the walls, and put on the roof. My offer, and the offers of others in this town, are simply us saying, 'We're ready to be part of your crew.'"

He gestured towards the far end of the hall, where a section of the ceiling was showing signs of water damage. "See that? That's a problem that needs a roofer's eye. And down in the basement, the old boiler is making some peculiar noises. That's a job for someone who understands heating systems. I can swing a hammer, I can fix a leaky faucet, and I know a thing or two about wood. Others in town have different skills. We can bring those skills to bear on this project, not because we're charity cases, but because we believe in this hall, and we believe in you, leading the charge."

His words resonated with a deeper truth, a calling to something beyond mere bricks and mortar. Clara had been so focused on the physical restoration of the building, on the meticulous planning and execution, that she had perhaps overlooked the very essence of what a community hall represented. It was a hub, a gathering place, a living monument to the shared experiences and connections of the people who called Cedar Ridge home. To restore the hall was to restore that sense of shared identity, that collective spirit.

"You're saying that... accepting help isn't a sign of weakness, but a sign of wisdom?" she asked, the question a tentative step towards embracing his perspective.

"Exactly," Jonah confirmed, his smile widening. "It's recognizing that none of us are islands. We're all connected, and our collective strength is far greater than our individual capabilities. Cedar Ridge understands that. We've learned it over the years, through good times and bad. We lean on each other. It's not about owing anyone anything; it's about building something together that's bigger and better than any one of us could build alone. This hall is a testament to that. It was built by the hands of this community, and it will be restored by the hands of this community."

He met her gaze, his blue eyes clear and steady, a quiet challenge and a gentle invitation. "So, Clara, what do you say? Are you ready to be a part of what we build together?"

The weight on Clara's shoulders didn't vanish entirely, but it shifted. It was no longer the solitary burden of her own ambition, but the shared responsibility of a collective endeavor. The can of penetrating oil, once a symbol of her limited resources, now felt like a key, unlocking a door to a richer, more connected future for both herself and the Cedar Ridge Community Hall. She looked at the stubborn window, then back at Jonah, a nascent understanding dawning in her eyes. Perhaps, just perhaps, the most important restoration wouldn't be of the building itself, but of her own rigid perception of what it meant to be strong, to be capable, and to be a part of something larger than herself.

The afternoon sun, which had begun to slant through the dusty panes of the Community Hall, now cast long, dramatic shadows that stretched across the worn floorboards. Clara stood by the stubborn window, her fingers still tingling from their brief contact with the cool metal of the oil can. Jonah's words, a gentle but persistent tide, had eroded some of the granite-hard walls she'd built around her independence. He hadn't just offered oil; he'd offered a different perspective, a vision of Cedar Ridge that was communal, interwoven, and, dare she admit it, appealing. The idea of "building together" was still a foreign concept, but it was no longer entirely unwelcome.

She glanced at the window again, the warped wood stubbornly refusing to yield. Her usual approach would be to apply more force, more pressure, until something gave way—either the wood or her own patience. But Jonah's analogy of the carpenter and the borrowed tool echoed in her mind. Was it truly a sign of weakness to accept a tool that would make the job easier, faster, and less likely to cause further damage? The grant funding was for the substantial repairs, the materials, the permits. It wasn't for the small, often overlooked, but crucial tasks that required a specific touch, a particular skill, or a specialized implement.

"Alright," she said, the word a small surrender, barely audible above the whisper of the wind rustling the leaves outside. It felt like a significant concession, a single, deliberate crack in the carefully constructed armor of her self-reliance. She'd always prided herself on her ability to tackle any problem, to find a solution with the resources at hand. To ask for help, even for something as seemingly minor as a stuck window, felt like admitting a deficiency. Yet, the alternative was to risk damaging the frame further, an outcome that went against the very meticulous nature of her restoration plan.

Jonah's expression remained open and patient. He didn't press, didn't make a show of her agreement. He simply nodded, a quiet acknowledgment. "Good," he said, his voice even. "Let me see if I have just the thing."

He disappeared for a moment, his footsteps echoing faintly from somewhere outside the main hall. Clara watched the dust motes swirl in the sunlight, her thoughts a tangled mess of apprehension and a nascent curiosity. What kind of tool would he have? What would it look like? And more importantly, what would it feel like to accept assistance, to share the burden, even in this small, tangible way? Her mother's voice, a constant internal whisper, reminded her of the importance of self-sufficiency, of never appearing to need anyone. But Jonah's vision of Cedar Ridge, of a community where mutual support was not a weakness but a strength, was beginning to take root, a delicate seedling pushing through the hardened earth of her ingrained beliefs.

He returned carrying a small, flat metal object, something that looked more like a specialized scraper than a tool she'd ever encountered. It had a thin, almost blade-like edge, but with a subtle curve to it, and a comfortable wooden handle. "This," he explained, holding it out for her inspection, "is a sash tool. It's designed to gently pry apart window sashes that have been painted shut or warped by humidity. You can get a lot of leverage without gouging the wood."

He knelt beside the window, his movements economical and precise. Clara watched, her breath held captive in her chest. He didn't ask for permission again; he simply began to work. He carefully inserted the narrow edge of the tool into the thin gap between the sash and the frame, where decades of paint and wood expansion had fused them together. He worked it back and forth with a steady, rhythmic motion, applying just enough pressure to encourage the separation.

There was no dramatic creaking, no splintering of wood, no strained grunts of effort. Instead, a faint, almost imperceptible give. Jonah continued, his focus absolute. He moved the tool along the edge, his touch sure and confident. Clara found herself studying his hands, the way his fingers gripped the handle, the controlled strength in his forearms. He wasn't just wielding a tool; he was employing a skill, a knowledge of materials and mechanics that she, with all her research and planning, hadn't anticipated.

Then, with a soft sigh of relief from the wood, the sash began to move. It wasn't a dramatic shift, but a gentle loosening, a freeing of the obstruction. Jonah worked the tool a little further, and then, with a quiet, satisfying slide, the window sash moved upward by a few inches. He repeated the process on the other side, and soon the entire window was no longer sealed shut. A small draft of cool, fresh air, carrying the scent of pine and damp earth, wafted into the hall, a welcome change from the stagnant, musty air.

He then carefully wiped the tool with a clean cloth he produced from his pocket, removing any traces of paint or debris. He didn't boast, didn't seek her praise. He simply stood, offering the tool back to her with a nod. "There you go," he said, his voice still low and calm. "Sometimes, you just need the right implement for the job."

Clara took the tool, her fingers brushing his as she accepted it. The metal felt cool and smooth against her skin. The ease with which he had accomplished the task was both reassuring and, she had to admit, a little humbling. It was a small thing, a single window, but it represented a significant shift in her approach. She had been so determined to prove her capability, to handle everything herself, that she had almost overlooked the simple efficiency of accepting a helping hand, or in this case, a helping tool.

A strange mix of emotions swirled within her. There was relief, certainly. The window was no longer a problem she had to wrestle with alone, a problem that might have required more force and potentially caused more damage. But there was also a subtle disquiet, a faint tremor of unease that rippled through her carefully constructed sense of self-reliance. It was the disquiet of admitting that she didn't have all the answers, that there were skills and knowledge beyond her own, and that it was okay, perhaps even beneficial, to tap into them.

"Thank you, Jonah," she said, her voice a little steadier this time. She looked at the tool in her hand, then at the now-movable window. "That... that was remarkably efficient."

He offered a small, genuine smile. "Just trying to lend a hand where I can. It's good to see this place coming back to life." He glanced around the hall, his gaze lingering on the peeling paint and the water-stained ceiling. "That's a bigger job than a stuck window, of course. But every bit helps."

He didn't linger. He didn't ask if she needed anything else, didn't try to prolong the interaction. He simply gave a final, amicable nod and turned to leave, his presence a quiet force that had momentarily altered the atmosphere of the hall. "I'll be around if you need anything else," he said over his shoulder as he walked towards the main entrance. "Just give a holler."

And then he was gone, leaving Clara alone once more with the echoes of his words and the subtle scent of the fresh air that now filled the hall. She looked down at the sash tool in her hand, its weight a tangible reminder of the interaction. It was a simple tool, but it had opened something more significant than a window. It had opened a small, tentative door in her own defenses, a doorway through which the possibility of collaboration, of shared effort, and of community could begin to enter. The disquiet remained, a faint hum beneath the surface, but it was now accompanied by a growing sense of relief, and perhaps, just a whisper of hope.

The restoration of the Cedar Ridge Community Hall was a monumental task, and she was beginning to suspect that perhaps, just perhaps, she didn't have to face it entirely alone. The offer of partnership, once so alien, was starting to feel less like a burden and more like an invitation. She carefully placed the sash tool on a nearby ledge, a silent acknowledgment of its usefulness, and turned back to the window, a new resolve settling over her. The next step, she knew, would be to actually begin the repairs that the grant funding would cover, and the thought of tackling them, with the possibility of future assistance, felt a little less daunting.

The gentle sigh of the wind, now carrying the scent of the newly opened window, felt like a whispered confession of defeat. Clara traced the cool, smooth grain of the sash tool still resting on the ledge, its presence a stark contrast to the splintered frustration she'd felt only moments before. Jonah's effortless solution to her persistent problem, the problem that had tied her in knots for what felt like an eternity, had been... disarming. It was more than just the efficiency of his method; it was the quiet confidence with which he'd approached it, the innate understanding of the wood's stubborn resistance and the precise tool to coax it into submission.

Her own approach, a brute-force insistence on moving the unyielding material, now seemed almost comically inefficient. She'd been so focused on the *act* of overcoming, on proving her own strength and capability, that she'd overlooked the simpler, more elegant path. It was a humbling realization, a small tremor beneath the bedrock of her carefully cultivated self-reliance. Her mother's voice, a familiar refrain of "do it yourself, rely on no one but yourself," seemed to fade slightly, replaced by the quiet hum of the wind and the memory of Jonah's steady hands.

She watched as Jonah, his work here done, gathered his belongings with the same unhurried grace he'd shown throughout their interaction. He offered a final, brief nod in her direction, a silent acknowledgment that spoke volumes. There was no expectation, no plea for further conversation, just a simple, polite departure. He moved with a grounded purpose, his boots crunching softly on the gravel outside, a sound that gradually receded, leaving Clara alone with the silence and her burgeoning thoughts.

As he walked away, disappearing around the side of the Community Hall and heading towards what she assumed was his workshop, Clara found herself observing his retreating figure with a new perspective. It wasn't just the competence she'd witnessed; it was the underlying philosophy, the unspoken belief in shared effort that seemed to permeate his very being. He hadn't just fixed a window; he had, in a subtle but profound way, demonstrated the value of community.

His earlier words about "building together," about Cedar Ridge being a place where people helped each other, had previously seemed like quaint, almost naive notions. She'd filed them away as the idle musings of a man perhaps too comfortable with the idea of interdependence. But now, holding the evidence of his practical assistance in her hand – the sash tool, a tangible symbol of borrowed expertise – those words began to resonate with a different kind of weight.

She pictured him in his workshop, a space she'd never seen but imagined filled with the scent of sawdust and the quiet industry of skilled hands. He'd likely have a collection of such specialized tools, each one a testament to years of learning, of problem-solving, of honing his craft. He didn't hoard that knowledge, didn't keep those tools locked away as personal treasures. He readily offered them, even to a relative newcomer like herself, someone who had, admittedly, approached him with a degree of suspicion and a wall of guarded independence.

A flicker of unease, a familiar ghost of her ingrained self-sufficiency, began to stir. What if his offer of help wasn't just about a single window? What if it was an opening, a subtle invitation to lean on him, and by extension, on others in the community? The thought was both tempting and terrifying. Her entire adult life had been a testament to her ability to stand on her own two feet, to navigate challenges without seeking external validation or support. Admitting that she *might* need help, that she *could* benefit from the collective wisdom of Cedar Ridge, felt like a betrayal of the very principles she lived by.

Yet, the evidence was undeniable. The window was open. The air was fresh. And her own frustration had been replaced by a quiet sense of... possibility. She found herself replaying the interaction, not with a critical eye, but with a dawning curiosity. Jonah hadn't *taken over*. He hadn't dismissed her efforts or made her feel inadequate. He had simply applied his knowledge, his tools, his experience, to a problem that was blocking her progress. It was a partnership, albeit a brief and unsolicited one, and it had yielded a result she couldn't have achieved on her own, at least not without significant effort and potential damage.

She picked up the sash tool, its cool metal a reassuring weight in her palm. It was a simple instrument, yet its impact was far-reaching. It had not only opened a window but had also begun to pry open a few of the tightly sealed shutters of her own resistance. The grant money was secured, a substantial sum that would allow for the major renovations: the new roof, the electrical upgrades, the restoration of the façade. But those were the bones of the project. The soul, she was beginning to realize, lay in the smaller, more intricate details – the kind of details that required not just funding, but also skill, knowledge, and perhaps, a helping hand.

She glanced back towards the path Jonah had taken, a faint smile touching her lips. He had offered more than just a tool; he had offered a glimpse into a different way of doing things, a way that acknowledged the strength found in shared endeavor. She wasn't ready to abandon her independence, not by a long shot. The walls she had built were thick and deeply rooted. But for the first time, she could see a small, almost imperceptible crack in their formidable structure, a crack through which the light of community might, just might, begin to filter in.

The idea of Cedar Ridge, once a place she was merely restoring, was starting to feel like a place she might actually *belong*, if only she could learn to accept the outstretched hands, or the offered tools, that came with it. The task ahead was still daunting, but the prospect of facing it, with the faintest whisper of shared purpose in the air, was no longer quite so solitary. She would proceed with the grant work, meticulously and independently, but she would also keep her eyes and ears open, a cautious acknowledgment that sometimes, the most efficient path wasn't the one walked alone.

CHAPTER FOUR

Contrasting Approaches

The Community Hall, with its freshly unjammed window now framing a sliver of the late afternoon sun, had become a silent testament to a nascent understanding for Clara. She stood in her small, rented office above the bakery, the scent of yeast and sugar a comforting counterpoint to the crisp, official paper spread before her. Her workbench, usually a controlled chaos of blueprints and historical photos, was now dominated by thick binders labeled with meticulous, color-coded tabs: "Cedar Ridge Historical Preservation Society – Bylaws," "Municipal Building Codes – Appendix C: Structural Integrity," and "Recommended Repair Protocols for 19th Century Timber Frames." This was her domain, the world of rules, regulations, and the ironclad certainty of documented procedures.

Her approach was systematic, bordering on monastic. Every decision, every potential expense, had to be vetted, cross-referenced, and approved according to a rigid framework. The grant money, a lifeline for the beleaguered Hall, came with its own set of stringent guidelines, and Clara intended to meet them with unwavering precision. She'd spent the better part of the morning poring over the stipulations, her brow furrowed in concentration as she highlighted clauses pertaining to vendor selection and material sourcing. "All contractors and sub-contractors must provide three (3) written bids for services exceeding five hundred dollars ($500)," she read aloud to the empty room, her voice echoing slightly in the confined space. "Documentation of all bids, including rationale for final selection, must be appended to the project ledger."

She meticulously noted down the requirement, her pen scratching decisively on her notepad. For the minor repairs needed on the Hall's plumbing – a few leaky pipes and a temperamental faucet – she'd already begun compiling a list of local plumbers. Her research, which involved more than just a quick online search, had led her to several names mentioned in various town archives and online business directories. Each one would receive a formal request for a detailed quote, a process she intended to repeat for even the smallest of tasks. The warped floorboards in the west wing, for instance, would require a carpenter, and she'd need at least three distinct proposals for their replacement, outlining materials, labor costs, and estimated timelines. It wasn't just about due diligence; it was about demonstrating to the grant committee, and to herself, that this project was being managed with the utmost professionalism and accountability.

Her personal philosophy, honed over years of navigating corporate bureaucracy and academic research, was rooted in the belief that structure and order were the bulwarks against chaos. In her experience, deviations from established protocols invariably led to unforeseen problems, missed deadlines, and ultimately, financial overruns. The world, as she understood it, operated on a system of checks and balances, of clear expectations and measurable outcomes. This was how projects were successfully completed, how trust was earned, and how reputations were built. The Community Hall, a symbol of Cedar Ridge's past and a beacon for its future, deserved nothing less than this rigorous, data-driven approach.

She paused, tapping her pen against her chin. The initial assessment of the electrical system was also due for a detailed breakdown. While the grant covered significant upgrades, the specifics of the rewiring, the type of conduits, and the number of new outlets, needed to be determined by a licensed electrician. Again, the three-bid rule would apply. She envisioned herself meticulously comparing the figures, scrutinizing the fine print, and making a decision based solely on objective criteria. It was a painstaking process, but one that guaranteed transparency and minimized risk. She even planned to document the exact specifications of the lumber needed for any structural repairs, cross-referencing them with approved materials lists to ensure compliance. Every nail, every plank, every length of wire would have its place in the grand, meticulously kept record.

As she worked, a faint image of Jonah's hands, calloused and steady, flickered in her mind. His solution to the window problem had been so... unburdened by paperwork. He'd simply assessed the situation, reached for a specific tool, and with a few deft movements, resolved the issue. It was an approach that seemed to bypass the very layers of procedure she was currently immersed in. He hadn't asked for a quote; he hadn't filled out any forms. He had simply *done*. And it had worked. Beautifully.

The thought was a persistent whisper at the edge of her consciousness, a subtle counterpoint to the rustle of paper. She remembered his casual mention of "just grabbing a few guys from town" for larger tasks, of calling up familiar faces who'd done work for him, and for their neighbors, for years. There was an implied trust, a reliance on established relationships that seemed to operate on an entirely different currency than the one she was dealing with. It was a currency of reputation, of mutual respect, and of a shared understanding that went beyond the written word.

She sighed, a soft exhalation that disturbed the precise stacks of documents. Her gut instinct, honed by years of practical experience in her own field, told her that Jonah's way, while perhaps less document-heavy, was undeniably effective within the context of a small town like Cedar Ridge. But her professional responsibility, her ingrained sense of how things *should* be done, kept her tethered to the rulebook. The grant committee wouldn't be impressed by a handshake deal or a promise based on community goodwill. They expected a paper trail, a clear audit of every dollar spent.

She continued to refine her system, creating spreadsheets for estimated costs, comparing them against the grant's allocation for each category. She even began sketching out a timeline, marking milestones and potential bottlenecks, all based on her current understanding of the necessary steps. Each step, in her mind, was a carefully planned maneuver, requiring specific approvals and documented evidence of completion.

The sheer volume of paperwork was daunting, but it was a necessary evil, a price to pay for legitimacy and successful funding. She was building the Hall anew, not just with brick and mortar, but with meticulous planning and an unwavering commitment to protocol. It was the right way, the only way, she knew how to build.

Meanwhile, in the heart of Cedar Ridge, a different kind of enterprise was unfolding, one that operated less on the meticulously drafted pages of municipal bylaws and more on the well-worn pages of shared experience and unspoken agreements. Jonah, with his sleeves rolled up and a faint sheen of sawdust on his forearms, was standing on the porch of Mrs. Gable's small cottage, listening with patient attention. Mrs. Gable, a woman whose eighty years had etched a roadmap of gentle kindness onto her face, was explaining a recurring issue with her porch railing. It had a tendency to sag, particularly after a heavy rain, and no amount of tightening screws seemed to keep it in place permanently.

"It's the old oak post, dear," she explained, her voice raspy but warm. "Been there since the house was built, I reckon. Wonderful old thing, but it's settled a bit, I think, and the wood's taken on a bit of a swell."

Jonah nodded, his eyes scanning the weathered timber, the slight angle of the railing, the way the boards met. He didn't pull out a tape measure or consult a technical manual. His assessment was immediate, intuitive, born from decades of working with the very materials that formed the bones of Cedar Ridge. He'd seen this before, felt it in his hands, understood the subtle language of aging wood.

"I know just the thing, Mrs. Gable," he said, a gentle smile easing the lines around his eyes. "There's a trick to it. Nothing that'll cost you much, and it'll hold it firm as a rock. I'll just need to fetch my tools and perhaps pop over to Silas's lumber yard. He'll have just the right kind of bracing we'll need, the old-fashioned kind that doesn't mind a bit of moisture."

Silas, a man whose family had been in the lumber business in Cedar Ridge for three generations, was more than just a supplier; he was a trusted colleague. Jonah didn't need to provide Silas with a detailed requisition form. A phone call, a brief explanation of the problem, and Silas would know exactly what Jonah needed, and at what price. There would be no competitive bidding, no multi-page quotes for a few feet of seasoned timber and a length of steel rod. There would simply be an exchange, based on years of mutual respect and a shared commitment to the well-being of the town's aging structures.

"Oh, that would be a blessing, Jonah," Mrs. Gable said, her hands fluttering with relief. "I was just about to call that young man Clara's hired for the Hall. He sounded very official, you know, asking all sorts of questions about permits and professional certifications. But I'm not sure he'd understand about old oak posts and a bit of settling."

Jonah suppressed a chuckle. He knew the young man Clara had hired – or rather, the young woman. Clara herself. He respected her dedication, her drive, her clear commitment to doing things properly. But he also saw the inherent disconnect, the fundamental difference in their operating systems. Clara approached problems like a surgeon with a scalpel, meticulously dissecting each component, charting every variable, and ensuring every action was documented for posterity. Jonah, on the other hand, was more like a seasoned mechanic, relying on his intuition, his vast reservoir of practical knowledge, and his network of skilled hands to diagnose and repair.

"Clara's got a good head on her shoulders," Jonah said diplomatically, his gaze returning to the porch. "She's making sure everything's by the book for the Hall. That's important, especially with the grant. But for things like your railing, or a leaky faucet at the church, or a fence that's gone askew at the schoolhouse... well, that's where folks like me and Silas and the others come in. We know the town, we know its quirks, and we know each other."

He envisioned the process for Mrs. Gable's railing. He'd likely need to find a few sturdy pieces of hardwood, perhaps some specialized joinery screws that wouldn't corrode. He'd then brace the post from the inside, using a technique that allowed for expansion and contraction without stressing the surrounding wood. It would be a repair that was both effective and discreet, designed to blend seamlessly with the existing structure. And the cost? It would be fair, a reflection of the materials and his time, but not an amount that would burden Mrs. Gable. It would be the Cedar Ridge way: practical, community-minded, and efficient.

He knew Clara was meticulously gathering quotes for every faucet washer and every roof shingle. He could imagine her creating detailed spreadsheets, comparing not just prices, but also the specifications of each item, the warranties offered, the delivery timelines. It was a Herculean effort, and while he admired her diligence, he couldn't help but feel a pang of something akin to pity. She was expending so much energy on processes that, in Cedar Ridge, were often streamlined by trust and established relationships.

"I'll bring the materials by this afternoon," Jonah continued, turning back to Mrs. Gable. "And I'll do the work while I'm here. Shouldn't take too long. And then, perhaps, we can sit on that newly stable porch with a cup of tea and watch the world go by."

Mrs. Gable's face lit up. "Oh, Jonah, you're a treasure. A real treasure. Not like those fellows who charge you an arm and a leg just to look at the problem."

He smiled, the familiar warmth of community service settling over him. This was his rulebook: the unwritten code of neighborliness, the ingrained understanding that in a town like Cedar Ridge, looking out for each other was not just an option, but an essential part of the fabric of life. He didn't need three bids for a helping hand; he just needed to know it was needed. And for Mrs. Gable, it was clearly needed.

He'd make sure Silas had the right kind of wood, and then he'd head over, ready to lend his expertise, his tools, and his time, without a single form in sight. He was sure Clara was doing a sterling job on the Hall, in her own way, but he also knew that the Hall, like the rest of Cedar Ridge, would benefit from a different kind of touch, a touch that understood the value of a well-placed brace as much as a meticulously documented invoice.

The scent of aged paper and the faint metallic tang of ink had become Clara's constant companions. Her office, perched above the rhythmic hum of the bakery, was a sanctuary of order in the burgeoning chaos of the Community Hall's restoration. But even this haven, meticulously organized with its color-coded binders and detailed spreadsheets, was beginning to feel the strain. The grant money, a lifeline she'd fought tooth and nail to secure, was proving to be a surprisingly tight leash, especially when confronted with the capricious reality of a building constructed over a century ago.

Her latest hurdle involved the intricate plaster moldings that adorned the Hall's main chamber. During her initial survey, they had been noted as needing "minor cosmetic attention." However, as the dust of countless decades was gently dislodged, it became apparent that "minor" was a gross understatement. Large sections had crumbled, revealing not just water damage but a surprising lack of structural integrity in some areas.

The original plaster, a unique blend likely sourced locally with materials long since unavailable, was far too delicate to be replicated with standard modern compounds. The grant stipulated only approved materials, and after consulting with a specialist, Clara discovered that a specific, custom-mixed lime-based plaster, designed to mimic the original composition and setting properties, was the only viable option. The cost, however, was staggering.

"Three thousand, five hundred dollars for enough plaster to cover forty linear feet?" Clara murmured, rereading the quote from 'Heritage Plastering Specialists,' a firm renowned for its historical restoration work. The figure seemed astronomical, far exceeding her allocated contingency for decorative elements. She tapped her pen against the document, a frown creasing her brow. "And that's *before* the specialized artisan who knows how to apply it without causing further damage. Another two thousand, minimum."

This was precisely the kind of unforeseen expense that sent a chill down her spine. She'd budgeted meticulously, allocating funds for every foreseeable issue, from structural repairs to new wiring. But the Hall, it seemed, was a master of surprise. Her instinct was to demand more bids, to scrutinize this quote with the same rigor she applied to every other aspect of the project. She opened another binder, flipping to the section on vendor selection. "All bids for services exceeding $500 must be submitted in triplicate," she read aloud, her voice tight. "Comparison of bids, including material specifications and estimated labor hours, must be documented."

She reached for her phone, intending to draft a formal request to several other restoration companies. It was the sensible, the *proper* thing to do. But before she could dial, a different voice, a more pragmatic one, seemed to echo in the quiet room. It was Jonah's voice, laced with the easy confidence of someone who'd navigated the labyrinthine challenges of old buildings his entire life. She remembered their conversation about the warped floorboards in the west wing. She'd insisted on sourcing new, kiln-dried oak to match the original specifications, a process that involved significant lead time and a not-inconsiderable price tag.

"Why not just pull some good, solid planks from the old mill down by the creek?" Jonah had suggested, gesturing with a hand dusted with sawdust. "It's been empty for years. Plenty of good, seasoned wood in there. Might even find some that's already the right width. Just need to check it for rot, of course."

At the time, Clara had politely dismissed the idea. "But the mill isn't structurally sound, Jonah," she'd countered, picturing the leaning structure. "And I doubt Silas would allow us to just take lumber without proper authorization. Besides, the grant requires us to use approved suppliers and materials. We can't just salvage things."

He'd shrugged, a hint of a smile playing on his lips. "Clara, that mill's been standing longer than most folks in town. The wood in there is harder than nails. And Silas? Silas owes me a favor or two. He'd be happy to let us 'borrow' a few planks if it meant keeping them from going to waste. It's about resourcefulness. It's about knowing the town, knowing who to ask, and knowing what's worth saving."

Now, staring at the exorbitant quote for the plaster, Jonah's words resurfaced with an almost irritating persistence. Resourcefulness. Knowing the town. These were concepts that felt alien to her by-the-book approach. Her world was built on contracts, on verified specifications, on paper trails that guaranteed accountability. The idea of "calling in favors" or "borrowing" materials from a derelict building felt... unprofessional. It skirted the edges of propriety, and more importantly, it bypassed the very oversight the grant committee demanded.

She sighed, pushing the plaster quote aside. It was just one more battle in a war that seemed to be escalating with every passing day. The foundation had required more underpinning than initially anticipated, and the plumbing, while not catastrophic, was a tangled mess of ancient lead pipes that needed complete replacement. Each unearthed problem brought with it a new wave of unforeseen costs, a new demand on her carefully constructed budget.

She opened a separate spreadsheet, meticulously detailing each expense. The "Contingency Fund" line item, once a comfortable buffer, was rapidly shrinking. She'd allocated a standard 10% for unforeseen issues, a figure that felt laughably optimistic now. The grant's stipulations were clear: all expenses must be documented, justifiable, and approved. Deviations from the budget, particularly significant ones, would require a formal amendment, a process that involved lengthy explanations and, potentially, a reduction in future funding. The thought of having to explain to the grant committee why she needed an extra $5,500 for a few decorative moldings was enough to make her stomach clench.

Just then, the door to her small office creaked open, and Jonah's familiar silhouette filled the frame. He carried a small, canvas bag, and his presence seemed to inject a dose of grounded reality into the room, a stark contrast to the abstract figures on her screen.

"Just wanted to check in," he said, his voice a low rumble. "See how things are coming along in the lion's den." He gestured vaguely at the stacks of paper.

Clara managed a weak smile. "The lion's den is proving to be rather... expensive, Jonah." She gestured at the plaster quote. "This came in today. For the moldings. It's... significant."

Jonah's gaze shifted to the document, his brow furrowing slightly as he took in the figure. He didn't flinch, but a subtle tension entered his posture. "Yeah, that's... quite a number. Heritage Plastering Specialists, huh? They're good, real good, but they charge for every grain of sand, I reckon."

"They use a specific blend for historical restorations," Clara explained, feeling the need to defend the quote, even as she balked at its size. "It's the only thing that will work with the original composition. Apparently, modern materials would be too aggressive and could damage what's left."

Jonah leaned against the doorframe, his arms crossed. He looked thoughtful, not surprised. "Look, Clara, I get it. You've got the grant people breathing down your neck, and they want everything by the book. But sometimes, the book doesn't account for the way things *really* are. That plaster mix they're talking about? It's probably a specialty lime-based product, right? Takes a long time to cure, needs a specific touch."

Clara nodded, her pen poised, ready to jot down any practical advice he might offer, though she doubted it would align with her prescribed methods.

"My Uncle Ben," Jonah continued, his gaze drifting out the window, as if he could see the Community Hall from here, "he used to do a lot of work on the old houses in the neighboring county. He had a knack for that kind of stuff. Used to mix his own plaster. Said it was just lime, horsehair, and water, but he had his own ratios. He swore by it. Said it was stronger, more forgiving, and a fraction of the cost."

Clara's pen stopped mid-air. "He... mixed his own? But... what about the specifications? The approval process?"

Jonah chuckled, a dry, rasping sound. "Clara, Uncle Ben wasn't exactly one for paperwork. He was more of a 'get it done right' kind of guy. And when he did work for folks, they didn't ask for invoices with itemized lists of horsehair. They paid him because his work lasted. And he'd often 'borrow' a bit of lime from the old quarry, or get some horsehair from the stables down the road. It was just how it worked back then. How it still works for a lot of us."

He pushed himself off the doorframe and walked further into the room, his boots making soft thuds on the wooden floor. He picked up a stray piece of paper from her desk, not a quote, but a list of potential contractors. "You've got 'Artisan Plastering' on here, and 'Historical Finishes Inc.'," he observed. "They're going to be in the same ballpark as Heritage. They're all professionals, and they all charge professional rates for specialized work."

He placed the paper back down, his expression earnest. "But what if we looked at it differently? That grant is for restoring the Hall, right? For bringing it back to its former glory. Does it *have* to be that exact, expensive blend if we can achieve a similar result using materials that are still historically appropriate, even if they're not directly from the original recipe?"

Clara's shoulders stiffened. "The grant is for restoring it *to its original condition*, Jonah. That means using materials that are as close as possible to what was originally there. That's what the committee expects. That's what my reputation hinges on." She thought of the hours she'd spent researching historical building techniques, her dedication to authenticity.

"And what if some of those moldings are beyond repair, Clara?" Jonah pressed gently. "What if the original structure is too deteriorated to take that delicate plaster? You'll end up paying a fortune for something that crumbles again in five years. Wouldn't it be better to salvage what we can, carefully document it, and then use a very good, durable replica for the irreparable sections? We could even get Silas to mill some of the original timber we find on site and incorporate it into the repair mix. He's got a good eye for that sort of thing."

His suggestion, while practical, felt like a direct affront to her core principles. "Silas? Salvaged timber?" Clara shook her head. "Jonah, that's not how grant-funded projects work. We need traceability. We need to know where every dollar is going and why. If we start using salvaged materials, even if they're suitable, it's going to raise red flags. It looks... informal. It looks like corners are being cut."

"Corners aren't being cut, Clara," Jonah countered, his voice firm but not angry. "Resourcefulness is being employed. That's what people *did* in this town for generations. When the old general store needed a new awning, Mr. Henderson didn't call three different awning companies. He went to his neighbor, Joe, who was a whiz with canvas and a sewing machine, and they worked something out. Joe got paid a fair price, Mr. Henderson got a good awning, and the town kept its money circulating locally."

He paused, letting his words sink in. "That plaster quote? It's a budget breaker. It's a significant chunk of your contingency, and likely more. And for what? A cosmetic fix that might not even hold. What if we called the local historical society? They might know of someone who's worked with similar materials on a smaller scale, someone who wouldn't charge an arm and a leg. Or what about finding some of that old, reclaimed wood that's been salvaged from other demolitions in the area? We could grind that down, mix it with a modern, compatible binder. It would give that historical feel without the astronomical cost."

Clara felt a wave of exasperation wash over her. "Reclaimed wood? Grinding it down? Jonah, you're talking about... creative accounting, and that's not my forte. My forte is following the rules, ensuring transparency, and delivering a project that meets all the grant's requirements. If that means spending more money on the right materials, then that's what needs to happen." She tapped the problematic quote again. "I need to get at least two more formal bids for this. It's the only way I can justify the expenditure, or perhaps find a more reasonable alternative within the approved vendor list."

"And if those other bids are just as high, or even higher?" Jonah asked, his tone laced with a hint of challenge. "What then? You'll just keep throwing money at it until your contingency is gone and you're begging for more? Or are you going to consider the possibility that there's a way to do this without bankrupting the project?"

His directness was unsettling. Clara knew he wasn't trying to undermine her; he was genuinely trying to help, to find a solution that made sense to him. But his solutions were rooted in a world she was still trying to understand, a world where relationships and ingenuity trumped regulations and line items.

"I'm not asking for handouts, Jonah," she said, her voice tighter than she intended. "I'm asking for adherence to protocol. This grant is for a significant restoration. It needs to be done right, and 'right' involves proper documentation and approved materials. I can't just... call around to friends and see who's willing to 'do me a favor.' It's not how this works."

"It's not just about favors, Clara," Jonah said, his gaze unwavering. "It's about community. It's about understanding that in a town like Cedar Ridge, people have skills. They have resources. And sometimes, the most efficient and cost-effective way to get something done is to tap into that existing network, not to reinvent the wheel with every single task. Those companies you're calling? They're likely going to use standard industry practices.

They'll factor in their overhead, their travel time, their profit margins. We can do this ourselves, with the right guidance, and save a significant amount. Think about the plumbing. You're getting quotes for entirely new copper pipe, right? What if we found some of that old, lead pipe that's been decommissioned from other houses? It's perfectly usable for certain applications, and it's free for the taking if you know who to ask. It's still a historically appropriate material."

Clara shuddered internally. Lead pipes. Salvaged lumber. Homemade plaster. It sounded like a recipe for disaster, or at least, for a catastrophic audit. "Jonah, that's precisely the kind of thing I *cannot* do. The grant has specific requirements for materials, especially for plumbing. Lead is often prohibited due to health concerns, even if it's decommissioned. And even if it weren't, using it without proper documentation would be a direct violation of the terms. I'm trying to *save* this Hall, not put it in jeopardy with questionable practices."

He ran a hand through his hair, a gesture of mild frustration. "So, you're going to spend, what, seven, eight thousand dollars on decorative plaster that's just going to sit on a wall, when you could probably achieve a similar, if not better, result for a fraction of that by using a different approach? An approach that still respects the historical integrity of the building, but also respects the budget?"

Clara finally pushed her chair back, standing to face him. "It's not about 'just decorative plaster,' Jonah. It's about authenticity. It's about doing it the way it was done. And it's about accountability. I have a responsibility to the grant committee, and to this town, to ensure that every dollar is spent wisely and according to the established guidelines. My approach might be slower, it might be more expensive in the short term, but it's the only way I know how to guarantee the integrity of the project and the funding."

She picked up the phone again, her fingers hovering over the keypad. "I need to make those calls. I need to get those bids. And I will not be swayed by suggestions of... borrowing materials or employing unconventional methods. This is a professional restoration, and it will be managed as such."

Jonah watched her for a moment, his expression a mixture of respect and something akin to exasperation. He knew, with a certainty born from years of experience, that Clara's rigid adherence to protocol was both her greatest strength and her most significant potential weakness when it came to a project as complex and unpredictable as the Community Hall.

He also knew that sometimes, the most "proper" way was not always the most practical, or the most beneficial for the long-term health of a building that had weathered more than just time. It had weathered generations of Cedar Ridge's unique brand of resourceful, community-driven problem-solving. And he couldn't shake the feeling that Clara, in her earnest pursuit of perfect procedure, was about to miss out on the very essence of what made this town, and its beloved Hall, truly resilient.

The scent of aged paper and the faint metallic tang of ink had become Clara's constant companions. Her office, perched above the rhythmic hum of the bakery, was a sanctuary of order in the burgeoning chaos of the Community Hall's restoration. But even this haven, meticulously organized with its color-coded binders and detailed spreadsheets, was beginning to feel the strain. The grant money, a lifeline she'd fought tooth and nail to secure, was proving to be a surprisingly tight leash, especially when confronted with the capricious reality of a building constructed over a century ago.

Her latest hurdle involved the intricate plaster moldings that adorned the Hall's main chamber. During her initial survey, they had been noted as needing "minor cosmetic attention." However, as the dust of countless decades was gently dislodged, it became apparent that "minor" was a gross understatement. Large sections had crumbled, revealing not just water damage but a surprising lack of structural integrity in some areas.

The original plaster, a unique blend likely sourced locally with materials long since unavailable, was far too delicate to be replicated with standard modern compounds. The grant stipulated only approved materials, and after consulting with a specialist, Clara discovered that a specific, custom-mixed lime-based plaster, designed to mimic the original composition and setting properties, was the only viable option. The cost, however, was staggering.

"Three thousand, five hundred dollars for enough plaster to cover forty linear feet?" Clara murmured, rereading the quote from 'Heritage Plastering Specialists,' a firm renowned for its historical restoration work. The figure seemed astronomical, far exceeding her allocated contingency for decorative elements. She tapped her pen against the document, a frown creasing her brow. "And that's *before* the specialized artisan who knows how to apply it without causing further damage. Another two thousand, minimum."

This was precisely the kind of unforeseen expense that sent a chill down her spine. She'd budgeted meticulously, allocating funds for every foreseeable issue, from structural repairs to new wiring. But the Hall, it seemed, was a master of surprise. Her instinct was to demand more bids, to scrutinize this quote with the same rigor she applied to every other aspect of the project. She opened another binder, flipping to the section on vendor selection. "All bids for services exceeding $500 must be submitted in triplicate," she read aloud, her voice tight. "Comparison of bids, including material specifications and estimated labor hours, must be documented."

She reached for her phone, intending to draft a formal request to several other restoration companies. It was the sensible, the *proper* thing to do. But before she could dial, a different voice, a more pragmatic one, seemed to echo in the quiet room. It was Jonah's voice, laced with the easy confidence of someone who'd navigated the labyrinthine challenges of old buildings his entire life. She remembered their conversation about the warped floorboards in the west wing. She'd insisted on sourcing new, kiln-dried oak to match the original specifications, a process that involved significant lead time and a not-inconsiderable price tag.

"Why not just pull some good, solid planks from the old mill down by the creek?" Jonah had suggested, gesturing with a hand dusted with sawdust. "It's been empty for years. Plenty of good, seasoned wood in there. Might even find some that's already the right width. Just need to check it for rot, of course."

At the time, Clara had politely dismissed the idea. "But the mill isn't structurally sound, Jonah," she'd countered, picturing the leaning structure. "And I doubt Silas would allow us to just take lumber without proper authorization. Besides, the grant requires us to use approved suppliers and materials. We can't just salvage things."

He'd shrugged, a hint of a smile playing on his lips. "Clara, that mill's been standing longer than most folks in town. The wood in there is harder than nails. And Silas? Silas owes me a favor or two. He'd be happy to let us 'borrow' a few planks if it meant keeping them from going to waste. It's about resourcefulness. It's about knowing the town, knowing who to ask, and knowing what's worth saving."

Now, staring at the exorbitant quote for the plaster, Jonah's words resurfaced with an almost irritating persistence. Resourcefulness. Knowing the town. These were concepts that felt alien to her by-the-book approach. Her world was built on contracts, on verified specifications, on paper trails that guaranteed accountability. The idea of "calling in favors" or "borrowing" materials from a derelict building felt... unprofessional. It skirted the edges of propriety, and more importantly, it bypassed the very oversight the grant committee demanded.

She sighed, pushing the plaster quote aside. It was just one more battle in a war that seemed to be escalating with every passing day. The foundation had required more underpinning than initially anticipated, and the plumbing, while not catastrophic, was a tangled mess of ancient lead pipes that needed complete replacement. Each unearthed problem brought with it a new wave of unforeseen costs, a new demand on her carefully constructed budget.

She opened a separate spreadsheet, meticulously detailing each expense. The "Contingency Fund" line item, once a comfortable buffer, was rapidly shrinking. She'd allocated a standard 10% for unforeseen issues, a figure that felt laughably optimistic now. The grant's stipulations were clear: all expenses must be documented, justifiable, and approved. Deviations from the budget, particularly significant ones, would require a formal amendment, a process that involved lengthy explanations and, potentially, a reduction in future funding. The thought of having to explain to the grant committee why she needed an extra $5,500 for a few decorative moldings was enough to make her stomach clench.

Just then, the door to her small office creaked open, and Jonah's familiar silhouette filled the frame. He carried a small, canvas bag, and his presence seemed to inject a dose of grounded reality into the room, a stark contrast to the abstract figures on her screen.

"Just wanted to check in," he said, his voice a low rumble. "See how things are coming along in the lion's den." He gestured vaguely at the stacks of paper.

Clara managed a weak smile. "The lion's den is proving to be rather... expensive, Jonah." She gestured at the plaster quote. "This came in today. For the moldings. It's... significant."

Jonah's gaze shifted to the document, his brow furrowing slightly as he took in the figure. He didn't flinch, but a subtle tension entered his posture. "Yeah, that's... quite a number. Heritage Plastering Specialists, huh? They're good, real good, but they charge for every grain of sand, I reckon."

"They use a specific blend for historical restorations," Clara explained, feeling the need to defend the quote, even as she balked at its size. "It's the only thing that will work with the original composition. Apparently, modern materials would be too aggressive and could damage what's left."

Jonah leaned against the doorframe, his arms crossed. He looked thoughtful, not surprised. "Look, Clara, I get it. You've got the grant people breathing down your neck, and they want everything by the book. But sometimes, the book doesn't account for the way things *really* are. That plaster mix they're talking about? It's probably a specialty lime-based product, right? Takes a long time to cure, needs a specific touch."

Clara nodded, her pen poised, ready to jot down any practical advice he might offer, though she doubted it would align with her prescribed methods.

"My Uncle Ben," Jonah continued, his gaze drifting out the window, as if he could see the Community Hall from here, "he used to do a lot of work on the old houses in the neighboring county. He had a knack for that kind of stuff. Used to mix his own plaster. Said it was just lime, horsehair, and water, but he had his own ratios. He swore by it. Said it was stronger, more forgiving, and a fraction of the cost."

Clara's pen stopped mid-air. "He... mixed his own? But... what about the specifications? The approval process?"

Jonah chuckled, a dry, rasping sound. "Clara, Uncle Ben wasn't exactly one for paperwork. He was more of a 'get it done right' kind of guy. And when he did work for folks, they didn't ask for invoices with itemized lists of horsehair. They paid him because his work lasted. And he'd often 'borrow' a bit of lime from the old quarry, or get some horsehair from the stables down the road. It was just how it worked back then. How it still works for a lot of us."

He pushed himself off the doorframe and walked further into the room, his boots making soft thuds on the wooden floor. He picked up a stray piece of paper from her desk, not a quote, but a list of potential contractors. "You've got 'Artisan Plastering' on here, and 'Historical Finishes Inc.',," he observed. "They're going to be in the same ballpark as Heritage. They're all professionals, and they all charge professional rates for specialized work."

He placed the paper back down, his expression earnest. "But what if we looked at it differently? That grant is for restoring the Hall, right? For bringing it back to its former glory. Does it *have* to be that exact, expensive blend if we can achieve a similar result using materials that are still historically appropriate, even if they're not directly from the original recipe?"

Clara's shoulders stiffened. "The grant is for restoring it *to its original condition*, Jonah. That means using materials that are as close as possible to what was originally there. That's what the committee expects. That's what my reputation hinges on." She thought of the hours she'd spent researching historical building techniques, her dedication to authenticity.

"And what if some of those moldings are beyond repair, Clara?" Jonah pressed gently. "What if the original structure is too deteriorated to take that delicate plaster? You'll end up paying a fortune for something that crumbles again in five years. Wouldn't it be better to salvage what we can, carefully document it, and then use a very good, durable replica for the irreparable sections? We could even get Silas to mill some of the original timber we find on site and incorporate it into the repair mix. He's got a good eye for that sort of thing."

His suggestion, while practical, felt like a direct affront to her core principles. "Silas? Salvaged timber?" Clara shook her head. "Jonah, that's not how grant-funded projects work. We need traceability. We need to know where every dollar is going and why. If we start using salvaged materials, even if they're suitable, it's going to raise red flags. It looks... informal. It looks like corners are being cut."

"Corners aren't being cut, Clara," Jonah countered, his voice firm but not angry. "Resourcefulness is being employed. That's what people *did* in this town for generations. When the old general store needed a new awning, Mr. Henderson didn't call three different awning companies. He went to his neighbor, Joe, who was a whiz with canvas and a sewing machine, and they worked something out. Joe got paid a fair price, Mr. Henderson got a good awning, and the town kept its money circulating locally."

He paused, letting his words sink in. "That plaster quote? It's a budget breaker. It's a significant chunk of your contingency, and likely more. And for what? A cosmetic fix that might not even hold. What if we called the local historical society? They might know of someone who's worked with similar materials on a smaller scale, someone who wouldn't charge an arm and a leg. Or what about finding some of that old, reclaimed wood that's been salvaged from other demolitions in the area? We could grind that down, mix it with a modern, compatible binder. It would give that historical feel without the astronomical cost."

Clara felt a wave of exasperation wash over her. "Reclaimed wood? Grinding it down? Jonah, you're talking about... creative accounting, and that's not my forte. My forte is following the rules, ensuring transparency, and delivering a project that meets all the grant's requirements. If that means spending more money on the right materials, then that's what needs to happen." She tapped the problematic quote again. "I need to get at least two more formal bids for this. It's the only way I can justify the expenditure, or perhaps find a more reasonable alternative within the approved vendor list."

"And if those other bids are just as high, or even higher?" Jonah asked, his tone laced with a hint of challenge. "What then? You'll just keep throwing money at it until your contingency is gone and you're begging for more? Or are you going to consider the possibility that there's a way to do this without bankrupting the project?"

His directness was unsettling. Clara knew he wasn't trying to undermine her; he was genuinely trying to help, to find a solution that made sense to him. But his solutions were rooted in a world she was still trying to understand, a world where relationships and ingenuity trumped regulations and line items.

"I'm not asking for handouts, Jonah," she said, her voice tighter than she intended. "I'm asking for adherence to protocol. This grant is for a significant restoration. It needs to be done right, and 'right' involves proper documentation and approved materials. I can't just... call around to friends and see who's willing to 'do me a favor.' It's not how this works."

"It's not just about favors, Clara," Jonah said, his gaze unwavering. "It's about community. It's about understanding that in a town like Cedar Ridge, people have skills. They have resources. And sometimes, the most efficient and cost-effective way to get something done is to tap into that existing network, not to reinvent the wheel with every single task. Those companies you're calling? They're likely going to use standard industry practices.

They'll factor in their overhead, their travel time, their profit margins. We can do this ourselves, with the right guidance, and save a significant amount. Think about the plumbing. You're getting quotes for entirely new copper pipe, right? What if we found some of that old, lead pipe that's been decommissioned from other houses? It's perfectly usable for certain applications, and it's free for the taking if you know who to ask. It's still a historically appropriate material."

Clara shuddered internally. Lead pipes. Salvaged lumber. Homemade plaster. It sounded like a recipe for disaster, or at least, for a catastrophic audit. "Jonah, that's precisely the kind of thing I *cannot* do. The grant has specific requirements for materials, especially for plumbing. Lead is often prohibited due to health concerns, even if it's decommissioned. And even if it weren't, using it without proper documentation would be a direct violation of the terms. I'm trying to *save* this Hall, not put it in jeopardy with questionable practices."

He ran a hand through his hair, a gesture of mild frustration. "So, you're going to spend, what, seven, eight thousand dollars on decorative plaster that's just going to sit on a wall, when you could probably achieve a similar, if not better, result for a fraction of that by using a different approach? An approach that still respects the historical integrity of the building, but also respects the budget?"

Clara finally pushed her chair back, standing to face him. "It's not about 'just decorative plaster,' Jonah. It's about authenticity. It's about doing it the way it was done. And it's about accountability. I have a responsibility to the grant committee, and to this town, to ensure that every dollar is spent wisely and according to the established guidelines. My approach might be slower, it might be more expensive in the short term, but it's the only way I know how to guarantee the integrity of the project and the funding."

She picked up the phone again, her fingers hovering over the keypad. "I need to make those calls. I need to get those bids. And I will not be swayed by suggestions of... borrowing materials or employing unconventional methods. This is a professional restoration, and it will be managed as such."

Jonah watched her for a moment, his expression a mixture of respect and something akin to exasperation. He knew, with a certainty born from years of experience, that Clara's rigid adherence to protocol was both her greatest strength and her most significant potential weakness when it came to a project as complex and unpredictable as the Community Hall.

He also knew that sometimes, the most "proper" way was not always the most practical, or the most beneficial for the long-term health of a building that had weathered more than just time. It had weathered generations of Cedar Ridge's unique brand of resourceful, community-driven problem-solving. And he couldn't shake the feeling that Clara, in her earnest pursuit of perfect procedure, was about to miss out on the very essence of what made this town, and its beloved Hall, truly resilient.

As Clara meticulously documented the escalating costs, her focus, usually so sharp and unwavering, began to blur at the edges. The spreadsheets and budgets, once her clear allies in the fight to preserve the Community Hall, now felt like a cage, trapping her in a world of numbers that seemed increasingly detached from the reality of the building itself. The sheer volume of paperwork, the constant need to justify every expenditure, was beginning to wear her down. She found herself staring at the figures, the dollar signs swimming before her eyes, and a profound weariness settled in.

She picked up a file, not for a contractor or a material quote, but for the Community Food Pantry. It was an ancillary project, one that had been incorporated into the broader scope of the Hall's restoration as a way to highlight the building's ongoing importance to the town. The grant had allocated a modest sum for its refurbishment and stocking, a detail Clara had initially treated with the same detached professionalism as the roof repairs or the electrical upgrades. It was another line item, another set of requirements to meet.

But as she sifted through the inventory lists, the donation logs, and the tentative schedules for volunteers, something shifted within her. The Pantry wasn't just about shelving and cans of soup; it was about people. She found a handwritten note tucked into a binder, a thank you from someone named Mrs. Gable. It was brief, simply expressing gratitude for a box of fresh vegetables.

Clara remembered hearing the name Gable mentioned in passing – an elderly woman who lived in one of the smaller cottages on Elm Street, known for her quiet dignity and her perpetually modest means. She imagined Mrs. Gable, her hands gnarled with age, carefully tending a small, sun-starved garden that likely yielded little. The idea of her relying on the Hall's pantry for fresh produce, for the simple sustenance that Clara took for granted, pricked at something within her.

Then there were the requests for baby formula and diapers. The names on these requests were often accompanied by brief notes – young mothers struggling to make ends meet, families facing unexpected job losses. Clara pictured these young parents, their faces etched with worry, turning to the Community Hall not for a dance or a town meeting, but for the essential necessities that allowed their children to thrive. This wasn't just about historical preservation; it was about immediate, vital human need.

Jonah's words, which had so recently grated on her sense of propriety, began to echo in a different context.

Resourcefulness. Community. Knowing the town. He spoke of these things as practical tools, as the natural way of getting things done. Clara had always seen them as... softer, less quantifiable concepts, secondary to the robust framework of grants, contracts, and regulations. But now, looking at the tangible needs of the Pantry's clients, those 'softer' concepts began to acquire a sharp, undeniable weight.

The Hall, she realized, was more than just a historic structure in need of repair. It was a living, breathing entity within the community, a hub of support and assistance. The restoration project, while crucial for its future, was just one aspect of its multifaceted role. Her purely logistical approach, her laser-like focus on the building's structural and historical integrity, felt increasingly incomplete. It was like admiring the intricate framework of a bridge without acknowledging the people who would cross it, the traffic it would carry, the connections it would forge.

She found herself pausing, her pen hovering over the budget for the Pantry's small refrigerator. The quote was for a new, energy-efficient model, well within the allocated funds. But for the first time, she wondered about the *type* of food that would be kept there. Would it be perishable goods? Fresh produce, like the kind Mrs. Gable might have received? The thought of a brand-new refrigerator, gleaming and efficient, sitting empty or holding only a few sad-looking items, suddenly felt like a waste, not just of money, but of potential.

A new question, one she hadn't even considered before, began to form in her mind: what *kind* of restoration was truly needed? Was it solely about returning the building to its past glory, or was it also about ensuring it could continue to serve the evolving needs of the present and future community? The grant, in its very wording, spoke of preserving it *for the benefit of the people.* Had she, in her meticulous adherence to the 'how,' neglected the 'for whom'?

She remembered a conversation she'd overheard at the bakery earlier that week. Two women, discussing the upcoming bake sale to raise funds for the Pantry's deficit. They weren't discussing architectural authenticity or specialized plaster mixes; they were talking about who could donate cakes, who had the best pie recipes, and how to best spread the word. It was a spontaneous, unscripted mobilization of community effort, driven by a direct understanding of need.

Jonah, she mused, lived and breathed this kind of understanding. He navigated the town's social fabric with an intuitive ease that Clara could only envy. He didn't just see a building; he saw the people connected to it, the history they carried, the support systems they relied upon. His suggestions about salvaged materials and local expertise, while initially jarring to her structured sensibilities, were rooted in this deeper understanding of community resilience. They were practical solutions born from a world where resourcefulness wasn't just an option, but a necessity, and where helping a neighbor wasn't an obligation, but a way of life.

Clara looked back at the plaster quote, then at the Pantry inventory. The disparity felt stark. Thousands of dollars for decorative moldings, while essential services for vulnerable residents relied on community donations and a perpetually stretched budget. It wasn't that the restoration wasn't important; it was vital. But perhaps, just perhaps, her definition of "restoration" had been too narrow, too focused on the bricks and mortar and not enough on the heart and soul of the building.

She knew she couldn't simply abandon the grant's stipulations. The money was earmarked, and its use was strictly defined. But as she began to draft a new email, requesting more detailed bids for the plaster work, a subtle shift had occurred. Her questions were still focused on materials and costs, but beneath the professional veneer, a new awareness was dawning. She started to think about the Hall not just as a project, but as a place where Mrs. Gable could find fresh produce, where young families could access essential supplies, where the heart of Cedar Ridge continued to beat, nourished and supported by the very structure she was fighting to preserve. The community's needs were no longer abstract data points; they were beginning to emerge, not as challenges to her plan, but as an integral part of it. And Clara, in her quiet, methodical way, was starting to listen.

The very act of processing the various requests and needs related to the Community Hall's multifaceted role began to subtly alter Clara's perspective. The grant, while its primary focus was on the physical restoration of the historic building, also encompassed elements that spoke to its ongoing utility. Among these was the refurbishment and stocking of the Community Food Pantry, a service that Clara had initially categorized as a secondary, albeit important, aspect of the project. Now, however, as she delved deeper into the operational requirements of the Pantry, she found herself confronted with a series of needs that transcended mere logistical considerations.

She found herself rereading correspondence from various individuals and families who relied on the Pantry's services. There was a recurring mention of a Mrs. Gable, an elderly woman whose pension barely covered her rent, and who depended on the Pantry for access to fresh produce. Clara pictured her, a solitary figure in a modest cottage, her meager income stretched thin. The thought of Mrs. Gable being able to supplement her diet with fresh fruits and vegetables, something Clara herself took for granted, resonated with a quiet poignancy. This wasn't just about food; it was about dignity, about ensuring that an elderly resident could maintain a degree of independence and well-being.

Beyond Mrs. Gable, Clara's attention was drawn to the consistent demand for infant supplies – diapers and baby formula. These requests came from young families, many of whom were navigating the precarious terrain of low wages and unexpected financial setbacks. The Pantry served as a crucial safety net, providing these essential items that allowed parents to care for their children without succumbing to overwhelming financial strain. Clara began to understand that the Hall, through the Pantry, was a lifeline, a tangible expression of community care that directly impacted the lives of its youngest and most vulnerable members.

This growing awareness of the human element behind the Pantry's operations began to create a subtle friction with Clara's strictly procedural approach. She had meticulously allocated funds for the Pantry's refurbishment, ensuring all materials met building codes and were aesthetically appropriate for the historic setting. She had even drafted a detailed inventory of needed supplies, based on historical usage patterns and projected demand. However, the emotional weight of these needs, the tangible impact on individuals like Mrs. Gable and young families, was something her spreadsheets and project plans had not fully captured.

Jonah's influence, though often presented as a counterpoint to her methods, began to surface in her thoughts. His inherent understanding of the town's social fabric, his ability to see beyond the physical structure to the people it served, was a stark contrast to her own initial focus on structural integrity and grant compliance. While Clara grappled with the complex budgetary implications of unforeseen restoration costs, Jonah seemed to possess an intuitive grasp of how to leverage community resources and local expertise to overcome obstacles. His suggestions, though sometimes unconventional, were always grounded in a pragmatic understanding of how things *actually* got done in Cedar Ridge.

Clara found herself re-examining the budget for the Pantry. The grant provided a set amount for its operational needs, but it was clear that this amount, while adequate for basic stocking, would not stretch to meet every potential need. The constant requests for specific items, the fluctuating demand, and the inherent variability of donations presented a challenge that a fixed budget struggled to address. She realized that the Pantry's effectiveness was not solely dependent on the Hall's physical condition but on its ability to adapt and respond to the ever-changing needs of the community it served.

She thought about the local farmers' market, a weekly event that brought fresh, seasonal produce to the town. Could there be a way to integrate that into the Pantry's supply chain? Perhaps a partnership, a donation program, or even a small purchasing fund that could be managed with greater flexibility than the grant's rigid disbursement protocols allowed. These were not questions she had anticipated when she first took on the restoration project. Her initial objective had been to ensure the Hall's structural soundness and historical accuracy. Now, however, she was beginning to see that a truly successful restoration involved more than just preserving the past; it involved equipping the building to serve the present and future needs of the community.

The emotional resonance of the Pantry's needs began to soften Clara's purely logistical mindset. She started to see the Hall not just as a collection of beams, plaster, and wiring, but as a vessel for community support. The faces behind the requests – Mrs. Gable, the young mothers, the families facing hardship – began to take precedence over the mere numbers in her financial projections. She understood, with a growing clarity, that the true value of the Community Hall lay not only in its architectural heritage but in its capacity to foster connection, provide assistance, and embody the spirit of communal care.

This realization did not, however, translate into an immediate abandonment of her systematic approach. Clara was, by nature, a planner and a pragmatist. She still believed in the importance of adhering to the grant's guidelines and ensuring fiscal responsibility. But now, those principles were being viewed through a new lens, one that acknowledged the human dimension of the project. She began to consider how she could achieve the grant's objectives while also being more responsive to the tangible needs of the community, needs that were becoming increasingly evident through her work with the Food Pantry.

She found herself rereading the grant proposal, not just for the sections pertaining to structural repairs and historical preservation, but also for the clauses that addressed community benefit and ongoing usage. Were there opportunities within the grant's framework, she wondered, to establish more sustainable support mechanisms for the Pantry? Could a portion of the contingency fund, if strategically allocated, be used to address immediate needs that the regular budget could not cover? These were questions that required careful consideration, consultation with the grant committee, and perhaps even a willingness to explore some of the more unconventional, community-based solutions that Jonah so readily embraced.

The tension between her structured methodology and the emergent human needs was palpable. She was caught between the necessity of following established protocols and the growing imperative to address the very real struggles of the people who relied on the Hall's services. It was a complex challenge, one that required a delicate balancing act. Clara knew that any deviation from the grant's terms would need to be meticulously justified, supported by data and rationale that spoke to both fiscal prudence and demonstrable community benefit.

As she continued to review the Pantry's operational data, Clara began to sketch out potential solutions in a separate notebook, a departure from her usual digital spreadsheets. She noted down ideas for partnerships with local agricultural producers, potential volunteer recruitment drives specifically for the Pantry, and even ways to reallocate existing resources to create a more flexible fund for emergency supplies. These were nascent ideas, far from fully formed plans, but they represented a significant shift in her thinking. She was no longer just managing a restoration project; she was becoming an advocate for the broader community that the Hall served. The pragmatic, often-unseen needs of Cedar Ridge's residents were no longer distant data points; they were becoming the driving force behind her evolving approach to the Community Hall's future.

Jonah's vision for the Community Hall was, in a word, alive. It wasn't a sterile museum piece destined for preservation under glass, but a breathing entity, capable of evolving and adapting to the needs of Cedar Ridge. He spoke with a quiet passion, his hands sketching invisible blueprints in the air as he leaned against the doorframe of Clara's office. The late afternoon sun, filtering through the dusty panes, cast long shadows that seemed to dance with the energy of his ideas.

"Think about it, Clara," he began, his voice carrying a warmth that had been absent from their previous, more practical discussions. "Right now, we're focused on making sure the walls don't fall down, and the roof doesn't leak. And that's crucial, absolutely. But what happens *after* we've done all that? What's the point of a beautifully restored building if it's just... empty?"

Clara, who had been poring over a particularly complex set of electrical schematics, looked up, her brow furrowed. "The point, Jonah, is that it's *preserved*. It's a historical asset for the town. It meets the grant's objectives."

He gave a soft, almost imperceptible sigh, a sound that was less of annoyance and more of a gentle disagreement. "Preserved, yes. But what about *utilized*? What about making it a place people *want* to be, not just a place they're obligated to maintain?" He gestured vaguely towards the back of the building, where a patch of overgrown land lay neglected. "Imagine that space, cleared out.

We could put in a few raised garden beds. Community plots. People could grow their own vegetables, share the bounty. It'd be a beautiful thing, wouldn't it? Fresh produce, right there, accessible to everyone. Maybe even tie it into the food pantry donations. Imagine a little sign, 'From the Hall's garden to your table.'"

Clara's mind, trained to see potential problems rather than opportunities, immediately flagged the practicalities. "Garden plots? That's... outside the scope of the restoration grant, Jonah. And who would manage it? What about liability? And the soil quality? We'd need to get it tested."

Jonah chuckled, a low, rumbling sound that seemed to vibrate through the small office. "Clara, we're talking about a vision here. The details can be worked out. That's what committees are for, right? And Silas, down at the hardware store, he's got all sorts of soil amendments and tools he'd probably donate or let us borrow. He loves a good garden." He paused, his gaze sweeping across the room, as if mentally reconfiguring the Hall's interior. "And that main hall itself. It's big, it's got good acoustics. We could create a little performance space. Not a stage, exactly, but a designated area. For local musicians, poets, maybe even a small theater group that's been struggling for space."

He was painting a picture so vivid, so full of life, that it began to chip away at Clara's rigid adherence to the grant's parameters. Her focus had been so intently on the 'how' of preservation that she'd neglected the 'why' of its continued existence.

"Local artists," Clara murmured, jotting down a note, not as a concrete plan, but as a fleeting acknowledgment of his idea. "The grant is primarily for structural restoration and historical accuracy. A performance space… it's not in the original proposal."

"But it *should* be part of the Hall's future, Clara," Jonah insisted, his tone earnest. "It's about making the building relevant again. And then there's the old kitchen. It's currently just… a storage room, isn't it? Think of what we could do with that. We could get it up to code, maybe get some local chefs to run cooking classes. Imagine teaching people how to make sourdough bread, or how to preserve jams, using ingredients from those garden plots. It becomes a hub of activity, a place where people learn, connect, and share skills."

He paced a few steps, his boots thudding softly on the old wooden floorboards. "It's about building community, Clara. That's what this place was always meant to be. A place for everyone. Not just a relic of the past, but a vibrant part of Cedar Ridge's present and future. Your spreadsheets are essential, don't get me wrong. They're the backbone of making sure this gets done properly. But a backbone needs a body, and a heart. And that's what we need to build now."

Clara felt a familiar tightening in her chest, a sensation that usually accompanied the discovery of a new budget deficit or a structural anomaly. His ideas, while compelling, represented a significant departure from the meticulous, box-ticking approach she had adopted. They were fluid, adaptable, and deeply rooted in the idea of community engagement – concepts that were difficult to quantify and even harder to justify to a grant committee primarily concerned with concrete deliverables.

"Jonah," she began, carefully choosing her words, "the grant funding is very specific. We're allocated funds for structural repairs, electrical upgrades, plumbing, and the restoration of original architectural features. Ideas like community gardens, performance spaces, and cooking classes, while wonderful, would require separate funding streams and extensive planning outside the scope of this particular project."

He stopped pacing and turned to face her, his expression thoughtful rather than dismissive. "I understand that, Clara. I do. But sometimes, the most effective way to secure future funding, or even to garner local support for a project, is to demonstrate its potential beyond the minimum requirements. People are more likely to invest their time, their money, and their enthusiasm in something that they can see themselves being a part of. If the Hall is just a restored building, it's a project. If it's a place for gardens, for music, for learning new skills... it becomes a necessity."

He walked over to her desk, his gaze falling on the plaster quote, still lying there like a unwelcome guest. "This plaster issue you're dealing with," he said, tapping the paper lightly. "Your instinct is to get the most expensive, most specialized solution, because it's 'approved.' And that's fair, given the grant. But what if there's a way to achieve a similar historical look, a similar durability, using materials and methods that are more accessible, more cost-effective, and still respect the building's integrity?

What if we talked to Silas about sourcing a high-quality, naturally aged lime plaster from a smaller, regional supplier? Or what if we worked with a local artisan who might not have the 'Heritage Plastering Specialists' name, but has decades of hands-on experience with traditional techniques? They might be willing to work within a more reasonable budget if they understand the broader vision for the Hall."

Clara felt a familiar defensive posture rising within her. "But the grant requires approved vendors and materials. It's about accountability, Jonah. It's about ensuring that the funds are used appropriately and that the work meets a certain standard."

"And what if that standard is too high, or too rigid, to allow for the building's true potential?" he countered gently. "What if the 'approved' solution is so expensive that it starves other, equally important aspects of the Hall's revitalization? You're spending thousands on a specific type of plaster, and I'm trying to suggest that for a fraction of that cost, we could potentially achieve a result that is historically congruent, durable, and frees up funds for other things. Things that make the building *useful*."

He picked up a pencil from her desk, turning it over in his fingers. "Think about the kitchen again. You said it's just a storage room now. What if we could make it functional for a cooking class, not necessarily a full commercial kitchen, but something simple and effective? We could use salvaged materials, maybe some older cabinetry from a renovation elsewhere in town, refitted and refinished. It would still look appropriate, it would still be functional, and it would cost a fraction of what a brand-new, grant-approved kitchen would cost. It's about flexibility, Clara. It's about seeing problems not as insurmountable obstacles, but as opportunities to innovate."

Clara found herself torn. On one hand, Jonah's ideas were undeniably appealing, painting a picture of a Community Hall that was more than just a historical footnote. On the other hand, her entire professional existence was built on a foundation of meticulous planning, adherence to regulations, and the unwavering pursuit of documented compliance. The very notion of "salvaged materials" or "regional suppliers not on an approved list" sent a shiver of unease down her spine. It felt... risky. Unprofessional, even.

"I appreciate your... enthusiasm, Jonah," she said, her voice carefully measured. "And I understand the desire to make the Hall a vibrant community center. But my role here is to ensure that the restoration project is completed to the highest standards, within the framework of the grant. Deviating from that framework, even with the best intentions, could jeopardize the entire funding."

"And what if sticking to the framework too rigidly means we end up with a beautifully preserved shell that no one uses?" Jonah asked, his gaze steady. "What if the cost of that plaster, or the rewiring, or whatever else comes up, is so high that it leaves nothing for anything else? A building needs to serve its community to truly thrive. It needs to adapt. My vision isn't about cutting corners; it's about finding smarter, more resourceful ways to achieve the goals. It's about leveraging what we *have* in Cedar Ridge, not just what we can buy from a catalog."

He walked back towards the door, his presence still filling the room with a tangible sense of possibility. "Imagine those garden plots, Clara. People working together, sharing what they grow. Imagine a local band playing on a Saturday afternoon, filling the hall with music. Imagine Mrs. Gable, who you mentioned earlier, coming to a cooking class and learning how to make her favorite jam. That's not just a restored building; that's a thriving community."

He paused at the threshold, turning back to her. "Your vision is about preserving the past. Mine is about building a future *within* that preserved past. They're not mutually exclusive. They just require a different kind of flexibility. A willingness to see the potential, not just the problems."

Clara watched him go, the echo of his words lingering in the quiet office. She looked at the plaster quote, then at her spreadsheets, then at the image of Mrs. Gable she'd conjured in her mind. Jonah saw a canvas, ripe for new life. She saw a framework, needing to be filled according to strict instructions. His approach was organic, community-driven, and inherently adaptable.

Hers was structured, compliance-focused, and, she was beginning to realize, potentially too narrow to truly serve the enduring spirit of the Community Hall. He saw a living, breathing organism; she saw a meticulous blueprint. And the growing realization that the blueprint might be missing the very essence of what made the building, and the town, special, settled heavily upon her. The grant required her to restore the Hall; Jonah's vision inspired her to *revitalize* it. The distinction, she was starting to understand, was everything.

The conversation with Jonah had unsettled Clara more than she cared to admit. His vision of the Community Hall was so expansive, so deeply ingrained in the fabric of community life, that it challenged the very core of her project management philosophy. She had spent months meticulously dissecting the grant requirements, ensuring every task, every expenditure, was justifiable and aligned with the stated objectives of historical preservation. Jonah, however, saw the Hall not just as a historical artifact, but as a living, breathing entity, capable of continuous growth and adaptation.

He spoke of the neglected patch of land behind the Hall with an almost reverent tone, envisioning it transformed into a vibrant community garden. He described raised beds bursting with fresh produce, a place where residents could cultivate their own food, share their bounty, and perhaps even contribute to the Food Pantry's supplies. "Imagine," he'd said, his eyes alight with the possibility, "a sign that reads, 'From the Hall's garden to your table.' It's not just about preserving history, Clara; it's about nurturing the future, about fostering self-sufficiency and connection."

Clara, ever the pragmatist, had initially recoiled. "Community gardens are wonderful, Jonah, but they fall outside the scope of this restoration grant. We'd need separate funding, new permits, and a comprehensive management plan. And then there's the issue of soil testing and irrigation..." Her mind, a well-oiled machine of logistical hurdles, had immediately begun to catalog the potential complications.

Jonah, however, wasn't deterred. He waved a dismissive hand. "Silas at the hardware store would probably donate the soil and seeds. He's always looking for ways to support the town. And a few volunteer hours could handle the irrigation. It's about resourcefulness, Clara. Not about adhering to a rigid plan that prevents us from doing good things."

His words, though intended to be encouraging, had felt like a mild rebuke to her by-the-book approach. She was so focused on ticking the boxes dictated by the grant committee that she risked missing the opportunities to truly enrich the Hall's impact on the community.

Then there was his idea for a small performance space. He spoke of utilizing the main hall's natural acoustics, creating a designated area for local musicians, poets, and amateur theater groups. "It's about making the Hall a place where people *create*, Clara," he'd explained, gesturing with his hands to illustrate the flow of an audience. "Not just a place where they remember the past. Think of the energy, the life it would bring back into this building."

Clara had mentally filed that away as "potential future development, requiring separate funding." The grant was for restoration, not for the creation of new amenities. Yet, the image of a local band playing in the grand hall, their music echoing through the restored space, tugged at something within her. It was a vision of vibrancy, of renewed purpose, that her spreadsheets and historical documents hadn't captured.

And the kitchen. The dusty, disused room at the back, relegated to storage. Jonah saw not a forgotten space, but a potential hub for community learning. He painted a picture of cooking classes, where residents could learn to bake bread, preserve fruits, or prepare healthy meals. "Imagine folks learning new skills, sharing recipes, connecting over food," he'd enthused. "It's about building practical knowledge, about strengthening the community's ties."

He even suggested using salvaged cabinetry and refurbished fixtures, a notion that made Clara's internal alarm bells ring louder than ever. "Approved materials and vendors are crucial, Jonah," she'd countered, her voice tight. "We can't just use... whatever we find."

"But 'whatever we find' can often be just as good, if not better, and a fraction of the cost," he'd replied patiently. "It's about recognizing value, Clara. It's about seeing the potential in things that others might discard.

The grant is for restoring the Hall, yes. But what if 'restoring' also means making it a place that can actively serve the community in new and meaningful ways? A place that's not just a monument, but a resource."

His words lingered long after he'd left. Clara found herself staring at the plaster quote, the astronomical figure a stark reminder of the financial constraints she was operating under. Jonah's approach was fluid, adaptable, and community-centric. He saw potential where she saw problems and obstacles. He envisioned a revitalized Hall that was not just structurally sound but brimming with life and activity.

He understood that a building, to truly endure, needed to be more than just a preserved artifact; it needed to be a dynamic part of the community it served, a place that fostered connection, learning, and shared experiences. His vision was a stark contrast to her own, which was primarily focused on meeting the minimum requirements of the grant and ensuring historical accuracy. He saw a canvas for new life; she saw a meticulously drawn blueprint. The growing realization that his perspective might be the key to unlocking the Hall's true potential, beyond the grant's narrow definition of restoration, began to dawn on her, a subtle yet powerful shift in her understanding of what this project truly entailed.

The tremor of his words had barely subsided when the urgent shrill of Clara's phone shattered the quiet. A quick glance at the caller ID – the town's building inspector – sent a familiar jolt of anxiety through her. She answered, her voice carefully composed, but the conversation was brief and grim. A section of the west-facing wall, previously deemed stable, was showing signs of advanced deterioration, likely exacerbated by the recent heavy rains. The inspector's tone was unequivocal: immediate stabilization was required, or further demolition could occur, potentially compromising the entire structure.

Clara hung up, her hand trembling slightly. This was exactly the kind of unforeseen crisis that Jonah's flexible approach seemed designed to navigate, while her meticulous grant-driven plan felt increasingly like a flimsy shield against a raging storm. She looked at the pile of paperwork on her desk, the grant stipulations and budget allocations suddenly feeling utterly inadequate.

Jonah, who had been about to offer another suggestion about the Hall's outdated plumbing, noticed the shift in her demeanor. He recognized the look of a project manager facing an unexpected, significant obstacle. He stepped closer, his usual easygoing confidence tempered with a newfound concern. "Everything alright, Clara?"

She sighed, a weary sound that seemed to carry the weight of the old building itself. "Not entirely. The inspector just called. That west wall... it's worse than we thought. They're recommending immediate temporary support to prevent further collapse." She gestured towards the schematics spread across her desk, her finger tracing a section of the wall in question. "This means rerouting some of the planned electrical work, and it's going to eat into our contingency fund faster than I'd anticipated."

He leaned in, his gaze sharp as he examined the plans. "Temporary support. That means bracing, right? We'll need sturdy timber. I can get some quotes from Silas – he'll have the best quality lumber and can probably deliver it faster than any contractor we'd have to bring in from out of town." He paused, his eyes meeting hers. "And we'll need to assess the extent of the damage before we can even think about permanent repairs. That might mean bringing in someone with expertise in structural assessment, but who also understands old buildings. Not just a generic engineer who'll want to rip it all out and replace it with modern materials."

Clara found herself listening, not with her usual guarded skepticism, but with a surprising degree of attentiveness. Silas, the local hardware store owner, was indeed a known quantity – knowledgeable, reliable, and deeply invested in the town's welfare. And Jonah's point about finding someone who understood old buildings resonated. Her grant had specified approved engineering firms, but none of them, she suspected, had dealt with the unique challenges of a century-old structure like the Community Hall.

"Silas," she mused aloud, her pen hovering over her notepad. "Yes, he might be able to help with the timber. And the assessment... I'll have to check if any of the approved consultants have experience with historic structures. It's a long shot." She scribbled a note:

"Contact Silas re: lumber and potential structural assessment recommendations."

"And the cost of that temporary bracing," Jonah continued, his brow furrowed in thought. "We need to be smart about it. We don't want to spend so much on a temporary fix that it compromises the budget for the permanent repairs. Maybe we can salvage some of the old beams from the attic crawl space? If they're still sound, they could be repurposed for bracing. It would save us money and be in keeping with the spirit of using existing resources."

The suggestion of salvaging old beams, while potentially innovative, still made Clara's organizational instincts prickle. Her grant manual, a thick tome of regulations and procedures, was quite specific about the sourcing of materials. "Salvaging... I'm not sure that would be permissible under the grant's material procurement guidelines, Jonah. We need to ensure everything used for repair is up to code and documented."

He offered a small, understanding smile. "I know, Clara. I know the rules. But sometimes, the rules are written for a world that doesn't exist in a town like Cedar Ridge, where ingenuity and resourcefulness are just as important as a signed invoice. If we can prove that the salvaged beams are structurally sound – Silas can help us with that assessment – and that using them is a demonstrably more cost-effective solution that doesn't compromise the structural integrity, we might be able to get it approved.

We'd need to document the assessment, of course, and the process of their integration." He looked at her, a flicker of something akin to respect in his eyes. "You're good at documentation, aren't you?"

The implied compliment, and the logic behind it, disarmed her. He was right. Her strength lay in her meticulous record-keeping. If she could find a way to document the salvaging process in a manner that satisfied the grant's requirements for accountability and quality control, it might just be feasible. It was a compromise, a bridge between her rigid adherence to procedure and his practical, community-minded approach.

"I can... I can look into the documentation required for using salvaged materials," she admitted, her voice softer than before. "And Silas's assessment would be crucial. If he's confident in the beams, and we can get clear evidence of their suitability..." She trailed off, the wheels of her mind beginning to turn, not in outright opposition, but in exploration of possibility.

"Exactly," Jonah said, a subtle triumph in his tone, though it was tempered with a genuine desire to move forward collaboratively. "And while we're dealing with the wall, we can start planning for the other immediate needs. The pantry's shelves are practically groaning, and we've had a surge in demand lately. We need to reinforce them, maybe even add some extra shelving units, before they give way. That's something I can definitely help with, sourcing materials and managing the installation. It's straightforward, but it needs doing urgently."

Clara nodded, acknowledging the truth of his statement. The pantry was a constant source of concern, its limited space and resources stretched to their breaking point. The idea of adding more shelving, while not directly related to the Hall's structural restoration, was undeniably important for the community. "Yes, the pantry shelves," she agreed. "That's a practical necessity. If you can handle sourcing the materials and overseeing the installation, that would be a significant help. We'll need to stay within budget, of course, but I'll allocate a portion of the funds for that." She made another note:

"Allocate budget for pantry shelving. Jonah to oversee sourcing and installation."

He smiled, a genuine, warm smile that softened the worry lines around his eyes. "Great. And on the plumbing, we can start with the most critical areas. Leaks that are actively causing damage. We can prioritize those, get them repaired, and then look at upgrading the rest as funds allow. It's about managing the immediate crises while still planning for the long-term improvements."

Their conversation, which had begun with a jarring crisis, had slowly transformed into a tentative negotiation. Clara, though still firmly rooted in the grant's parameters, was beginning to see the value in Jonah's pragmatic, community-focused perspective. She saw his genuine desire to help, not just to push his own agenda, but to make the Hall functional and beneficial for Cedar Ridge. And Jonah, in turn, seemed to recognize Clara's unwavering dedication to the project's success, her commitment to seeing the restoration through, even when faced with daunting challenges. He saw that her meticulousness wasn't born of inflexibility, but of a deep sense of responsibility.

"Alright, Jonah," Clara said, her voice gaining a measure of resolve. "Let's try this. You handle the immediate structural support for the west wall, including getting quotes from Silas for lumber and any necessary bracing. I will contact the approved engineering firm to schedule an immediate assessment of the damage, and I'll also discreetly inquire about the possibility of using sound, salvaged materials for the temporary fix, provided we can document it thoroughly. For the pantry, your offer to manage shelving installation is accepted. We'll set a specific budget for that, and I'll need detailed invoices."

He nodded, his expression serious. "Understood. And for the plumbing, I'll focus on identifying and repairing the most critical leaks first. I can prepare a report detailing the issues, the proposed repairs, and the cost, for your approval before I proceed with anything beyond the immediate emergency containment."

It was an uneasy alliance, forged in the crucible of necessity. Clara still felt the pull of her established protocols, the ingrained habit of adhering strictly to the grant's every comma and clause. The idea of deviating, even slightly, made her stomach clench. But she also saw the pragmatic wisdom in Jonah's suggestions, the potential for greater efficiency and community benefit if they could find ways to blend their approaches.

Jonah, for his part, seemed to appreciate Clara's willingness to consider his ideas, to negotiate rather than simply dismiss them. He understood that her caution was born of experience and a heavy burden of responsibility. He saw that her dedication wasn't a barrier, but a foundation upon which they could build something stronger.

"We'll need to coordinate our efforts closely," Clara stated, her tone firm but not dismissive. "I'll need regular updates from you regarding the wall repairs and the pantry shelving. And I'll keep you informed of any developments with the engineering assessment and the grant administration side of things."

"Absolutely," Jonah replied. "I'll set up a shared document for progress reports and material costs. And we can have a brief check-in, maybe once a day, to go over what's been done and what's coming up."

The prospect of daily check-ins with Jonah, something she might have balked at a week ago, now felt like a practical necessity. It was a small step, a single thread in the complex tapestry of the Hall's revitalization, but it was a step forward. The deep-seated differences in their approaches remained, but they were no longer insurmountable walls. They were becoming more like diverging paths that, with careful navigation, could potentially converge towards a shared goal.

As Jonah began to gather his tools, a sense of quiet determination settled over Clara. The overwhelming feeling of being solely responsible for every aspect of the Hall's restoration had begun to dissipate, replaced by a fragile hope. This collaboration, born out of a crisis, was more than just a practical arrangement; it was a testament to the fact that even the most disparate individuals could find common ground when the needs of their community were at stake. Her focus had been on preserving the past; his, on building the future.

And now, it seemed, they were beginning to understand how those two visions could intertwine, creating something far more robust and enduring than either could achieve alone. The uneasy alliance was forming, not out of friendship, but out of a shared purpose, a mutual, if grudging, respect for each other's strengths, and a profound understanding that the Community Hall, and the town it served, needed them both.

CHAPTER FIVE

Cracks in the Facade

The scent of dust and forgotten time hung heavy in the air as Clara ventured into the Hall's seldom-used storage rooms. Her initial intention was a simple inventory, a necessary task to ascertain what usable materials might be salvaged for the ongoing repairs. The grant, after all, encouraged resourcefulness, a concept that felt increasingly relevant as the budget dwindled. Armed with a flashlight and a healthy dose of apprehension—the darkness often held more than just cobwebs—she began to systematically sift through the accumulated detritus of decades. Old banners drooped from the rafters, their once vibrant colors faded to muted ghosts. Shelves sagged under the weight of discarded furniture, forgotten theatrical props, and boxes that seemed to hold the collective memories of every town event the Hall had ever hosted.

It was in the furthest, darkest corner, tucked behind a towering stack of dusty hymnals, that she found it. A sturdy, dark wooden trunk, surprisingly well-preserved, its brass latches tarnished but intact. It wasn't on any of her inventory lists, nor did she recall seeing it before. Curiosity, a trait she usually managed to keep in check when focused on project management, tugged at her. With a determined grunt, she wrestled the trunk out into the faint light filtering through a grimy windowpane.

The latches sprang open with a protesting creak, revealing a treasure trove of a life lived and perhaps, unfulfilled. Inside, nestled amongst yellowed linens and a few moth-eaten shawls, was a shoebox. Not a modern, brightly colored one, but a vintage, unassuming grey cardboard box. It was filled with letters, tied with brittle, faded ribbon. Her heart gave a peculiar lurch. The handwriting on the envelopes was elegant, a flowing script that was achingly familiar. It was her Aunt Eleanor's.

Clara's aunt had been a quiet presence in her childhood, a woman of gentle smiles and often faraway eyes. She'd lived a solitary life in a small cottage on the outskirts of town, her visits to Clara's family few but cherished. Eleanor had passed away some years ago, and Clara hadn't been privy to many details of her life beyond the surface. She'd always assumed her aunt's life, while perhaps lonely, had been peaceful.

With trembling fingers, Clara untied the ribbon. The letters were dated from the late 1970s and early 1980s, a period Clara dimly remembered as a time of nascent economic hardship for many in the area. The first letter she unfolded was addressed to a bank manager, a formal request for a loan that spoke of dwindling savings and an unexpected medical expense. The tone was polite, almost apologetic, yet underscored by a desperate urgency. Clara's breath hitched. This wasn't the simple, quiet life she'd imagined.

She continued to read, each letter a further revelation. There were pleas to friends who never seemed to respond, requests for assistance that went unanswered. There were letters to distant relatives, hinting at a need for help that was never explicitly stated, a subtle dance around the shame of asking. One letter, penned in a shaky hand, spoke of a looming foreclosure, of the possibility of losing the cottage where she'd lived for over fifty years. The ink blurred as Clara's vision swam. She'd never known her aunt to be anything but self-sufficient, a pillar of quiet resilience. To see her so vulnerable, so clearly struggling, was like discovering a hidden facet of a well-known landscape, a chasm that had been there all along, unseen.

One letter, in particular, struck Clara with the force of a physical blow. It was addressed to her own mother, her aunt's younger sister. The date was just a few months before Eleanor's death. Clara remembered that period well. Her mother had been consumed with family matters, juggling Clara's father's failing business and her own demanding job. Clara herself had been wrestling with her own early career anxieties, feeling adrift and uncertain.

"Dearest Clara," the letter began, a stark deviation from the usual address. Clara frowned. This was unusual. Her aunt always addressed her mother as 'my dear sister'. Puzzled, she unfolded the letter. It was written not to her mother, but to Clara.

"My Dearest Clara," it started again, *"I know this is not how we usually communicate, and I hope you will forgive my forwardness. I find myself in a position I never thought I would be, a position of needing to ask for help. Not for myself, not entirely, but for the preservation of something I hold dear. The cottage, as you know, has been my sanctuary for so long. But recent... unforeseen circumstances have made it difficult to maintain. The roof, Clara, it needs significant repair, and the costs are... beyond my current means.*

I have explored every avenue, every polite request. But it seems pride, or perhaps a misplaced sense of propriety, has prevented me from making the most important call. The call to my niece. You have always been such a bright spark, Clara, so capable and so independent. I see so much of your father in you, his determination and his resourcefulness. It is these qualities I hope you will lend me. If there is any way you could... perhaps assist with the cost of the roof repairs, even a small loan, it would mean more than I can possibly express. I would, of course, repay you as soon as my situation improves. I will understand if this is not possible. Your own path is important, and I would never wish to burden you. But please, Clara, consider it. The thought of losing this place, of not having a roof over my head in my twilight years... it is a heavy burden to bear alone. I will be at the Hall on Saturday afternoon, helping with the bake sale. Perhaps we could speak then, away from prying eyes. If not, please know that my hope, however small, rests with you. With deepest affection, Eleanor."

Clara's hands began to shake, the paper rustling faintly. She reread the words, her mind struggling to reconcile the image of her quiet, stoic aunt with this raw, vulnerable plea.

"I will understand if this is not possible. Your own path is important, and I would never wish to burden you." Those words echoed in the cavernous storage room, a whisper of past disappointment that still held the power to wound.

She remembered that Saturday. She'd been so engrossed in a new project at work, so overwhelmed by the demands of her burgeoning career, that she had consciously avoided her aunt. She'd heard her mother mention Eleanor would be at the Hall, but she'd made an excuse, a flimsy fabrication about a late meeting. She hadn't wanted to be bothered. She'd been so focused on her own ascent, her own need to prove herself, that she hadn't seen her aunt's silent cry for help. She'd been so afraid of *being* a burden, of the perceived entanglement, that she'd actively, albeit unconsciously, pushed away someone who needed her.

A wave of guilt washed over Clara, cold and suffocating. She'd never known. Her aunt had never spoken of it again, and Clara, caught up in her own life, had never inquired. Eleanor had passed away a few months later, and Clara had attended the funeral, her heart heavy with a vague sense of regret she couldn't quite articulate, a feeling that she had somehow missed a crucial opportunity for connection. Now, holding this tangible evidence of her aunt's hidden struggles, the regret solidified into a sharp, painful shard of understanding. Her aunt had carried this burden alone, a burden that Clara, in her own self-absorption, had failed to alleviate.

The letters continued, a cascade of unspoken anxieties. Some were addressed to a lawyer, detailing attempts to sell some of her meager possessions. Others were to a local community fund, a desperate, last-ditch effort that seemed to have been met with refusal. Each word was a testament to a silent war fought within the confines of Eleanor's quiet life. Clara felt a profound kinship with the woman whose letters lay in her hands. Eleanor's fear of being a burden, her hesitation to ask for help, her desire to maintain her independence at all costs—these were all emotions that Clara understood on a visceral level.

She herself lived with a constant, gnawing fear of being a burden. Her meticulous grant management, her almost obsessive need for control, her reluctance to delegate or ask for assistance—all stemmed from this deep-seated anxiety. She had seen firsthand, in her own family, the corrosive effects of reliance, the way promises could be broken, leaving one stranded and vulnerable. Her father's business had failed, and the fallout had been immense, leaving her mother shouldering an overwhelming debt and Clara with a stark realization: you could only truly rely on yourself. Her aunt's letters were a chilling echo of that lesson, a confirmation that even the most loving intentions could be overshadowed by life's harsh realities.

Clara sat on the dusty floor, the shoebox open before her, the letters fanned out like a deck of sorrowful cards. The weight of her aunt's unspoken suffering pressed down on her, heavy and profound. It mirrored her own deepest fears. Her aunt had been afraid of losing her home, of facing destitution in her old age. Clara, in her own way, was terrified of losing her footing, of her carefully constructed professional life crumbling, leaving her exposed and alone. She saw in Eleanor's plight a reflection of her own vulnerability, a stark reminder that beneath the veneer of competence and control, everyone carried their own set of worries and anxieties.

She remembered the grant stipulations, the requirement for detailed financial transparency, the constant reporting to funding bodies. It felt like a pale imitation of the intense scrutiny Eleanor had faced. Her aunt had tried to manage her finances, to keep her struggles private, to maintain a façade of normalcy. Clara, too, strived for an outward appearance of control, of unflawfulness. But these letters proved that the reality could be far more complex, far more desperate.

The silence of the storage room amplified the turmoil within her. She imagined her aunt, sitting alone in her small cottage, penning these desperate notes, her heart heavy with a need that went unfulfilled. The thought that Eleanor had turned to *her*, Clara, with this plea, and that Clara had turned away—not out of malice, but out of a self-imposed isolation born of past hurt—was almost unbearable. It was a painful paradox: her aunt's desperate need for connection had been met with Clara's equally desperate need for independence.

She carefully gathered the letters, retying the brittle ribbon around them. This wasn't just a historical discovery; it was a personal reckoning. Her aunt's story had become intertwined with her own, a somber reminder of the unspoken burdens people carry and the profound impact of seemingly small choices. The Community Hall, with its own history of resilience and near collapse, felt like a fitting place for this revelation. It was a place that had weathered storms, that had seen its fair share of hardship and hope. And now, Clara was faced with her own storm, a tempest of guilt and regret, all stemming from a letter never truly answered.

She carefully placed the shoebox back into the trunk, the lid falling with a soft thud. The dust motes danced in the sliver of light, indifferent to the emotional upheaval unfolding before them. Clara knew she couldn't change the past. She couldn't go back and have that conversation with her aunt on Saturday afternoon. But she could learn from it. She could choose to break the cycle of unspoken anxieties, to reach out, to offer support when it was needed, even when it felt uncomfortable.

The project at the Community Hall, which had felt like a monumental task of structural repair and financial management, suddenly took on a new dimension. It wasn't just about preserving bricks and mortar; it was about honoring the legacy of the people who had poured their lives into this building, people like her aunt Eleanor, who had navigated their own challenges with quiet fortitude, and sometimes, with a desperate need for a hand to hold. Clara's fear of being a burden, so deeply ingrained, felt for the first time like a cage she could, perhaps, begin to unlock.

The discovery in the trunk wasn't just about her aunt's past; it was a catalyst for Clara's own future, a gentle, yet insistent, call to be more present, more open, and more willing to connect, even when the prospect felt daunting. The cracks in the facade of the Hall seemed to mirror the cracks that had just appeared in her own carefully constructed defenses.

Jonah watched Clara from across the almost-empty hall, the late afternoon sun slanting through the tall, arched windows, illuminating dust motes dancing in the stillness. She sat on the edge of the stage, a shoebox open at her feet, her shoulders hunched in a way that spoke volumes even from a distance. He'd seen that posture before, that particular set of the shoulders that telegraphed a heavy burden carried alone. It was a familiar ache he recognized in her, a pain he'd tried to outrun for years, only to find it waiting for him in the quiet corners of his own life.

He remembered the old library renovation project, a decade ago now. It had been his passion, a labor of love to restore the crumbling edifice on the town's main street. He'd envisioned it as a hub, a place for learning and gathering, a beacon of culture in a town that sometimes felt starved of it. He'd poured his energy, his savings, and his heart into it. He'd organized fundraisers, rallied volunteers, and even charmed the local bank into a modest loan. For a while, it had felt like a miracle was unfolding, brick by careful brick.

But then the momentum had stalled. People, once enthusiastic, started dropping away, their lives pulling them in different directions. The promised support from the town council dwindled to a trickle of lukewarm encouragement. The funds, so carefully pieced together, proved to be a mere fraction of what was truly needed. He'd found himself standing on the unfinished stage, surrounded by scaffolding and the ghosts of what could have been, the weight of it all crushing him. He'd felt like a failure, a man who had promised the moon and delivered only dust.

The memory resurfaced now, sharp and unwelcome, as he saw Clara's silent struggle. Her distress was palpable, a low hum in the air that resonated with his own past disappointments. He saw in her the same fierce protectiveness of something she cared about, the same underlying fear of seeing it crumble. He understood her guardedness, too. When you've felt the sting of letting people down, or worse, of being let down yourself, the instinct is to build walls, to keep the tender parts of yourself safe from the potential for pain.

He hadn't known Clara long, not really. Their interactions had been polite, professional, tinged with a carefully maintained distance. He'd observed her dedication to the Hall, her meticulous attention to detail, her unwavering focus on the grant requirements. He'd admired her competence, her ability to navigate the bureaucratic labyrinth with a steely resolve. But he'd also sensed a carefully constructed facade, a polished exterior that hinted at something deeper, something perhaps more fragile beneath the surface.

Now, witnessing this quiet unraveling, that sense of something hidden became undeniable. The letters spread before her, the crumpled tissues scattered around her feet—it was a tableau of raw, unvarnished emotion. He felt a pang of empathy, a deep-seated understanding of the loneliness that often accompanied such moments. He knew the temptation to retreat, to pull the blinds and shut out the world when the weight of responsibility felt too heavy to bear.

He found himself walking towards her, his footsteps echoing softly on the wooden floor. He didn't have words of wisdom, no magic solution to offer. But he knew, with a certainty that settled deep in his bones, that no one should have to carry such burdens alone. The memory of his own failed project, the gnawing sense of inadequacy that had lingered for years, made him acutely sensitive to Clara's pain. He didn't want her to experience that same crushing weight of isolation.

He stopped a respectful distance away, not wanting to intrude, but also unwilling to let her remain adrift in her sea of sorrow. "Clara?" he said, his voice soft, careful not to startle her.

She jumped, her head snapping up, her eyes wide and a little wild. She quickly tried to gather the scattered papers, her movements jerky, betraying her agitation. "Jonah," she managed, her voice tight. "I... I didn't hear you."

He offered a small, reassuring smile. "It's a quiet afternoon," he said. He gestured vaguely towards the shoebox. "Looks like you've unearthed some history." He kept his tone light, casual, hoping to ease the tension he felt radiating from her.

She nodded, her gaze dropping back to the letters. "You could say that," she murmured, her fingers tracing the faded ink on an envelope. There was a profound sadness in her eyes, a reflection of the pain he recognized all too well.

He hesitated for a moment, then took a step closer, his gaze steady on her face. "Are you alright?" The question was simple, but it carried the weight of his own unspoken experiences. He knew what it felt like to pretend everything was fine when it wasn't, to plaster a smile on your face while your insides churned with worry. He also knew the relief that could come from even a small acknowledgment of that struggle.

Clara's eyes flickered up to his, a hint of vulnerability in their depths before she quickly masked it. She managed a weak smile. "Just... a bit overwhelmed," she admitted, her voice a little steadier. "This project is bigger than I anticipated, and then finding... this..." She gestured to the trunk. "It's a lot to process."

He understood. He understood the feeling of being buried under the weight of something unexpected, something that shifted the ground beneath your feet. He remembered the library, how the initial excitement had been replaced by a relentless grind of problem-solving, of facing one setback after another. He'd felt that same sense of being overwhelmed, of questioning his own judgment and capabilities.

"I know the feeling," he said, his voice low. "Sometimes the past has a way of making itself known, doesn't it?" He didn't elaborate, didn't want to launch into his own story, but he hoped the shared sentiment would offer a sliver of comfort. He saw a flicker of recognition in her eyes, a brief moment where the carefully constructed walls seemed to soften.

He continued, his voice gentle. "This Hall... it's a special place. It's got a lot of history, a lot of heart. It deserves to be saved. And it will be." He met her gaze, his own conviction steady. "We just have to... keep at it. Even when it gets tough."

He saw the faint nod she gave, a subtle acknowledgment of his words. He knew he wasn't fixing anything, not really. But perhaps, just perhaps, he was offering a small anchor in the storm she was weathering. He remembered how, in the midst of his library struggles, a simple word of encouragement, a shared understanding, had sometimes been enough to keep him going for another day.

He knew her instinct would be to retreat, to try and handle this on her own. He recognized that fierce independence, that desire to prove herself capable. But he also knew, from his own painful lessons, that some battles were too big to fight alone. And that sometimes, the greatest strength lay not in carrying the burden by oneself, but in allowing someone else to share the load.

He looked at the letters again, the tangible evidence of her aunt's unspoken struggles. He imagined the quiet dignity with which Eleanor must have faced her own challenges, her own fears. And he saw in Clara a reflection of that same quiet strength, a strength that was now being tested. His own fear of letting people down, of failing to be the support he felt he should be, made him even more determined to offer what little he could. He didn't want Clara to feel the same crushing disappointment he had once felt, to be left standing alone in the quiet aftermath of something that had promised so much.

"If you need a hand with anything," he offered, his voice firm but not demanding, "anything at all, don't hesitate. Even just to talk. Sometimes it helps to just... say it out loud." He knew it was a cliché, but he also knew its truth. He'd learned it the hard way, by keeping his own struggles locked away until they threatened to consume him.

Clara finally looked up at him, a small, hesitant smile touching her lips. It was a fragile thing, but it was there. "Thank you, Jonah," she said, her voice softer now, a hint of genuine gratitude in its tone. "I appreciate that."

He returned the smile, a silent acknowledgment of her vulnerability. He didn't push, didn't pry. He simply stood there, a quiet presence, a reminder that she wasn't entirely alone in her struggle. He understood that the ghosts of the past could be powerful, and that sometimes, the best you could do was to offer a steady hand, a listening ear, and the quiet assurance that even in the face of disappointment, the work of building something worthwhile could continue.

He knew, from his own experience, that the fear of failure was a formidable adversary, and that the desire to protect oneself from further hurt could be just as strong as the need for help. He saw in Clara a mirror of his own past, and a hope for a different future, one where burdens were shared, and where the ghosts of the past could finally be laid to rest. He knew that the struggle to keep the Hall alive was more than just a practical challenge; it was a deeply personal one, intertwined with the history of the town and the unspoken narratives of the people who had loved it.

And he, Jonah, carried his own ghosts from past projects that had faltered, and he was determined, for Clara's sake, and for the Hall's, not to let history repeat itself. He knew that the fear of letting people down, a fear that had once crippled him, was now a quiet motivator, a spur to ensure that this time, the project would not falter due to a lack of support or understanding. He saw Clara's pain and recognized it as a familiar echo of his own, a testament to the emotional toll that such endeavors could take.

The calendar in Clara's office, once a cheerful splash of color, now felt like a ticking bomb. Each flip of the page brought the town council's deadline for the initial structural assessments and financial viability plans closer, and with it, a tightening knot of anxiety in her chest. The crisp white paper of the notice, pinned prominently above her desk, seemed to glare at her, the bold black lettering a constant reminder of the precarious position the Grand Hall, and by extension, her own reputation, occupied. It had been three weeks since the council had issued the ultimatum, a stark ultimatum born from a simmering dissatisfaction with the Hall's upkeep and the perceived drain on town resources. Three weeks felt like both an eternity and a blink of an eye, a frustrating paradox that kept her perpetually on edge.

The weight of the task had been substantial from the outset, but now, with the approaching deadline, it felt monolithic. Clara found herself working through the early mornings, the first hint of dawn painting the sky outside her window, and often burning the midnight oil, the only illumination the stark glow of her desk lamp. Sleep became a luxury she could barely afford, a fleeting respite before the relentless pressure resumed. Her office, once a sanctuary of focused work, was now a testament to her frantic efforts: stacks of blueprints teetered precariously, meticulously organized binders overflowed with reports and invoices, and half-empty mugs of rapidly cooling coffee dotted every available surface. The air was thick with the scent of old paper and a subtle undercurrent of her own exhaustion.

The discovery of Eleanor's letters, tucked away in that forgotten shoebox, had been a pivotal, albeit unsettling, turning point. While they had initially served as a poignant connection to her aunt, a way to understand the woman behind the legend, they had also become a stark, tangible warning. The carefully penned words spoke not only of Eleanor's love for the Hall but also of her own struggles, her own quiet battles against fading funds and dwindling support. Clara saw echoes of her own anxieties mirrored in those pages – the fear of not being enough, the dread of seeing something precious slip through one's fingers due to circumstances beyond one's complete control. Eleanor had faced similar challenges, and the fact that the Hall had still faced such precarious times, even with her aunt's devoted efforts, sent a shiver down Clara's spine. It was a stark reminder that dedication alone wasn't always enough to stave off decline.

This newfound understanding had fueled a desperate need for control, an almost obsessive drive to meticulously manage every aspect of the revitalization project. She found herself poring over every detail of the structural reports, scrutinizing every line item in the projected budgets, cross-referencing every potential grant application with a vigilance that bordered on paranoia. She knew that any perceived weakness, any overlooked detail, could be seized upon by the council as a reason to dismiss her proposal, to pronounce the Hall a lost cause. The fear of failure, a fear that had always lurked in the background of her professional life, now loomed larger than ever before. It wasn't just about the Hall anymore;

it was about proving that she was capable, that she could succeed where others, even her own aunt, had faced significant hurdles.

The social aspect of her life had become a casualty of this intensified focus. Invitations to coffee with friends went unanswered, phone calls were missed, and the casual, friendly banter that usually characterized her interactions with the townsfolk became increasingly strained. She'd catch herself zoning out during conversations, her mind replaying financial projections or worrying about the structural engineer's final assessment. The bright, engaged Clara that most people knew was slowly being eclipsed by a more harried, preoccupied version of herself. She noticed the concerned glances, the gentle inquiries about her well-being, but she brushed them aside, convinced that any display of vulnerability would be interpreted as weakness, further undermining her credibility.

One particularly trying afternoon, the air outside thick with the oppressive heat of late summer, Clara found herself staring at a complex diagram of the Hall's aging roof trusses. The engineer's report was thorough, detailed, and alarmingly expensive to rectify. The cost of repairs alone was a significant chunk of the initial projected budget, a figure that made her stomach clench. She'd spent hours trying to find alternative solutions, researching innovative materials, and exploring less invasive repair methods, but the reality remained stubbornly grim. The roof was a critical, costly component, and its extensive damage threatened to derail the entire financial plan. She felt a wave of despair wash over her, the sheer magnitude of the undertaking threatening to engulf her.

She leaned back in her chair, the worn leather groaning in protest, and closed her eyes, trying to summon a semblance of calm. The faces of the council members flashed through her mind – Mayor Thompson's perpetually skeptical expression, Mrs. Gable's sharp, discerning gaze, Mr. Henderson's quiet but firm demeanor. They represented the collective will of the town, a will that was increasingly leaning towards practicality and fiscal responsibility, and Clara knew, with a chilling certainty, that sentimentality wouldn't sway them. They wanted a solid, actionable plan, a guarantee of future stability, not a nostalgic plea for the past.

The image of her aunt, Eleanor, flickered in her mind's eye. She saw her aunt's determined chin, the slight crinkle of her eyes when she smiled, the unwavering commitment that had defined her. Clara felt a profound sense of responsibility to honor that legacy, to not let the Hall crumble under her watch. But the pressure was immense, and the specter of Eleanor's own struggles, the hints of her own quiet desperation evident in those letters, served as a constant, gnawing reminder of how easily even the most ardent efforts could fall short. She remembered one particular passage where Eleanor had written about a disheartening grant rejection, the words conveying a weariness that Clara now understood all too well. "The funding bodies seem to have lost faith in the dream," Eleanor had penned, her usual buoyant tone tinged with a deep sadness. "It is becoming harder and harder to convince them that this old place is worth the investment."

Clara sighed, running a hand through her already disheveled hair. She understood that feeling of fighting an uphill battle, of pouring one's heart and soul into something only to be met with indifference or outright rejection. The letters had provided a powerful, intimate glimpse into Eleanor's world, a world that was far more complex and fraught with challenges than Clara had ever imagined. Her aunt's carefully maintained public image of unwavering optimism had masked a deep well of worry and perseverance, and Clara now felt the weight of that legacy pressing down on her. She knew she had to be more than just optimistic; she had to be strategic, resourceful, and, above all, successful.

The days blurred into a relentless cycle of meetings, research, and endless calculations. She met with contractors, architects, and historical preservationists, each consultation adding another layer of complexity to the already daunting project. She learned more about arcane building codes, obscure zoning laws, and the intricate dance of municipal bureaucracy than she had ever thought possible. She discovered that the Hall, with its many historical quirks and original features, presented unique challenges that required specialized, and often expensive, solutions. The initial estimates had been optimistic, a necessary evil to secure initial interest, but the reality of the situation was proving to be far more demanding, both financially and logistically.

One evening, as the sun dipped below the horizon, casting long shadows across her office, Clara found herself staring at a particularly discouraging financial projection. The numbers simply refused to align. Even with the most optimistic fundraising scenarios, the projected costs of restoring the Hall to its former glory, while ensuring its long-term viability, far exceeded the available capital. The grant money she had so painstakingly researched was competitive, and the town's contribution, while pledged, was contingent on a detailed and convincing plan that demonstrated a clear return on investment – a concept that felt almost laughable when applied to a historic community building.

She felt a prickle of tears welling up, a raw frustration she'd been suppressing for weeks. She was so close, yet so impossibly far. The deadline loomed, a constant, oppressive presence, and the fear of disappointing not only the council but also her aunt's memory, and the community that held the Hall dear, was almost unbearable. She'd always prided herself on her competence, her ability to tackle challenges head-on and emerge victorious. But this... this felt different. This felt like a battle against insurmountable odds, a test of endurance that was pushing her to her absolute limits.

She remembered Jonah's quiet offer of support, his gentle acknowledgment of her struggle. He had seen her distress in the hallway that day, had recognized the familiar posture of someone carrying a heavy burden. His words, "No one should have to carry such burdens alone," had resonated deeply. At the time, she had been too consumed by her own internal turmoil to fully process his offer, too determined to prove her self-sufficiency. But now, in the lonely quiet of her office, surrounded by the stark reality of her situation, his words offered a sliver of comfort, a faint glimmer of hope that perhaps, just perhaps, she didn't have to face this alone. The thought of sharing her anxieties, of admitting the sheer overwhelming nature of the task, was terrifying, but the alternative – continuing to falter under the weight of it all – was becoming increasingly unbearable. The deadline was no longer just a date on a calendar; it was a crucible, testing not only her resolve but also her ability to accept help when it was most desperately needed.

The hum of the old fluorescent lights in Clara's office seemed to amplify the tension that had settled between her and Jonah. He stood leaning against her doorframe, arms crossed, a familiar stubbornness etched onto his features, while she sat behind her desk, the meticulously organized piles of papers a silent testament to her preferred method of tackling problems. The air crackled with an unspoken disagreement, the pleasant camaraderie they had shared just days before now feeling like a distant memory.

"I just don't see how a 'spontaneous' bake sale is going to generate the kind of funds we need, Jonah," Clara said, her voice carefully modulated, betraying none of the frustration simmering beneath the surface. "We need a structured approach. Pre-approved vendors, set price lists, a clear inventory. It needs to be professional, to demonstrate to the council that we're serious about this."

Jonah pushed off the doorframe, taking a step into the room. "Professional? Clara, this is a community bake sale, not a Wall Street merger. The charm is in the spontaneity, the idea that anyone can contribute, that everyone gets involved. Imagine Mrs. Henderson baking her famous apple pies, the Miller's kids selling lemonade, the bakery donating some of their day-olds. It's about bringing people together, not about bureaucratic red tape."

Clara felt a familiar tightening in her chest. His vision, while well-intentioned, felt utterly impractical to her. "But how do we control quality? What if someone brings something that's... not quite right? And what about pricing? If everyone sets their own prices, we could end up with a fifty-cent cookie next to a five-dollar cookie. It's chaotic, Jonah. It undermines the entire purpose of raising serious funds." She gestured to the spread of papers on her desk, her eyes sweeping over the detailed budget proposals and grant applications. "This project requires a level of precision and organization that a free-for-all bake sale simply cannot provide."

"Precision and organization are your strengths, Clara, and I respect that," Jonah said, his tone softening slightly, though the disagreement remained evident. "But sometimes, you have to trust the community. You have to believe that people want to help, that they'll contribute in their own way. My idea isn't about chaos; it's about organic support. It's about creating a ripple effect. People see their neighbors contributing, they feel a sense of ownership, and they're more likely to open their wallets. Your way feels... cold. Like you're trying to micromanage goodwill."

The word "micromanage" stung. Clara's jaw tightened. "It's not micromanaging, Jonah, it's ensuring accountability. It's about presenting a unified, professional front to the town council. They're looking for tangible evidence of viability, not a quaint display of community spirit. If we can't even organize a simple bake sale effectively, how can we expect them to trust us with the Grand Hall's future? They'll see it as proof that we're not capable of managing such a significant undertaking." The fear, the one that had been a constant companion since the council's ultimatum, surged within her. This wasn't just about a bake sale; it was about the entire project, about her own ability to deliver.

"And I'm telling you, Clara, that 'quaint display of community spirit' is exactly what will convince them," Jonah countered, his voice rising slightly. "They want to see that this Hall means something to the people of this town, that it's not just some dusty old building that a few people are trying to save. It's about passion, about connection. Your spreadsheets can't measure that. My approach allows for that to shine through. We can coordinate a central drop-off point, have volunteers manage the sales, and yes, we can even have a suggested donation list to guide people. But we can't shut down every spontaneous act of generosity with a checklist."

Clara felt a wave of exasperation. He simply didn't understand the pressure she was under, the scrutiny she was facing. "Suggested donation list? Jonah, that's even less structured! We need to know exactly how much money we're bringing in. We need to be able to account for every penny. If we're asking for public funds, we have a responsibility to be transparent and rigorous. Your idea sounds like a recipe for financial uncertainty." She pictured the council members, their brows furrowed as they reviewed her meticulously crafted reports. A bake sale with no clear financial controls would be an instant dismissal.

"And your meticulously crafted reports will gather dust if no one feels any real connection to the Hall," Jonah retorted, his own frustration surfacing. He took another step into the room, his voice firm. "You're so focused on the numbers, on the *how*, that you're forgetting the *why*. Why are we saving this Hall? Because it's a symbol of our town's history, because it's a place for community gatherings, because it holds memories for so many people. A rigid, over-organized event loses that magic. It becomes just another transaction."

"It's not just a transaction, it's an investment!" Clara exclaimed, her voice cracking with emotion. The carefully constructed facade of composure she had maintained for weeks began to crumble. "And I am trying to ensure that investment is sound! I'm trying to prevent this Hall from becoming another forgotten relic because someone couldn't be bothered to plan properly!" The words hung in the air, sharper than she intended. She saw a flicker of hurt in Jonah's eyes, and immediately regretted her outburst.

He recoiled slightly, his arms uncrossing. "So, my ideas are 'bothered' planning? My attempts to rally the town are just... a nuisance to your grand design?" His voice was laced with a wounded tone. "I thought we were a team, Clara. I thought we were working together to save this place."

"We are working together," Clara said, her voice softening as she tried to mend the rift. "But we have different ideas about the best way to achieve our goal. Your approach relies on... well, it relies on a level of community buy-in that I'm not sure we can guarantee. We're on a deadline. We can't afford to have this bake sale fall flat because it was too disorganized, or because people didn't understand what they were supposed to do." She wrung her hands under the desk, the anxiety about the looming deadline a suffocating weight. "I'm just trying to make sure we succeed. My aunt... she tried for years, and she faced so many setbacks. I don't want to fail her. I don't want to fail this town."

Jonah watched her, his expression shifting from anger to concern. He recognized the tremor in her voice, the way she clutched the edge of her desk. He saw the deep-seated fear that fueled her meticulousness, the overwhelming burden she carried. He understood, in that moment, that her resistance wasn't about control for its own sake, but about a desperate need to avoid the kind of failure that haunted her.

"Clara," he said, his voice gentle now, bridging the gap that had widened between them. "I know you're under immense pressure. And I admire your dedication, truly. But you can't carry all of this alone. This isn't just your responsibility. It's the town's. And my approach isn't about being careless; it's about harnessing the collective energy of those who care. We can make it work. We can have a bake sale that's both spirited and structured. We can have Mrs. Henderson's pies and a clear accounting system. We just need to find a way to blend our strengths, not let them pull us apart."

He walked closer to her desk, his gaze steady and earnest. "Think about it. What if we designate a few trusted volunteers – people you know and can rely on – to manage the financial side, to handle the collections and ensure everything is properly recorded? They can work with your systems. And at the same time, we can put out a call to the entire town, letting everyone know *how* they can contribute – what kind of baked goods are welcome, what time to drop them off, where the proceeds will go. We can create a central hub, a focal point for the effort. It doesn't have to be either-or. We can have your organization *and* the community's heart."

Clara looked at him, really looked at him, and saw not just a differing opinion, but a genuine desire to collaborate. His idea, when framed that way, didn't sound as terrifyingly unstructured. The thought of delegating the financial tracking, of entrusting a small, vetted group with that crucial aspect, eased some of the pressure. It was a compromise, a bridge between her need for control and his vision of community engagement.

"So, you're saying... we can have designated 'official' bakers who follow certain guidelines, and then also a general call for anyone who wants to contribute, with a central collection point?" she clarified, cautiously exploring the possibility. "And these trusted volunteers would be accountable to me?"

Jonah smiled, a genuine, hopeful smile that reached his eyes. "Exactly. They'd be accountable to the project, and by extension, to you. We can set clear expectations for them. They'd be the gatekeepers of quality and organization on the day, working *with* your plans, not against them. And the rest of the town gets to feel like they're part of something bigger, something more personal. It's about building enthusiasm, Clara, not just collecting donations."

Clara leaned back in her chair, a sigh escaping her lips, but this time it was one of relief, not despair. The confrontation had been difficult, exposing the stark contrast in their approaches and the anxieties that lay beneath. But in the shared space of that disagreement, they had found a path forward, a way to weave their disparate threads into a stronger, more resilient fabric. The Grand Hall, she realized, needed both its meticulously crafted blueprints and the warm, beating heart of the community to truly thrive. And perhaps, just perhaps, she needed Jonah's perspective to see that the most effective solutions often lay in the delicate balance between order and spirit.

The idea of a collaborative bake sale, one that honored both her need for structure and his belief in community, began to take root, a small but significant crack in the facade of her overwhelming anxiety. It was a compromise, yes, but it was also a testament to the power of working together, a lesson she was slowly, but surely, learning. The journey to save the Grand Hall was proving to be as much about personal growth as it was about bricks and mortar.

The silence that followed Jonah's last words was thick with unspoken emotions. Clara's gaze, which had been fixed on the detailed budget proposal before her, slowly lifted to meet his. The raw vulnerability in his eyes, mirroring the tremor she felt within herself, was disarming. It was in that quiet space, between the lingering echoes of their argument and the nascent understanding, that the carefully constructed walls around Clara's heart began to show their true fragility.

"It's not that I don't trust the community, Jonah," she began, her voice a little softer, a little more hesitant than before. "It's... it's just that sometimes, people let you down. They make promises, they seem so sure, and then... nothing. Or worse, they make things worse." Her fingers, which had been tracing the neat lines of a financial projection, now curled inward, a subconscious attempt to hold herself together. "I learned a long time ago that relying too much on others can be... dangerous. It leaves you exposed. And when you're responsible for something as important as the Grand Hall, exposure is a luxury you can't afford."

She paused, swallowing the lump in her throat. The memory, sharp and painful, resurfaced with an almost physical ache. It was from her early days in the town, when she'd been full of youthful idealism, eager to contribute, to be a part of something. She'd joined a committee, full of bright-eyed individuals who'd sworn they would revitalize the old community gardens. They'd spoken of shared responsibility, of communal effort, and Clara, trusting in their enthusiasm, had poured her energy into it. She'd meticulously planned planting schedules, researched soil enrichment, even rallied donations for new tools. Then, one by one, people had drifted away. Excuses became commonplace, then silence. The project, so full of promise, had withered and died, leaving Clara feeling foolish, betrayed, and utterly alone in her disappointment. The garden had become an overgrown, neglected testament to broken commitments.

"There was a project, years ago," she confessed, her gaze drifting towards the window, as if the answer lay in the sunlit street outside. "A group of us wanted to... well, it doesn't matter what it was. What matters is that I believed in it. I believed in the people involved. And when it all fell apart, because everyone else just... stopped caring, I felt like a fool. Like I'd been naive.

It taught me that if you want something done right, if you want it to actually *happen*, you have to be the one driving it. You can't depend on others to carry the weight, because they'll eventually put it down. And you'll be left holding it all, alone." The words were a confession, a plea for understanding, an explanation for the rigid structure she so fiercely clung to. It was the core of her fear – the fear of being left holding the bag, of another well-intentioned dream crumbling into dust.

Jonah listened, his initial defensiveness softening into something akin to empathy. He saw the flicker of pain in her eyes, the tightening of her jaw as she recounted her past. He recognized the deep-seated fear that drove her meticulousness, the almost desperate need for control that stemmed from a profound sense of being let down. It wasn't just about the bake sale, or even the Grand Hall; it was about a lifetime of learned caution, of building protective walls after painful experiences.

"I understand," he said, his voice low and steady, a stark contrast to the earlier tension. "I've felt that too, in a different way. That crushing weight of responsibility when you feel like you're the only one holding things together. The fear that you're not good enough, that you're going to let everyone down." He shifted his weight, his gaze meeting hers directly. "My dad... he was a builder. Built half the houses in this town, his hands strong, his reputation solid. But there was this one big project, years ago. A community center. He poured everything into it – his time, his savings, his reputation. He was so sure it would be his legacy."

His expression grew distant, a shadow passing over his features. "But there were... complications. With permits, with suppliers, with unforeseen costs. Things spiraled. He worked himself to the bone, trying to keep it all afloat, trying to fix every problem that came up. He believed, right up until the end, that he could make it work. That he could pull it all back." He let out a ragged sigh. "He couldn't. It ended up bankrupting him. And it broke him, too. Not just financially, but... inside. He never really recovered. He always blamed himself. Said he wasn't strong enough, wasn't smart enough. He carried that failure like a shroud for the rest of his life."

Jonah ran a hand through his hair, a gesture of restless energy that seemed to stem from the resurfacing memory. "I saw firsthand what that kind of pressure does. What it does to a person when they feel like they've failed. And I swore I'd never let that happen. To me, or to anyone I cared about.

So, yeah, I get the fear. I get the urge to try and control every single variable, to preempt every possible disaster."

He took a step closer, his gaze earnest. "But sometimes, Clara, the biggest risk isn't in trying something a little less controlled. Sometimes, the biggest risk is in trying to control *everything* and ending up suffocating the very thing you're trying to save. My dad... he was too proud to ask for help, too focused on his own perceived failure. He tried to carry the whole burden alone. And it destroyed him."

The raw honesty in his words, the shared vulnerability, created a new kind of connection between them. Clara saw not just Jonah, the man who disagreed with her methods, but Jonah, a man who carried his own burdens, his own ghosts. His story resonated with her own deep-seated fear of failure, of the devastating consequences that came when responsibilities became too heavy, too isolating.

"So, your approach," she began, her voice barely a whisper, testing the waters of this new emotional landscape, "it's not about carelessness, or a lack of appreciation for... for the importance of getting it right. It's about... about preventing that isolation? About not letting the responsibility crush the people trying to shoulder it?"

Jonah nodded, a small, grateful smile touching his lips. "Exactly. It's about building a net, not just a foundation. My dad tried to build a fortress, and when the walls came down, there was nothing to catch him. I believe in this Hall. I believe in the idea of saving it. But I also believe that we can't do it alone. And more importantly, we shouldn't have to. The effort should be shared, the joy of it should be shared, and yes, the burden of it should be shared too. If we can get the whole town excited about this bake sale, if they feel like they're a part of it, then when things get tough, when unexpected problems arise – and they will – we'll have more than just our own two hands to rely on. We'll have the community's. And that, Clara, is a strength no spreadsheet can ever quantify."

Clara looked at him, truly looked at him, and saw a depth of understanding she hadn't expected. His past, his father's story, had provided a crucial piece of the puzzle, explaining his passionate belief in community spirit, his insistence on an approach that felt more organic, more inclusive. It wasn't a dismissal of her concerns; it was a different perspective, born from a different kind of pain, a different kind of learned lesson.

"It's just... the thought of it all going wrong," she admitted, her voice still laced with a hint of the anxiety that had become her constant companion. "The thought of letting everyone down, especially after... after everything my aunt tried, after seeing how much this Hall means to people. It feels like a tremendous weight. And I've always been the one to try and lift it all by myself."

"I know," Jonah said, his voice gentle. "And I admire you for that. But you don't have to. Not anymore. This isn't just your aunt's legacy, Clara. It's the town's. And it can be ours to build, together. We can honor her memory by doing this right, but doing it *together*. We can create a bake sale that's both successful and meaningful. We can have your meticulous planning, and the community's boundless enthusiasm. We can find that balance."

He extended a hand, not in a gesture of truce, but of genuine connection. "So, what do you say? Can we try to find a way to build that net? A way that honors your need for structure, and my belief in the power of community? A way that allows us to be accountable, but also to invite everyone in?"

Clara hesitated for a moment, her fingers still curled inward. The offer was an olive branch, a pathway out of the rigid box she had built around herself. It wasn't just about the bake sale anymore; it was about the possibility of shared vulnerability, of trusting someone else with a piece of the burden. Her past had taught her caution, but perhaps, just perhaps, her present was offering her a chance to learn something new.

Slowly, tentatively, she unfurled her fingers, her gaze still locked with Jonah's. The fear was still there, a low hum beneath the surface, but it was now accompanied by a flicker of something else – hope. The cracks in her facade were widening, not from the force of an argument, but from the quiet power of shared experience, of two wounded souls finding common ground. The path ahead was still uncertain, but for the first time in a long time, Clara felt a sense of possibility, a quiet understanding that perhaps, she didn't have to carry the weight of the world, or the Grand Hall, all by herself. The unveiling of their past hurts had, paradoxically, opened the door to a shared future.

CHAPTER SIX

Shared Labors, Quiet Conversations

The hum of the circular saw cut through the cavernous space of the Grand Hall, a sound that had become an almost comforting counterpoint to the focused silence that had settled between Clara and Jonah. The air, once thick with dust and the scent of old wood, now carried the sharp, clean aroma of freshly cut lumber and the faint, metallic tang of the reinforcing brackets. Their shared project, the monumental task of shoring up the Hall's aging support beams, had demanded a new kind of partnership, one built not on shared anxieties or past traumas, but on the tangible, honest labor of their hands.

Clara, consulting her meticulously drawn blueprints, moved with a precise efficiency that spoke of hours spent poring over structural diagrams and consulting with engineers. Her instructions were clear, concise, and always delivered with an unwavering focus on the task at hand. "Jonah, that joist needs to be seated flush against the existing beam. Make sure there's no gap. I don't want any wiggle room, no matter how slight." Her voice, though firm, lacked the edge of the earlier disagreements. There was a new steadiness to it, a quiet confidence that stemmed from seeing her plans take physical form, from witnessing the very structure of the Hall begin to strengthen under their collective effort.

Jonah, for his part, moved with a powerful, unhesitating physicality. He was the embodiment of practical application, his strong hands, calloused from years of work, manipulating tools with an innate understanding. He'd spent the morning meticulously preparing the lumber, his movements economical and sure as he measured, sawed, and drilled. Now, he was the one hoisting the heavy, newly cut beams into place, his muscles coiling and uncoiling with each effort. He'd learned to anticipate Clara's needs, to gauge the precise moment she would signal for him to position a beam, to understand the subtle shift in her stance that indicated a need for a specific tool. It was a silent language, forged in the shared rhythm of their work.

The process of reinforcing the beams was a delicate dance between Clara's intellectual precision and Jonah's practical strength. She guided, he executed. She envisioned, he built. There were moments of intense concentration, where the only sounds were the sharp *thwack* of a hammer driving a nail home, the low growl of the saw, and the soft scrape of metal against wood. Each action was deliberate, each placement critical. Clara would trace the lines of her plans with a fingertip, then point to a specific point on the existing beam, her gaze meeting Jonah's. He would nod, his eyes assessing the weight, the angle, the best way to maneuver the lumber into its designated position.

"This one needs to bear the primary load from the north-facing wall," Clara explained, her voice echoing slightly in the vast space. "We're essentially creating a new, stronger spine for that section. It has to be perfectly aligned, or the stress will transfer to the weaker points, and we'll be back to square one."

Jonah grunted, hefting the heavy timber. Sweat beaded on his forehead, but his focus never wavered. "Got it. Just tell me where you want it to land. I'll make sure it's secure." He braced himself, his legs set wide, and with a deep breath, he guided the beam into position. Clara, holding a level against the wood, called out minute adjustments. "A millimeter to your left, Jonah. That's it. Now hold it steady."

The silence that followed as Jonah held the beam in place was different from the tense quiet that had previously existed between them. This was a shared anticipation, a collective holding of breath as Clara meticulously secured the beam with heavy-duty brackets and bolts. The metallic clang of the wrench tightening the bolts echoed with a satisfying finality. It was a sound of progress, of stability being created, of weakness being overcome.

Later, as they worked on a different section, involving the installation of steel bracing, Clara found herself observing Jonah. He was moving with a fluid grace that belied the sheer physicality of his work. He'd learned to work *with* the grain of the wood, to anticipate the resistance, to find the most efficient path for his tools. There was a quiet competence about him that was undeniably appealing. He wasn't just strong; he was intelligent in his strength, his movements economical and purposeful.

"You've got a good eye for this, Jonah," she commented, her voice softer than intended. She'd been about to point out a slight misalignment, but he'd already corrected it, his intuition seemingly kicking in before she even had to speak.

He paused, wiping a bead of sweat from his brow with the back of his hand. A genuine smile touched his lips, a rare sight that softened the rugged lines of his face. "My dad always said a good builder listens to the wood. And to the structure. They tell you what they need if you're quiet enough to hear them." He gestured to the beam he'd just secured. "This old girl's been telling us she's tired for a long time. Needs a bit of help to stand tall again."

Clara found herself nodding, a small smile mirroring his. His words resonated with her own deep-seated respect for the Hall, for its history, for the countless memories it held. It wasn't just about wood and nails; it was about preserving something vital, something that connected them all. The shared labor had, in a quiet, unassuming way, been building something else between them: a foundation of mutual respect, a burgeoning camaraderie built on shared effort and a common purpose.

As the day wore on, the rhythmic clang of hammer against metal, the scrape of sandpaper smoothing rough edges, and the low rumble of their movements became the soundtrack to their renewed connection. There were no grand pronouncements, no dramatic confessions, just the steady, reliable rhythm of work. Clara found her own anxieties beginning to recede, replaced by the satisfying ache in her muscles and the quiet pride of seeing tangible progress. She'd always tackled her responsibilities with a fierce, solitary determination, but in the echoing expanse of the Grand Hall, with Jonah working diligently by her side, the weight of it all felt... lighter.

She noticed small details: the way Jonah carefully cleared away sawdust from her workspace before she needed it, the way he'd instinctively moved to shield her from a falling piece of debris, the quiet hum he sometimes made when he was particularly focused. These were not grand gestures, but they spoke volumes, weaving a subtle thread of consideration into the fabric of their shared labor.

"We should consider reinforcing this cross-beam as well," Clara said, pointing to another section of the Hall's framework. "The calculations show it's under significant stress from the weight of the roof on the west side."

Jonah squinted, following her gaze. He walked over, placed his hands on the beam, and gave it a gentle push. "Yeah, I can feel it. It's got a bit of a give to it. Nothing dangerous yet, but it'll only get worse." He looked back at Clara, his expression thoughtful. "We'll need another length of lumber, maybe two inches thicker than what we've used so far, and some heavier-duty bracing. I know a place down in Oakhaven that might have exactly what we need. We could head over there first thing tomorrow morning?"

The suggestion itself was a testament to their evolving dynamic. He wasn't just waiting for her instructions; he was actively problem-solving, anticipating needs, and proposing solutions. It was a partnership in its purest form, a seamless blend of her planning and his practical initiative.

"That sounds like a good plan," Clara replied, a genuine sense of ease settling over her. She met his gaze, and for the first time, she saw not just the competent tradesman, but a man who was willing to invest his time and energy, his skill and his strength, into something he believed in. It was a silent acknowledgment of shared commitment, a quiet understanding that they were in this together.

As the afternoon light began to slant through the tall, arched windows, casting long shadows across the floor, a sense of accomplishment settled over them. The Hall, though still unfinished, felt sturdier, more secure. The beams they had worked on were now solid anchors, their presence a silent testament to their combined efforts. The rhythmic sounds of their labor had faded into a comfortable quietude, a shared understanding that transcended words.

They had, through sheer hard work and a willingness to trust each other's strengths, begun to rebuild more than just the physical structure of the Grand Hall. They had begun to build something between themselves, something strong and resilient, forged in the crucible of shared effort and the quiet satisfaction of a job well done. The work was far from over, but the path forward, illuminated by the late afternoon sun, felt undeniably brighter, and considerably less daunting, with a partner by her side.

The rhythmic clang of tools had finally subsided, replaced by the low hum of anticipation for a much-needed respite. The afternoon sun, softened by the accumulated dust on the Grand Hall's expansive windows, cast a warm, golden glow across the vast space. Clara found herself wiping a smudge of sawdust from her cheek, the physical exertion of the morning leaving a pleasant ache in her limbs. Jonah, his brow damp with sweat that caught the light, was already gathering the thermos and two chipped enamel mugs from the makeshift workbench.

"Think that's enough for today," he said, his voice a low rumble that didn't quite fill the cavernous hall, but was nonetheless a welcome sound. He poured the coffee, the rich aroma mingling with the ever-present scent of aged wood and fresh lumber. Clara accepted the mug, its warmth seeping into her chilled fingers. They found a relatively clean spot on a stack of sawhorses, the uneven surface a temporary throne in their kingdom of restoration.

The coffee, as expected, was lukewarm and tasted faintly of metal from the thermos, but in that moment, it was nectar. They sat in comfortable silence for a few minutes, the only sounds the distant chirping of birds outside and the occasional creak of the Hall settling around them. It was a silence born not of awkwardness, but of shared effort and a burgeoning understanding. Clara watched Jonah as he took a slow sip, his gaze sweeping over the immense space, a quiet pride evident in the slight softening of his features.

"You know," Clara began, her voice a little hesitant, the words feeling fragile in the grand expanse, "this place... it reminds me of why I wanted to do this." She gestured vaguely with her mug, encompassing the high ceilings, the skeletal beams they had been working on, the very air thick with history. "When I was a kid, I used to imagine all sorts of stories happening in rooms like this. Big parties, secret meetings... you name it."

Jonah turned his attention to her, his expression open and attentive. He didn't interrupt, simply waited for her to continue. The act of him listening, truly listening, without any hint of judgment or impatience, felt like a small, precious gift.

"I left Cedar Ridge for a long time," she admitted, the confession feeling both liberating and a little unnerving. The reason for her departure had always been a carefully guarded secret, a wound she had never been entirely comfortable exposing. "When I was in college, there was a... a situation. Something that made me feel like I'd outgrown this place, like I needed to prove I could make it on my own, far away from... from everyone." She trailed off, the memory of the suffocating small-town scrutiny still a faint echo. "I thought I was stronger if I didn't need anyone, if I could build my own life without relying on... on the expectations or the gossip of a place like this."

She took another sip of coffee, her gaze fixed on the swirling patterns of dust motes dancing in the sunlight. It felt like a confession, a laying bare of a vulnerable part of herself. She braced herself for a reaction, a polite nod, perhaps a shared platitude about independence. But Jonah's response was something entirely different.

He set his mug down with a soft clink. "Funny how life works, isn't it?" he said, his voice quiet and contemplative. "Sometimes it takes you far away to make you realize what you've been missing right here. Or maybe," he paused, a thoughtful frown creasing his brow, "it takes you going through something that makes you realize that being 'on your own' isn't the same as being 'alone'."

He looked out at the Hall again, and Clara sensed a shift in his demeanor, a subtle opening up. "My dad," he began, his voice taking on a softer, more introspective tone, "he was a builder, like me. Worked with his hands his whole life. But he always had this... this thing he'd do. Every time he'd finish a big project, he'd invite everyone. Not just the people who paid him, but the neighbors, the shopkeepers, even some folks who'd just been grumbling about the construction noise. He'd have a big pot of stew on the stove, maybe some of my mom's apple pie. Just... a gathering. To celebrate what was built, but also, I think, to celebrate being part of something."

Clara listened, captivated. This was a side of Jonah she hadn't seen, a glimpse into the foundations of his own character. The image of his father, a man of action and community, resonated deeply.

"He'd say," Jonah continued, a faint smile playing on his lips, "that a building stands strong not just because of its foundations and its beams, but because of the hands that built it and the lives it touches. He always believed that you couldn't really finish a job until you'd shared it with the people who would use it, or at least the people who lived around it." He looked back at Clara, his eyes clear and steady. "He used to say that pride in your work is good, but shared pride... that's something else entirely. That's what really makes a place feel like home."

His words hung in the air, not heavy with expectation, but light with understanding. He hadn't pried into the specifics of her past, hadn't asked for details she wasn't ready to give. Instead, he had offered a parallel, a quiet affirmation that her desire for independence didn't negate the value of connection, and that sometimes, the very places we tried to escape were the ones that held the truest sense of belonging.

"My dad," Jonah added, his gaze drifting back to the Hall, "he would have loved this place. He'd have seen the potential, the history. He'd have rolled up his sleeves and gotten right to work with us." A wistful note entered his voice, and Clara understood without him having to say it that his father was no longer with them. The shared project, the act of restoration, was clearly a way for him to honor his father's legacy.

"It sounds like he was a good man," Clara said softly, her heart aching a little for the shared grief that often lay beneath the surface of strong, capable individuals. The Grand Hall, in its silent grandeur, seemed to absorb their confessions, providing a neutral ground for their cautious confessions. It was a sanctuary, a place where the weight of their individual histories could be momentarily set aside, replaced by the shared task and the emerging comfort of each other's presence.

"He was," Jonah confirmed, his voice firm. "And my mom, she was the glue. Always made sure there was food on the table, and that no matter how tough things got, we knew we were loved. She'd bring us sandwiches and thermoses of soup out to the job sites when we were kids, helping Dad. She'd have this way of making even the dustiest, messiest work site feel... like a family outing." He chuckled softly, a sound of fond remembrance. "She's still here, though. Still making the best darn apple pie in three counties, and always ready with a listening ear."

Clara felt a warmth spread through her that had nothing to do with the coffee. It was the warmth of empathy, of seeing her own struggles reflected in his stories, and of recognizing the quiet strength that came from a supportive family, even in its absence. She had always viewed her own family ties as a source of obligation, a burden she had been eager to shed. Jonah's perspective, however, painted a picture of family as a source of resilience, a wellspring of unconditional support.

"It's important, isn't it?" Clara mused, swirling the remaining coffee in her mug. "To have that. That sense of... of belonging. Even if you're trying to stand on your own two feet, it's easier when you know there's a foundation to fall back on." She looked at him, a newfound respect blooming in her chest. "You've handled this restoration with so much... care. It's not just about fixing the building, is it? It's about honoring its past, and making sure it has a future."

Jonah nodded, his gaze meeting hers. "That's it exactly. This Hall... it's seen a lot. Good times and bad. It's been a gathering place, a place of celebration, a place of solace. To let it fall into disrepair... that feels like a disrespect to all those stories, to all those people who walked these floors." He picked up his mug again, the enamel chipped on the rim. "My dad always said, 'You build it right, and it'll stand for generations.' I guess that applies to more than just wood and nails."

The implication hung in the air, unspoken but deeply felt. They were, in their own ways, building something more than just a structurally sound building. They were building trust, understanding, and perhaps, a future for themselves, both individually and perhaps, as a nascent partnership. The Grand Hall, with its echoes of the past and its promise of renewal, was becoming more than just a project; it was becoming a testament to their shared labor and their quiet, burgeoning connection. The lukewarm coffee, the scent of sawdust, and the vulnerability shared in the hushed grandeur of the Hall had woven a new thread into the tapestry of their relationship, a thread of candor and quiet empathy. It was a fragile thread, but in the sturdy embrace of the Grand Hall, it felt strong enough to hold.

"You know," Clara said, her voice lighter now, the earlier hesitancy replaced by a newfound ease, "when I first agreed to work on this with you, I was... I was mostly doing it because I felt obligated. And because I knew no one else would be as thorough, or understand the historical significance as well as I did." She offered a small, self-deprecating smile. "I admit, I thought it would be a bit of a battle of wills, you and me, trying to impose our own ideas."

Jonah chuckled, a genuine, unforced sound. "I'm not going to lie, Clara. I had a few of those thoughts myself. You've got a reputation for being... particular." He met her gaze, his eyes twinkling with amusement. "And I figured a fancy architect would be more interested in drawing pretty pictures than getting her hands dirty."

Clara felt a blush creep up her neck, but it was a blush of amusement rather than embarrassment. "And you," she retorted, her smile widening, "you strike me as someone who prefers to just get the job done, without too much fuss or explanation. I imagined you'd be impatient with my detailed plans, my endless checking and rechecking."

"Well," Jonah conceded, leaning back slightly against the wall, his posture relaxed, "I'll admit, I've been surprised. You know your stuff, Clara. You see things I wouldn't even think to look for. And you're not afraid to get dirty, that's for sure." He gestured to her hands, still smudged with grime. "You've got a good feel for this place, too. A real respect for it."

"And you," Clara said, her voice softening, "you're incredibly skilled. Your instincts are spot on, and you work with such... efficiency. I've learned a lot from watching you. More than I expected, honestly." She paused, gathering her thoughts. "It's not about battling wills, is it? It's about... combining our strengths. My eye for detail and your... your practical expertise. We're actually a pretty good team, aren't we?"

The question hung in the air, not as a challenge, but as a simple, honest observation. Jonah held her gaze for a long moment, the warmth of his eyes reaching her. The sunlight seemed to catch the subtle flecks of gold in his irises, making them shimmer.

"Yeah, Clara," he said, his voice a little deeper than before. "I think we are."

The simple affirmation was more potent than any grand declaration. It was a recognition of their shared journey, of the unexpected synergy that had developed between them amidst the dust and the timbers of the Grand Hall. The shared labor, which had initially felt like an obligation, had morphed into something far more rewarding: a testament to their individual capabilities and their surprising compatibility. The coffee break had transitioned from a moment of mere physical rest to a profound emotional connection, a quiet acknowledgment of their shared progress, both in the restoration of the Hall and in the delicate rebuilding of their own trust and understanding.

As they gathered their mugs and thermos, the silence that settled between them now was a comfortable, companionable one. The sun dipped lower, painting the Hall in even richer hues of amber and rose. The work ahead was still significant, the challenges numerous, but the path forward felt undeniably clearer, illuminated by the shared understanding that had blossomed in the quiet conversations of their coffee breaks, a testament to the power of candor and the unexpected strength found in shared vulnerability. The Grand Hall was not just a building they were restoring; it was a space where something new was being carefully constructed, piece by piece, between two souls who had learned to listen, to share, and to trust.

The rhythmic clang of tools had finally subsided, replaced by the low hum of anticipation for a much-needed respite. The afternoon sun, softened by the accumulated dust on the Grand Hall's expansive windows, cast a warm, golden glow across the vast space. Clara found herself wiping a smudge of sawdust from her cheek, the physical exertion of the morning leaving a pleasant ache in her limbs. Jonah, his brow damp with sweat that caught the light, was already gathering the thermos and two chipped enamel mugs from the makeshift workbench.

"Think that's enough for today," he said, his voice a low rumble that didn't quite fill the cavernous hall, but was nonetheless a welcome sound. He poured the coffee, the rich aroma mingling with the ever-present scent of aged wood and fresh lumber. Clara accepted the mug, its warmth seeping into her chilled fingers. They found a relatively clean spot on a stack of sawhorses, the uneven surface a temporary throne in their kingdom of restoration.

The coffee, as expected, was lukewarm and tasted faintly of metal from the thermos, but in that moment, it was nectar. They sat in comfortable silence for a few minutes, the only sounds the distant chirping of birds outside and the occasional creak of the Hall settling around them. It was a silence born not of awkwardness, but of shared effort and a burgeoning understanding. Clara watched Jonah as he took a slow sip, his gaze sweeping over the immense space, a quiet pride evident in the slight softening of his features.

"You know," Clara began, her voice a little hesitant, the words feeling fragile in the grand expanse, "this place... it reminds me of why I wanted to do this." She gestured vaguely with her mug, encompassing the high ceilings, the skeletal beams they had been working on, the very air thick with history. "When I was a kid, I used to imagine all sorts of stories happening in rooms like this. Big parties, secret meetings... you name it."

Jonah turned his attention to her, his expression open and attentive. He didn't interrupt, simply waited for her to continue. The act of him listening, truly listening, without any hint of judgment or impatience, felt like a small, precious gift.

"I left Cedar Ridge for a long time," she admitted, the confession feeling both liberating and a little unnerving. The reason for her departure had always been a carefully guarded secret, a wound she had never been entirely comfortable exposing. "When I was in college, there was a... a situation. Something that made me feel like I'd outgrown this place, like I needed to prove I could make it on my own, far away from... from everyone." She trailed off, the memory of the suffocating small-town scrutiny still a faint echo. "I thought I was stronger if I didn't need anyone, if I could build my own life without relying on... on the expectations or the gossip of a place like this."

She took another sip of coffee, her gaze fixed on the swirling patterns of dust motes dancing in the sunlight. It felt like a confession, a laying bare of a vulnerable part of herself. She braced herself for a reaction, a polite nod, perhaps a shared platitude about independence. But Jonah's response was something entirely different.

He set his mug down with a soft clink. "Funny how life works, isn't it?" he said, his voice quiet and contemplative. "Sometimes it takes you far away to make you realize what you've been missing right here. Or maybe," he paused, a thoughtful frown creasing his brow, "it takes you going through something that makes you realize that being 'on your own' isn't the same as being 'alone'."

He looked out at the Hall again, and Clara sensed a shift in his demeanor, a subtle opening up. "My dad," he began, his voice taking on a softer, more introspective tone, "he was a builder, like me. Worked with his hands his whole life. But he always had this... this thing he'd do. Every time he'd finish a big project, he'd invite everyone. Not just the people who paid him, but the neighbors, the shopkeepers, even some folks who'd just been grumbling about the construction noise. He'd have a big pot of stew on the stove, maybe some of my mom's apple pie. Just... a gathering. To celebrate what was built, but also, I think, to celebrate being part of something."

Clara listened, captivated. This was a side of Jonah she hadn't seen, a glimpse into the foundations of his own character. The image of his father, a man of action and community, resonated deeply.

"He'd say," Jonah continued, a faint smile playing on his lips, "that a building stands strong not just because of its foundations and its beams, but because of the hands that built it and the lives it touches. He always believed that you couldn't really finish a job until you'd shared it with the people who would use it, or at least the people who lived around it." He looked back at Clara, his eyes clear and steady. "He used to say that pride in your work is good, but shared pride... that's something else entirely. That's what really makes a place feel like home."

His words hung in the air, not heavy with expectation, but light with understanding. He hadn't pried into the specifics of her past, hadn't asked for details she wasn't ready to give. Instead, he had offered a parallel, a quiet affirmation that her desire for independence didn't negate the value of connection, and that sometimes, the very places we tried to escape were the ones that held the truest sense of belonging.

"My dad," Jonah added, his gaze drifting back to the Hall, "he would have loved this place. He'd have seen the potential, the history. He'd have rolled up his sleeves and gotten right to work with us." A wistful note entered his voice, and Clara understood without him having to say it that his father was no longer with them. The shared project, the act of restoration, was clearly a way for him to honor his father's legacy.

"It sounds like he was a good man," Clara said softly, her heart aching a little for the shared grief that often lay beneath the surface of strong, capable individuals. The Grand Hall, in its silent grandeur, seemed to absorb their confessions, providing a neutral ground for their cautious confessions. It was a sanctuary, a place where the weight of their individual histories could be momentarily set aside, replaced by the shared task and the emerging comfort of each other's presence.

"He was," Jonah confirmed, his voice firm. "And my mom, she was the glue. Always made sure there was food on the table, and that no matter how tough things got, we knew we were loved. She'd bring us sandwiches and thermoses of soup out to the job sites when we were kids, helping Dad. She'd have this way of making even the dustiest, messiest work site feel... like a family outing." He chuckled softly, a sound of fond remembrance. "She's still here, though. Still making the best darn apple pie in three counties, and always ready with a listening ear."

Clara felt a warmth spread through her that had nothing to do with the coffee. It was the warmth of empathy, of seeing her own struggles reflected in his stories, and of recognizing the quiet strength that came from a supportive family, even in its absence. She had always viewed her own family ties as a source of obligation, a burden she had been eager to shed. Jonah's perspective, however, painted a picture of family as a source of resilience, a wellspring of unconditional support.

"It's important, isn't it?" Clara mused, swirling the remaining coffee in her mug. "To have that. That sense of... of belonging. Even if you're trying to stand on your own two feet, it's easier when you know there's a foundation to fall back on." She looked at him, a newfound respect blooming in her chest. "You've handled this restoration with so much... care. It's not just about fixing the building, is it? It's about honoring its past, and making sure it has a future."

Jonah nodded, his gaze meeting hers. "That's it exactly. This Hall... it's seen a lot. Good times and bad. It's been a gathering place, a place of celebration, a place of solace. To let it fall into disrepair... that feels like a disrespect to all those stories, to all those people who walked these floors." He picked up his mug again, the enamel chipped on the rim. "My dad always said, 'You build it right, and it'll stand for generations.' I guess that applies to more than just wood and nails."

The implication hung in the air, unspoken but deeply felt. They were, in their own ways, building something more than just a structurally sound building. They were building trust, understanding, and perhaps, a future for themselves, both individually and perhaps, as a nascent partnership. The Grand Hall, with its echoes of the past and its promise of renewal, was becoming more than just a project; it was becoming a testament to their shared labor and their quiet, burgeoning connection. The lukewarm coffee, the scent of sawdust, and the vulnerability shared in the hushed grandeur of the Hall had woven a new thread into the tapestry of their relationship, a thread of candor and quiet empathy. It was a fragile thread, but in the sturdy embrace of the Grand Hall, it felt strong enough to hold.

"You know," Clara said, her voice lighter now, the earlier hesitancy replaced by a newfound ease, "when I first agreed to work on this with you, I was... I was mostly doing it because I felt obligated. And because I knew no one else would be as thorough, or understand the historical significance as well as I did." She offered a small, self-deprecating smile. "I admit, I thought it would be a bit of a battle of wills, you and me, trying to impose our own ideas."

Jonah chuckled, a genuine, unforced sound. "I'm not going to lie, Clara. I had a few of those thoughts myself. You've got a reputation for being... particular." He met her gaze, his eyes twinkling with amusement. "And I figured a fancy architect would be more interested in drawing pretty pictures than getting her hands dirty."

Clara felt a blush creep up her neck, but it was a blush of amusement rather than embarrassment. "And you," she retorted, her smile widening, "you strike me as someone who prefers to just get the job done, without too much fuss or explanation. I imagined you'd be impatient with my detailed plans, my endless checking and rechecking."

"Well," Jonah conceded, leaning back slightly against the wall, his posture relaxed, "I'll admit, I've been surprised. You know your stuff, Clara. You see things I wouldn't even think to look for. And you're not afraid to get dirty, that's for sure." He gestured to her hands, still smudged with grime. "You've got a good feel for this place, too. A real respect for it."

"And you," Clara said, her voice softening, "you're incredibly skilled. Your instincts are spot on, and you work with such... efficiency. I've learned a lot from watching you. More than I expected, honestly." She paused, gathering her thoughts. "It's not about battling wills, is it? It's about... combining our strengths. My eye for detail and your... your practical expertise. We're actually a pretty good team, aren't we?"

The question hung in the air, not as a challenge, but as a simple, honest observation. Jonah held her gaze for a long moment, the warmth of his eyes reaching her. The sunlight seemed to catch the subtle flecks of gold in his irises, making them shimmer.

"Yeah, Clara," he said, his voice a little deeper than before. "I think we are."

The simple affirmation was more potent than any grand declaration. It was a recognition of their shared journey, of the unexpected synergy that had developed between them amidst the dust and the timbers of the Grand Hall. The shared labor, which had initially felt like an obligation, had morphed into something far more rewarding: a testament to their individual capabilities and their surprising compatibility. The coffee break had transitioned from a moment of mere physical rest to a profound emotional connection, a quiet acknowledgment of their shared progress, both in the restoration of the Hall and in the delicate rebuilding of their own trust and understanding.

As they gathered their mugs and thermos, the silence that settled between them now was a comfortable, companionable one. The sun dipped lower, painting the Hall in even richer hues of amber and rose. The work ahead was still significant, the challenges numerous, but the path forward felt undeniably clearer, illuminated by the shared understanding that had blossomed in the quiet conversations of their coffee breaks, a testament to the power of candor and the unexpected strength found in shared vulnerability. The Grand Hall was not just a building they were restoring; it was a space where something new was being carefully constructed, piece by piece, between two souls who had learned to listen, to share, and to trust.

The days that followed saw a subtle but significant shift in their working dynamic. Clara, initially focused on the meticulous sourcing of historically accurate materials – a process that often involved extensive research, precise ordering, and sometimes frustratingly long lead times – began to see the wisdom in Jonah's more fluid, community-driven approach. He had a knack for knowing who to ask, where to find reclaimed lumber that was just the right age and character, and how to barter for services rather than paying top dollar. One afternoon, while Clara was poring over architectural salvage catalogs, trying to locate a specific type of wrought iron hinge, Jonah returned from a trip into town with a satisfied grin, carrying a dusty, but perfectly matched set of hinges.

"Old Man Hemlock down at the hardware store," he explained, holding one up for her inspection. "Said he had a box of 'em tucked away in his back room for twenty years. Said he'd been meaning to throw them out, but I told him they belonged right here." He winked. "A little bit of charm, a little bit of good ol' fashioned negotiation, and here we are. Saved us a pretty penny, too."

Clara examined the hinges, running her thumb over the intricate scrollwork. They were exactly what she had envisioned, perhaps even better, bearing the patina of age that no reproduction could replicate. "Jonah, this is... this is remarkable," she admitted, a genuine sense of awe in her voice. "I've been spending hours searching online, and I'd never have thought to check with Mr. Hemlock."

"That's the thing about Cedar Ridge, Clara," he said, leaning against a sturdy support beam. "There's history in every corner, and more often than not, the answer you're looking for is just a conversation away. People here, they like to feel useful. They like to know their old stuff, their knowledge, is still valued." He gestured around the Hall. "This place, it's not just wood and stone; it's woven into the fabric of this town. And the people who've lived here, they're part of its story, just like the bricks and mortar."

He then showed her how he'd approached other suppliers, not just looking for the cheapest price, but for those who had a vested interest in the project's success, those who understood the significance of restoring the Grand Hall. He'd spoken with local carpenters who offered their time for specific tasks, with a retired stonemason who was happy to lend his expertise on repairing the foundation, and with a local farmer who had a surplus of sturdy oak that he was willing to sell at a discount. It was a web of interconnectedness that Clara, accustomed to the more transactional nature of urban restoration projects, found both novel and deeply effective. She began to understand that Jonah's resourcefulness wasn't just about saving money; it was about building relationships and fostering a sense of collective ownership.

In turn, Clara found her meticulous planning and organizational skills proving invaluable when it came to the more complex, long-term aspects of the restoration, particularly the grant applications. Jonah had a clear vision and a wealth of practical knowledge, but the process of drafting formal proposals, detailing budgets, and outlining timelines felt less intuitive to him. He'd often present her with scribbled notes and rough estimates, his eyes alight with ideas, but struggling to translate them into the coherent, persuasive language required by funding bodies.

"I can tell them what we need," he'd say, gesturing with his hands, "and I can tell them why it's important, but putting it all down on paper so it makes sense to someone who's never even *seen* this place... that's where I get lost."

Clara, however, thrived in that space. She would take his enthusiastic, often fragmented explanations, and weave them into polished, compelling narratives. She'd meticulously break down the restoration phases, create detailed budget spreadsheets that accounted for every screw and every hour of labor, and research and identify potential funding sources that Jonah hadn't even considered. She developed a grant proposal for the historical society that was so comprehensive and well-argued, it brought a tear to the eye of the grant committee chairman, a notoriously stern man.

"You've articulated the soul of this project, Ms. Hayes," he'd said, his voice thick with emotion. "We rarely see proposals that not only understand the structural needs but also the emotional and historical significance of a place."

Clara, blushing slightly at the praise, felt a surge of pride that wasn't solely her own. She knew that the 'soul' he spoke of was something Jonah had breathed into the project, a passion that she had simply helped to translate into words. She found herself enjoying the challenge of translating his practical vision into a language that would secure the necessary resources, and Jonah, in turn, was visibly impressed by her ability to navigate the bureaucratic labyrinth.

"You've got a way with words, Clara," he'd told her, shaking his head in admiration after reviewing a particularly successful funding application. "Makes it sound like we're not just fixing a building, but saving a piece of history. And I guess... I guess we are." He'd paused, his gaze thoughtful. "It's a good thing we've got you for the paperwork. I'd probably just end up writing a strongly worded letter of intent and calling it a day."

They began to develop a rhythm, a collaborative dance. Jonah would bring his hands-on knowledge, his understanding of local resources, and his innate ability to connect with people. Clara would bring her architectural expertise, her meticulous planning, and her talent for articulating the project's value. He'd show her how to leverage the goodwill of the community for material donations and skilled labor, while she'd refine his project outlines and presentations to secure the financial backing needed for the larger, more costly aspects of the restoration.

There were still moments of gentle friction, of course. Clara would sometimes find herself gently nudging Jonah towards a more structured approach to material procurement, reminding him of the potential for delays if certain items weren't ordered well in advance. And Jonah would occasionally have to remind Clara that sometimes, a perfectly good, slightly imperfect, reclaimed beam was more practical and cost-effective than waiting six weeks for a custom-milled piece. But these were not conflicts; they were conversations, opportunities for each to learn from the other.

One evening, as they were packing up after a long day, Jonah picked up a beautifully carved wooden corbel that Clara had painstakingly cleaned and repaired. "Remember this beauty?" he asked, turning it over in his hands. "You spent two solid days on this, didn't you? I thought you were going to polish it right out of existence."

Clara laughed. "It deserved it. Look at the detail, Jonah. This was crafted by someone with incredible skill. It's a piece of art. We can't just rush through these things and call it done."

"I know, I know," he conceded, his grin softening. "And you were right. It looks fantastic. It's just... sometimes I see something like this, and I think about how much simpler it would be to just replace it with something new, something sturdy and functional, and move on to the next problem." He handed the corbel back to her carefully. "But then I see you working on it, and I remember why we're doing this. It's not just about making it stand up; it's about making it *be* what it was, and what it can be again."

Clara accepted the corbel, its weight solid and reassuring in her hands. She looked at Jonah, at the genuine respect in his eyes, and felt a warmth spread through her. He saw the value in her dedication, just as she was beginning to see the profound wisdom in his practical, community-focused approach. They were, she realized, learning each other's language, not just of construction and design, but of values and priorities.

"And I've learned from you too, Jonah," she said softly. "About how much can be achieved when you bring people together, when you trust in the community's willingness to help. I used to think that building something meant controlling every single element, ensuring perfection through rigid planning. But you've shown me that true strength often comes from collaboration, from weaving together different threads of skill and passion." She gestured to the corbel. "This is beautiful because of the hands that carved it and the care that's gone into its restoration. It's a testament to both the past and the present."

Jonah nodded, a quiet understanding passing between them. The Grand Hall, in its ongoing transformation, was becoming more than just a building they were restoring. It was becoming a crucible where their differing perspectives were being forged into a stronger, more unified vision. They were discovering that their strengths, when combined, created something far more resilient and beautiful than either could have achieved alone. The shared labor was indeed leading to quiet conversations, and those conversations were slowly but surely bridging the gap between their worlds, building a foundation of mutual respect and a shared purpose that felt as solid and enduring as the stone and timber of the Grand Hall itself.

The task of reorganizing and restocking the Community Pantry became an unexpected, yet deeply rewarding, shared project. It started, as so many things did lately, with a casual observation. Clara, while walking past the small, unassuming building on the edge of town square, noticed its dim, dusty interior and the sparsely filled shelves. She remembered it as a bustling hub during her childhood, a place where families could always find a helping hand. Now, it looked tired, neglected.

"I was thinking about the pantry yesterday," Clara mentioned to Jonah a few days later, as they were meticulously sanding down an old wooden balustrade in the Grand Hall. The rhythmic scrape of sandpaper was a familiar soundtrack to their days, punctuated by the occasional exchange of ideas or quiet observations. "It's really struggling. The shelves are practically bare, and it looks like no one's really been in to organize it properly in years."

Jonah paused his work, his brow furrowed in thought. "Yeah, I've seen that," he replied, his voice carrying the usual calm assurance. "My mom used to help out there when I was a kid. She always said it was important for a town to have a place like that, a safety net for folks when things got tough." He set down his sandpaper. "What are you thinking?"

A spark ignited in Clara's eyes. "I was thinking," she began, her voice gaining momentum, "that maybe we could help. I mean, my organizing skills are... well, you've seen them at work in this place. And you know everyone in town, and all the local suppliers. Together, we could probably make a real difference." She looked at him, a hopeful plea in her gaze. "It wouldn't be glamorous, I know, but it feels like the kind of work that *matters*."

Jonah met her gaze, a slow smile spreading across his face. He saw not just the architect's meticulous approach, but the compassionate heart that had driven her to return to Cedar Ridge. He understood the quiet satisfaction that came from restoring something broken, from giving a forgotten place a new lease on life. "You know what, Clara? I think that's a fantastic idea." He clapped his hands together, a decisive sound. "Let's do it. When do you want to start?"

The following Saturday, armed with cleaning supplies, an eagerness to tackle a new challenge, and a shared sense of purpose, they descended upon the Community Pantry. The air inside was stagnant, carrying the faint, musty scent of disuse. Dust motes danced in the slivers of light that managed to penetrate the grimy windows. The shelves, made of sturdy but plain wood, were a haphazard collection of dented cans, faded boxes, and a few sad-looking bags of pasta. It was clear that the pantry hadn't seen a true inventory or a dedicated restocking effort in a very long time.

Clara, with her innate talent for order, immediately began to survey the space, her mind already devising a system. "Okay," she announced, her voice cutting through the quiet. "First, we need a complete inventory. We'll sort everything by category – canned goods, dry goods, toiletries, baby items, that sort of thing. Then, we'll see what we have, what's still good, and what needs to be disposed of." She pulled a notepad and pen from her bag, already sketching out sections for shelves.

Jonah, meanwhile, was already examining the structure of the shelving and the overall layout. He pointed out areas that needed reinforcement, suggested ways to reconfigure the existing shelves to maximize space, and noted where new shelving might be beneficial. "This back wall here," he said, tapping a solid section of wood, "could easily support a couple of more rows. We could build them ourselves. And we should get some proper bins for things like rice and flour, to keep them fresh and pest-free."

The initial sorting was a monumental task. They unearthed expired goods, dented cans, and items that were clearly past their prime. Clara, with her sharp eye for detail, meticulously checked expiration dates, while Jonah, with his pragmatic approach, made quick work of discarding anything that was unsalvageable. It was slow, sometimes tedious work, but neither of them complained. As they cleared the shelves, a sense of purpose, of creating order from chaos, began to build.

"It's amazing how much this place has been overlooked," Clara murmured, wiping sweat from her brow with the back of her hand. She held up a can of peaches, its label faded but still readable. "Imagine someone really needing this, and finding it hidden away, or not being able to find what they needed because it's all jumbled together."

"That's why we're here," Jonah said, his voice earnest. He placed a stack of cleaned cans onto a makeshift sorting table. "To make sure that when someone *does* need it, everything is easy to find, well-organized, and fresh." He looked around at the growing piles of salvageable items. "We've got a good start. Now, we need to think about getting more in."

This was where Jonah's connections came into play. The following Monday, Clara returned to the pantry to find a delivery truck parked outside. Jonah, looking more at home amongst crates of produce than he ever had in a dusty old library, was busy unloading boxes of fresh vegetables and fruit from local farms. He'd contacted several farmers he knew – the ones he'd previously sourced wood from for his building projects, or whose produce he regularly bought at the farmer's market. He'd explained the situation, and the response had been immediate and generous.

"Farmer McGregor dropped off a whole load of potatoes and onions," Jonah announced, his face alight with enthusiasm as he entered the pantry, carrying a heavy box. "And Mrs. Gable from the apple orchard said she'd have a truckload of apples ready for us by Wednesday. Said she had a surplus this year and was happy to share." He grinned. "Looks like Cedar Ridge remembers how to take care of its own."

Clara was impressed, and deeply moved. She'd spent hours researching grant applications and looking for bulk purchasing discounts, but Jonah's ability to tap into the goodwill of the community was far more immediate and impactful. "This is incredible, Jonah. I was trying to figure out how we'd afford even a fraction of this."

"It's not just about money, Clara," he said, setting the box down gently. "It's about people wanting to help. They just need to know where to direct that help. And who better to tell them than us?" He gestured around the now-tidier space. "You've made this place look so welcoming. Now we're filling it with good things."

Over the next few weeks, the Community Pantry underwent a remarkable transformation. Clara, with her systematic approach, established a clear inventory system, labeling each shelf and bin with clear, easy-to-read signs. She created a logbook for incoming donations and outgoing supplies, ensuring accountability and helping them track what was most needed. Jonah, true to his word, continued to leverage his network. He'd visit local grocery stores, asking for donations of day-old bread, dented cans, or excess produce. He spoke to butchers about surplus meats, to bakers about slightly imperfect pastries. He even organized a small collection drive at his own construction sites, encouraging his workers to contribute non-perishable items.

One afternoon, Clara found herself carefully arranging rows of canned goods, her heart swelling with a quiet satisfaction. The shelves, once sparse and forlorn, were now full, neatly organized, and bursting with an array of essentials. The scent of fresh produce, delivered by Jonah that morning, mingled with the faint, clean aroma of disinfectant. It was a tangible representation of their shared effort, a testament to what they could achieve when they combined their strengths.

Jonah entered the pantry, carrying a large cardboard box filled with various items. He paused, his gaze sweeping across the re-stocked shelves. A look of genuine pride settled on his face. "You've done an amazing job, Clara. It looks... it looks like a real place now. A place people can rely on."

"We did it," Clara corrected, smiling up at him. "It was your connections, your ability to bring in these donations, that made it possible. I just... organized it."

"Nonsense," Jonah countered, setting the box down. "You gave it structure. You made it functional. Without your system, all those donations would just be piled up, just like before. You gave it purpose." He picked up a can of soup, examining the label. "This is what it's all about, isn't it? Making sure people have what they need. Giving them a little bit of hope when they're going through a tough time."

He then explained how they would handle distribution, outlining a simple sign-out sheet and a discreet collection process, designed to maintain the dignity of those who sought assistance. He spoke of his mother's quiet dedication, the hushed conversations she'd have with families, the way she'd offer a word of encouragement along with the food. Clara listened, understanding that this project was more than just stocking shelves; it was about honoring a legacy of compassion and community support.

As they continued to work, filling the last few empty spaces on the shelves, a comfortable silence settled between them. It was a silence born of shared accomplishment, of a deep, unspoken understanding that transcended the practicalities of their task. They had come together to restore a building, and in doing so, they had inadvertently restored a vital part of the town's heart, and in the process, had deepened their own connection.

"You know," Clara said, her voice soft, as she placed a bag of rice onto a designated shelf, "I used to think that all I cared about was preserving the past, the historical integrity of places like the Grand Hall. But seeing this... seeing how we can directly impact people's lives, right now... it's a different kind of reward."

Jonah nodded, leaning against a sturdy shelf. "It is. Building something beautiful is important, no doubt about it. But building a strong community, one that looks out for its own... that's the real foundation." He looked at her, his gaze steady and warm. "You've got a good heart, Clara. You see the value in things, not just in their age or their architecture, but in their purpose. And you're not afraid to get your hands dirty to make that purpose a reality."

Clara felt a blush creep up her neck, a familiar sensation that was no longer born of awkwardness, but of genuine appreciation. She had initially seen Jonah as a skilled laborer, a pragmatic builder. But through their shared work, both on the Hall and now the pantry, she was discovering a depth to him, a genuine commitment to the well-being of his community that mirrored her own growing desire to contribute.

"And you, Jonah," she replied, her voice imbued with a newfound warmth, "you have a way of making things happen. You see a need, and you don't hesitate. You rally people, you bring them together. It's inspiring. I used to think restoration was all about meticulously planning every detail, but you've shown me the power of collaboration, of relying on the generosity and goodwill of others."

The pantry, now fully stocked and gleaming, felt like a beacon in the town square. It was a symbol of what could be achieved when people worked together, when individual skills and passions were woven into a collective effort. Clara found herself looking at the neatly arranged cans, the bags of flour and sugar, the neatly folded toiletries, and feeling a profound sense of accomplishment. This was not just about charity; it was about empowerment, about ensuring that no one in Cedar Ridge felt entirely alone or without support.

As they finally closed up the pantry for the day, the setting sun cast a warm, golden light across the town square, illuminating the small building and making it shine. The work was far from over; ongoing donations and restocking would be crucial for its continued success. But the foundation had been laid, both literally and figuratively. They had breathed new life into a forgotten space, and in doing so, had reinforced their own burgeoning partnership, built on shared labor, quiet conversations, and a mutual respect for the things that truly mattered. The pantry's revival was a quiet testament to their combined efforts, a tangible reminder that even the most overlooked places, and the most unlikely of collaborators, could bloom with renewed purpose.

The last of the donated canned goods had been neatly placed on the shelves, and the final sweep of the Community Pantry floor had been completed. Clara dusted off her hands, a smudge of something indeterminate on her cheek, and looked around at the transformed space. It was more than just organized; it felt alive, infused with the promise of renewed purpose. Jonah, his usual quiet presence a comforting anchor, was securing the pantry's door, his movements efficient and sure. A sense of profound satisfaction settled over Clara, a feeling that reached beyond the completion of a task and touched something deeper within her.

"We did it," she said, her voice a little breathless, the exhaustion of the day finally catching up to her.

Jonah turned, a slow smile softening the lines of his tired face. "We did. And it looks... it looks really good, Clara. You should be proud."

She shrugged, a faint blush rising on her cheeks. "It was a team effort. I just... I organized the chaos."

"You brought order to it," he corrected gently, stepping out onto the worn wooden steps of the pantry's entrance. The air outside was beginning to cool, carrying the sweet scent of honeysuckle and damp earth. Dusk was painting the sky in hues of soft lavender and rose, the first stars beginning to prick through the deepening blue. "And you did it with that incredible eye of yours. I'm still amazed at how you figured out that storage system in the back. I never would have thought of it."

They stood there for a moment, the sounds of the small town – a distant dog bark, the faint hum of traffic from the main road – fading into a gentle murmur. The day had been long, filled with the physical labor of sorting and cleaning, punctuated by the focused energy of their collaboration. Now, as twilight embraced Cedar Ridge, a different kind of energy began to emerge between them, one that was quieter, more reflective.

"It's funny," Clara began, her gaze drifting upwards, following the fading light. "I used to come here with my grandmother. She was one of the original volunteers, back when this place was first started. I remember being a little girl, standing on these very steps, and watching the families come and go. It always felt like a place of hope." She sighed, a soft sound lost in the quiet evening. "It broke my heart to see it fall into such disrepair."

Jonah leaned against the porch railing, his posture relaxed but attentive. "My mom talked about it, too. Said it was a lifesaver for a lot of folks during the lean years. She always said community wasn't just about building houses, but about building connections, about making sure everyone had a safety net." He paused, his gaze sweeping across the familiar, comforting landscape of Cedar Ridge. The rolling hills that cradled the town, the patchwork of fields, the warm glow of lights beginning to flicker on in the houses. "It's a good town, Clara. It's got its quiet moments, sure, but there's a lot of heart here."

Clara felt a warmth spread through her, a response to his words that was more than just agreement. It was a shared sentiment, a recognition of the subtle beauty and enduring spirit of their town. She had returned to Cedar Ridge with a mission to preserve its history, to meticulously restore its past. But in the process, she was discovering a deeper appreciation for its present, for the living, breathing community that was its true legacy.

"It is a good town," she agreed, her voice soft. "And seeing the pantry like this again... it feels like we've given it back a piece of its heart. A piece that was missing." She tilted her head, her eyes scanning the darkening sky. "Look," she pointed, her voice hushed with a childlike wonder, "the first stars are out. Orion, I think. My grandmother used to point him out to me."

Jonah followed her gaze, his expression softening. "Yeah, that's Orion. And see, just to the left of him, that's Taurus, the Bull. And if you look a little further, you can make out the Big Dipper, even with the lights starting to come on." He spoke with a quiet ease, as if the constellations were old friends he'd known for years. He didn't just see them; he seemed to understand them, their patterns and movements etched into his mind like the blueprints of a familiar building.

As he spoke, Clara felt a subtle shift in the air between them. The lingering exhaustion of the day was replaced by a gentle intimacy, a shared appreciation for the quiet spectacle unfolding above them. The practicalities of their shared labor, the lists, the inventory, the organizing – all of it receded, making way for something more profound. They were no longer just two people who had worked on a project; they were two souls, standing under an infinite sky, finding common ground in the vastness of the universe.

"I haven't really looked at the stars like this since I was a kid," Clara confessed, her voice barely above a whisper. "Back home, the city lights always drowned everything out. It's one of the things I missed most about coming back here."

"It's hard to escape the noise and the glare, isn't it?" Jonah mused, his gaze still fixed on the celestial display. "Sometimes you have to get away from it all to really see what's there. To see what's truly beautiful." He turned his head, his eyes meeting hers in the dim light. "Like the quiet strength of this town. Or... or the quiet determination in someone who sets out to fix what's broken."

His words, spoken with such sincerity, resonated deeply within Clara. She had always been driven by a need to restore, to preserve. But her return to Cedar Ridge, and her interactions with Jonah, were challenging her to redefine what "restoration" truly meant. It wasn't just about the stone and mortar of old buildings; it was about mending the fabric of a community, about nurturing the intangible threads that held people together.

"I think," Clara said slowly, choosing her words carefully, "that sometimes, when you're so focused on the details, on the preservation, you can miss the bigger picture. You can forget that a building, or a place, is more than just its physical structure. It's about the people who use it, the lives that are lived within it."

Jonah nodded, a thoughtful expression on his face. "That's what I try to remember when I'm building. It's not just about putting up walls. It's about creating a space where people can live, and grow, and make memories. A place that feels like home." He paused, then added, his voice a touch softer, "And sometimes, it's about creating something new, something that's needed right now, even if it's not made of ancient stone. Like the pantry."

The shared work on the pantry had, indeed, opened up a new dimension to their connection. It had moved them beyond the formal interactions of their roles in the Grand Hall renovation and into a space of genuine collaboration, of shared purpose that extended beyond the project itself. Clara found herself drawn to Jonah's quiet strength, his innate understanding of the town and its people. He, in turn, seemed to appreciate her meticulousness, her passion for detail, and her underlying compassion.

"You know," Clara confessed, a hint of vulnerability in her tone, "I was so worried when I first came back. Worried that I wouldn't fit in, that I'd be seen as an outsider, someone who just wanted to change things without understanding them."

Jonah's gaze was steady and reassuring. "You've done more than just change things, Clara. You've brought back something important. You've reminded people that this town is worth investing in, that its history matters, and that its future matters, too. And you've done it with a respect that's... well, it's rare." He offered a small, genuine smile. "You fit in just fine. More than fine."

His words were a balm to her unspoken fears. She had long prided herself on her independence, her ability to rely on herself. But the truth was, she craved connection, a sense of belonging. And in Jonah, she was finding a quiet, steady anchor in the often-turbulent waters of her own emotions.

"And you," Clara said, her voice warm with appreciation, "you've been... well, you've been a constant. Always there, with your steady hands and your calm approach. You make things happen, Jonah. You always have. You make me feel like... like Cedar Ridge is truly a place I can call home again."

The twilight had deepened, and the stars were now a brilliant tapestry across the inky sky. The world around them had faded into a gentle blur, their focus narrowed to the intimate space between them, a space filled with unspoken understanding and burgeoning warmth. The air was still, carrying the faint scent of pine from the surrounding woods.

"It's a good place to call home," Jonah said, his voice a low rumble. "Especially when you've got good people to share it with." He shifted his weight, his gaze lingering on her face. There was a question in his eyes, a gentle curiosity that made Clara's heart beat a little faster. "Are you... are you happy here, Clara?"

The question hung in the air, simple and profound. Clara considered it, her mind sifting through the layers of her return, the professional challenges, the personal reassurances. She had come back seeking purpose, seeking to reconnect with her roots. She had found that, and so much more. She had found a sense of community, a renewed appreciation for the quiet beauty of her surroundings, and in Jonah, a burgeoning connection that felt both unexpected and deeply right.

"Yes," she answered, her voice firm, a genuine smile gracing her lips. "Yes, I am. I think... I think I'm finally starting to feel like I'm where I'm supposed to be."

Jonah's smile widened, a look of quiet contentment settling over his features. He reached out, his hand hovering for a moment before gently touching her arm. The contact was light, tentative, yet it sent a ripple of warmth through Clara. It was a touch that spoke of comfort, of shared understanding, of a nascent connection that was just beginning to bloom.

"That's good to hear," he said, his thumb brushing lightly against her sleeve. "That's really good to hear."

They stood there for a long moment, bathed in the soft glow of the emerging stars, the quiet intimacy of the evening wrapping around them like a warm embrace. The barriers that had once seemed so formidable were slowly dissolving, replaced by a sense of shared comfort, a burgeoning understanding that spoke of a connection that was both deeply rooted and beautifully new.

The stars above bore witness to their quiet conversation, to the unspoken promises whispered in the twilight, and to the gentle unfolding of a future that held the promise of shared dreams and quiet joys. The work on the pantry had been a labor of necessity, but the evening under the stars was a labor of the heart, a testament to the quiet magic that could blossom in the most unexpected of places, and in the most unlikely of companionships.

CHAPTER SEVEN

External Setbacks

The crisp autumn air that had invigorated Clara's spirit just hours before now felt heavy, laden with a dread she couldn't quite shake. She sat at her grandmother's old oak desk, the same desk where Clara had poured over historical documents and architectural plans, now illuminated by the harsh glare of her laptop screen. The grant application, a document she had meticulously crafted, a testament to weeks of research, late nights, and unwavering optimism, lay open before her. It was a comprehensive proposal, detailing the critical structural needs of the Grand Hall, outlining a phased approach to restoration, and most importantly, underscoring the deep historical and cultural significance of the building to Cedar Ridge.

She had poured her heart and soul into it, weaving together her professional expertise with her burgeoning love for the town and its people. Jonah, with his practical insights and understanding of local needs, had been instrumental in ensuring the proposal reflected the community's genuine desire for the Hall's revival. They had anticipated potential hurdles, addressed every conceivable question, and presented a case that felt, to Clara at least, irrefutable.

The email notification had arrived innocuously, a standard update from the Historical Preservation Fund. She'd clicked it open with a sense of eager anticipation, ready to celebrate the impending approval that would finally set the Grand Hall's extensive repairs into motion. Instead, her eyes scanned lines that seemed to blur, words that felt like a physical blow.

"Regrettably, your application for the Grand Hall Restoration Project has been denied." The sentence hung in the digital air, stark and unforgiving. She read on, her breath catching in her throat. The reasons cited were a cold, impersonal critique that stung more than any technical flaw: "Insufficient evidence of broad community involvement and a lack of a demonstrably sustainable long-term operational plan."

Clara reread the offending phrases, her mind struggling to process the disconnect. Insufficient community involvement? She'd spoken to dozens of townspeople, gathered countless testimonials, and the recent revitalization of the Community Pantry, a project she and Jonah had spearheaded, was a tangible demonstration of grassroots engagement. A sustainability plan? They had outlined a multi-pronged approach, including rental income from events, potential partnerships with local businesses, and a robust volunteer program, all designed to ensure the Hall's viability for generations to come. It felt as if the reviewers had looked at the proposal through a different lens, one that completely missed the spirit of what they were trying to achieve.

A wave of cold despair washed over her. This wasn't just a setback; it felt like a fundamental misunderstanding of their entire endeavor. The grant was meant to cover the most critical, expensive structural work – the foundation repairs, the crumbling brickwork, the compromised roof that threatened to buckle under the weight of winter snows. Without that funding, the restoration, as she had envisioned it, would stall indefinitely, leaving the Grand Hall vulnerable to further decay. She leaned back in her chair, the worn leather creaking in protest, and closed her eyes, trying to ward off the rising panic.

She thought of Jonah, his quiet confidence, his unwavering support. He had invested his time, his reputation, and his belief in this project. He had shared his vision of the Grand Hall as a vibrant hub once more, a place for celebrations, for town meetings, for connecting the generations. The pantry project had been a small victory, a taste of what was possible when they worked together. This grant denial felt like a direct repudiation of that shared hope.

The specific wording gnawed at her. "Lack of community involvement." Had they not done enough to showcase the town's support? She recalled the interviews she'd conducted, the handwritten notes from seniors eager to see the Hall restored, the enthusiastic endorsements from local business owners who recognized its potential economic impact. She had included many of these in the appendices, believing they painted a clear picture of widespread support. Perhaps the sheer volume of physical evidence – architectural surveys, historical significance reports – had overshadowed the human element. Or perhaps the reviewers simply didn't grasp the unique, organic way community operated in a place like Cedar Ridge, where support often manifested in quiet gestures and long-standing traditions rather than formal committees and public rallies.

Then there was the sustainability plan. Clara had spent hours researching best practices for historic building management, consulting with preservation experts, and adapting their strategies to Cedar Ridge's specific economic landscape. They had projected realistic revenue streams, accounted for ongoing maintenance costs, and proposed a tiered membership program for Hall patrons. It was a solid, well-researched plan. Yet, the rejection letter implied it was unproven, perhaps too ambitious, or not sufficiently detailed to inspire confidence. Was it possible they had been too focused on the immediate needs, the pressing repairs, and not enough on the long-term operational realities?

A knot of anxiety tightened in Clara's stomach. She knew, intellectually, that rejection was a part of any ambitious undertaking. But this felt different. This felt personal, and it struck at the core of her professional identity. She had always prided herself on her thoroughness, her ability to anticipate challenges and craft effective solutions. To be told her efforts were insufficient, that she had missed crucial elements, was a bitter pill to swallow.

She thought about the conversations she'd had with Jonah about the future of Cedar Ridge. He believed in the town's inherent strength, its capacity for resilience. He had spoken about how the Grand Hall could be a catalyst for economic growth, a place to draw people in, to create opportunities. She had shared that vision, adding her own layer of historical preservation and cultural significance. Now, that shared vision felt a little more fragile, a little more distant.

The denial also raised a more uncomfortable question: was their approach, focused on meticulous restoration and historical accuracy, truly what the community needed most, or what *she* thought they needed? The grant reviewers' comments about community involvement and sustainability hinted at a potential disconnect. Perhaps the town's true sustainability lay not just in preserving the past, but in adapting it to meet present-day needs in a way that was economically viable and community-driven. Jonah understood this intrinsically. He built things that served a purpose, that made life better for the people of Cedar Ridge. Had she, in her passion for historical preservation, overlooked the practical realities of what made a community thrive?

She traced the outline of the rejection letter on her screen. This wasn't a time for despair, she told herself. It was a time for reassessment, for recalibration. The Grand Hall was still standing, albeit precariously.

The community still desired its restoration. And she and Jonah were still committed. But the path forward had just become infinitely more complex. The grant had been their primary funding source, the key to unlocking the most urgent repairs. Without it, they would have to find a new way, a more creative, perhaps more challenging, way to move forward.

She looked out the window at the darkening sky, the first stars beginning to appear, just as they had the night before. The beauty of the constellations, the quiet peace of Cedar Ridge, felt like a distant echo of the hope she'd felt then. Now, a new urgency pulsed beneath the surface. The Grand Hall wasn't just a historical artifact; it was a vital part of Cedar Ridge's future, and its present was in peril. She knew, with a dawning certainty, that this denial, while devastating, was not the end. It was simply an unexpected, and incredibly difficult, turn in the road.

They would have to find another way. They would have to prove that their commitment to Cedar Ridge, and to the Grand Hall, was deeper and more resilient than any funding rejection. The challenge, she knew, had just begun. She would need to talk to Jonah. He always had a way of finding solutions, of seeing possibilities where she saw only obstacles. This was one of those times.

The words on the screen swam before Clara's eyes, each one a tiny shard of ice. "Regrettably, your application for the Grand Hall Restoration Project has been denied." The impersonal, clinical tone of the email was a stark contrast to the passion and conviction she had poured into the proposal. It wasn't just a rejection; it felt like a dismissal of everything she and Jonah had worked towards, a testament to the deep, unwavering belief they held in the Grand Hall's potential to revitalize Cedar Ridge.

She reread the reasons cited: "Insufficient evidence of broad community involvement and a lack of a demonstrably sustainable long-term operational plan." Clara's mind reeled. She had spoken to so many people, meticulously gathered testimonials, documented the enthusiasm for the project at every turn. The recent success of the Community Pantry, a project she and Jonah had spearheaded, was a living, breathing example of grassroots engagement. And the sustainability plan – she had spent weeks researching best practices, consulting experts, and tailoring their proposals to Cedar Ridge's unique economic landscape. It was solid, well-researched, and, she believed, utterly achievable.

A cold knot of anxiety tightened in her stomach. This wasn't just a bureaucratic misstep; it was a direct challenge to her professional competence. She had always prided herself on her thoroughness, her foresight. To be told she had fallen short, that she had missed crucial elements, was a bitter blow. She thought of Jonah, his steady encouragement, his shared vision of the Grand Hall as the heart of Cedar Ridge once more. This denial felt like a shadow cast over their shared hope.

The weight of this setback pressed down on her, heavy and suffocating. She leaned back in her grandmother's worn oak chair, the familiar creak a small, comforting sound in the otherwise silent room. The crisp autumn air outside, which had always invigorated her, now seemed to carry a whisper of foreboding. The grant had been their lifeline, the crucial funding that would allow them to tackle the most urgent, and expensive, structural issues. Without it, the Grand Hall, already teetering on the edge of decay, would remain vulnerable.

She closed her eyes, trying to push back the rising tide of panic. She had to reframe this. This wasn't the end; it was a detour. A significant, daunting detour, but a detour nonetheless. The Grand Hall was still standing, albeit precariously. The community still yearned for its revival. And her commitment, and Jonah's, remained unwavering. But the path forward had just become infinitely more complicated.

The thought of Jonah brought a flicker of reassurance. He possessed an almost innate understanding of Cedar Ridge, a grounded practicality that complemented her more academic approach. He knew how to connect with people, how to rally support, how to make things happen. She would need to talk to him, to share the devastating news and begin the arduous task of charting a new course.

As the initial shock began to recede, replaced by a more focused, albeit still anxious, resolve, Clara knew that the biggest challenge wasn't just finding new funding. It was proving that their vision for the Grand Hall was not just about preserving a historical artifact, but about investing in the future of Cedar Ridge. It was about demonstrating that their commitment was deeper, more resilient, and more community-rooted than any single grant application could ever fully convey.

The following morning, the atmosphere at the Town Hall was thick with an unspoken tension, a low hum of anticipation that Clara recognized all too well. She had requested an emergency meeting with the Town Council, a desperate attempt to explain the situation, to plead for understanding, and to begin the long, arduous process of rebuilding. She sat at the polished, yet slightly scuffed, long table, the same one where countless town meetings and lively debates had unfolded over the decades. To her left sat Mayor Thompson, his brow furrowed with a weariness that seemed to have settled permanently upon him. To her right, Councilwoman Albright, her arms crossed, her expression unreadable but radiating an air of pragmatic impatience. The other council members, familiar faces from years of community events and casual encounters, were present, their gazes shifting between Clara and their notepads.

"Clara, we appreciate you coming here on such short notice," Mayor Thompson began, his voice a low rumble, carefully modulated to convey both concern and authority. "We've all been... expecting some news regarding the grant for the Grand Hall. The town's been buzzing with anticipation, as you know."

Clara took a deep breath, the recycled air of the council chambers feeling suddenly thin. "Mayor, members of the council," she started, her voice steadier than she'd expected, "I... I have some difficult news. The application for the Historical Preservation Fund grant was denied."

A collective sigh rippled through the room, a tangible wave of disappointment. Councilwoman Albright's arms remained crossed, but a slight tightening around her eyes betrayed her reaction. "Denied?" she echoed, her tone clipped. "And why, precisely?"

Clara launched into her explanation, carefully articulating the reasons cited in the rejection letter. She spoke of the reviewers' concerns about insufficient community involvement and the lack of a robust sustainability plan. As she spoke, she felt a familiar surge of frustration, the disconnect between her meticulous efforts and the reviewers' abstract criticisms. She tried to convey the depth of support she had already garnered, the testimonials, the local business endorsements, the sheer passion of Cedar Ridge's residents. She spoke of the sustainability proposals they had developed, the projected revenue streams, the partnerships they had envisioned.

"But we *did* have community involvement," Clara insisted, her voice rising slightly. "We spoke to dozens of people. The Community Pantry project, which Jonah and I spearheaded, is a testament to that. We have appendices filled with letters of support, endorsements from local businesses who see the economic potential..."

"Letters and endorsements are one thing, Clara," Councilwoman Albright interjected, her voice cutting through Clara's explanation. "But the reviewers clearly felt it wasn't enough. And the sustainability plan... frankly, while your proposal was detailed, it relied heavily on projections that, to an outside observer, might seem a bit... optimistic for a town like Cedar Ridge."

Mayor Thompson nodded slowly. "Eleanor has a point, Clara. The grant was substantial. It was our best hope for addressing the critical structural issues. We all want the Grand Hall restored, but we also need to see a clear path forward, a plan that's not just aspirational, but achievable and sustainable in the long run."

Clara's heart sank. She had anticipated their concern, but the immediate shift in their tone, the unspoken urgency, was palpable. The town, like the council, was eager for action. They had seen the Grand Hall's slow decline for years, and the promise of restoration had become a beacon of hope. But with that hope came impatience, a weariness of delays and setbacks.

"I understand your concerns," Clara said, forcing herself to maintain a calm demeanor. "And I agree that we need a solid plan. But this denial... it's a significant setback, and the timeframe for addressing the most critical structural issues is becoming increasingly urgent. The roof, in particular, is a serious concern before winter sets in."

It was then that Mayor Thompson delivered the ultimatum, his voice grave. "Clara, we've been patient. We've supported your efforts. But the council has discussed this extensively. We can't afford to pour more town resources into a project that has, thus far, failed to secure the necessary external funding. We need to see tangible progress, and we need it soon." He paused, letting the weight of his words settle. "Therefore, the council's decision is this: we are giving you two weeks.

Two weeks to present a revised plan. A plan that demonstrates not only a viable funding strategy – and I mean *secured* or at least demonstrably within reach – but also concrete evidence of broader community buy-in and a clear, actionable operational strategy. If, in two weeks, we don't see a plan that satisfies these criteria, then the council will have no choice but to re-evaluate the future of the Grand Hall project entirely. We may have to consider other options... options that don't involve this particular restoration effort."

The words hung in the air, heavy and sharp. Two weeks. It was an impossibly short timeframe, a tight deadline that felt designed to crush any lingering hope. Clara's mind raced, a familiar panic beginning to claw at her throat. It was the same feeling she'd had before – the precipice, the brink of failure. The council's ultimatum was a stark, unyielding ultimatum, leaving little room for error, and even less for the organic, sometimes slow-burning, process of community building that was so vital to Cedar Ridge.

Councilwoman Albright leaned forward, her gaze direct. "We need to know that this project has the full backing of the town, Clara. Not just a few enthusiastic individuals. We need to see that the community is truly invested, willing to contribute their time, their resources, their ideas. And we need to be convinced that once restored, the Grand Hall will be a self-sustaining entity, not a perpetual drain on the town's budget."

Clara's gaze swept across the faces of the council members. She saw a mixture of apprehension and a deep-seated desire for a solution. They were not malicious; they were pragmatic, and perhaps, a little weary. They had seen projects stall before, promises fade. The Grand Hall, with its crumbling facade and faded glory, had become a symbol of past aspirations that hadn't materialized. They needed proof, not just promises.

"Two weeks is... a very short time, Mayor," Clara managed to say, her voice barely a whisper. The panic was threatening to consume her. "Especially to secure funding and demonstrate such broad community backing."

"We understand that, Clara," Mayor Thompson replied, though his tone offered little solace. "But the situation is urgent. The building's condition requires immediate attention, and we can't afford to wait indefinitely. This is our opportunity to show the town, and ourselves, that this project is viable. That it's worth the investment, not just of money, but of the town's collective will."

Councilwoman Albright offered a thin, tight smile. "Think of it as a challenge, Clara. A chance to galvanize the town in a way that perhaps the grant application didn't fully capture. Show us what Cedar Ridge can do when it truly rallies behind a cause."

Clara nodded, a tight, almost imperceptible movement of her head. She felt a strange sense of detachment, as if she were observing the scene from afar. The weight of the council's ultimatum pressed down on her, a physical sensation that stole her breath. It was a race against time, a desperate scramble to salvage a dream that was rapidly slipping through her fingers. She knew, with a chilling certainty, that this was a turning point.

The Grand Hall's fate, and perhaps her own place in Cedar Ridge, now rested on her ability to meet this formidable challenge head-on, to prove them all wrong. The familiar dread, the chilling whisper of failure, threatened to engulf her, but beneath it, a flicker of defiance began to ignite. She would not let the Grand Hall crumble. She would not let Cedar Ridge lose this vital piece of its soul. But two weeks... it felt like an eternity, and yet, impossibly short. The immense pressure of the ultimatum settled over her, a suffocating blanket, yet it also sparked a desperate, urgent resolve. She had to find a way. She *had* to.

Leaving the Town Hall, the crisp autumn air felt less like a gentle caress and more like a bracing slap. The weight of the council's ultimatum pressed down on Clara, each ticking second a reminder of the impossibly short deadline. Two weeks. It was a stark, unyielding timeframe, a judgment on the project and, by extension, on her efforts. The town's impatience was a palpable force, a collective sigh of weariness that she had sensed in the council chambers. They wanted action, not more studies, more proposals that seemed destined to gather dust. They had watched the Grand Hall decline for years, a slow, agonizing erosion of a once-proud landmark, and now, any further delay felt like a betrayal of their long-held hopes.

Clara's mind raced, a chaotic whirl of potential solutions and looming obstacles. The grant, their primary hope, was gone. Now, they needed a plan that not only secured funding but also demonstrated an undeniable, broad-based community commitment. The council had made it clear: the abstract evidence she had presented in the grant application was no longer sufficient. They needed something tangible, something that resonated with the heart of Cedar Ridge.

She walked along Main Street, the familiar storefronts blurring past her. The aroma of freshly baked bread from Miller's Bakery, the cheerful chime of the bell above the door at The Book Nook, the steady rhythm of daily life – it all felt so fragile now, so vulnerable to the potential loss of the Grand Hall. She had always believed in the power of community, in the shared spirit that bound Cedar Ridge together. But had she truly captured that spirit in her grant proposal? Had she effectively conveyed the deep, intrinsic connection the town had to this decaying edifice?

The council's words echoed in her mind: "Insufficient evidence of broad community involvement." It stung, but it also held a kernel of truth. While she had spoken to many, had she truly mobilized them? Had she tapped into the deeper wellspring of collective will that existed in Cedar Ridge? She thought of Jonah, his natural ability to connect with people, to inspire action. He understood that community wasn't just about surveys and testimonials; it was about shared experiences, about mutual reliance, about a collective stake in the town's future.

And the sustainability plan. The council's skepticism about its viability was a valid concern, even if it felt like a personal critique. Cedar Ridge wasn't a bustling metropolis; its economy was built on small businesses, agriculture, and a strong sense of local interdependence. A grand, ambitious operational plan, while theoretically sound, needed to be grounded in the reality of this town. It needed to reflect Cedar Ridge's unique strengths and resources.

Clara stopped in front of the dry cleaner's, her reflection in the window a pale, anxious face. She felt the familiar pressure, the cold grip of panic threatening to seize her. The feeling of being on the brink, of staring into the abyss of failure, was overwhelming. She had poured so much of herself into this project, her professional reputation, her personal hopes for Cedar Ridge. To have it all crumble within two weeks felt like an impossible burden.

But then, a different sensation began to stir within her – a nascent defiance. The council's ultimatum, while daunting, was also a clear mandate. It wasn't a death knell; it was a call to action. It demanded a different approach, a more direct, more personal engagement with the heart of Cedar Ridge. She couldn't rely on external grants anymore. She had to find a way to harness the town's own potential, its own resilience.

She thought of the conversations she'd had with Jonah over the past few months. He'd spoken about the untapped potential of local artisans, the desire of younger generations to find sustainable livelihoods within the town, the willingness of older residents to share their skills and knowledge. Perhaps the sustainability plan needed to be less about projections and more about people. Perhaps the community involvement needed to be less about surveys and more about shared action, about tangible contributions.

The two-week deadline was a brutal constraint, but it also forced a clarity that had been absent before. There was no room for indecision, no time for second-guessing. She needed to be bold, to be innovative, to be unafraid of asking for what the Grand Hall, and Cedar Ridge, truly needed. She pictured the Grand Hall, its skeletal structure silhouetted against the darkening sky, a silent plea for rescue. She couldn't let it fall.

The panic hadn't entirely receded, but it was now tempered by a growing sense of purpose. The council had presented them with a challenge, a seemingly insurmountable obstacle. But Clara knew that Cedar Ridge, and she and Jonah, had a knack for finding strength in adversity. The Grand Hall was more than just a building; it was a symbol of their shared history, their collective aspirations. And she was determined to prove, in these next two weeks, that it was also a symbol of their enduring resilience. She needed to talk to Jonah, immediately. He would understand.

He would know how to translate this daunting ultimatum into a galvanized movement, how to transform the town's weariness into a renewed sense of purpose. This was their moment to prove that the heart of Cedar Ridge beat strong, and that its future, like the Grand Hall itself, was worth fighting for. The clock was ticking, but for the first time since reading that rejection email, Clara felt a flicker of genuine hope, a fragile ember glowing in the face of overwhelming darkness. She had to believe that together, they could find a way. They had to.

The walk from the Town Hall back to her grandmother's house was a blur of hurried footsteps and a mind racing at a thousand miles an hour. The two-week deadline loomed like a guillotine, its shadow falling across every aspect of her life. Clara's initial shock had morphed into a frantic energy, a desperate need to *do something*. She replayed the council meeting in her head, the councilwoman's clipped pronouncements, the mayor's weary but firm ultimatum. The words "insufficient community involvement" and "lack of a demonstrably sustainable long-term operational plan" hammered at her, each a testament to a perceived failure she was determined to rectify.

She'd always believed in meticulous planning, in building a case brick by solid brick. The grant application had been her magnum opus of research and strategy. To have it dismissed so summarily, based on what felt like a superficial reading, was maddening. It wasn't just about her pride; it was about the Grand Hall, about Cedar Ridge's heart. The building was deteriorating at an alarming rate, and the winter storms were fast approaching, a natural enemy to already compromised structures. The council's impatience, while understandable, felt like a cruel twist of fate, a demand for miracles on an impossibly tight schedule.

Clara let herself into the quiet house, the scent of old wood and dried lavender a familiar comfort. She found Jonah in the backyard, tinkering with a stubborn carburetor on his ancient pickup truck, his brow furrowed in concentration. The late afternoon sun cast long shadows across the lawn, painting the scene in hues of gold and amber. He looked up as she approached, a smudge of grease on his cheek, his smile immediate and warm.

"Hey, you," he said, wiping his hands on a rag. "How'd the council meeting go? Any news?"

Clara's carefully constructed composure began to fray. She could feel the lump in her throat, the sting of unshed tears. She took a deep breath, trying to find her voice. "It... it wasn't good, Jonah."

His smile faltered, replaced by a look of concern. He put down his wrench and stepped towards her, his eyes searching hers. "What happened?"

"They denied the grant," she said, the words tumbling out in a rush. "The Historical Preservation Fund. Denied. And they... they gave us two weeks. Two weeks to come up with a new plan, a plan that shows *secured* funding, or at least something demonstrably within reach, and concrete evidence of broader community buy-in. Otherwise..." Her voice cracked. "Otherwise, they'll re-evaluate the whole project. They might even consider other options."

Jonah's jaw tightened. He reached out, his calloused hand gently touching her arm. "Two weeks? Clara, that's... that's insane. How can anyone secure significant funding and mobilize a whole town in two weeks?"

"I don't know," she admitted, her voice barely a whisper. "I tried to explain about the support we *do* have, the letters, the business endorsements, the

Community Pantry project... but they weren't convinced. Councilwoman Albright was particularly... firm. She said the reviewers felt it wasn't enough, that my sustainability plan was too optimistic."

A low growl rumbled in Jonah's chest. "Optimistic? We have a solid plan, Clara. We've done our homework. It's just... they don't see the spirit of Cedar Ridge. They see numbers on a page, not the heart of this town." He shook his head, his gaze fixed on the distant, darkening silhouette of the Grand Hall against the horizon. "This is exactly what I was afraid of. Relying on some bureaucratic committee to decide the fate of our town's landmark."

"But it was our best shot, Jonah!" Clara's voice rose, frustration bubbling to the surface. "We needed that funding. Without it, we can't even begin the critical repairs. The roof alone is a disaster waiting to happen."

"And this ultimatum is just another obstacle," Jonah countered, his tone hardening. "They want to see tangible proof of community buy-in? Fine. They want to see us rally? Then we'll show them."

Clara looked at him, a knot of anxiety tightening in her stomach. She could already sense the direction of his thoughts, a familiar divergence in their approaches. "Show them how, Jonah?"

"A community event," he said, his eyes lighting up with a spark of his usual enthusiasm. "A big one. A fundraiser, a festival. We'll have local bands, food stalls, craft vendors – everything that makes Cedar Ridge special. We'll get the whole town involved, show the council, show everyone, exactly how much this place means to us. We'll sell tickets, raffle off donations from businesses, hold a silent auction. We'll prove our commitment through our actions, not just our words."

Clara felt a wave of dread wash over her. A community event. It sounded chaotic, unpredictable, and, in her mind, entirely insufficient to meet the council's stringent demands for *secured* funding. "A festival, Jonah?

That's your plan? To throw a party and hope to raise enough money to fix a collapsing roof and a crumbling foundation? The grant was for a significant amount. A bake sale isn't going to cut it."

"It's not just a bake sale, Clara," Jonah said, his voice tinged with impatience. "It's a demonstration of unity. It's showing the council that the people of Cedar Ridge are willing to invest their own time, their own money, their own efforts. We can get pledges, commitments. We can show them a groundswell of support that no grant reviewer could ever ignore."

"But the grant reviewers aren't the ones we need to convince anymore, Jonah. It's the Town Council. And they want to see *secured* funding. A festival is great for goodwill, for community spirit, but it's not a guarantee. What if we don't raise enough? What if it rains? What if people just don't show up in the numbers we need? Then we've wasted precious time, and we'll be right back where we started, only with less time left."

Clara's voice was tight with controlled panic. She felt the familiar pull towards her usual methods – seeking professional help, appealing to higher authorities, navigating the established channels. "I was thinking we could try to appeal the decision. Or look for other grants, perhaps at a state level, or from private foundations that focus on historical preservation. We need a more formal, strategic approach."

Jonah scoffed. "Appeal? Another committee, another endless wait. And more grants? We just got rejected by one. You think another application is going to be a magic bullet in two weeks? Clara, you're trying to fight this with paperwork and procedures. That's not how Cedar Ridge works. This town responds to action, to people coming together. My way is immediate. It's tangible. It's something we can control."

"Control?" Clara's voice sharpened. "Throwing a festival is hardly something we can control entirely. There are a million variables, Jonah. Weather, attendance, the sheer logistical nightmare of organizing something like that in such a short timeframe. My way is about building a solid, defensible case. It's about proving our viability through rigorous planning and strategic alliances. It's about appealing to the systems that are in place to provide this kind of support."

"And your systems just failed us!" Jonah retorted, his voice rising to match hers. "That grant was supposed to be our lifeline, and it dried up. Now we're left with nothing but deadlines and demands. I'm talking about tapping into the real power of this town, Clara. The power of its people. When everyone pitches in, when everyone feels like they have a stake, that's when things get done. That's what the council *should* have seen in your application, but didn't. We need to *show* them. We need to rally the troops, not fill out more forms."

"Rallying the troops doesn't pay for structural repairs, Jonah," Clara said, her voice cold. "It doesn't magically reinforce a failing roof. We need money. Real money. And we need a plan that shows we can manage that money effectively and ensure the building's long-term viability. A festival might raise a few thousand dollars, but it won't secure the hundreds of thousands we need. Appealing to a state preservation board, or even looking at private donors with a proven track record in historical restoration, that's where the real funding lies."

"So, what? We just wait and hope some faceless foundation in another state decides to throw us a bone? While our Grand Hall crumbles around us?" Jonah's frustration was evident. He ran a hand through his already tousled hair. "That's not a plan, Clara. That's just passing the buck. We need to be proactive. We need to show initiative, ingenuity. We need to leverage the resources we *do* have, which is the spirit and the hard work of the people of Cedar Ridge."

"And what if that spirit and hard work isn't enough to meet the council's financial requirements?" Clara challenged, her own fear and desperation fueling her argument. "What if the festival raises only a fraction of what we need? Then we've exhausted our options. We've made a spectacle of ourselves and still failed. My approach, while it might seem slower, is about building a solid, sustainable solution. It's about ensuring the Grand Hall isn't just restored, but that it *stays* restored. That requires a long-term operational plan, a sound financial strategy, not just a one-time surge of goodwill."

"And your 'sound financial strategy' just got us a two-week deadline!" Jonah shot back. "We're already behind. This is about survival now, Clara. And the best way to survive, to fight back against this kind of pressure, is to show them we're a force to be reckoned with. A united town, working together for a common cause. That's a powerful statement. It's something that money can't buy."

"But it's not what the council is asking for," Clara insisted, her voice strained. "They're asking for financial guarantees, for evidence of a viable operational model. They're not asking for a street fair. They're asking for a business plan. And while I admire your passion, Jonah, and I believe in the spirit of this town, we need to be realistic about what it takes to secure significant funding for a project of this magnitude. We need to engage with the professional avenues that are designed for this very purpose."

"Professional avenues that just told us we didn't cut it!" Jonah paced a few steps, his hands balled into fists at his sides. "They want broad community involvement? Fine. We'll give them broad community involvement, on a scale they can't ignore. We'll have every business in town contribute, every willing hand. We'll create a buzz, an event that people will be talking about for years. And in the process, we'll raise money, we'll gather pledges, we'll create a visible, undeniable demonstration of support. It's proactive. It's engaging. It's *us* taking charge, not waiting for someone else to bail us out."

"But it's also risky," Clara countered, her voice laced with anxiety. "Terribly risky. What if we fail? What if the event doesn't generate enough, or if the council sees it as just a charming but ultimately insufficient gesture?

They've laid down a clear marker, Jonah. They want quantifiable results, not just enthusiasm. I believe we need to pursue all avenues simultaneously, but my focus needs to be on the more structured, formal appeals. I need to be crafting that revised proposal, identifying potential alternative funding sources, and demonstrating a more robust operational strategy. That's what will ultimately satisfy the council's requirements."

"And while you're doing that, who's going to ignite the town? Who's going to make people *feel* the urgency, the importance of the Grand Hall?" Jonah stopped pacing and faced her, his gaze intense. "Your grant proposals, as thorough as they are, don't capture the soul of this place. They don't show the history, the memories, the sheer love the people have for that building.

A festival will. It will remind everyone *why* we're fighting for it. It will create a tangible connection, a sense of shared ownership that no amount of carefully worded prose can replicate. You can craft your strategy, Clara, but I'll be out there, rallying the people. We need both, but right now, the most immediate need is to demonstrate that the *town* is behind this project with everything it has."

Clara felt a familiar tug-of-war within her. Her mind, trained in logic and structured problem-solving, recoiled at the perceived chaos of Jonah's plan. Yet, she couldn't deny the power of his conviction, the inherent truth in his understanding of Cedar Ridge's heart. He saw the town as a living entity, a collective spirit that could be roused to action. She saw it as a complex system that needed careful navigation and strategic planning.

"But what if my proposal, the one that focuses on securing actual funds and a sustainable operational model, is what they ultimately need to see?" she argued, her voice laced with a plea for understanding. "What if the festival, as wonderful as it might be for morale, doesn't provide the concrete financial assurances they're demanding? We can't afford to put all our eggs in one basket, Jonah, especially when that basket is a community fair."

"And we can't afford to sit here waiting for a miracle grant to materialize when our town is in crisis!" Jonah's voice was firm, unyielding. "The council's ultimatum is a direct challenge to the community. They want to see if we're truly invested. A festival is the most direct, most visible way to answer that challenge. It's about demonstrating commitment through action.

Your meticulous approach is vital, Clara, I know that. But right now, we need to show them the fire in our belly, the collective will of Cedar Ridge. That's what will make them reconsider, that's what will buy us the time and the goodwill we need to implement your more long-term strategies. We need to create a sense of urgency, a unified front, that speaks louder than any rejection letter. Think of it as building the foundation of support that will allow your more formal proposals to succeed. Without that groundswell, your plans will remain just that – plans. We need to make them believe, not just read."

The tension between them crackled in the air, a palpable manifestation of their differing visions for tackling this crisis. It was a recurring theme in their relationship, a fundamental difference in how they approached challenges: Clara's methodical, rule-based approach versus Jonah's intuitive, resourceful, often rule-bending methods. And now, with the fate of the Grand Hall hanging in the balance, their disagreement felt more critical, more deeply felt, than ever before.

The silence in the house was a stark contrast to the turmoil that had erupted in the backyard. Clara moved through the rooms like a ghost, her mind still replaying the council's decision, the stark ultimatum, and the ensuing clash with Jonah. She found herself in the kitchen, the scent of baking bread, a constant in her grandmother's home, doing little to soothe her frayed nerves. She stared out the window at the sprawling oak tree in the yard, its branches bare against the darkening sky, a silent sentinel to the passage of time and the quiet strength that could weather any storm. But right now, she felt anything but strong. She felt exposed, vulnerable, and the weight of doubt, both her own and that she suspected would soon be cast by others, pressed down on her.

She knew how these things worked in small towns. News, even unwelcome news, traveled with the speed of gossip. The council meeting, while not broadcast live, would undoubtedly become the subject of hushed conversations at the general store, the post office, and over backyard fences. Clara had always prided herself on her ability to navigate such social currents, to maintain a composed public persona. But this was different. This wasn't about a minor social gaffe or a local dispute. This was about the Grand Hall, a symbol of Cedar Ridge's past and its potential future, and her leadership in its preservation was now being openly questioned, even before she'd had a chance to fully regroup.

The whispers would start subtly, she imagined. A raised eyebrow here, a knowing nod there. "Did you hear about the grant?" someone would murmur, their voice laced with a faux sympathy that masked a deeper skepticism. "Clara put so much into that application, didn't she? Such a shame it didn't pan out." And then, inevitably, the inevitable follow-up: "She's always been so organized, so by-the-book. I wonder if this kind of... *passion project* is really her strong suit. Remember that community garden idea a few years back? It never really took off, did it?"

The ghost of the community garden incident, a well-intentioned but ultimately faltering endeavor that Clara had spearheaded before the grant application, loomed in her mind. She'd been younger then, perhaps less experienced, and the project had indeed fizzled out due to a lack of sustained volunteer interest. It had been a painful lesson in the complexities of mobilizing a community, a lesson she'd vowed to never repeat. Now, it felt like a weapon that could be wielded against her, a testament to a perceived inability to translate vision into lasting reality.

And then there was Jonah. His plan, the rally-the-troops, festival-style approach, while undeniably appealing to the town's spirit, also opened him up to scrutiny. He was a known quantity in Cedar Ridge – a skilled mechanic, a generous neighbor, a man who could fix anything mechanical. But was he the right man to lead a complex preservation project? Some might see his impulsiveness, his tendency to bypass established protocols, as a weakness, a sign that he wasn't taking the seriousness of the situation as profoundly as Clara did.

They might wonder if his boisterous enthusiasm was merely a superficial gloss over a lack of strategic depth. "Jonah's always got a good idea," she could already hear the murmurs, "but can he actually *deliver* when it counts? He's good with engines, but this is about... history. And money." The subtle implication would be that his commitment, while genuine, was perhaps misguided, a romantic notion that would ultimately fail to contend with the hard realities of funding and preservation.

Clara sighed, leaning her forehead against the cool glass of the window. The immediate aftermath of the council meeting had been a whirlwind of adrenaline and argument. Now, in the quiet solitude of her grandmother's house, the true weight of the situation began to settle. The external pressures were mounting, and they weren't just from the Town Council anymore. They were from the very community they were trying to save.

She pictured Sarah Jenkins, the owner of the popular bakery on Main Street, a woman who had been effusive in her support of the Grand Hall project during the initial grant application phase, her business providing the delicious pastries for Clara's grant-writing retreats. Sarah was a pillar of the community, her opinion carrying considerable weight. Clara could envision Sarah, her hands dusted with flour, discussing the news with a neighbor. "Clara's always been so bright," she might say, her voice soft, regretful. "Such a shame. I really thought she had it in the bag.

But then, this whole grant thing... it felt a bit too... *official* for our town, didn't it? And Jonah's idea for a festival... bless his heart, he means well, but is that really going to secure the kind of funds we need? We're talking about a historic building, not a village fête." The underlying question, Clara knew, would be whether Clara, with her structured approach, or Jonah, with his grassroots enthusiasm, truly understood the magnitude of the task.

Then there was Mr. Abernathy, the retired history teacher who had been instrumental in providing historical context for Clara's initial grant proposal. He was a man of meticulous detail and unwavering adherence to academic rigor. While he had been supportive, Clara suspected his quiet nature masked a keen analytical mind that would be dissecting every aspect of their current predicament. He might voice his concerns privately, perhaps to Jonah's father, old man Peterson, a man known for his pragmatism and his deep roots in Cedar Ridge's logging industry.

"Peterson," Abernathy might begin, his voice measured, "I respect young Jonah's drive, truly I do. But the council's demands are quite specific. Secured funding, a sustainable plan. A town festival, while admirable for its spirit, rarely translates into the capital required for major structural repairs. I worry we are mistaking enthusiasm for solvency. Clara, for all her meticulousness, may have underestimated the sheer scale of the financial undertaking required."

The doubts would spread like a subtle poison, seeping into the foundations of trust that Clara and Jonah had been so diligently trying to build. It wasn't maliciousness, not at its core. It was the inherent human tendency to question, to second-guess, especially when faced with uncertainty and potential disappointment. It was the fear of another failed promise, another grand vision that crumbled under the weight of reality.

Clara ran a hand over the smooth, cool surface of the kitchen counter. She remembered the pride she'd felt when the initial letters of support had poured in, the endorsements from local businesses, the enthusiastic participation in the preliminary planning meetings. That had been tangible proof of community buy-in, of a shared desire to see the Grand Hall restored. But it seemed, in the eyes of the grant reviewers, and now perhaps in the eyes of some of their neighbors, it hadn't been enough. What did "enough" even look like? W

as it a written guarantee from every business owner? Was it a town-wide pledge drive that guaranteed specific monetary contributions? The council's demand for "demonstrably sustainable long-term operational plan" was already a labyrinth, and now, layered on top of that, was the equally daunting requirement for "insufficient community involvement" to be rectified.

She thought of Mrs. Gable, who ran the yarn shop. Mrs. Gable was a notoriously sharp-tongued woman, but she had a soft spot for Clara, often knitting small, thoughtful gifts for her. Clara could imagine Mrs. Gable talking to her knitting circle. "Clara's a good girl," she'd say, her needles clicking a rhythm of skepticism. "But bless her heart, she's trying to save a building with idealism. And Jonah... well, Jonah's a good mechanic, but he's not exactly a financial wizard, is he? This Grand Hall needs serious money, not just good intentions. And two weeks? It's a tight squeeze, and I'm not sure this town is ready to dig that deep. We've got our own bills to worry about." The underlying sentiment would be a pragmatic concern for individual livelihoods, a gentle nudge back to reality that Clara's grand vision, and Jonah's boisterous plan, might be out of touch with the everyday struggles of Cedar Ridge residents.

The external noise of doubt wasn't just a threat to their efforts; it was a direct assault on the fragile partnership that had begun to form between Clara and Jonah. They had their differences, their opposing approaches, but they were united in their core objective. Yet, as the whispers of skepticism began to circulate, they risked creating a fissure between them, a subtle erosion of mutual trust. If the community started to question Jonah's methods, would Clara begin to doubt his judgment? And if they doubted Clara's ability to secure funding, would Jonah start to feel she was too slow, too cautious, too detached from the town's emotional needs?

She pictured the general store, the heart of Cedar Ridge's daily commerce and gossip. Old Man Hemlock, perched on his stool behind the counter, would be dispensing wisdom and, no doubt, commentary. He'd seen it all in Cedar Ridge, the boom times and the lean years, the grand pronouncements and the quiet collapses. He'd probably shake his head, a wry smile playing on his lips. "Grant denied, eh? Told you that Historical Preservation Fund was a long shot.

Too many rules, not enough heart. Now this festival idea... it's got spirit, I'll give Jonah that. But spirit don't pay the bills. Clara's got the brains, bless her. But can she rally enough cash in two weeks? And will people even come out? Times are tight, Clara. People gotta eat. They gotta keep their roofs from leaking. Saving an old building... it's a noble cause, but it's a luxury for some." His words, laced with a lifetime of hard-earned pragmatism, would resonate with many, echoing the very doubts that Clara fought to suppress.

The fear was that these whispers, these seeds of doubt, would take root. That they would fester and grow, turning into open skepticism and, eventually, outright opposition. The urgency of the two-week deadline was already a crushing weight. Adding the burden of public opinion, of facing questioning glances and whispered criticisms, felt almost unbearable. Clara's strength had always lain in her meticulous preparation, her ability to anticipate challenges and formulate solutions. But this was a challenge she couldn't control through sheer logic or rigorous planning. This was about perception, about belief, about intangible community sentiment.

She looked at her hands, suddenly feeling small and inadequate. She had stepped into this role with a sense of duty, a deep-seated love for

Cedar Ridge and its history. She had believed in her ability to make a difference. But now, the external forces were pushing back, threatening to undermine not just her efforts, but her very confidence. She thought of Jonah's conviction, his unwavering belief in the power of the people. It was infectious, inspiring. But the whispers would try to chip away at that, too. They would question his motives, his capabilities, his understanding of the stakes. They would paint him as an impulsive dreamer, a man who was leading them on a wild goose chase.

Clara closed her eyes, taking a deep, shaky breath. She had to find a way to navigate this. She couldn't let the doubts of others dictate the fate of the Grand Hall. She and Jonah had a plan, albeit one with different facets. They needed to believe in their plan, and more importantly, they needed to convince the town to believe in them. It wouldn't be easy. The whispers were already starting, subtle and insidious. But she was Clara Donovan, and she wouldn't let Cedar Ridge's heart crumble without a fight. The external setbacks were not just the council's decision; they were the burgeoning doubts that threatened to dismantle the very spirit they needed to rally.

The grand, cavernous space of the Grand Hall, usually alive with the echoes of history and the promise of revival, now felt like a tomb. Dust motes danced in the slivers of late afternoon sun that pierced through the grimy, arched windows, illuminating the scene of their recent, disheartening defeat. Clara sat on an overturned wooden crate, the rough surface a stark contrast to the smooth, polished feel she usually associated with the Hall's elegant furniture, now packed away or damaged.

The air hung heavy with the scent of damp plaster and decaying wood, a mournful perfume for a dream on the brink of extinction. Around her, the debris of their efforts lay scattered: a half-unrolled blueprint, discarded proposal drafts, and a stack of brightly colored flyers for a festival that now seemed like a cruel joke. The fight had drained out of her, leaving an aching hollowness in its wake. The council's stern faces, their dismissive pronouncements, Jonah's frustrated outburst – it all swirled in a vortex of defeat. She felt a profound sense of loss, not just for the building, but for the hope she had so desperately clung to.

She heard the creak of the heavy oak door behind her, a sound that usually announced Jonah's energetic presence. But this time, it was a hesitant, weary sound. She didn't turn, didn't move. She knew it was him. No one else would venture into the Hall's silence with such a heavy heart. He didn't speak, and Clara didn't prompt him. He simply walked further into the space, his footsteps slow and deliberate on the dusty floorboards.

She could feel his presence, a familiar warmth that now felt tinged with shared desolation. He moved past her, not intruding, but settling a short distance away, near a grand, dusty fireplace that had once warmed generations of Cedar Ridge residents. He sat down, not on a crate, but on the cold stone hearth, his shoulders slumping, the usual spark in his eyes dimmed to a flicker.

For a long time, the only sounds were the wind sighing through the cracks in the walls and the faint chirping of unseen birds outside. The silence between them was not an awkward one, nor was it a void. It was a shared space, thick with unspoken emotions. Clara could feel the weight of their mutual disappointment pressing down, a tangible force in the dim light. She imagined Jonah replaying the council meeting in his mind, the frustrated arguments, the feeling of being misunderstood, the sting of being dismissed. She knew he'd been ready to fight, to rally, to push harder. And she, in her quiet determination, had believed in the power of her carefully constructed plan. Their differing approaches, usually a source of dynamic energy, now felt like two sides of a coin that had landed face down.

Finally, Jonah stirred. He didn't look at her, his gaze fixed on a loose floorboard at his feet. "They... they just didn't get it, Clara," he said, his voice rough, stripped of its usual optimism. It was a simple statement, but it held the universe of their current predicament. He wasn't blaming her, nor was he seeking blame himself. It was a shared observation of a universal truth – sometimes, despite best efforts, understanding eludes those who hold the power.

Clara finally turned her head, her eyes meeting his across the expanse of the dusty hall. His face, usually animated and quick to smile, was etched with a weariness that mirrored her own. There was no anger in his gaze, no trace of the frustration that had flared between them earlier. Instead, she saw a profound sadness, a shared recognition of the immense task they had undertaken and the seemingly insurmountable obstacles that now stood in their way.

"No, Jonah," she replied softly, her voice barely a whisper. "They didn't." She didn't add anything else. There was nothing else to add. The grant, the funding, the council's conditions – they were all secondary to this fundamental disconnect. They had tried to explain, to persuade, to demonstrate the value of the Grand Hall, not just as a building, but as the heart of Cedar Ridge. And it had fallen on deaf ears.

He let out a slow breath, a sound that seemed to carry the weight of the entire town's history. "All that work... the meetings, the research, getting everyone excited..." He trailed off, the unfinished sentence hanging in the air. It was a lament, not just for their personal efforts, but for the collective hope they had managed to kindle, only to see it doused by the cold water of official disapproval.

Clara found herself nodding, a slow, almost involuntary movement. She remembered the initial spark of excitement, the way ideas had flowed, the shared vision that had begun to crystallize between her and Jonah. She remembered the late nights spent poring over documents, the brainstorming sessions filled with both her methodical planning and his inspired leaps of imagination. It had felt so close, so tangible. And now... now it felt like a ghost.

"It's... a lot," she admitted, the understatement hanging in the vast space. A lot felt like an inadequate descriptor for the crushing weight of this setback.

Jonah finally looked directly at her, and in his eyes, she saw a flicker of something more than just disappointment. It was a raw, unvarnished vulnerability that mirrored her own. They had been so focused on their individual approaches, on proving their respective merits, that perhaps they had forgotten the core of what they were trying to achieve. They were a team, two disparate forces united by a common cause. And in this moment of shared defeat, that realization began to dawn with a quiet, profound clarity.

"Yeah," he said, his voice still low but steadier now. "It's a lot. But... you know what?" He paused, and Clara waited, her gaze fixed on him. "It's not over."

She searched his face, looking for any hint of bravado or false optimism, but found none. It was a statement of quiet defiance, born not of anger, but of a deep-seated resilience. He wasn't suggesting a new plan, not yet. He was simply refusing to concede defeat.

"We put everything into that grant," Clara said, a ghost of her usual analytical tone returning, but softer now. "And it wasn't enough. The council... they've given us a very tight deadline to prove 'insufficient community involvement.' Two weeks. To turn a perceived deficit into overwhelming proof of public engagement." The numbers, the logistics, the sheer impossibility of it all, threatened to reassert themselves, but she pushed them back.

Jonah pushed himself up from the hearth, his movements still a little stiff, and walked towards one of the large, faded windows. He ran a hand over the grimy glass, leaving a clear streak that offered a slightly less obscured view of the dying light outside. "So we prove it," he said, his back to her. "We show them. We're not just talking about a building, Clara. We're talking about... this. About Cedar Ridge. About what this place means."

There was a new note in his voice, a quiet conviction that resonated more deeply than his usual boisterous pronouncements. It wasn't about charming the council or winning them over with logic. It was about reminding them, and more importantly, reminding themselves, of the true stake.

Clara stood up, dusting off her skirt. The weariness was still there, a heavy blanket, but something else was beginning to stir beneath it. A faint warmth, a nascent flicker of defiance. "But how, Jonah? The whispers have already started. People are going to doubt us. They'll see this as a lost cause, a wasted effort." She thought of the subtle skepticism she'd already sensed, the polite but firm dismissal from some of the council members.

He turned from the window, and a ghost of his usual smile touched his lips. It wasn't a triumphant smile, but a weary acknowledgment of the challenge. "We'll answer the whispers with shouting, Clara. We'll answer the doubt with action. We'll make them see that this isn't just *our* project. It's *their* Grand Hall." He took a step towards her, and for the first time, Clara saw not the impulsive mechanic, but the leader he was capable of being. His eyes, though shadowed with fatigue, held a determined glint.

"They want community involvement?" he continued, his voice gaining a quiet strength. "They'll get it. More than they ever imagined. We'll show them that Cedar Ridge still has a heart, and that heart beats for this place." He looked around the vast, empty hall, and Clara could see the wheels turning in his mind, the familiar spark rekindling, albeit with a newfound depth. He wasn't just thinking about a festival anymore; he was thinking about legacy.

"It's not about winning them over with a song and dance," he said, anticipating her unspoken concern. "It's about showing them what's at stake. It's about reminding them why we fell in love with this place in the first place." He extended a hand, not in a gesture of reconciliation, but of partnership. "We're in this together, Clara. Win or lose, we're in it together."

Clara looked at his outstretched hand, then back at his face. The fight had drained out of her, but in its place, something more enduring had begun to grow. It was a quiet understanding, a shared resolve forged in the crucible of disappointment. She hadn't expected this – this moment of shared despair that wasn't about blame, but about mutual recognition and a renewed sense of purpose.

It was in this bleak, dusty hall, surrounded by the remnants of their setback, that their partnership solidified, not through grand pronouncements, but through the quiet acknowledgment of shared struggle and a dawning, unwavering commitment. She placed her hand in his, her grip firm. "Together," she echoed, the word a silent promise in the vast, waiting space. The road ahead was still daunting, the odds still stacked against them, but for the first time since the council meeting, Clara didn't feel utterly alone. The shared despair had, paradoxically, ignited a new, steady flame.

CHAPTER EIGHT

Rebuilding Trust

The hum of conversation in the town hall was a low thrum, a familiar sound that usually filled Clara with a sense of belonging. Tonight, however, it felt distant, alien. The scent of coffee and baked goods, a comforting hallmark of Cedar Ridge's community gatherings, did little to soothe the nervous flutter in her stomach. She watched as familiar faces – Mrs. Gable with her ever-present knitting, Mr. Henderson, the retired postman, the young families who had expressed such enthusiasm for the Grand Hall's revival – settled into their seats. Each one represented a thread in the intricate tapestry of their small town, a tapestry that had felt so fragile in the wake of the council's decision.

Jonah sat beside her, his presence a solid anchor. He'd given her a reassuring squeeze of her hand earlier, a silent promise of support, but the weight of the moment was hers to bear. The council's ultimatum—a stark two-week deadline to demonstrate overwhelming community involvement to counter their claims of insufficient public engagement—felt like an insurmountable mountain. She had spent the past few days wrestling with the setback, the sting of rejection, and the gnawing realization that her own reservations had perhaps played a part in the council's perception.

Clara rose from her seat, the scrape of the chair on the polished wooden floor echoing slightly in the momentary lull. A hush fell over the room, all eyes turning towards her. She took a deep breath, trying to steady her nerves, to push back the tremor that threatened to betray her. This wasn't just about the Grand Hall anymore; it was about honesty, about rebuilding trust, and about admitting her own shortcomings.

"Good evening, everyone," she began, her voice a little softer than she'd intended, but clear enough to carry. She offered a small, self-deprecating smile. "I... I wanted to start by saying a few words tonight. Not about blueprints, or budgets, or council meetings. But about... about me. And about us."

She could feel the collective gaze, a mixture of curiosity and concern. She knew that many had been privy to the heated exchange between her and Jonah after the council's verdict, and perhaps even overheard some of the more pointed critiques from the council members themselves. The grant denial had been a public humiliation, a stark confirmation of the doubts that had been whispered behind closed doors.

"When I first came to Cedar Ridge," Clara continued, her gaze sweeping across the faces, seeking out those who had been so eager, so hopeful, "I was... guarded. I came with a plan, a very detailed, very structured plan, and I believed, perhaps too much, in my ability to execute it on my own. I saw the Grand Hall, and I saw its potential, and I wanted to bring it back to life. But in my focus on the 'how,' I think I may have overlooked the importance of the 'who.'"

Her voice began to gain a steadier rhythm, the initial nervousness giving way to a quiet sincerity. "I'm not good at asking for help. It's not something I've had to do much of in my life. My instinct is always to find the solution myself, to analyze, to strategize, and to execute. And I realize now, looking back at how things unfolded, that my tendency to operate independently, to keep my cards close to my chest, might have sent the wrong message. It might have looked like I didn't trust any of you. And that's the last thing I ever wanted."

She paused, letting her words settle. This was the hardest part, admitting the fear that lay beneath her determined exterior. "The truth is, I was afraid. Afraid of failing, yes, but also afraid of being disappointed. Afraid of relying on others, only to have that reliance not be met. It's easier, in a way, to try and control every variable yourself. But that's not how community works, is it?"

A few people shifted in their seats, their expressions softening. She saw Mrs. Gable nod, her knitting momentarily forgotten. Mr. Henderson leaned forward, his brow furrowed in thought.

"I want to apologize," Clara said, her voice now imbued with a raw honesty that resonated through the hall. "I apologize for my initial aloofness. I apologize if I made any of you feel like your input wasn't valued, or that your support wasn't crucial. Because it is. It's everything." She looked directly at Jonah, her gaze filled with a gratitude that went beyond their shared project. He offered a small, encouraging smile.

"The council's decision," she went on, her voice gaining a quiet strength, "was a blow. It felt like a definitive statement that our vision wasn't shared, that the community wasn't behind it. And in my pride, in my disappointment, I almost let myself believe it. But then... then I remembered why we were doing this in the first place. Not for a grant, not for council approval, but for Cedar Ridge. For all of us."

She took another breath, her gaze returning to the faces of her neighbors. "They've given us a challenge. Two weeks to prove that this isn't a pipe dream, that the Grand Hall isn't just a decaying building, but a vital part of our town's soul. And I know that after the disappointment, after the uncertainty, it might feel like a difficult, even impossible task. You might be wondering if it's worth the effort, if we can really turn this around."

Clara's voice began to tremble, not from fear this time, but from the depth of her emotion. She had spent so long compartmentalizing her feelings, presenting a composed front, and now, in this moment, she was letting it all out. "I don't have all the answers," she admitted, her voice barely a whisper. "I don't have a magic plan that will instantly win everyone over. What I have is a belief. A belief in the spirit of this town. A belief in all of you."

She clasped her hands together, her knuckles turning white. "The council said we lacked community involvement. I know that's not true. I've seen the enthusiasm, I've heard the ideas, I've felt the shared desire to see this place thrive. But perhaps we haven't articulated it well enough. Perhaps we haven't shown them, truly *shown* them, what this project means to Cedar Ridge."

Clara stepped forward, her posture shifting from a defensive stance to one of open invitation. "So, I'm asking you, not just as your project leader, but as a resident of this town, as someone who has come to care deeply about this place and its people... I'm asking for your help. I'm asking for your support. I'm asking for you to stand with me, with Jonah, with all of us who believe in the Grand Hall, and show them what Cedar Ridge is truly made of."

Her gaze met Mr. Henderson's. He gave a slow, deliberate nod, his eyes kind. Mrs. Gable put her knitting down entirely now, her hands clasped in her lap, her expression one of quiet encouragement. A young woman in the front row, someone Clara recognized from the library's book club, offered a hesitant smile and a small wave.

"It's not too late," Clara continued, her voice gaining a renewed strength, a fragile hope blooming within her. "We have a chance to prove them wrong. Not with anger, not with arguments, but with action. With unity. With the overwhelming power of a community that believes in its own future." She looked at Jonah, and he rose to stand beside her, his presence a silent testament to their shared commitment.

"We've been talking about revitalizing the Grand Hall," she said, her voice ringing with a newfound conviction. "But maybe, what we've really been doing is revitalizing our own sense of community. And that's something worth fighting for. That's something worth showing the world." She extended her hands, palms up, a gesture of vulnerability and an open invitation. "So, what do you say, Cedar Ridge? Are you with us?"

The question hung in the air, pregnant with anticipation. It wasn't a demand, but a plea, a heartfelt invitation to join them in a shared endeavor. Clara's heart pounded in her chest, a nervous rhythm that now felt like a drumbeat of hope. She had laid bare her own fears and insecurities, acknowledging her own part in the perceived lack of connection. Now, the ball was in their court. She had offered her vulnerability, her honest struggle, and in doing so, she hoped she had paved the way for genuine trust, for the kind of open collaboration that could truly make the Grand Hall project, and Cedar Ridge itself, rise from the ashes of disappointment. The silence that followed wasn't one of hesitation, but of contemplation, of a town beginning to reckon with the power of their collective voice, and the quiet strength found in admitting when you need each other.

Jonah remained standing beside Clara, his presence a steady, quiet counterpoint to her impassioned plea. He hadn't spoken a word during her address, but his gaze had been fixed on her, a silent testament to his unwavering support. He had watched her lay bare her vulnerabilities, her fears, and her newfound understanding of community. He saw the way her voice had cracked, then strengthened, the way her initial nervousness had transformed into a quiet power. When she finally extended her hands, an open invitation to her neighbors, his heart swelled with a pride he hadn't anticipated. He knew, in that moment, that she had not only spoken to the town but had spoken directly to him, acknowledging their shared journey and his place within it.

As Clara's final question, "Are you with us?" hung in the air, Jonah stepped forward, his hand gently resting on the small of her back, a grounding touch. He didn't need to say anything yet; the atmosphere in the room had shifted. The initial silence wasn't one of doubt, but of consideration, a collective inhale as the townspeople processed Clara's words. He could feel the weight of their attention turn to him, a familiar sensation, but one he welcomed. He believed in Clara, not just as a project leader, but as a woman who was learning to open her heart, and he believed in Cedar Ridge.

When the murmur of agreement began to ripple through the hall, a collective hum of assent, Jonah stepped to the microphone that Clara had just vacated. He cleared his throat, the small click amplified in the sudden quiet. He looked out at the faces, familiar, friendly, some etched with concern, others alight with a dawning hope. He saw Mrs. Gable, her eyes glistening, and Mr. Henderson, his expression one of quiet resolve. He saw the young families, their earlier enthusiasm rekindled.

"Thank you, Clara," Jonah began, his voice resonating with a warmth that filled the room. He met her gaze for a fleeting moment, a silent acknowledgment of their shared moment. "You've said it all, in many ways. You've spoken with courage and honesty, and that's exactly what Cedar Ridge needed to hear." He paused, letting her words settle, allowing the foundation she had laid to solidify. He knew that Clara, in her own way, had begun the process of rebuilding trust, not just with the town, but with herself.

"I know that after the council's decision, there was a sense of disappointment," Jonah continued, his tone shifting to one of gentle reflection. "A feeling of being overlooked, of our efforts not being seen. And I understand that. I've been there. I've felt that sting myself, right here in Cedar Ridge." He saw a few heads nod in understanding; they knew his history, the challenges he'd faced.

"When I first moved back here, after... well, after things hadn't worked out the way I'd planned down south," he admitted, a hint of a self-deprecating smile touching his lips, "I felt lost. I felt like a failure. I'd poured everything I had into a business, and it had crumbled. And I came back here, to my hometown, feeling like I had nothing left to offer. I was reluctant to get involved, to put myself out there again. I was afraid of failing again, of disappointing the people I grew up with."

He let the confession hang in the air, a shared vulnerability that mirrored Clara's. "It's easy to withdraw when you're hurting," he confessed. "It's easy to build walls. And I know I did that. I kept to myself, I focused on getting by, and I didn't engage. I didn't see the potential around me, not really. I was too busy looking backward."

His gaze swept across the room again, his expression earnest. "But then," he said, his voice gaining a quiet strength, "things started to happen. Little things, at first. Mr. Henderson organizing the summer picnic, Mrs. Gable spearheading the library book drive, the young families starting that little community garden behind the general store. Small acts of people reaching out, not because they had to, but because they wanted to. Because they believed in the power of Cedar Ridge."

He remembered those days vividly. He had watched from his quiet corner, a reluctant observer, as the threads of community began to weave themselves back together. He'd seen the warmth in their interactions, the genuine concern they had for one another, the simple joy they found in shared effort. It had chipped away at his own isolation, slowly but surely.

"And slowly," Jonah went on, "I started to see it. I saw that Cedar Ridge isn't defined by its setbacks, or by any one person's ambition. It's defined by its people. By our willingness to show up for each other, even when it's hard. Even when we've been disappointed." He gestured towards Clara. "Clara came here with a vision for the Grand Hall, a vision for its future. And she's poured her heart and soul into it. But it's not just her vision anymore. It's our vision. It's our town's history, our town's future."

He met the eyes of a few of the council members who were present, their expressions stoic, perhaps a little surprised by his candor. "The council has asked us to demonstrate community involvement. They've given us a challenge. And I'm here to tell you, without a shadow of a doubt, that we will meet that challenge. Not because Clara and I are pushing for it, but because this town has a spirit that refuses to be diminished. A spirit that understands the value of a shared space, of a gathering place, of a cornerstone that holds our memories and our dreams."

Jonah stepped away from the microphone, moving closer to Clara. He didn't take her hand, but he stood beside her, a clear indication of their partnership. "When I heard Clara speak tonight, I heard a woman who has faced her own doubts and fears, and has come out on the other side with a renewed commitment. She's not afraid to admit when she needs help, and that, my friends, is a sign of strength, not weakness. And I know, because I've seen it firsthand, that when Clara sets her mind to something, with the support of this incredible community, there's nothing she can't achieve."

He looked back at the assembled townspeople, his expression earnest. "The Grand Hall isn't just a building. It's a symbol. It's a place where generations have celebrated, where futures have been planned, where our collective story has unfolded. To let it fall into disrepair, to let it be forgotten, would be to lose a piece of ourselves. And I, for one, am not ready to let that happen."

He raised his voice, a quiet conviction ringing through it. "We have two weeks. Two weeks to show the council, and more importantly, to show ourselves, what Cedar Ridge is capable of when we stand together. Let's flood the planning office with letters of support. Let's organize work parties to clear out the old dust and debris, to show them we're ready to roll up our sleeves. Let's share our memories of the Hall, our hopes for its future, and let's make our voices heard. Not with anger, but with a unified passion. With the quiet, steadfast power of a community that knows its own worth."

He turned to Clara, a genuine smile finally breaking through. "And I want to assure everyone here tonight, especially Clara, that I am fully committed to this project. I'm not just supporting it; I'm all in. I believe in the Grand Hall, and I believe in this town. And I know that together, we can make this happen. We *will* make this happen."

He offered a nod to the crowd, a gesture of respect and shared purpose. The air in the hall felt different now, charged with a renewed energy, a tangible shift in the collective mood. Clara felt a wave of relief wash over her, so potent it made her knees weak. Jonah's words, born from his own experiences of doubt and eventual re-engagement, had resonated deeply. He hadn't just offered support; he had shared a piece of his own healing journey, weaving it into the narrative of their shared endeavor. His unwavering belief, now openly declared, felt like a second anchor, solidifying the fragile hope she had managed to ignite.

As the initial applause began to build, a steady, enthusiastic wave, Clara leaned towards Jonah, her voice a soft murmur only he could hear. "Thank you," she whispered, her eyes shining with unshed tears. "You didn't have to do that. You didn't have to share... all of that."

Jonah's gaze softened as he looked at her. "Of course, I did," he replied, his voice low and steady. "You were brave enough to be honest. The least I could do was be honest too. And besides," he added, a playful glint in his eyes, "I figured if I didn't speak up, you might try to do all the heavy lifting yourself again, and we both know how well that works out."

Clara laughed, a light, relieved sound that surprised even herself. The tension that had coiled in her stomach for days began to unravel. It was the sound of trust being rebuilt, not just between her and the town, but between her and Jonah. His teasing, his easy camaraderie, was a balm to her soul. It was a testament to the connection they were forging, a connection built on shared vulnerability and a mutual desire for something real.

As the crowd began to disperse, buzzing with renewed purpose, a small group, including Mrs. Gable and Mr. Henderson, approached Clara and Jonah. Their faces were alight with a genuine enthusiasm that had been subdued by the council's rejection.

"That was wonderful, Clara!" Mrs. Gable exclaimed, her eyes twinkling. "And Jonah, your story... it gave me goosebumps. We all have our moments of doubt, don't we?"

Mr. Henderson nodded in agreement. "Indeed, we do. But it's what we do *after* those moments that truly matters. And tonight, you both showed us that the heart of Cedar Ridge is still beating strong." He looked from Clara to Jonah, a knowing smile on his face. "It's good to see you two working together. Really working together."

Clara felt a blush creep up her neck, but she met Mr. Henderson's gaze with a confident smile. "We're learning," she said softly, glancing at Jonah. "We're definitely learning."

Jonah added, his arm brushing lightly against Clara's, a gesture of unconscious solidarity, "We're a good team. And we have a lot of work to do."

The conversation flowed easily then, the initial awkwardness of the past few weeks dissolving in the shared energy of their collective goal. People offered ideas, suggestions, and commitments – a promise to organize a town-wide clean-up day, a baker who offered to donate goods for a fundraising bake sale, a carpenter who volunteered his skills for repairs. Each offer was a small victory, a tangible step forward, a thread woven into the growing tapestry of their renewed commitment.

Later that evening, as the last of the townspeople had departed, leaving behind the lingering scent of coffee and the quiet hum of a hall filled with renewed hope, Clara and Jonah found themselves alone. The hushed silence of the town hall felt different now, charged with the echoes of their conversations, the promise of their collective endeavor.

Clara turned to Jonah, her expression one of quiet gratitude. "I couldn't have done that without you," she admitted, her voice barely above a whisper. "Your words... they gave me the courage to be as honest as I was. And hearing you share your own experience... it made me feel less alone in all of this."

Jonah's gaze was warm and steady. He reached out, his fingers gently brushing a stray curl from her cheek. The contact sent a familiar shiver through her, a quiet acknowledgment of the growing connection between them. "You would have been fine, Clara," he said, his voice a low rumble. "You have a strength all your own. But yes," he admitted with a soft smile, "it's good to have someone watching your back. And knowing you're watching mine makes it even better."

He stepped a little closer, the space between them charged with an unspoken energy. "Seeing you up there tonight," he continued, his voice dropping, "seeing you lay it all out there... it was incredible. You've got this town in the palm of your hand, Clara. They believe in you."

Clara's heart fluttered at his words, at the genuine admiration in his eyes. "They believe in *us*," she corrected softly, her gaze meeting his. "And thanks to you, they believe in what we can do together." She looked around the hall, the place that had once felt like a symbol of her potential failure, now brimming with the promise of a shared future. "This grant... it was a setback. But maybe," she mused, "it was also an opportunity. An opportunity to truly connect with this town, to build something real, something that isn't dependent on outside funding, but on our own collective will."

Jonah nodded, his thumb gently stroking her cheek. "That's exactly it," he agreed. "The council wanted proof of community involvement. And tonight, we gave them that. And we gave ourselves that, too. We reminded ourselves what we're capable of when we stop trying to do it all alone." He paused, his gaze deepening. "And for me," he added, his voice laced with a quiet intensity, "it's been... refreshing. To see you open up, Clara. To see you let your guard down. It's been... really good."

The intimacy of the moment was palpable, a silent conversation passing between them. The challenges ahead were still significant, the work still daunting, but in that quiet space, amidst the fading echoes of the town hall meeting, a new foundation was being laid. It was a foundation of trust, of shared purpose, and of a burgeoning connection that promised to be as steadfast and enduring as the very community they were working to rebuild. The Grand Hall, with all its history and its future, was no longer just a project; it was becoming a symbol of their shared journey, a testament to the power of vulnerability, and the unwavering strength found in unwavering support.

The air in the town hall, still humming with the afterglow of Clara's heartfelt plea and Jonah's resonant testament, felt palpably lighter. The shift Clara had so desperately hoped for was not a sudden, dramatic upheaval, but a gentle, steady tide turning. It began with the quiet murmurs that followed their departure from the microphone, growing into a more robust hum of conversation as people gathered in small groups, their faces animated with a renewed sense of purpose. The initial hesitancy that had clouded many eyes was being replaced by a spark of determination, a flicker of 'what if' that was rapidly igniting into a flame of 'we can.'

Clara found herself caught in a swirl of interactions, each one a small confirmation of the momentum they had generated. Mrs. Gable, her eyes still a little moist but now shining with a practical resolve, approached Clara, a worn leather-bound notebook clutched in her hand. "Clara, dear," she began, her voice warm and familiar, "I've been thinking. The pantry, you know. It's going to get hectic with all the work parties and events we'll be organizing.

We'll need sustenance. I can coordinate the donations. I've got a system for it, have had for years, for the church bazaars and the harvest festivals. I can make sure everyone's fed, well-fed, and that nothing goes to waste. Just point me to where you'd like it set up." Her offer was practical, grounded, and perfectly in line with her nature, a comforting anchor in the sea of possibilities. Clara felt a genuine warmth spread through her at the ease with which Mrs. Gable had stepped into a role, transforming a potential logistical headache into a well-oiled operation before Clara had even fully processed the idea herself. It was the kind of proactive engagement that defined Cedar Ridge at its best.

Then came Mr. Henderson, his usual stoic demeanor softened by a smile that crinkled the corners of his eyes. He wasn't one for grand pronouncements, but his words carried the weight of years of dedication to the town. "Clara," he said, extending a calloused hand, "you've put a fire under us. And Jonah's right, we've all had our moments of feeling... sidelined. But that Grand Hall, it's seen a lot of life. My father helped lay some of those floorboards, you know. So, the lumber. For the repairs, the new supports you'll need, anything structural... I can talk to Ben over at the hardware store.

He'll give us a good price. Maybe even donate some of it. We'll make sure you get the best quality materials without breaking the bank." He clasped Jonah's shoulder briefly as he spoke, a silent acknowledgment of their shared commitment. The fact that Mr. Henderson, a man who usually operated with a quiet reserve, was already making connections and leveraging his influence spoke volumes about the shift in sentiment. It wasn't just about the building; it was about preserving their shared heritage, and Mr. Henderson was clearly invested in that.

As Clara and Jonah spoke with a few more residents, a group of boisterous teenagers, the very ones who had been idly kicking a soccer ball outside the hall just weeks prior, approached them. Their initial awkwardness was replaced by an eager energy. "Ms. Clara, Mr. Jonah," the tallest one, a boy named Liam, began, his voice still a little rough, "we heard what you said. About the cleanup. We're strong, and we've got plenty of energy. We can haul out the old stuff, move furniture, help with the landscaping around the hall. We're free most afternoons after school and all day Saturday. Just tell us what needs doing."

Their offers were genuine, unburdened by the complex histories and hesitations that might weigh on the older generation. They saw a project, a challenge, and a chance to contribute. It was a stark reminder that Cedar Ridge had a vibrant future, embodied in its youth, and that future was now looking towards the Grand Hall. Clara felt a pang of guilt for her initial assumptions about them, for seeing them as anything less than potential allies. Their eagerness was a powerful antidote to her lingering doubts.

The weight on Clara's shoulders, which had felt crushing just a few hours earlier, began to dissipate with each new offer, each shared memory, each hand extended in solidarity. The Grand Hall was no longer solely her burden, nor even just Jonah's. It was transforming, organically, into a communal project, a collective undertaking that resonated with the very spirit of Cedar Ridge. The council's challenge, intended to divide and perhaps even discourage, was inadvertently forging a new kind of unity.

Jonah, standing beside Clara, his presence a constant, reassuring force, observed the unfolding interactions with a quiet satisfaction. He saw the way Clara's shoulders had relaxed, the way her smile now reached her eyes, reflecting the genuine enthusiasm of the townspeople. He had known, deep down, that this was possible, that the heart of Cedar Ridge was still beating, but witnessing it firsthand was incredibly moving. He caught Clara's eye, a silent exchange passing between them – a shared understanding, a mutual acknowledgment of the profound shift occurring.

"It's happening, isn't it?" Clara murmured, a hint of wonder in her voice, as a small group of volunteers, armed with brooms and trash bags, began to gather near the entrance of the town hall, clearly eager to start the preliminary cleanup of the Grand Hall's exterior.

Jonah nodded, his gaze sweeping over the scene. "It is. It's always been here, Clara. That spirit. Sometimes it just needs a little nudge, a reminder of what it's capable of." He turned his attention back to her, his expression warm. "You gave them that nudge. And then you provided the spark. I just... fanned the flames a bit."

"You did more than fan them, Jonah," Clara replied, her voice soft. "You built a bonfire." She felt a surge of gratitude, not just for his words, but for his presence, for his willingness to stand by her, to believe in her when her own belief had wavered. His vulnerability earlier in the evening had opened the door for others, and his continued support was a constant reassurance.

As the evening wore on, the informal gatherings continued, spilling out onto the sidewalk in front of the town hall. People weren't just offering abstract support; they were identifying concrete needs and volunteering their specific skills. A young woman, Sarah Jenkins, who worked as a graphic designer in a neighboring town but lived in Cedar Ridge, approached Clara with a tablet in hand. "I saw you needed flyers, posters, something to get the word out about workdays and fundraisers," she explained, her eyes bright with enthusiasm.

"I can design them for you. Professionally. I can handle all the printing costs myself. I want this Hall to be saved, and I know good design can make a difference in getting people involved." Her offer was a godsend. Clara had been stressing about how to effectively communicate their plans, how to reach even more people, and Sarah's talent and generosity eliminated that worry entirely.

Later, a retired carpenter, a Mr. Silas Gable (no relation to Mrs. Gable, though they shared a similar warm disposition), who had been a quiet observer for most of the evening, approached Jonah. "Heard you talking about structural integrity," Silas said, his voice raspy but firm. "My hands aren't as steady as they used to be, but I know wood. I can tell you what's sound and what's rotten.

I can help supervise the younger folks, make sure they're doing it right, safely. Got a good set of tools in my workshop, too, if you need anything specific." Jonah's own experience with construction, while not as extensive as Silas's, allowed him to immediately recognize the value of such an offer. Silas wasn't just offering labor; he was offering decades of expertise, a living repository of the town's building history and wisdom.

The conversation flowed effortlessly between Clara, Jonah, and the various townspeople who came forward. Each interaction was a testament to the power of community, the deep-seated desire to protect and preserve what was meaningful. The Grand Hall, once a symbol of potential loss and division, was rapidly becoming a beacon of unity and shared purpose. The council's decision, which had initially felt like a insurmountable obstacle, was now being viewed as an opportunity – an opportunity to prove the resilience and collective strength of Cedar Ridge.

Clara noticed the subtle yet significant ways the town's perspective was shifting. The hesitations that had been evident at the initial town council meeting were slowly melting away. Those who had been uncertain, those who had been waiting to see if anyone else would step up, were now stepping forward themselves. It was as if Clara's and Jonah's vulnerability had given them permission to be vulnerable too, to express their own hopes and concerns, and to find solace and strength in shared commitment.

The young people, who Clara had initially seen as a potential challenge to engage, were proving to be some of the most enthusiastic participants. Liam and his friends weren't just offering to help with the cleanup; they were brainstorming fundraising ideas. "We could do a car wash," one of them suggested, "or maybe a bake sale, but like, a really big one. Or a talent show! Everyone in Cedar Ridge has some kind of talent, right?" Their energy was infectious, their ideas practical and achievable. Clara realized that these young people were not just the future of Cedar Ridge; they were an integral part of its present, and their commitment to the Grand Hall was a powerful statement of their connection to their hometown.

As the evening drew to a close, Clara and Jonah stood on the steps of the town hall, watching the last of the townspeople depart, their steps lighter, their conversations filled with plans and possibilities. The air was no longer heavy with uncertainty, but alive with the promise of shared endeavor. The Grand Hall was no longer just a project on a grant application; it was a living, breathing testament to the spirit of Cedar Ridge.

"You know," Clara said, turning to Jonah, a soft smile playing on her lips, "I was so focused on the grant, on the external validation. I thought if we could just get the funding, everything else would fall into place. But you were right. The real work, the real foundation, it's not about the money. It's about this." She gestured around them, to the quiet street now dotted with the warm glow of porch lights, to the distant sound of laughter from a neighbor's home. "It's about us. All of us."

Jonah's gaze met hers, and the warmth in his eyes was a silent echo of her sentiment. "That's the beauty of it, Clara," he said, his voice a low, steady rumble. "You came here to save a building, but I think you're helping to save something even more important. You're reminding us what it means to be a community, to rely on each other, to believe in something bigger than ourselves." He paused, a gentle smile gracing his lips. "And watching you do it, seeing you open your heart to this town... it's been one of the most inspiring things I've ever witnessed."

The sincerity in his voice sent a tremor through Clara, a familiar warmth that had nothing to do with the cool evening air. His belief in her, so consistently and openly expressed, was becoming a cornerstone of her own renewed confidence. She realized that their journey, much like the Grand Hall's restoration, was about more than just fixing something broken; it was about building something new, something stronger, from the ground up, on a foundation of trust and shared purpose. The path ahead would undoubtedly be filled with challenges, but with this newfound sense of unity, and with Jonah by her side, Clara felt a quiet, unshakeable certainty that Cedar Ridge, and the Grand Hall, were in good hands. The perspective had indeed shifted, and the future, once a hazy unknown, was beginning to take shape, illuminated by the collective will of a town ready to rebuild, together.

The initial wave of enthusiasm that had swept through Cedar Ridge following Clara and Jonah's town hall address was beginning to settle into a rhythm, a tangible momentum that required careful steering. The outpouring of support, while incredibly heartening, also presented a new set of challenges. Clara, accustomed to meticulously organized grant proposals and structured project timelines, found herself juggling a delightful but somewhat chaotic array of offers.

Mrs. Gable's pantry coordination was a godsend, but it also meant designating storage space and creating inventory lists. Mr. Henderson's promise of discounted lumber required precise measurements and material specifications. The teenagers' eagerness to help needed to be channeled into specific tasks with clear instructions. It was exactly the kind of community involvement she had dreamed of, yet it demanded a different kind of leadership than she was used to.

Jonah, ever the pragmatist with a deep understanding of the town's informal networks, saw this transition period as critical. He recognized Clara's inherent strength in strategic planning and her meticulous attention to detail, qualities essential for securing the long-term viability of the Grand Hall project. However, he also understood that Cedar Ridge operated on a foundation of relationships and immediate, actionable needs.

He knew that the town council, comprised of individuals who often favored established procedures, would eventually require more than just enthusiastic volunteer hours. They would need quantifiable progress, documented contributions, and a clear roadmap that demonstrated accountability. This was where his understanding of the town's practical workings and his own network could bridge the gap between community spirit and bureaucratic requirements.

Their first joint planning session was held in the quiet of Clara's borrowed office above the bakery. The afternoon sun cast long shadows across the worn wooden table, illuminating the scattered notes, sketches, and coffee cups that represented the nascent stages of their endeavor. Clara had come prepared with spreadsheets detailing potential renovation phases, projected costs, and timelines that would impress even the most seasoned grant administrator. Jonah, meanwhile, had a mental Rolodex of individuals, suppliers, and potential shortcuts, all gleaned from years of living and working in Cedar Ridge. He listened patiently as Clara laid out her structured approach, her voice clear and confident, outlining the need for a formal volunteer sign-up system, categorized tasks, and a system for tracking material donations.

"So, for the roof repairs," Clara explained, pointing to a section of her elaborate timeline, "we'll need to identify the specific sections requiring attention, estimate the amount of shingles needed, and then secure bids from at least three roofing contractors, even if we plan to do some of the work ourselves. We'll need to document every material purchase, every volunteer hour spent on that phase. It needs to be transparent and auditable." She looked at Jonah, her brow slightly furrowed, half-expecting him to find her approach too rigid.

Jonah, however, didn't dismiss her meticulously crafted plan. Instead, he leaned forward, his gaze thoughtful. "That's all good, Clara. Really good. And we'll need it for the grant. But 'auditable' doesn't always translate directly to 'done' in Cedar Ridge. Take the roof, for example. Mr. Abernathy, up on Maple Street? His family's been in the roofing business for three generations. He's got a stack of perfectly good leftover shingles from jobs he's done this year. He's not going to bid on a contract; he's just going to say, 'Here, take 'em, they're just gathering dust.' That's a material donation, a significant one, but it won't fit neatly into a 'bid from three contractors' box."

Clara paused, considering his words. She had been so focused on the formal channels that the informal, but equally valuable, contributions had been harder for her to quantify. "So, how do we account for that?" she asked, genuinely curious. "How do we integrate Mr. Abernathy's generosity into a plan that the council can understand and approve?"

"That's where we merge," Jonah said, a hint of a smile playing on his lips. "You provide the framework, the structure that shows we're organized and serious. I'll work on the ground, identifying those 'dusty stacks' of resources. My job will be to connect the dots between what people are willing to offer and what we actually need, and then translate that into your documentation. So, Mr. Abernathy's shingles become a documented donation. We'll get a letter from him, you'll log it, and that reduces our projected material cost. I'll talk to him, get the details, maybe even arrange for someone to help him haul them over to the Hall. You make sure the paperwork reflects it."

This was the crux of their collaboration. Clara's structured methodology, designed for external validation and long-term sustainability, could seem overwhelming and impersonal to the townspeople. Jonah's intuitive, relationship-based approach, while highly effective in galvanizing immediate support, lacked the formal rigor required by institutions like the town council. By working together, they could create a hybrid strategy that leveraged the strengths of both.

"Okay," Clara conceded, a spark of understanding igniting in her eyes. "So, for every concrete offer, every donation of time, materials, or expertise, we need a process. I'll create a template for a 'Community Contribution Record.' It will need the donor's name, the nature of the contribution, an estimated value if possible, and a signed acknowledgment. That way, when we present our progress reports, we can show not just money spent, but resources gained through community effort."

Jonah nodded enthusiastically. "Exactly. And I'll be the one out there, collecting those signatures. I'll talk to Mrs. Gable about her pantry system, ask her to keep a log of donated food items and their estimated retail value. I'll explain to the teenagers that while their energy is invaluable, we need to assign them specific tasks with clear start and end times, so we can track progress. Maybe we can create a 'Task Board' in the Hall itself, where they can sign up for specific jobs each day."

He paused, then added, "And for the more technical aspects, like structural assessments or electrical work, we need to be smart. You're right, we'll need professional input eventually. But for now, I know a few retired electricians and carpenters who might be willing to do a preliminary assessment, a 'goodwill check,' as they call it. They won't charge, but they'll be happy to lend their expertise, and their written opinion will carry weight with the council, especially if it's on official letterhead."

This realization was a turning point for Clara. She began to see how her structured approach and Jonah's flexible network could not only coexist but actively enhance each other. His ability to tap into the town's goodwill and personal connections meant that resources would flow in more readily. Her ability to document, categorize, and present these contributions in a professional manner would ensure that their efforts were recognized and valued by the town council and any potential funding bodies.

"This is... actually incredibly efficient," Clara admitted, a genuine smile replacing her earlier uncertainty. "My biggest fear was that the council would see our community-driven approach as disorganized or unprofessional. But if we can quantify and document everything, if we can demonstrate that this grassroots support translates into tangible progress and cost savings, then we're not just building a hall; we're building a case for why it matters."

Jonah chuckled, a warm, rumbling sound. "That's the idea. We're showing them that the heart of Cedar Ridge is beating, and it's strong. And that strength can be a powerful asset. Think of it this way: you're building the scaffolding, making sure the entire structure is sound and meets all the codes. I'm out there, making sure the best materials and the most skilled hands are available to help build it, and then I'm bringing those pieces back to you to be integrated."

Their planning sessions evolved from this initial discussion into a dynamic exchange of ideas. Clara would present a logistical challenge – for instance, the need for a temporary weatherproofing solution for the west-facing wall before the rainy season. Jonah would then brainstorm potential solutions based on local resources – perhaps a retired farmer who had surplus tarpaulin, or a group of teenagers looking for a project that didn't require specialized tools. Clara would then formalize the need, specifying dimensions and expected duration, and Jonah would go out and secure the resource, returning with a signed acknowledgment from the farmer or the teenager's team leader.

This collaborative approach extended to how they communicated with the town. Clara began drafting clear, concise updates for a new section of the town's website, detailing upcoming workdays, specific needs, and progress made. Jonah, meanwhile, would use his personal connections, phone calls, and casual conversations at the diner to ensure that everyone, including those less digitally inclined, was kept in the loop. He'd translate Clara's formal announcements into language that resonated with long-time residents, adding personal anecdotes and reassurances.

One afternoon, while discussing the need for volunteers for a major cleanup day, Clara expressed her concern about turnout. "We advertised it everywhere, but what if only a handful of people show up? The council will see that as a lack of public support."

Jonah's response was immediate. "That's where the personal touch comes in. I've already spoken to the families of about twenty of those teenagers you were so worried about. Their parents remember the Hall from their own childhoods. They're excited to see it revitalized. I've also talked to the folks at the senior center. They can't do the heavy lifting, but they've offered to provide refreshments for the volunteers, organize a bake sale to raise some funds on the day, and even help with sorting through salvaged materials. It's not just about putting up a flyer, Clara. It's about making calls, having conversations, reminding people what this place means to them."

Clara found herself increasingly relying on Jonah's insights. She learned to anticipate the kinds of informal resources that might be available and to frame her requests in a way that resonated with the community's shared history and pride. She began to understand that the council's requirements, while seemingly bureaucratic, were often a reflection of a need for demonstrable commitment and a clear plan for stewardship. By integrating Jonah's community-focused approach with her own structured methodology, they were creating something stronger than either could achieve alone.

The joint planning sessions became more fluid. Clara would bring a problem, Jonah would offer a community-based solution, and together they would refine it into a concrete action plan. For example, when discussing the need for new interior paint, Clara identified the required quantity and quality. Jonah, knowing the local hardware store owner, Mr. Peterson, had a reputation for being community-minded, suggested approaching him directly for a donation or a significant discount. Clara then drafted a formal proposal to Mr. Peterson, outlining the project's significance and the benefits of his involvement, while Jonah simultaneously dropped by the store to chat with him informally, reinforcing the message and emphasizing the town's collective enthusiasm. This dual approach, blending the official with the personal, proved remarkably effective. Mr. Peterson, influenced by both the well-crafted proposal and Jonah's personal appeal, agreed to donate a substantial portion of the paint needed, a contribution that significantly boosted their budget.

As they continued to refine their strategy, Clara realized that their differing perspectives were not a point of conflict, but a source of innovation. Jonah's innate understanding of the town's social fabric allowed him to anticipate potential roadblocks and leverage existing relationships. Clara's analytical mind provided the structure and accountability needed to transform good intentions into tangible results. This synergy was the key to bridging the ideological divide that had so often characterized town council meetings and community initiatives in the past. They were proving, through their actions, that a project could be both deeply rooted in community spirit and rigorously planned for long-term success. The

Grand Hall, once a symbol of division, was becoming a testament to the power of their combined vision, a beacon of what Cedar Ridge could achieve when its past and future, its heart and its structure, were brought together in harmony.

The air in Cedar Ridge, once thick with the scent of neglect and forgotten dreams, was now alive with a vibrant hum. It was the sound of hammers striking wood, of laughter echoing through dusty rafters, of countless feet treading the worn floorboards of the Grand Hall, each step a testament to a community reawakening. The initial surge of support, sparked by Clara and Jonah's town hall address, had not dwindled into a ripple; it had blossomed into a full-fledged tide, carrying with it a palpable sense of optimism. Clara found herself marveling at the sheer volume of hands eager to help, the sheer volume of hearts invested in this shared vision. The Grand Hall, a skeletal frame of its former glory just weeks before, was beginning to shed its shroud of decay, its windows, once opaque with grime, now gleaming as volunteers meticulously cleaned them, letting in shafts of sunlight that illuminated the dust motes dancing like tiny, hopeful sprites.

Mrs. Gable's pantry was no longer just a collection of wilting cans; it was a well-organized hub of sustenance, a testament to her tireless efforts and the town's generosity. Every donated loaf of bread, every carefully packed box of dry goods, was meticulously logged by Clara, her spreadsheets now a vibrant tapestry of community contributions. The lumber Mr. Henderson had pledged arrived in steady streams, not just as raw materials, but as meticulously measured planks, each one a silent promise of structural integrity. Clara, who had once found solace in the predictable rhythm of grant proposals, now navigated a more fluid, dynamic landscape, a symphony of diverse talents and willing hands. She had envisioned this kind of involvement, of course, but witnessing it unfold was an experience far richer and more profound than any imagined scenario. It was a constant dance between structure and spontaneity, a beautiful ballet of organization and heartfelt enthusiasm.

Jonah, with his innate understanding of Cedar Ridge's unspoken language and its intricate web of relationships, saw the transformation with a keen, appreciative eye. He understood that the town council, with its penchant for order and its adherence to protocol, needed more than just spirited volunteers; they needed a clear, demonstrable narrative of progress. Clara's meticulous planning provided the framework, the irrefutable evidence of diligence and foresight. His role, he knew, was to bridge that formal structure with the town's deeply ingrained sense of community. He was the conduit, the translator, ensuring that the spontaneous acts of kindness and the informal exchanges of resources were recognized and integrated into the larger, auditable plan.

Their joint planning sessions, once confined to Clara's borrowed office, now often spilled out into the very spaces they were working to restore. The scent of fresh wood mingled with the lingering aroma of old polish, a unique perfume of rebirth. Today, they stood near the grand staircase, its once-splintered banister now smooth and gleaming under Jonah's careful sanding, Clara's notes spread on a makeshift table nearby. The afternoon sun, slanting through the newly cleaned windows, cast a warm glow, highlighting the dust motes that danced with renewed vigor.

"The electrical rewiring is going to be a bigger undertaking than we initially thought," Clara said, tapping a finger against a diagram detailing the Hall's internal layout. "We've got the wiring and some of the basic fixtures donated, thanks to Mr. Silas and his team from the electrical supply company, but the actual installation requires a licensed electrician. I've reached out to a few firms, but their quotes are... steep. Even with the donated materials, it's a significant chunk of our budget."

Jonah nodded, his gaze sweeping over the intricate network of wires and conduits Clara had sketched. He understood the necessity of professional expertise. "Mr. Silas was amazing," he conceded. "And he's promised to help us with the planning and oversee the actual delivery of the supplies, but you're right, the labor is the sticking point. Hmm." He paused, his mind already sifting through the town's hidden talents. "You know, old Mr. Henderson, the one who donated the lumber? His son, Mark, used to be an electrician. He moved away years ago, got a good job out west, but I heard he's back in town for a while, visiting his folks. He's not doing it professionally anymore, but he's still got the skills. He's also got a soft spot for this place; his parents had their wedding reception here, back in the day."

Clara's eyes brightened. This was precisely the kind of connection Jonah excelled at, the kind that bypassed formal channels and tapped directly into the town's history and sentiment. "You think he'd be willing to help?" she asked, a hopeful lilt in her voice. "Even just for a few days? We could frame it as a 'community service' opportunity, maybe?"

"I don't know about 'service'," Jonah chuckled, a warm sound that resonated in the cavernous space. "But I know Mark. He's a good guy. He remembers this Hall as a place where good things happened. I'll give him a call. See if he's open to coming by, taking a look, maybe lending a hand for a bit. It might not cover the whole job, but even a few days of his expertise could save us a significant amount. And his word on the quality of the work, even if it's informal, would carry a lot of weight with the council. They know Mark Henderson, they know his family."

"That would be incredible, Jonah," Clara said, her voice filled with genuine gratitude. She jotted down a note, a small 'Henderson – Electrician?' beside the budget line item for electrical work. "It's these connections, these personal histories, that make Cedar Ridge unique. I'm so used to the impersonal nature of grant applications, where the strength of your proposal is measured by quantifiable data and statistical projections. Here, it's about relationships, about shared memories."

"And you're learning to leverage that," Jonah said, his gaze meeting hers. There was a new depth to their partnership, a comfortable rhythm that had emerged from the shared challenges. They had weathered storms, both literal and figurative, and in doing so, their trust had solidified, their respect had deepened. The initial hesitations, the subtle differences in their approaches, had smoothed out, replaced by an understanding of how their individual strengths complemented each other. Clara's meticulous planning, her ability to anticipate every contingency and document every detail, provided the bedrock. Jonah's intuitive grasp of the town's social fabric, his ability to connect with people on a personal level, was the vibrant, ever-flowing current that kept the project alive and energized.

"It's you," Clara admitted, a genuine smile gracing her lips. "You make it... accessible. You translate my spreadsheets into stories. You turn my proposed budget cuts into opportunities for community generosity. I was so focused on the 'how,' on the technicalities and the logistics, that I almost forgot the 'why' – the people, the shared history, the sense of belonging that this Hall represents."

"And you," Jonah countered, his voice soft, "you give us the 'how.' You ensure that when those stories are told, they're backed by tangible progress, by a plan that's not just passionate, but practical. You're building the trust with the council, with potential funders, by showing them we're serious, that we're organized, that we're not just dreaming, we're building. We're a team, Clara. You build the blueprint, I find the materials and the builders, and together, we're making this Hall stand again."

The sentiment was echoed in the very atmosphere of the Hall. Gone was the pervasive quiet of abandonment. It was replaced by a cacophony of activity, a joyful noise that spoke of renewed hope and unwavering determination. On any given day, a steady stream of volunteers, from teenagers with boundless energy to seasoned craftsmen with decades of experience, could be seen bustling through the doors. The local scout troop had adopted the task of refurbishing the old park benches that had once graced the Hall's exterior, their small hands carefully sanding and repainting, each stroke imbued with a sense of pride. The knitting circle, led by Mrs. Gable herself, had organized a campaign to create new curtains for the smaller meeting rooms, their needles clicking a steady rhythm, weaving together threads of community spirit.

Clara, armed with her clipboard and a smile that seemed to have permanently settled on her face, moved amongst them, offering words of encouragement, clarifying tasks, and ensuring that every contribution, no matter how small, was acknowledged. She'd learned to anticipate the ebb and flow of volunteer energy, to schedule the more physically demanding tasks for the mornings and the lighter, more social activities for the afternoons. She'd even initiated a "Volunteer Spotlight" initiative, featuring a different individual or group each week in the town newsletter, highlighting their specific contribution and the personal connection they felt to the project. It was a small touch, but one that fostered a sense of individual value and collective achievement.

Jonah, meanwhile, was the omnipresent force on the ground, his worn flannel shirt perpetually smudged with sawdust or paint. He was the one offering a steady hand to a wobbly ladder, the one who knew who had a surplus of roofing nails in their shed, the one who could convince Mr. Abernathy to lend his trusty wheelbarrow for the tenth time that week. He possessed an uncanny ability to read the room, to sense when a volunteer needed a break, a word of encouragement, or simply a friendly ear. He'd often lead impromptu singalongs during lunch breaks, his deep baritone a familiar anchor that brought a sense of camaraderie and shared purpose.

One crisp autumn afternoon, as they stood on the newly repaired balcony, overlooking the bustling town square, Clara expressed a quiet awe. "It's... more than I ever imagined," she confessed, her gaze sweeping over the scene below, the vibrant activity within the Hall a stark contrast to the quiet decay that had once defined it. "I remember when we first walked through here, the silence was almost deafening. It felt like a tomb. Now..."

"Now it feels like a heartbeat," Jonah finished, his voice resonating with a profound understanding. "It's the sound of Cedar Ridge remembering who it is, and who it can be. The Hall was always more than just a building, Clara. It was the heart of this town, the place where memories were made, where celebrations were held, where the community came together. And for a while, that heart was silent. But it was never truly gone. It was just... waiting."

"And we're helping it beat again," Clara said, a sense of profound purpose settling within her. The weight of responsibility, which had once felt like an unbearable burden, now felt like a privilege. She had learned to delegate, to trust the skills and enthusiasm of others, and in doing so, she had freed herself to focus on the bigger picture, on the overarching vision.

Jonah inclined his head, a gentle smile playing on his lips. "We are. And the best part is, we're not doing it alone. Look around, Clara." He gestured with a sweep of his hand towards the Hall, where the rhythmic thud of a hammer could be heard, punctuated by bursts of laughter. "Every single person here, they're not just volunteers. They're owners. They're stakeholders. They're invested, heart and soul. And that, my friend, that's a foundation stronger than any concrete. That's what makes this project, and this town, truly resilient."

The renewed hope wasn't just an abstract concept; it was a tangible force, visible in the determined set of every jaw, in the bright spark in every eye. The Grand Hall, once a symbol of Cedar Ridge's fading glory, was now a beacon of its future, a testament to what could be achieved when a community rediscovered its shared purpose, guided by a blend of meticulous planning and heartfelt connection. Clara and Jonah, standing side by side amidst the vibrant chaos, felt the exhilaration of genuine collaboration, a bond forged in shared adversity and cemented by the burgeoning possibility of success.

The task ahead was still immense, the challenges still present, but the spirit of Cedar Ridge had been rekindled, and with it, a renewed determination to see this dream rise from the ashes, stronger and more beautiful than ever before. The very air crackled with this revitalized energy, a testament to the fact that when people come together with a common goal, driven by shared memories and a hopeful vision, even the most dilapidated structures can be brought back to life, echoing with the vibrant pulse of a community's spirit. The journey had been arduous, marked by moments of doubt and setbacks, but each obstacle overcome had only served to strengthen their resolve, and the palpable sense of optimism that now pervaded Cedar Ridge was a testament to their unwavering commitment.

CHAPTER NINE

The Community Rallies

The air in Cedar Ridge pulsed with a different kind of energy now. It wasn't just the rhythmic clang of hammers or the hum of spirited conversations; it was the palpable excitement that hummed beneath every interaction, the shared anticipation of something truly grand. The Grand Hall was no longer just a restoration project; it was becoming a symbol, a beacon, and its resurgence was to be celebrated with an event that would capture the heart of the community and showcase its renewed spirit to the wider world.

The idea had been sparked in one of their late-night planning sessions, born from Clara's meticulous budget projections and Jonah's intuitive understanding of what truly made Cedar Ridge tick. They needed more than just donations; they needed an experience, a demonstration of unity that would not only raise funds but also rekindle pride.

"We need to put Cedar Ridge on the map again, Clara," Jonah had said, his eyes alight with an idea that was already taking shape. "Not just for the Hall, but for who we are. People have forgotten how vibrant this town can be. We need a day where everyone comes out, where the town square is alive, where we can show off what we're made of."

And so, the Grand Fundraising Event was conceived. It was to be more than a simple bake sale or a car wash; it was to be a festival, a full-blown celebration of Cedar Ridge's comeback. Jonah, with his innate flair for the dramatic and his deep well of connections, took the reins on the creative vision. He envisioned a town square transformed, a kaleidoscope of color and sound.

His mind conjured images of local bands whose music would fill the air, of artisans showcasing their crafts, their stalls brimming with handcrafted treasures, and of course, the quintessential small-town staple – a chili cook-off, where friendly rivalries would simmer and tantalizing aromas would draw crowds. He spoke of string lights draped between trees, of laughter echoing through the night, of a shared experience that would leave everyone feeling a little closer, a little prouder.

Clara, ever the pragmatist, embraced the vision but immediately began to map out the logistical labyrinth it entailed. Permits, insurance, vendor coordination, security, sanitation – the list was as long as it was daunting. Yet, there was a glint in her eye, a spark of challenge met. She saw the potential, the immense power of such an event to galvanize the town and to fill the coffers needed for the Hall's final push. Her spreadsheets, once filled with projected costs for lumber and wiring, now accounted for stage rentals, sound systems, and the licensing fees for public gatherings.

"We'll need to start early, Jonah," she'd cautioned, her finger tracing a line on a draft schedule. "The town council will want detailed proposals. And we need to make sure we have enough volunteers to manage everything. This isn't just a fun day out; it has to be a flawlessly executed event."

"And it will be," Jonah had assured her, his confidence unwavering. "Because everyone in this town wants this Hall to be saved. They'll step up. We just need to give them a reason, a focal point, and a clear plan. You build the framework, Clara, and I'll fill it with life."

He wasn't wrong. The announcement of the Grand Fundraising Event spread through Cedar Ridge like wildfire, igniting a collective enthusiasm that Clara had only dared to dream of. Jonah's proposal for the town square's transformation was met with cheers, the idea of a vibrant festival a welcome antidote to the quiet resignation that had begun to settle over the town in recent years.

He presented his vision to the town council with his usual charisma, weaving a narrative of community spirit, economic revitalization, and a spectacular celebration of Cedar Ridge's resilience. He spoke of the acoustic duo, The Willow Creek Ramblers, whose heartfelt folk melodies had serenaded countless local gatherings; of Sarah Jenkins, whose pottery was renowned throughout the county; and of old Jedediah, whose secret chili recipe had won him bragging rights for over a decade.

Clara, meanwhile, was a whirlwind of activity behind the scenes. She meticulously drafted the permit applications, her clear, concise language leaving no room for doubt. She liaised with local businesses, securing sponsorships and in-kind donations. The bakery offered to donate a portion of their day's sales, the hardware store pledged a significant amount of disposable goods for the food vendors, and even the usually taciturn Mrs. Peterson from the antique shop offered to loan out a collection of charming vintage decorations.

Clara's organizational skills were the bedrock upon which Jonah's vibrant vision was being built. She created volunteer sign-up sheets, assigning specific roles and responsibilities, ensuring that no task, however small, was overlooked. She organized a pre-event meeting for all vendors, outlining health and safety regulations and providing them with maps of their designated spaces. Her detailed budget was a masterpiece of fiscal responsibility, showing a clear path from projected income to essential expenditures, with a healthy allocation for the Grand Hall's restoration fund.

The days leading up to the event were a blur of organized chaos. Jonah, with a team of eager volunteers, transformed the usually quiet town square. Stages were erected, each one designed to showcase a different facet of local talent. The main stage, a sturdy wooden platform built by a team of volunteers from the local construction company, would host the musical acts. Smaller booths were set up for the artisans, their wares ranging from intricate quilts and handcrafted jewelry to whimsical garden ornaments and homemade jams. The air grew thick with the scent of sawdust and fresh paint, but also with the sweet anticipation of what was to come. String lights, salvaged and refurbished by the scout troop, were strung between lampposts and trees, promising a magical ambiance once dusk settled.

Clara, armed with clipboards and walkie-talkies, was the central nervous system of the operation. She coordinated deliveries, resolved minor crises with a calm demeanor, and ensured that every volunteer knew their role. She'd even managed to secure a few extra porta-potties from a neighboring town, a logistical victory that earned her a grateful nod from Jonah. She learned to anticipate potential problems, to have backup plans for backup plans, and to trust the people around her. The initial apprehension she'd felt about such a large-scale event had been replaced by a quiet confidence, a belief in the collective power of Cedar Ridge.

The chili cook-off, under Jonah's enthusiastic direction, became a legendary undertaking. Over twenty contestants vied for the coveted "Golden Ladle" award. There was Jedediah, the reigning champion, with his slow-simmered beef and bean concoction; young Maria Rodriguez, whose fiery jalapeño chili promised a kick; and the Henderson brothers, who presented a surprisingly delicate white chicken chili. Each contestant was provided with a designated cooking station, complete with a propane burner and a small table for their ingredients and secret spices. The aroma of simmering chili began to fill the air hours before the official judging, a tantalizing prelude to the main event. Tasters, armed with small cups and spoons, eagerly sampled their way through the competition, their faces a mixture of delight and thoughtful deliberation.

"This is what it's all about, isn't it?" Jonah said, leaning against a lamppost, his eyes sweeping over the bustling scene. He'd traded his usual flannel for a clean, pressed shirt, but a faint smudge of paint still adorned his cheek, a testament to his hands-on approach. "Seeing everyone come together, sharing their passions, their talents. It's more than just raising money for the Hall; it's about reminding ourselves what a special place Cedar Ridge is."

Clara smiled, a genuine, unrestrained smile that reached her eyes. She held a clipboard, but her gaze was fixed on the vibrant tapestry of the town square. "It's incredible, Jonah. I've never seen anything like it. The energy is... infectious." She paused, watching a group of children chase balloons near the main stage. "I was so focused on the spreadsheets and the budgets, on making sure everything was accounted for, that I almost forgot the intangible element. The joy. The sense of belonging."

"That's my job," Jonah quipped, a playful glint in his eyes. "To add the intangible. You provide the solid foundation, Clara, and I get to paint the sky with stars."

As the afternoon sun began its slow descent, casting long shadows across the square, the festival reached its zenith. The first band, a lively bluegrass ensemble, took to the main stage, their spirited tunes drawing smiles and spontaneous dancing from the crowd. Children, their faces painted with whimsical designs, weaved through the legs of adults, their laughter mingling with the music. Artisan stalls reported brisk sales, their owners beaming as they wrapped up purchases for satisfied customers. The scent of popcorn and grilled sausages mingled with the ever-present aroma of chili, creating a sensory feast.

Clara found herself drawn to the craft stalls. She admired a hand-knitted scarf, its intricate pattern a testament to hours of patient work. She spoke with the artisan, a young woman named Emily who had recently moved to Cedar Ridge. Emily explained that she'd contributed a portion of her stall's earnings to the Grand Hall fund, her voice filled with a quiet pride. "It's important," Emily had said simply. "This Hall represents the heart of the town. I wanted to be a part of bringing it back."

Jonah, meanwhile, had his hands full with the chili cook-off. He announced the finalists, his voice booming through the portable microphone, and then introduced the judges – the mayor, the owner of the local diner, and a renowned food critic who had driven over from the neighboring city, intrigued by the buzz surrounding Cedar Ridge's revival. The tension in the air was thick as the judges deliberated, their faces serious as they sampled the final contenders.

The evening was drawing in, and the string lights began to twinkle, casting a warm, magical glow over the square. Families spread out blankets on the grass, sharing picnic dinners and enjoying the festive atmosphere. The second band, a more mellow acoustic group, took the stage, their soulful melodies providing a soothing backdrop to the fading light.

Clara found Jonah standing near the edge of the crowd, his arms crossed, a contented smile on his face. The day had been a resounding success. The fundraising thermometer, displayed prominently near the main stage, showed a significant increase, and the sheer volume of people who had turned out was a testament to the community's engagement.

"We did it, Jonah," Clara said softly, a sense of quiet triumph settling over her. "We really did it."

He turned to her, his smile widening. "We did. And look at them, Clara. Look at this town. It's alive again." He gestured with his head towards the scene unfolding before them – laughter, music, the shared enjoyment of a community coming together. "This is the real treasure we're unearthing. This spirit. This connection."

"It's more than I ever imagined," she admitted, her voice filled with a profound sense of gratitude. "I was so focused on the mechanics of rebuilding, on the tangible structure of the Hall, that I sometimes lost sight of what it truly represents."

"And I sometimes get lost in the spectacle," Jonah admitted, his gaze meeting hers. "The music, the food, the atmosphere. But you always bring me back to the purpose. You're the anchor, Clara. You make sure the magic has a solid foundation."

He took a step closer, the glow of the string lights illuminating their faces. The noise of the festival seemed to fade, leaving them in a quiet bubble of shared accomplishment and something more, something that had been building between them, subtly, over weeks of shared challenges and triumphs. The air between them seemed to thrum with an unspoken awareness, a gentle recognition of the partnership they had forged.

"Thank you, Clara," he said, his voice low and sincere. "For making this happen. For believing in this town, and in me."

Clara felt a warmth spread through her, a feeling far more potent than the ambient glow of the festival lights. "Thank *you*, Jonah. For showing me what's possible when you combine passion with purpose, and when you have a community that's willing to rally."

As the music swelled and the laughter continued, Clara and Jonah stood together, a silent acknowledgment of their shared journey and the bright future they were building, not just for the Grand Hall, but for Cedar Ridge itself. The festival was a resounding success, a vibrant testament to the town's indomitable spirit, and a significant step forward in their ambitious endeavor. The money raised was substantial, exceeding even Clara's most optimistic projections, but the true win was the rekindled sense of unity and pride that now permeated every corner of Cedar Ridge. The Grand Hall was no longer a forgotten relic; it was a symbol of hope, a testament to their collective strength, and the Grand Fundraising Event had been the dazzling spark that illuminated its path forward.

The sheer volume of contributions that began to arrive at the Grand Hall was nothing short of astonishing. It was a testament to the power of a shared vision, a collective desire to see Cedar Ridge not only restored but thriving. The initial trickle of donations, which had been steady but manageable, transformed into a joyous deluge in the days following the successful fundraising event. Clara, armed with her detailed inventory sheets and a newfound, almost exhilarating sense of purpose, found herself coordinating a logistical ballet that would have impressed even the most seasoned event planner.

The first wave came from the local agricultural backbone of Cedar Ridge. Farmer McGregor, a man whose weathered hands had coaxed life from the rich soil for generations, arrived with a truck overflowing with crates of ripe tomatoes, crisp lettuces, and plump zucchini. He'd declared, with a gruff but hearty laugh, that his harvest was too abundant to sit idle, and a good portion of it would go to nourishing the town. Following his lead, the Miller family, known for their sweet corn and tender green beans, sent their bounty in a similarly generous fashion.

Even the usually reserved old Mr. Henderson, whose apple orchard was legendary, sent over three bushels of his finest Honeycrisps, a rare treat for anyone in Cedar Ridge. These weren't just donations; they were edible embodiments of the land, the sweat, and the unwavering spirit of the farmers who sustained the town. Clara meticulously logged each item, noting the freshness and abundance, a silent prayer of gratitude forming on her lips with every entry. The aroma of fresh earth and sun-ripened produce filled the air around the Hall, a vibrant counterpoint to the lingering scent of sawdust and popcorn from the festival.

Then came the contributions from the town's commercial heart. The Cedar Ridge General Store, a fixture on Main Street for as long as anyone could remember, delivered a veritable cornucopia of non-perishable goods. Boxes upon boxes of pasta, rice, canned vegetables, and soups were stacked precariously in the loading bay, their labels a colorful testament to the store's commitment. Mrs. Gable, the owner, a woman of sharp wit and a surprisingly soft heart, personally oversaw the delivery, her usual stern expression softened by a genuine smile. "It's the least we can do, Clara," she'd said, her voice carrying a touch of pride. "Seeing everyone pull together... it's something special. We wanted to do our part to keep that momentum going."

The hardware store, which had so readily supplied goods for the event setup, now contributed cases of bottled water and cleaning supplies, recognizing the practical needs of a well-stocked pantry. Even the local bakery, which had already donated generously to the festival, sent over a selection of day-old breads and pastries, still perfectly good and a welcome addition for those who might not otherwise have access to such treats. Each donation, no matter the size, was a brick in the foundation of this burgeoning support system.

But perhaps the most heartwarming contributions were those that came directly from the residents themselves. Inspired by the success of the festival and the tangible good it had brought about, people began to open their cupboards and their hearts. Small, carefully folded notes accompanied many of these donations, offering words of encouragement and hope. There were jars of homemade preserves – strawberry, plum, and even a few adventurous elderberry concoctions – lovingly labeled and sealed with wax. Knitted scarves and mittens, their fibers soft and warm, appeared, a silent promise of comfort against the approaching chill. Hand-stitched dish towels, their patterns simple but cheerful, were folded neatly into bags.

One elderly gentleman, who lived alone and rarely ventured out, presented Clara with a meticulously carved wooden bird, its delicate wings poised for flight. He'd spoken quietly, his voice raspy with age, about how he remembered the Hall being a place of gathering and celebration for his own family, and how he wanted to contribute to its revival in any way he could. Clara found herself deeply moved by such personal expressions of generosity; they spoke of a deeper connection to the Hall and to the town's shared history.

The task of organizing this influx of generosity fell to Clara, Jonah, and a growing army of enthusiastic volunteers. The Grand Hall, which had so recently been a hive of festival preparations, now transformed into a bustling hub of organization. The main floor, cleared of temporary staging and vendor booths, became a vast sorting and stocking area. Long tables were set up, each designated for a specific category of goods: produce, canned goods, dry goods, baked goods, toiletries, and clothing.

Jonah, his usual boisterous energy now channeled into a more focused, methodical approach, took charge of the physical labor. He and a team of burly volunteers, many of whom had helped with the Hall's initial renovations, moved boxes with practiced ease, their movements efficient and coordinated. They built sturdy shelving units from salvaged lumber, creating order from the chaos of incoming supplies. Jonah, with a grin that stretched across his paint-smudged face, directed the placement of each shelf, ensuring that the layout was logical and accessible.

"We want people to be able to find what they need easily, Clara," he'd explained, gesturing with a hammer. "No one should feel lost or overwhelmed when they come here for help." He'd even devised a simple color-coded system for the shelves, using painted strips of wood, to make navigation even more intuitive.

Clara, meanwhile, was the conductor of this benevolent orchestra. With her clipboard in hand, she moved between the tables, overseeing the sorting, checking expiration dates on canned goods, and ensuring that the fresh produce was stored correctly to maximize its longevity. She trained new volunteers with patience and clarity, explaining the importance of each task. There was Mrs. Gable's daughter, who volunteered her afternoons after her shift at the General Store, meticulously organizing the toiletries.

Young Tommy Peterson, who had been so eager to help with the festival decorations, now helped unpack boxes of donated socks and hats, his small hands surprisingly adept at folding and stacking. Even Sarah Jenkins, the talented potter whose creations had graced the artisan stalls, spent her spare hours carefully unpacking and arranging delicate preserves, her gentle touch ensuring nothing was broken.

The sheer variety of donations meant that Clara's inventory sheets grew exponentially. She meticulously cataloged every item, from a single can of beans to a dozen loaves of bread. She created a digital database, a testament to her foresight, that would allow them to track stock levels and identify immediate needs. This wasn't just about collecting items; it was about creating a sustainable system, a reliable resource for the community. She worked late into the evenings, the soft glow of a single lamp illuminating her focused expression as she cross-referenced incoming items with her ever-expanding list.

Jonah would often find her there, surrounded by towering stacks of boxes, a faint weariness etched on her features, but a deep satisfaction radiating from her. He'd bring her a cup of coffee, brewed from the communal coffee maker they'd set up, and sit beside her, his presence a silent reassurance. "You're building something incredible here, Clara," he'd say, his voice soft, a rare moment of quiet contemplation in his usually energetic demeanor. "More than just a pantry. You're building hope."

Clara would look up, a genuine smile gracing her lips, the exhaustion momentarily forgotten. "It's because of you, Jonah. Because you made everyone believe that this was possible. That *we* were possible. And because of all these people," she gestured around them at the organized shelves, the diligently working volunteers, "who stepped up when they were needed most. The Hall truly is becoming a hub, isn't it? A place where we can all support each other."

The pantry itself was a marvel of efficiency and care. The fresh produce, carefully sorted and displayed on long, cool tables, looked vibrant and inviting. The canned goods were arranged by type, their labels facing forward, creating neat rows of sustenance. Shelves dedicated to personal care items were stocked with soaps, shampoos, toothbrushes, and toothpaste, along with gently used clothing, sorted by size and type. There was even a small corner designated for children's items – diapers, baby formula, and a few carefully chosen donated toys. Each section was clearly marked with signs Clara had designed herself, simple and clear, ensuring that anyone needing assistance could easily find what they were looking for.

The process wasn't without its challenges, of course. There were the occasional mislabeled items, the unexpected spoilage of a few crates of produce despite their best efforts, and the constant need to replenish supplies as the pantry began to serve its purpose. But with each minor setback, the team learned and adapted. Jonah's organizational skills, combined with Clara's meticulous planning, created a system that was both robust and responsive. They established a schedule for volunteer shifts, ensuring that the pantry was always staffed and ready to receive donations or assist those in need. They also began to develop partnerships with local organizations, like the school's guidance counselor and the local church, to ensure that those who could benefit most from the pantry were aware of its existence and accessibility.

The Grand Hall was no longer just a building undergoing restoration; it had taken on a new life, a deeper purpose. It had become a symbol of Cedar Ridge's resilience, a tangible manifestation of its community spirit. The shelves, once bare and echoing with the emptiness of neglect, now brimmed with the generosity of its people, a silent testament to their shared commitment. Clara and Jonah, standing amidst the organized abundance, felt a profound sense of accomplishment. They had set out to save a building, but in doing so, they had helped to rebuild a community, one donation, one delivery, one act of kindness at a time. The pantry was ready, a beacon of support, a place where the heart of Cedar Ridge could truly be felt, warm and sustaining, ready to nourish its people for months to come.

The Grand Hall was buzzing with a new kind of energy, one that was less about grand gestures and more about quiet, consistent effort. The pantry, a monument to the town's immediate generosity, was stocked and running smoothly, but the restoration of the Hall itself was an ongoing endeavor. Jonah, ever the pragmatist, recognized that the momentum generated by the festival and the subsequent outpouring of donations needed to be channeled into tangible, sustainable progress. "We can't just rely on people bringing us things, Clara," he'd stated one afternoon, wiping sweat from his brow after a long day of reinforcing a support beam. "We need to teach people how to *do* things. How to fix, how to build, how to maintain. That's how this place truly becomes ours, and stays ours."

And so, the idea for skill-sharing workshops was born, a natural extension of the collaborative spirit that had already taken root. Jonah, with his knack for bringing people together and his own diverse set of practical skills, took the lead in organizing them. He envisioned a series of informal sessions, held right there in the Grand Hall, where residents could share their expertise with one another. It wasn't about formal classes or certifications;

it was about passing down knowledge, fostering self-sufficiency, and empowering the community to take ownership of their shared space.

The first workshop focused on the most immediate need: basic repairs. A small group of experienced carpenters, including old Mr. Abernathy, whose hands had built half the homes in Cedar Ridge, and Sarah's Uncle Mike, who was known for his meticulous woodworking, volunteered to lead. They gathered in the main hall, armed with their tools and a collection of salvaged lumber. Jonah had arranged for a steady supply of wood scraps and various broken items – a wobbly chair leg, a loose door hinge, a cracked shelf – to serve as practice materials. He'd also ensured that a good selection of basic tools, from hammers and screwdrivers to measuring tapes and levels, were readily available for anyone who didn't have their own.

"Alright, folks," Mr. Abernathy's voice, raspy with age but still commanding, echoed through the hall. "We're going to start with the fundamentals. Understanding your wood grain, knowing how to make a clean cut, the difference between a nail and a screw, and when to use each. This isn't rocket science," he chuckled, his eyes twinkling, "but it's the kind of knowledge that keeps a house, or a town hall, from falling apart." He demonstrated how to properly measure and mark a piece of wood, emphasizing the importance of accuracy. Uncle Mike then took over, showing the proper technique for hammering a nail without bending it, and explaining the subtle art of using wood glue effectively.

The participants, a mix of eager young adults and seasoned residents looking to refresh their skills, watched with rapt attention, their hands itching to try. Jonah moved among them, offering encouragement and lending a hand where needed, his presence a constant source of energy and positive reinforcement. He ensured that everyone had a chance to practice, guiding them through each step, offering gentle corrections, and celebrating every small success. The air filled with the rhythmic tap-tap-tapping of hammers and the soft hum of sawdust being created, a testament to the tangible progress being made.

Next, Jonah enlisted the help of the town's licensed electrician, a quiet but highly competent woman named Emily Carter. Emily, who had been hesitant at first about sharing her specialized knowledge, was eventually persuaded by Jonah's earnestness and the clear need for electrical safety awareness. Her workshop, held in a cordoned-off section of the hall to ensure maximum safety, focused on the absolute basics of home electrical systems and, more importantly, on recognizing and avoiding hazards. She began by demystifying the common symbols on electrical diagrams, explaining how electricity flowed through wires and circuits. She then moved on to practical demonstrations, using a safe, low-voltage setup.

"This," she explained, pointing to a visual aid of a frayed wire, "is a disaster waiting to happen. The insulation is compromised, leaving the conductor exposed. This can lead to shocks, fires, and a whole lot of trouble." She showed the participants how to identify signs of wear and tear on cords and plugs, the importance of not overloading outlets, and the critical role of circuit breakers. Her most vital lesson, however, was about when *not* to attempt a repair. "If you're unsure, if you see anything that looks suspect, if you smell burning plastic, please, for your own safety and the safety of others, call a professional.

There's no shame in knowing your limits. In fact, knowing them is the smartest thing you can do." The participants, many of whom had admitted to a certain trepidation around anything electrical, left Emily's session with a newfound respect for the power flowing through their homes and a clearer understanding of how to stay safe. Jonah made sure to have a list of recommended electricians, including Emily, readily available for those who needed professional assistance.

The workshops weren't confined to the indoor restoration. As spring began to coax life from the earth, the focus shifted outdoors to the newly designated community garden plots behind the Hall. This initiative, spearheaded by the town's most dedicated gardeners, had quickly become a symbol of hope and fresh beginnings. Martha Gable, the General Store owner's wife and a woman whose green thumb was legendary throughout Cedar Ridge, volunteered to lead a series of gardening workshops. Her sessions were held on Saturday mornings, drawing a crowd of all ages, from curious children to seasoned horticulturalists eager to share their wisdom.

Martha's approach was nurturing and inclusive. She'd set up demonstration beds within the community garden, showcasing different planting techniques and soil enrichment methods. Her first workshop focused on preparing the soil. "You can have the best seeds in the world," she'd explained, her voice warm and encouraging as she turned over a clump of rich, dark earth, "but if your soil isn't healthy, your plants won't thrive. We need to give them the best foundation possible." She demonstrated how to compost effectively, using kitchen scraps and yard waste, and explained the benefits of adding organic matter to the soil. She spoke about the importance of understanding soil pH and how to test it using simple kits.

Subsequent workshops delved into specific planting techniques, from direct sowing of seeds to transplanting seedlings. Martha shared her knowledge of companion planting, explaining how certain plants could benefit each other when grown in close proximity. She discussed pest control, emphasizing natural and organic methods that wouldn't harm beneficial insects or the environment. One particularly popular session focused on attracting pollinators, with Martha demonstrating how to create habitats for bees and butterflies, and discussing the best flowers to plant for these essential garden visitors. The laughter of children chasing butterflies and the contented murmurs of adults sharing planting tips became a regular soundtrack to the life blooming around the Grand Hall.

Clara, who had initially felt a pang of anxiety at the thought of delegating such crucial tasks, found herself increasingly drawn to overseeing these workshops. She'd always been a planner, an organizer, the one who made sure all the pieces fit. But here, she was witnessing a different kind of leadership emerge, one that involved empowerment and shared responsibility. She'd stand at the back of the carpentry session, a notebook in her hand, not to critique, but to learn. She'd observe the questions being asked, the hands-on engagement, the growing confidence in the participants' eyes. She saw how Jonah, with his infectious enthusiasm and practical guidance, made even the most daunting tasks seem achievable. She witnessed Martha's gentle encouragement, her ability to make every novice gardener feel like they could cultivate a thriving patch of earth.

It was a revelation. Clara realized that her role wasn't just about managing resources and logistics; it was about fostering an environment where skills could flourish, where knowledge could be exchanged, and where the community could grow stronger, together. She began to actively participate in the planning of future workshops, suggesting topics based on conversations she'd overheard or needs she'd identified during her work with the pantry. She saw how the electrician's safety protocols complemented the carpenters' repair techniques, and how the gardeners' understanding of natural resources could be applied to the Hall's own landscaping plans.

She started seeing herself not as the sole operator, but as a facilitator, a connector. She recognized that by empowering others to teach, she was multiplying the impact of their collective efforts. The Hall was becoming more than just a building; it was becoming a living, breathing center for community growth and development. The workshops were tangible proof that the spirit of generosity ignited by the festival had evolved into something deeper and more enduring: a commitment to shared learning, mutual support, and the collective act of rebuilding not just a structure, but a way of life. Clara found a profound satisfaction in this shift, a quiet joy in watching the community's skills blossom, knowing that she was playing a part in cultivating that growth. The Grand Hall was no longer just a project; it was becoming a classroom, a workshop, a garden, and a testament to the enduring power of Cedar Ridge to reinvent itself, brick by brick, skill by skill, hand in hand.

Each completed repair, no matter how minor, was met with a chorus of encouragement and genuine appreciation. A mended windowpane, once a jagged hole letting in the wind, now offered a clear view of the budding spring landscape. The collective sigh of relief and the murmur of congratulatory remarks that followed its installation felt almost as satisfying as the smooth, unhindered flow of air. It was a small victory, yes, but in the context of months of disrepair, it was a significant one. Similarly, a freshly painted wall, its former peeling, water-stained facade replaced by a clean, even coat of neutral primer, became an instant focal point. A small group of volunteers, armed with brushes and rollers, had spent an entire Saturday meticulously preparing the surface and applying the paint. The transformation was striking, a visual representation of the progress they were making.

Clara found herself instinctively pausing after each significant step, her gaze sweeping over the newly improved section. She'd clap her hands together, a bright smile on her face, drawing the attention of those working nearby. "Look at that!" she'd exclaim, her voice filled with genuine delight. "That wall looks brand new. Martha, your team did a wonderful job with the prep work. And thank you, David, for lending your steady hand with the roller." These acknowledgments weren't mere formalities; they were heartfelt tributes, designed to ensure that no effort went unnoticed. She'd make a point of seeking out each individual who had contributed, offering a handshake, a word of thanks, and sometimes, a simple, knowing glance that communicated the depth of her gratitude.

Jonah, ever the steady presence, echoed her sentiments. He possessed an uncanny ability to identify the core contributors to each success and to articulate their specific roles. When a particularly stubborn floorboard, warped and creaking ominously, was finally pried loose and replaced with a sturdy, perfectly fitting piece, Jonah was the first to publicly praise the individuals who had painstakingly worked on it. "That was no easy feat, gentlemen," he announced, addressing the small knot of men gathered around the repaired section, their faces flushed with exertion and pride. "You wrestled that old wood into submission. That floor will hold strong for years to come, thanks to your perseverance." He'd then detail the process, highlighting the challenges overcome – the rusted nails, the stubborn adhesion, the need for precise measurements – making everyone aware of the skill and effort involved.

These moments, these small celebrations, were the mortar that held the bricks of their collective effort together. They were more than just acknowledgments; they were fuel for the ongoing work. Each completed repair, each aesthetically pleasing improvement, served as tangible proof of their capabilities. The Grand Hall, once a symbol of decline and neglect, was slowly but surely transforming into a testament to what Cedar Ridge could achieve when united. The atmosphere within its walls shifted from one of weary obligation to one of hopeful anticipation. The hum of activity was no longer a somber drone but a vibrant symphony of purposeful action, punctuated by laughter, shared advice, and the satisfying sounds of creation and repair.

Clara observed this shift with a deep sense of satisfaction. She saw how the initial enthusiasm of the festival donations had matured into something more profound: a sustained engagement fueled by visible results and a shared sense of accomplishment. The pantry shelves were still stocked, a testament to immediate need and quick generosity, but the ongoing restoration of the Grand Hall offered a different kind of reward. It was the reward of seeing something broken made whole again, of contributing to something lasting, and of witnessing the community's collective spirit manifest in physical form.

She recalled a particular afternoon when a group of teenagers, initially volunteering out of a sense of civic duty or perhaps even parental pressure, had been tasked with sanding down a series of wooden benches. The work was tedious, repetitive, and not particularly glamorous. Yet, as the hours wore on, a subtle transformation occurred. They began to work together, passing sanding blocks, sharing the task of clearing away dust, and even finding a rhythm in their movements. When they finished, the benches gleamed with a smooth, polished finish, a stark contrast to their former rough, splintered state.

Clara, who had been overseeing the pantry that day, made a point of going to see their handiwork. She gathered them together, not for a formal lecture, but for a simple acknowledgment. "Look at this," she said, running her hand over the smooth surface of a bench. "You've completely revitalized these. They're beautiful now. You should all be incredibly proud of what you've accomplished today. This is the kind of work that makes a real difference." The pride that bloomed on their young faces was palpable, a quiet but powerful validation of their efforts. It was a small victory, a sanded bench, but it represented a significant shift in their perception of their own capabilities and their connection to the Hall.

Jonah, too, actively fostered this sense of ownership. He'd often initiate conversations that went beyond the immediate task, connecting the current work to the Hall's history and its future. While supervising the repair of a section of the tin roof, he'd explain to the volunteers how generations of Cedar Ridge residents had maintained it, passing down the knowledge of how to patch leaks and prevent rust. He'd frame the current efforts not as a burden, but as an honorable continuation of a legacy. "This roof has sheltered countless town gatherings," he'd say, his voice carrying over the rhythmic clang of hammers. "It's our turn to ensure it can do the same for the next generation. Every patch we put in now is an investment in our town's future." This framing elevated the work from a chore to a meaningful contribution, imbuing each successful repair with a sense of historical weight and communal responsibility.

The momentum built from these small victories was undeniable. It wasn't just about the physical improvements; it was about the renewed sense of optimism and capability that permeated Cedar Ridge. People who had previously felt disconnected or overwhelmed by the scale of the Hall's disrepair now saw tangible evidence of their collective power. They understood that even the most daunting tasks could be broken down into manageable steps, and that each step, when taken together, led to significant progress. The Grand Hall was no longer just a building in need of repair; it was a living, breathing project, a symbol of resilience and a testament to the enduring strength of a community that knew how to rally.

Clara found herself reflecting on this evolution often, a quiet sense of awe settling over her as she witnessed the transformation, both of the Hall and of the people within it. The initial outpouring of support had been extraordinary, but this sustained, hands-on engagement was something even more profound, a deeper commitment born from shared effort and the sweet taste of hard-won success.

The scent of fresh paint and newly polished wood still hung in the air, a testament to the relentless dedication of Cedar Ridge. But as the last of the major repairs drew to a close, a new atmosphere began to settle within the Grand Hall. It was an atmosphere less of urgent mending and more of hopeful anticipation, a quiet hum of possibility that Clara found herself breathing in with a deep, contented sigh. She leaned against a newly secured window frame, the afternoon sun warming her face, and watched Jonah as he meticulously organized a collection of donated books destined for the Hall's repurposed library alcove. The shelves, once bare and dusty, now brimmed with stories, a kaleidoscope of worn spines promising adventures and knowledge.

"It's incredible, isn't it?" Clara murmured, her voice soft, almost reverent. "Just a few weeks ago, this was all just... a dream. A desperate hope."

Jonah looked up, a rare, unreserved smile crinkling the corners of his eyes. He brushed a stray strand of hair from his forehead, his movements imbued with a familiar, steady grace. "It's more than a dream now, Clara. It's real. Look at it." He gestured with a sweep of his hand, encompassing the vast, revitalized space. "It's not just a building anymore. It's... us. It's everything we've poured into it."

Clara nodded, her gaze drifting to the meticulously restored stage, where the worn velvet curtain, painstakingly cleaned and rehung, now promised to conceal and reveal countless future performances. She imagined the laughter of children attending a play, the hushed anticipation before a community concert, the earnest delivery of a local historian sharing tales of Cedar Ridge's past. This wasn't just about saving a structure; it was about breathing life back into its very soul.

"And it's going to be so much more than just a performance space," she said, her voice gaining a confident lilt. "I've been thinking, Jonah. With the pantry stocked and the Hall itself looking so... alive, we can start looking at the bigger picture. What else can this place *be* for Cedar Ridge?"

Jonah set down a stack of books and walked towards her, his expression thoughtful. "That's exactly what I've been mulling over myself. The initial crisis, the immediate need to prevent closure and feed our neighbors, that was crucial. But now..." He paused, his gaze sweeping across the room as if he could already see the spectral outlines of future events. "Now, we can dream a little bigger. What kind of community center do we want this to be?"

"A hub," Clara declared, the word resonating with her own burgeoning vision. "A place where people don't just come for a meal, but where they connect, learn, and grow. I've been sketching out some ideas." She reached into the canvas tote bag she always seemed to have at hand and pulled out a worn notebook, its pages filled with her characteristic neat, yet energetic script. "For starters, I've been thinking about educational workshops. We have so many talented people in Cedar Ridge. Imagine knitting circles, cooking classes using ingredients from our own community garden, maybe even basic carpentry or repair workshops for those who want to learn how to tackle their own home projects."

Jonah's eyebrows rose, a spark of genuine interest igniting in his eyes. "That's a fantastic idea, Clara. We could tap into the skills of our retired tradespeople, the gardeners, even some of the younger folks who are already demonstrating real aptitude." He leaned closer, peering at her sketches. "And what about outreach? You mentioned that earlier."

"Absolutely," Clara confirmed, her enthusiasm building. "I envision this place as a bridge. We could host events specifically for families who might be struggling, offering resources and support in a welcoming, non-judgmental environment. Perhaps even a 'welcome to Cedar Ridge' program for new residents, helping them integrate and feel connected from day one." She traced a diagram in her notebook. "And this space, the former annex, it's perfect for a small community library, not just for books, but for resources too – local history archives, information on town services, even a bulletin board for local events and services."

Jonah picked up a stray pencil and tapped it against his chin, his mind clearly working at a rapid pace. "A community library... yes. That would fill a real gap. And the workshops, Clara, you're onto something. It's about empowerment. Giving people the tools and the knowledge to feel more self-sufficient, to build confidence." He paused, a flicker of something akin to vulnerability crossing his face. "I know firsthand how much a simple skill, or the knowledge of how to fix something, can mean. It's not just about the object repaired; it's about the feeling of capability it instills."

Clara met his gaze, a quiet understanding passing between them. She knew the unspoken weight of his past, the quiet struggles that had shaped him. "Exactly," she said softly. "And this Hall can be a place where people discover that capability. Imagine the impact on our youth, too. Instead of just after-school programs that are purely recreational, we could offer apprenticeships in skills that could actually lead to jobs, or at least provide a strong foundation. Think about it, Jonah: woodworking, basic mechanics, even digital literacy workshops. We have the space, and with the community's continued support, we can find the instructors."

He ran a hand through his hair, a gesture of profound contemplation. "The potential is... immense. It's not just about maintaining a building anymore, is it? It's about nurturing the heart of this town. Creating a place where everyone feels they belong, where they can contribute and be valued." He looked at her directly, his gaze steady and earnest. "This vision you're painting, Clara, it's ambitious. But it's also exactly what Cedar Ridge needs. It's a vision that extends far beyond the immediate crisis."

"And it's a vision we can build together," Clara replied, her voice firm with conviction. "The energy and generosity that poured into saving this Hall... that can be channeled into making it a vibrant, thriving center. It's about sustainability, not just of the building, but of the community itself." She pointed to a section of her notebook. "I was even thinking about partnerships with local businesses. Could they sponsor a workshop series? Could they offer internships to some of the young people who show promise in certain skills? It's a reciprocal relationship. They support us, and in turn, we provide them with a more skilled and engaged workforce, a stronger community to operate within."

Jonah chuckled, a warm, genuine sound. "You've clearly been putting a lot of thought into this, Clara. And every idea you share just builds on the last. It's infectious." He picked up a loose plank, examining its grain. "This Hall has seen so much. Decades of town meetings, celebrations, even struggles. It's been the backdrop to so many lives in Cedar Ridge. To see it transformed into a place that actively fosters new memories, new skills, and new connections... it's truly something."

"It's about legacy, isn't it?" Clara mused, her gaze distant. "We're not just repairing the Hall; we're building upon the legacy of everyone who ever used it, who ever cared about it. We're ensuring that it continues to serve Cedar Ridge for generations to come, not just as a building, but as a vital part of our shared life." She turned back to him, her eyes shining. "And this partnership, Jonah... it's not just about saving the Hall anymore. It feels like something more. Something... foundational."

He met her gaze, a subtle shift occurring between them. The pragmatic, crisis-driven dynamic that had characterized their interactions for so long was evolving, softening into something warmer, more layered. "I agree," he said, his voice a low rumble. "This has been... more than just a project. It's forged something between us, Clara. A shared understanding, a shared purpose. And this vision for the future, this ambitious plan for the Hall... it solidifies that. It extends beyond the immediate challenges."

Clara felt a blush creep up her neck, a warmth that had nothing to do with the afternoon sun. She knew what he was implying, and she felt it too – a growing connection, a mutual respect that was blossoming into something deeper, something more personal. "It does," she confirmed, her voice barely above a whisper. "It's about building a future, not just for the Hall, but... for all of us. For Cedar Ridge."

"And I can't think of anyone I'd rather build that future with," Jonah said, his gaze holding hers. The words hung in the air between them, charged with unspoken emotion. It was a simple statement, delivered with his characteristic sincerity, yet it held the weight of their shared journey, of the challenges overcome, and the promise of what was yet to come. The

Grand Hall, once a symbol of Cedar Ridge's potential decline, was now poised to become a beacon of its enduring strength and its vibrant future, a future Clara and Jonah were now clearly committed to building, side by side. The vast space around them, filled with the tangible results of their collective effort, suddenly felt like a canvas, ready for the vibrant strokes of their shared vision. The scent of possibility was stronger now, mingling with the lingering aroma of paint and wood, promising a new chapter, not just for the Hall, but for them.

CHAPTER TEN

Facing the Finish Line

The air in Cedar Ridge buzzed with a nervous energy that Saturday, a palpable tension woven through the usual weekend calm. It was the day of the final town council inspection. For months, the Grand Hall had been a whirlwind of activity – hammering, sanding, painting, and a relentless surge of community spirit that had breathed life back into its weary bones. Now, it was time for the official stamp of approval, the moment of truth that would determine not just the fate of the building, but the tangible realization of so many hopes and dreams. Clara felt it in her own chest, a flutter that was equal parts anxiety and exhilaration. She clutched the worn binder, its contents a testament to countless hours of meticulous planning, fundraising, and coordination. It was more than just a collection of documents; it was the story of Cedar Ridge's resilience, a narrative she had helped to write.

She arrived early, the Grand Hall bathed in the soft, diffused light of a mid-morning sun. Jonah was already there, his presence a quiet anchor in the grand space. He was systematically checking the latches on the newly installed windows, his movements efficient and familiar. Seeing him, a sense of calm settled over Clara. He was a steady force, a man who understood the weight of responsibility and the satisfaction of seeing a job done right. He offered her a small, reassuring smile as she approached, a silent acknowledgment of the momentous occasion.

"Ready?" he asked, his voice a low, steady tone that cut through the expectant silence.

Clara took a deep breath, the scent of beeswax polish and fresh lumber filling her lungs. "As I'll ever be," she replied, managing a confident smile. "I've got everything cross-referenced, signed, and sealed. The pantry is overflowing, the volunteers have done an incredible job with the final clean-up, and I even have a photo album chronicling the entire transformation, from the dusty beams to... this." She gestured around the revitalized hall, a sense of pride swelling within her. "It's all here."

Jonah nodded, his gaze sweeping across the expanse of the main hall, the restored stage, the gleam of the polished floor. "It looks good, Clara. Really good. You've poured your heart and soul into this, and it shows." He met her eyes, his own filled with a quiet admiration. "Whatever happens today, you should be incredibly proud of what you've accomplished."

His words were a balm, easing some of the tight knot of nerves in her stomach. It was true; she had poured everything she had into this project, and seeing the tangible results was deeply gratifying. But the finality of the inspection, the oversight of the town council, loomed large. She knew that behind their stoic facades, the council members represented the varying opinions and concerns of the town, some of whom had been skeptical of the project from the outset.

The arrival of the town council members was signaled by the rumble of a familiar car pulling up outside. Clara straightened her shoulders, the binder held firmly in her hands. Mayor Thompson, a man whose weary pragmatism often masked a deep affection for Cedar Ridge, led the contingent. Beside him walked Mrs. Gable, the sharp-eyed treasurer known for her meticulous attention to detail, and Mr. Henderson, the council's elder statesman, whose quiet approval carried considerable weight. The atmosphere shifted, the hopeful hum of the Hall's readiness becoming a more charged, expectant silence.

"Clara, Jonah," Mayor Thompson greeted, his voice gruff but not unkind. "We're here to see the results of your considerable efforts." He cast a sweeping glance around the Hall. "Impressive, certainly. Let's have a look."

Clara stepped forward, her voice steady as she addressed them. "Welcome, Mayor Thompson, Mrs. Gable, Mr. Henderson. We're so pleased to finally be able to show you the completed restoration of the Grand Hall. As you know, the community's response has been overwhelming, and the volunteer hours and donations have far exceeded our initial projections." She opened her binder, her fingers expertly navigating the tabs. "I've prepared a comprehensive overview, detailing the repairs completed, the safety certifications, and the financial records. I've also included a proposal for the Hall's future use, which I believe will demonstrate its vital role in revitalizing Cedar Ridge."

She began with the structural integrity, pointing to the detailed reports from the engineers who had assessed and overseen the foundation and roof repairs. "As you can see," she explained, projecting a few key images from her laptop onto a portable screen, "the structural issues have been entirely remediated. The building is now sound, safe, and ready for occupancy." She moved on to the electrical and plumbing upgrades, highlighting the modern, energy-efficient systems installed. "We've brought all systems up to current code, ensuring reliability and safety for all who will use the Hall."

Mrs. Gable, her pen poised over her notepad, interjected, "And the budget, Clara? We've seen the preliminary figures, but the final accounting is crucial."

"Of course, Mrs. Gable," Clara responded, her confidence unwavering. She turned to a section filled with receipts, invoices, and a meticulously itemized ledger. "Here is the final financial breakdown. As you can see, we came in under our revised budget, thanks to the extraordinary generosity of our community and the incredible dedication of our volunteers who provided skilled labor at no cost. The detailed breakdown of every expenditure is included, from materials to the specialized contracting work that was essential." She paused, allowing them a moment to absorb the figures. "We also have a significant amount of funds remaining, which will be allocated towards the initial operational costs and the programming initiatives we've outlined."

Jonah, who had been quietly observing, stepped forward as they moved towards the pantry. "The pantry is fully stocked, Mayor," he said, opening the heavy door. "We've received donations from local farms, the town grocery store, and many individuals. It's organized for easy access, and we have a system in place for ongoing inventory and distribution to ensure it continues to serve the community effectively." He gestured to the neatly stacked shelves of canned goods, fresh produce, and essential supplies. The sheer volume was a testament to the town's renewed spirit.

Mayor Thompson peered inside, a flicker of surprise crossing his face. "Well, I'll be. That's... substantial. Much more than I anticipated." He turned to Clara. "And this is all sustained by continued community effort?"

"Absolutely," Clara confirmed. "We have a dedicated team of volunteers who have committed to ongoing food drives and distribution. We're also exploring partnerships with local food banks and agricultural initiatives to ensure a consistent supply. The pantry isn't just a temporary solution; it's designed to be a permanent fixture of support for Cedar Ridge."

They moved through the main hall again, Clara pointing out the restored seating, the pristine bathrooms, the newly painted walls adorned with historical photographs that had been carefully restored. She spoke of the acoustics, now improved by the soundproofing measures taken, and the accessibility features that had been incorporated, ensuring the Hall was welcoming to everyone.

"We've also made significant progress on the proposed programming," Clara continued, leading them towards the smaller annex that was designated as the future library and community hub. "As you saw in the proposal, we've secured a commitment from retired librarian, Mrs. Albright, to help establish and manage the library. We've already received hundreds of book donations, and we're creating a cataloging system that will make these resources readily available." She gestured to the empty shelves, which were waiting for their literary cargo. "We envision this as more than just a place for books; it will be a resource center, offering access to computers, educational materials, and information on local services."

Mr. Henderson, who had been observing quietly, finally spoke. His voice was gentle, tinged with the wisdom of age. "This is all commendable, Clara. You and Jonah, and all the volunteers, have done a remarkable job. The transformation is... profound. It speaks to the heart of this town." He paused, his gaze thoughtful. "But the council needs to be confident in the ongoing viability of this project. The maintenance, the programming, the staffing – these are ongoing costs."

"And we have a solid plan for that," Clara assured him, turning to a section of her binder detailing the operational budget and projected revenue streams. "We anticipate revenue from facility rentals for private events, community workshops with a nominal fee, and ongoing fundraising initiatives. We've also established a community fund specifically for the Hall's upkeep and programming.

Furthermore, the town council's endorsement today will be instrumental in securing grants and further donations from larger foundations and corporations who are looking to invest in community revitalization projects like this one." She met Mr. Henderson's steady gaze. "We're not just looking at the immediate completion, Mr. Henderson; we're building a sustainable future for this Hall, one that will benefit Cedar Ridge for decades to come."

Mayor Thompson studied the financial projections, his brow furrowed in concentration. Mrs. Gable made a few more notes, her expression unreadable. The silence stretched, punctuated only by the distant chirping of birds. Clara felt her heart pound in her chest, the anticipation almost unbearable. This was it, the culmination of so much effort, so much hope.

Finally, Mayor Thompson looked up, a slow smile spreading across his face. He turned to Mrs. Gable and Mr. Henderson, a subtle nod passing between them. "Clara," he began, his voice carrying a new warmth, "your dedication, your vision... it's been nothing short of extraordinary. And Jonah, your steady hand and practical expertise have been invaluable." He gestured around the Hall. "What you have achieved here is a testament to the spirit of Cedar Ridge. You've not only restored a building; you've reignited a sense of purpose, of community pride."

He extended his hand towards Clara. "The town council is unanimous. The Grand Hall is officially deemed safe, functional, and a vital asset to our community. Your proposals for its future use are sound and inspiring. We are pleased to grant our full endorsement and support for the Grand Hall's continued operation as a community center."

A wave of relief washed over Clara, so profound it almost buckled her knees. She felt a happy tear escape and trace a path down her cheek. She accepted the Mayor's handshake, her own grip firm with emotion. "Thank you, Mayor Thompson. Thank you to the entire council. This means the world to Cedar Ridge."

Jonah placed a gentle hand on her shoulder, a silent gesture of shared triumph. He offered a rare, broad smile to the council members. "We won't let you down. This Hall will thrive."

As the council members departed, their earlier tension replaced by a palpable sense of optimism, Clara turned to Jonah, her eyes shining. The binder felt suddenly lighter, its purpose fulfilled. "We did it, Jonah," she whispered, her voice thick with emotion. "We actually did it."

He met her gaze, his eyes reflecting the same joy and relief. "We did, Clara," he said softly. "Thanks to you. You were the driving force, the one who never gave up. I was just... along for the ride."

Clara shook her head, a laugh bubbling up. "Don't be ridiculous. This was a team effort, and you were an essential part of it. Your practicality, your insights... I couldn't have done it without you." The afternoon sun streamed through the large windows, illuminating dust motes dancing in the air, turning the Grand Hall into a golden sanctuary. It was no longer just a building; it was a promise, a tangible symbol of what Cedar Ridge could achieve when its people came together. The final inspection was more than just a bureaucratic hurdle; it was the official christening of a new era for the Grand Hall, and for the town it served.

And as Clara stood there, bathed in the warm light, with Jonah beside her, she knew this was only the beginning. The finish line had been crossed, but the real journey, the one of building and nurturing this vibrant community hub, was just about to begin. The weight of responsibility had lifted, replaced by an exhilarating sense of possibility. She looked at Jonah, at the quiet strength in his eyes, and felt a new kind of warmth bloom within her, one that had nothing to do with the sunshine. The Grand Hall had been saved, and in the process, something equally precious had begun to blossom between them. The air, once thick with anticipation and a touch of fear, now felt light, filled with the sweet scent of success and a future brimming with shared purpose.

The council members, having completed their official assessment, were gathering their notes. Mayor Thompson's declaration of approval had been met with a collective exhale of relief from Clara and Jonah, but the feeling of accomplishment was amplified by the unexpected presence of several other familiar faces. They hadn't been privy to the inspection itself, but their arrival at the Grand Hall moments after the council's departure was a clear indication of their keen interest and unwavering support.

Mrs. Gable, the town treasurer whose sharp gaze had seemed to dissect every financial detail during the inspection, was now offering Clara a warm, genuine smile. She approached Clara, her usual businesslike demeanor softened by an undeniable pride. "Clara," she said, her voice carrying a note of genuine admiration, "I must say, I was impressed. Thoroughly impressed. Not just with the restoration itself – which is a marvel, truly – but with the foresight you've shown. The pantry, for instance. I've always been a pragmatist, and when I first heard the whispers about a community pantry, I admit I had my reservations. Food security is a serious matter, and setting up something like that requires more than just good intentions. It requires planning, organization, and a real understanding of need. But seeing it today, seeing the sheer volume and the sensible organization... it's more than just a collection of donations. It's a lifeline. A tangible manifestation of our town looking out for its own. And the fact that you have a system in place for ongoing management... that speaks volumes about your commitment and your competence."

Her words, coming from a woman known for her fiscal prudence and exacting standards, were a powerful endorsement. Clara felt a flush of gratitude. "Thank you, Mrs. Gable. That means a great deal coming from you. The pantry truly wouldn't be what it is without the generosity of so many. The farmers, the grocers, the individuals who have been dropping off bags of groceries every single day. It's a testament to the people of Cedar Ridge."

Beside Mrs. Gable stood Mr. Davies, the owner of Davies' Hardware, a man whose gruff exterior hid a heart as solid as the oak planks he sold. He'd been a quiet but consistent presence throughout the renovation, offering discounted materials and lending tools whenever they were needed. He clapped Jonah on the shoulder, a hearty sound that echoed in the still-newly-polished hall. "Jonah, you and your crew have done yeoman's work," he boomed, his voice resonating with honest approval. "I saw some of the original framing in the attic when I delivered those roof trusses. Looked like it was about to give up the ghost.

You've brought this old girl back to life, and then some. And Clara," he turned to her, his gaze direct, "you've got a fire in your belly, lass. A good fire. I've been in this town a long time, seen projects come and go. Most of them fizzle out. But this? This Grand Hall project, it's got roots. And it's got you, making sure those roots are strong and deep. That pantry you've put together... it's already making a difference. I've had folks stop by the store, mention how they've been able to supplement their tables thanks to the Hall. That's not just charity, that's community. Real, honest-to-goodness community."

His acknowledgment of the pantry's tangible impact resonated deeply with Clara. She'd spent countless hours organizing inventory, coordinating volunteers, and ensuring that the donations were distributed efficiently and with dignity. It was often a behind-the-scenes effort, unseen by many, so hearing Mr. Davies speak of its impact directly was incredibly affirming.

"Mr. Davies, that's wonderful to hear," Clara replied, a genuine smile lighting up her face. "We've had so many volunteers step up to help with the pantry. It's become a hub of activity in itself, and the goodwill it's fostering is incredible. We've seen families helping families, neighbors looking out for neighbors. It's truly heartwarming."

The sentiment of community was echoed by others who had also lingered, drawn by the buzz of the inspection's conclusion. Mrs. Peterson, who ran the local bakery and had donated countless batches of her famous cinnamon rolls for volunteer workdays, approached Clara, her apron dusted with flour. "Oh, Clara, it looks absolutely beautiful!" she exclaimed, her eyes wide with delight as she surveyed the main hall. "It's like stepping back in time, but with all the modern comforts. And the plans for it... a place for the children to learn, for us all to gather. It's going to be the heart of Cedar Ridge again, I just know it." She leaned in conspiratorially. "And that pantry! My goodness. We've had a few more elderly folks in town who've been struggling a bit, and knowing they have a reliable source of good food... it's a huge relief. I've been telling everyone at church about it, encouraging them to contribute whatever they can. It's such a vital service."

Her words painted a picture of the Hall's impact far beyond its physical restoration. It was becoming a symbol of hope, a tangible representation of collective care and mutual support. Clara felt a swell of emotion, a profound sense of satisfaction that went far beyond the professional approval of the town council. This was about people, about connections, about building a stronger, more resilient community.

Even old Mr. Abernathy, who had been one of the most vocal skeptics in the early stages, muttering about wasted money and a folly of youthful idealism, was present. He stood a little apart from the main group, his arms crossed, but his expression was no longer one of outright disapproval. There was a grudging respect in his eyes as he looked around the Hall. When Clara caught his gaze, he gave a curt nod. "Hmph. Looks... solid," he grumbled, his voice gruff, but the edge of negativity was gone. "You youngsters certainly put in the elbow grease. And that pantry... heard good things. Good things." It was high praise from Mr. Abernathy, and Clara knew it. It was a quiet acknowledgment that the project, against his initial doubts, had proven its worth.

The collective voice of these community members, their spontaneous testimonials and heartfelt expressions of support, spoke volumes. They weren't just bystanders; they were stakeholders, invested in the success of the Grand Hall. Their presence and their words underscored the fact that this project had transcended Clara and Jonah's individual efforts, becoming a genuine community endeavor. It was a testament to the power of shared vision and collective action.

Clara exchanged a glance with Jonah. In his eyes, she saw a mirrored reflection of her own deep satisfaction. The council's approval was the official seal of success, the culmination of months of hard work and painstaking detail. But the quiet affirmation from Mrs. Gable, the booming praise from Mr. Davies, the hopeful words of Mrs. Peterson, and even the grudging nod from Mr. Abernathy – these were the true heartbeats of their achievement. They represented the tangible impact the Grand Hall would have on the lives of the people of Cedar Ridge, the renewed sense of pride and belonging it would foster.

This wasn't just about a building anymore. It was about the threads of connection that had been woven and strengthened throughout the process. The pantry, initially conceived as a practical solution to a growing need, had become a powerful symbol of communal care. It had brought people together, fostering empathy and encouraging generosity. The volunteers who staffed it, the donors who filled its shelves, the families who benefited from its provisions – they were all part of a larger narrative of resilience and compassion.

"It's more than just a building, isn't it?" Clara murmured to Jonah, her voice soft but filled with emotion. "It's a promise. A promise we've all made to each other."

Jonah's hand found hers, his thumb tracing gentle circles on her skin. "It is," he agreed, his gaze sweeping across the faces of the gathered townspeople. "And seeing them here, seeing how much it means to them... it makes all the long nights, all the setbacks, feel like nothing. This is why we did it."

The chatter around them was a tapestry of excited murmurs and satisfied exclamations. People were already discussing potential events, envisioning future gatherings, and expressing their eagerness to get involved. The Grand Hall, once a silent monument to a bygone era, was now alive with the vibrant energy of a community reawakened. The finishing line had been crossed, but as Clara listened to the collective voice rise around her, she knew their journey was far from over. It was, in fact, just beginning. The Grand Hall, revitalized and embraced, was poised to become the true heart of Cedar Ridge, a place where memories would be made, connections would be forged, and the enduring spirit of their small town would continue to shine. The sense of shared accomplishment, amplified by the presence of so many townspeople, was a powerful testament to what could be achieved when a community dared to dream together, and then worked together to make that dream a reality. Clara felt a profound sense of belonging, not just to the project, but to the very fabric of Cedar Ridge, a fabric that had been strengthened and beautified by the restoration of their beloved Grand Hall.

The air in the Grand Hall was still thick with the scent of lemon polish and aged wood, a testament to the meticulous work that had transformed the space. The murmur of satisfied townspeople, a comforting hum of approval, filled the expansive room. Clara, basking in the glow of success, felt a sense of profound peace settle over her. Mayor Thompson's pronouncement of approval had been the official stamp, but the genuine warmth emanating from Mrs. Gable, Mr. Davies, and Mrs. Peterson felt like the true validation. Even Mr. Abernathy's gruff acknowledgment was a victory in itself. She exchanged a look with Jonah, a silent acknowledgment of shared accomplishment and a future that felt bright and full of promise. The Grand Hall, resurrected from its slumber, was ready to embrace its role as the heart of Cedar Ridge once more.

Then, a question, sharp and unexpected, cut through the celebratory atmosphere. It came from Councilman Davies, a man whose reputation for scrutinizing details was as legendary as his meticulous record-keeping. He held a sheaf of papers, his brow furrowed as he pointed to a section of the blueprints Clara had painstakingly reviewed. "Clara," he began, his voice amplified by the acoustics of the hall, "I'm looking at the cross-bracing in the west wing's roof support. It seems... unconventional. Have you considered the long-term stress factors here? The original plans didn't feature this particular configuration."

A knot of anxiety tightened in Clara's stomach. This was it. The moment where her carefully constructed facade of competence might crumble under the weight of scrutiny. Her initial instinct was to retreat, to defend her decisions as solely her own. She had always prided herself on her independence, her ability to shoulder burdens alone. But as she opened her mouth to speak, a different feeling surfaced, a quiet strength that had been growing within her throughout this entire process. She took a deep breath, the scent of beeswax and old timber grounding her.

"Councilman Davies," she replied, her voice clear and steady, surprising even herself with its calm assurance. "You're absolutely right. That particular bracing configuration is not original. It's a modification we implemented to address a specific structural weakness discovered during the restoration." She met his gaze directly, her own eyes reflecting the polished gleam of the chandeliers. "Jonah, our lead contractor, identified a potential point of vulnerability in the joist system after he'd exposed the original beams. He explained that the load distribution was uneven, and under extreme weather conditions, it could lead to significant stress on the central support column."

She paused, allowing his words to sink in, then continued, her confidence growing with each spoken sentence. "Jonah's expertise in structural integrity is extensive, and he proposed a solution that involved reinforcing the cross-bracing. However, the original wooden beams, while sturdy, presented a challenge for the typical metal brackets he usually employs. That's where Mr. Henderson, one of our community volunteers, came in." Clara gestured towards a man standing a little apart from the main group, a retired carpenter with hands that bore the indelible marks of a lifetime's work. Mr. Henderson, a quiet man who had donated his time and considerable skill to countless projects in Cedar Ridge, offered a small, shy smile.

"Mr. Henderson has an unparalleled understanding of woodworking and historical building techniques," Clara explained, her voice filled with genuine respect. "He suggested a custom-fit wooden brace, intricately carved to seamlessly integrate with the existing beams. He meticulously calculated the angles and pressure points, drawing on decades of experience. He worked with Jonah to ensure the design was both aesthetically pleasing and structurally sound, creating a solution that respected the historical integrity of the hall while providing modern-day stability."

She turned back to Councilman Davies, a soft smile gracing her lips. "So, while the design might appear unconventional on paper, it's a testament to the combined knowledge of Jonah's modern engineering principles and Mr. Henderson's masterful craftsmanship. It was a collaborative effort, born out of a shared commitment to ensuring the long-term safety and durability of this building. We didn't just want to restore it; we wanted to make it stronger and more resilient for generations to come."

The silence that followed her explanation was not the tense quiet of an interrogation, but the thoughtful hush of genuine consideration. Councilman Davies slowly lowered his papers, his gaze shifting from the blueprints to Mr. Henderson, and then back to Clara. A subtle change passed over his features, the sharp edges of his skepticism softening.

"I see," he said, his voice losing its accusatory edge. "A collaborative approach. And you, Clara, you embraced that. You didn't feel the need to... assert your sole authorship of the design?"

The question hung in the air, more a reflection than an accusation. It was a pointed inquiry into Clara's long-held belief in self-reliance, her tendency to carry every responsibility on her own shoulders. For years, she had operated under the assumption that admitting a need for help was a sign of weakness. She had seen her father, a man who prided himself on his independence, struggle to accept assistance, and she had vowed to be different, to be stronger, to need no one. But this project had fundamentally altered her perspective.

"Councilman Davies," Clara began, her voice laced with a newfound vulnerability, "I've spent a lot of my life believing that the strongest person is the one who can stand entirely on their own. That asking for help, or admitting you don't have all the answers, is a failing. This project... it taught me otherwise. It showed me that true strength isn't about isolation; it's about connection. It's about recognizing the diverse talents and knowledge that exist within our community and weaving them together. Jonah's insight was invaluable. Mr. Henderson's skill was indispensable. Without their contributions, this hall might not be as safe or as beautiful as it is today."

She met the councilman's gaze again, her expression open and earnest. "I realized that my role wasn't to be the sole genius behind every decision, but to be the conductor of an orchestra. To listen, to understand, to synthesize the expertise of others, and to guide us all towards a shared goal. It's a more powerful, and ultimately more effective, way of working. It allows for innovation, for solutions that one person might never conceive of alone. And it fosters a sense of ownership and pride in everyone involved."

A ripple of quiet assent spread through the gathered townspeople. They had witnessed Clara's journey, her initial anxieties and her gradual blossoming into a leader who embraced collaboration. Mrs. Gable nodded thoughtfully, a knowing smile playing on her lips. Mr. Davies beamed, his gruff demeanor softening into genuine paternal pride. Mr. Henderson, typically reticent, stood a little taller, a quiet satisfaction evident in his posture.

"That's a remarkably insightful perspective, Clara," Councilman Davies conceded, his tone shifting from that of an examiner to that of an impressed observer. "It speaks to a maturity and a deep understanding of leadership that goes beyond mere technical competence. You haven't just restored a building; you've helped to foster a renewed sense of community interdependence. That, in itself, is a significant achievement." He gave a final, decisive nod. "The cross-bracing is approved."

A collective sigh of relief swept through the hall, but for Clara, the true victory wasn't in the approval of a structural detail. It was in the public declaration of her evolving philosophy, the open acknowledgment of her interdependence. She looked at Jonah, their eyes meeting across the space. In his gaze, she saw not just pride in their shared success, but a profound understanding of the personal transformation that had taken place. He knew how much this moment meant to her, how it represented a shedding of old limitations and an embrace of a more connected, collaborative future.

The applause that followed Councilman Davies's pronouncement was enthusiastic, but Clara's focus remained on the quiet realization blooming within her. She had always been driven by a fierce desire to prove herself, to demonstrate her capability, to be the one in control. This need stemmed from a deep-seated fear of being perceived as inadequate, a fear that had often led her to isolate herself, to shoulder burdens alone rather than risk asking for assistance. She had believed that vulnerability was a liability, a crack in the armor that would be exploited.

But the Grand Hall project had chipped away at those defenses, brick by painstaking brick. The initial skepticism of the townspeople, the unexpected challenges, the sheer scale of the undertaking – all of it had forced her to lean on others. She had discovered that Jonah's steady calm was a balm to her anxieties, that Mrs. Gable's sharp mind could untangle bureaucratic knots she couldn't navigate, that Mr. Davies's practical advice saved her from costly mistakes, and that the collective spirit of the volunteers was a wellspring of unwavering support.

And then there was Mr. Henderson. His quiet wisdom, his innate understanding of materials and techniques that predated modern engineering, had been a revelation. Clara recalled the initial discussions about the roof bracing. She had pored over engineering textbooks, trying to find a solution that fit the historical context. Jonah had offered his professional opinion, but it was Mr. Henderson who had truly bridged the gap. He hadn't just suggested a modification; he had envisioned a solution that was both technically sound and harmoniously integrated with the building's original character.

She remembered the afternoon she and Jonah had stood in the dusty attic, tracing the lines of the old beams. Jonah had pointed out the stress points, sketching diagrams in his notebook. Clara had felt a familiar wave of inadequacy wash over her, a fear that she was out of her depth. But then Mr. Henderson had arrived, his weathered hands gently touching the aged wood. He hadn't spoken much, but his observations were profound. He'd seen things in the grain, in the subtle wear patterns, that Jonah's calculations couldn't capture. He'd spoken of how the wood "breathed" and how it needed to be treated with respect.

He'd then proposed the idea of a custom wooden brace, not a crude addition, but a carefully crafted piece that would echo the existing joinery.

Clara had initially been hesitant. It felt... artisanal. Less predictable than a manufactured component. But Jonah, ever the pragmatist, had seen the merit in Mr. Henderson's approach. He'd explained to Clara that the beauty of such a solution lay in its adaptability, its ability to conform to the unique quirks of the old structure. He'd also pointed out that Mr. Henderson's involvement would likely be more cost-effective than fabricating a specialized metal bracket.

Clara had to admit, the thought of relying on Mr. Henderson's intuition, on his years of hands-on experience, had been daunting. It felt like relinquishing a degree of control, placing trust in something less tangible than a blueprint or a set of specifications. But she had seen the respect in Jonah's eyes, heard the quiet confidence in his voice as he vouched for Mr. Henderson's capabilities. And something within her had shifted. She had taken a deep breath and said, "Let's go with Mr. Henderson's design. I trust your judgment, Jonah, and I trust Mr. Henderson's skill."

Standing there now, listening to Councilman Davies's words, Clara felt a profound sense of liberation. She hadn't compromised the project by asking for help; she had elevated it. She had allowed the collective wisdom of Cedar Ridge to infuse the restoration with a richness and resilience that her solitary efforts could never have achieved. The defensive posture she had adopted for so long, the need to always be the one with the answers, had been a cage. And in that moment, she felt its bars dissolve.

She glanced at Jonah again, and this time, their shared smile was even more radiant. This was more than just a successful renovation; it was a testament to their evolving relationship, to the way they had learned to trust and rely on each other. It was a promise of a future where they would continue to build, to create, and to overcome challenges, not as individuals striving for sole credit, but as partners, drawing strength from their combined abilities and the unwavering support of their community.

The Grand Hall, standing proud and strong, was a physical manifestation of that very principle. It was a beacon, not just of Cedar Ridge's past, but of its collaborative, interconnected future. And Clara, for the first time, felt truly capable, not because she could do everything, but because she had learned the profound strength that came from knowing who to ask, and how to weave their gifts into something truly magnificent. This was the true meaning of completion, not just of a building, but of a personal transformation that would echo through every aspect of her life.

The hum of conversation in the Grand Hall began to ebb, replaced by a more directed buzz of final affirmations. Clara had navigated the inspection with a grace that still surprised Jonah, a testament to the seismic shifts happening within her. He watched her now, a soft smile playing on his lips, a quiet pride swelling in his chest. It wasn't just the restoration of Cedar Ridge's beloved gathering space that filled him with satisfaction; it was the profound transformation he'd witnessed in Clara herself.

When he'd first met her, Clara had been a fortress. Her independence was a carefully constructed wall, designed to keep the world at bay. She carried her burdens like a solitary soldier, convinced that the only way to succeed was to rely solely on her own strength. He'd seen the flicker of vulnerability in her eyes, the exhaustion that shadowed her features, but she'd always brushed away any offers of help with a polite, albeit firm, deflection. He understood, on some level, the roots of her self-reliance, the fear that admitting a need for assistance was a confession of inadequacy. He'd seen it in his own family, the stubborn pride that often masked a deeper loneliness.

But this project, this monumental undertaking of breathing life back into the Grand Hall, had been the catalyst for change. He remembered the early days, the hesitant consultations, the way she'd meticulously reviewed every detail, often working late into the night, her brow furrowed with the weight of responsibility. He'd watched her grapple with unexpected setbacks, with the delicate dance of community politics, and with her own ingrained reluctance to delegate.

Then, slowly at first, the cracks had begun to appear in her armor, not through any forceful breach, but through a gentle, almost imperceptible erosion. It started with small gestures: a shared cup of coffee during a long workday, a brief, genuine smile that reached her eyes, an openness to his suggestions that had gradually replaced her initial guardedness. He'd seen her begin to actively seek out the expertise of others, not out of desperation, but out of a growing understanding that collaboration was a source of strength, not weakness.

Her interaction with Councilman Davies today had been the most striking example of this evolution. Clara hadn't just answered his question about the cross-bracing; she had articulated a philosophy of leadership that was both profound and deeply personal. She had spoken of orchestrating a symphony, of weaving together diverse talents, of finding strength not in isolation but in connection. The vulnerability she had displayed, the honest admission of her past beliefs and her present understanding, had been courageous. And it had resonated. He'd seen the shift in the councilman's demeanor, the grudging respect morphing into genuine admiration.

More than that, he'd seen the way Clara had deferred to Mr. Henderson, not as a subordinate, but as a respected peer. She had openly acknowledged his invaluable contribution, her voice filled with genuine warmth and gratitude. It was a far cry from the Clara he had first encountered, the one who might have felt threatened by such specialized knowledge, who might have strived to maintain absolute control over every aspect of the design. Instead, she had embraced it, recognizing that Mr. Henderson's decades of experience with woodworking offered a perspective that no amount of engineering theory could replicate.

He recalled their conversations about the roof's structural integrity, the initial concern over the aging wooden beams and the potential for stress fractures. Clara had been poring over technical manuals, her mind a whirlwind of calculations and structural load capacities. Jonah had offered his professional assessment, identifying the need for reinforcement, but it was Mr. Henderson who had truly bridged the gap between modern engineering and historical preservation.

He remembered that afternoon in the attic, dust motes dancing in the shafts of light filtering through the grimy windows. Clara had been tracing the rough grain of the old oak beams, a faint frown etched on her face. He'd been sketching diagrams, pointing out potential weak points, but he'd sensed her underlying anxiety, her familiar unease when faced with a challenge that felt beyond her immediate grasp. Then Mr. Henderson had arrived, his presence quiet and unassuming, but his eyes sharp and knowing. He'd run his calloused hands over the wood, his touch reverent. He'd spoken not in technical jargon, but in the language of the wood itself, explaining how it had settled, how it breathed, how it needed to be treated with a respect born of understanding.

Mr. Henderson's proposal for a custom-fitted wooden brace had initially seemed unconventional to Clara, perhaps even less definitive than a manufactured solution. But Jonah had seen the brilliance in it. He'd explained to Clara that the beauty of Mr. Henderson's approach lay in its adaptability, its inherent ability to harmonize with the unique contours of the ancient beams. It was a solution that didn't impose itself upon the structure but rather became an integral part of it. And, as Jonah had pointed out, it was likely to be more cost-effective than fabricating a specialized metal bracket.

He remembered Clara's hesitation, the visible struggle between her ingrained need for control and her burgeoning trust in the collective wisdom of the community. He'd seen the moment of decision flicker in her eyes, the subtle shift as she finally allowed herself to lean into the expertise of others. "I trust your judgment, Jonah," she had said, her voice soft but firm, "and I trust Mr. Henderson's skill." That moment, he'd realized, was a turning point not just for the Grand Hall, but for Clara herself. It was a public declaration of her willingness to embrace collaboration, to acknowledge that her own strengths were amplified when they were woven with the strengths of others.

Now, standing here, watching her bask in the quiet approval of the townspeople, he felt a profound sense of peace. The Grand Hall was more than just a restored building; it was a symbol of what could be achieved when a community came together, when individual talents were recognized and honored. And Clara, the woman who had once stood so resolutely alone, was now the living embodiment of that principle. She had not only saved the hall; she had helped to mend the fabric of their town, fostering a renewed sense of interdependence.

He saw the genuine warmth in her smile as she exchanged a look with Mrs. Gable, a silent acknowledgment of shared effort and mutual respect. He noted the proud nod from Mr. Davies, a man not easily impressed, his gaze reflecting a paternal satisfaction that spoke volumes. Even Mr. Abernathy, usually so reserved, offered a brief, approving glance in Clara's direction, a gruff but meaningful testament to her success.

The journey had been arduous, marked by moments of doubt and uncertainty, but Clara had emerged from it not just as a competent project manager, but as a leader who understood the power of community. She had shed the weight of her self-imposed isolation, replacing it with the liberating understanding that true strength lay in connection, in the ability to trust and to be trusted.

And in her eyes, when they met his, he saw a reflection of that newfound freedom. There was a softness there, a warmth that had been absent before, a vulnerability that was no longer a weakness but a source of profound beauty. It was the look of a woman who had discovered the immense strength that came not from standing alone, but from standing together. He felt a deep, quiet satisfaction, a warmth spreading through him that had nothing to do with the polished wood or the grand architecture, but everything to do with the woman who had breathed life back into both. Their shared glances held a silent promise, a testament to a bond that had been forged in the fires of collaboration and tempered by shared success.

He saw in her the woman he had always hoped she would become, a woman who had finally allowed herself to be seen, to be known, and to be loved. The Grand Hall was complete, but for Jonah, the most beautiful restoration had been Clara herself. The journey had been long, and the finish line was finally in sight, but he knew, with a certainty that settled deep within his soul, that this was just the beginning of their shared story.

The air in the council chambers, thick with anticipation and the scent of polished oak, seemed to hold its breath. Clara's heart hammered a frantic rhythm against her ribs, each beat a desperate plea for a favorable outcome. Beside her, Jonah's presence was a steady anchor, his hand resting lightly on her elbow, a silent testament to their shared ordeal. She could feel the collective gaze of the townspeople, a palpable weight of hope and anxiety pressing in. Then, Councilman Davies cleared his throat, the sound echoing in the sudden, profound silence.

"We have deliberated," he began, his voice measured, "and considered all the evidence presented. We have heard from Ms. Vance regarding the viability of the Community Hall and Pantry, from Mr. Henderson regarding the structural integrity of the building, and from numerous members of our community about the hall's indispensable role." He paused, his gaze sweeping over the faces gathered before him, a flicker of something akin to pride softening his usually stern features. "The decision is unanimous."

Clara's breath hitched. The world seemed to narrow to the space between Davies' lips and the verdict he was about to deliver. She squeezed Jonah's hand, a silent plea for reassurance that he, in turn, offered with a reassuring squeeze of his own.

"The Community Hall and Pantry is approved," Councilman Davies declared, his voice resonating with a newfound clarity. "It will remain open, serving this community for years to come."

A collective gasp rippled through the room, followed almost instantly by an explosion of cheers and applause. The tension that had held everyone captive snapped, replaced by an almost overwhelming wave of elation. Clara felt her knees go weak, a giddy sense of relief washing over her so intensely that for a moment, she could barely stand. She looked at Jonah, her eyes welling up, and saw in his face the same dawning joy, the same profound sense of accomplishment.

The room erupted into a joyous chaos. People were hugging, laughing, tears streaming down their faces. Mrs. Gable, her face a mask of pure delight, threw her arms around Clara, her embrace warm and genuine. "Oh, Clara, we did it!" she exclaimed, her voice thick with emotion. "We really did it!"

Jonah turned to Clara, his eyes shining with an emotion that went far beyond the triumph of the moment. He gently cupped her face, his thumbs brushing away the stray tears that had escaped. "You did it, Clara," he murmured, his voice low and husky, filled with a depth of feeling that made her heart swell. "You saved it. You saved *us*."

In that moment, amidst the cacophony of celebration, their eyes met and held. It was a look that encapsulated everything they had been through: the sleepless nights, the moments of doubt, the unwavering support, the quiet understanding that had blossomed between them. It was a look that acknowledged the immense challenges they had faced together, the way they had leaned on each other, and the profound transformation that had occurred, not just in the Grand Hall, but within themselves.

Clara saw in Jonah's gaze the reflection of her own journey. She saw the woman she had been – guarded, fiercely independent, convinced she had to carry every burden alone – and the woman she was becoming – stronger, more open, capable of trusting and being trusted. She saw the architect who had meticulously planned and executed the restoration, but more importantly, she saw the man who had seen past her defenses, who had believed in her even when she doubted herself, and who had offered his unwavering support, not out of obligation, but out of a deepening affection.

He had witnessed her vulnerability, her struggles, and her eventual triumph. He had seen her learn to delegate, to collaborate, to weave the diverse talents of the community into a cohesive tapestry. He had been her confidante, her advisor, and her steadfast champion. And now, in the aftermath of their victory, she saw in his eyes a silent promise, a confirmation of the unspoken bond that had grown between them, strong and true.

The cheers of the crowd seemed to fade into a distant hum as Clara's world centered on Jonah. His touch was gentle, reassuring, and in its simplicity, spoke volumes. This was more than just a successful project; it was a shared victory, a milestone that had irrevocably altered the landscape of their relationship. The Grand Hall, restored to its former glory, was a testament to their collective effort, but the true restoration, Clara knew, had been within her own heart, a healing that had begun the moment Jonah had stepped into her life and gently, persistently, helped her to believe in the power of connection.

She reached up, her hand covering his on her cheek, her own fingers tracing the strong line of his jaw. "We did," she whispered, her voice barely audible above the din, but her gaze conveying a depth of gratitude and affection that transcended words. "We did."

The weight of months of hard work, of sleepless nights poring over blueprints, of tense meetings and unexpected setbacks, lifted from her shoulders. It was a feeling of profound relief, yes, but it was also something more. It was the exhilarating lightness of knowing that she hadn't had to face it all alone. It was the quiet joy of shared success, a success that felt all the sweeter because it was intertwined with the deepening feelings she held for Jonah.

He lowered his hand, but his gaze remained locked on hers, a silent conversation passing between them. It spoke of shared dreams, of unspoken desires, of a future that now seemed not only possible but inevitable. The Grand Hall was more than just a building; it was the crucible in which their relationship had been forged, a place where vulnerabilities had been exposed, strengths had been recognized, and a love, quiet and unassuming at first, had taken root and begun to flourish.

As the celebration continued around them, a joyous wave of community spirit, Clara and Jonah remained in their own bubble, the world outside their shared gaze momentarily forgotten. The cheers and laughter of their neighbors were the soundtrack to a private symphony, a melody of shared accomplishment and burgeoning love. They had faced the finish line, not just for the restoration of the Grand Hall, but for the beginning of something new, something beautiful, something that promised to endure long after the last echoes of celebration had faded.

The verdict was in, and it was a resounding yes. Yes to the hall, yes to the pantry, and yes, Clara knew with a certainty that settled deep within her soul, to a future shared with the man who had helped her discover the true meaning of strength, not in isolation, but in the profound and enduring power of connection. The promise in his eyes, the warmth of his touch, the shared silence between them – it was all a silent, beautiful declaration of love, a love that had been built, brick by painstaking brick, alongside the restoration of their beloved community hall. And as the jubilant crowd began to spill out of the chambers, eager to spread the good news, Clara knew that this was not an ending, but a beginning.

A beginning of shared mornings, of quiet evenings, of a life built on the foundation of trust, respect, and a love that had weathered every storm and emerged even stronger. The Grand Hall was safe, and in its safety, Clara had found a home, not just for her community, but for her heart, a home she was ready to build, brick by beautiful brick, with Jonah.

CHAPTER ELEVEN

A New Foundation

The cheers from the council chambers had long since subsided, replaced by a gentler, more pervasive hum of activity that pulsed through Cedar Ridge. The Grand Hall, bathed in the soft afternoon sun, was alive with a renewed energy, a vibrant testament to the community's collective will. Clara stood on the newly polished wooden floorboards, her heart still humming with the residual echo of their hard-won victory. Beside her, Jonah's presence was a comforting warmth, his shoulder brushing hers as they surveyed the scene unfolding before them.

It wasn't just a reopening; it was a resurrection. The very air seemed lighter, imbued with the scent of freshly baked bread from the pantry and the sweet perfume of wildflowers adorning every table. Laughter, genuine and unrestrained, cascaded through the hall, a melody Clara had longed to hear. Children, their faces alight with excitement, darted between the legs of adults, their joy infectious. The pantry shelves, once sparsely stocked and a stark reminder of their precarious situation, now groaned under the weight of donations. Jars of homemade preserves gleamed, bags of flour and sugar were stacked high, and baskets overflowed with fresh produce, each item a silent prayer answered, a tangible symbol of neighbors looking out for neighbors.

Clara watched Mrs. Gable, her face a roadmap of a life well-lived, engage in animated conversation with young Lily Peterson, her hands gesturing emphatically as she described the best way to ferment cucumbers. Nearby, Mr. Henderson, his usual gruff demeanor softened by the palpable joy of the occasion, was meticulously explaining the finer points of structural integrity – a gentle, humorous jab at his own earlier anxieties – to a group of curious teenagers. Even Councilman Davies, his stern posture relaxed, was seen sharing a quiet moment with Silas Croft, their heads bent together in conversation, a rare smile gracing his lips. It was a tapestry woven with threads of all colors and textures, each person a vital part of the whole.

"Look at them, Jonah," Clara murmured, her voice thick with emotion. "Look at what we've done."

Jonah's hand found hers, his fingers lacing through hers with a familiar ease that sent a shiver of contentment through her. "

We did," he corrected gently, his thumb stroking the back of her hand. "This is all of Cedar Ridge, Clara. You just reminded them what they were fighting for."

His words, as always, were grounding. It was true. The fight had been a collective one, a shared struggle that had unearthed a deep wellspring of resilience within the town. The Grand Hall, once a symbol of potential loss, had transformed into a beacon of hope, its restored walls echoing with the laughter and renewed purpose of its inhabitants. The pantry, no longer a symbol of desperation, was now a testament to abundance, a tangible demonstration of their shared commitment to one another.

Clara's gaze swept over the bustling room, cataloging the familiar faces, each one etched with a unique story of perseverance. She saw the quiet strength of Eleanor Vance, her tireless advocacy for the pantry a constant source of inspiration. She saw the unwavering support of the Miller family, who had opened their farm to supply fresh produce. She saw the quiet determination of the teenagers who had volunteered countless hours, their youthful energy a powerful force for good. And she saw the deep, abiding love for this town that resided in every heart present.

"It feels… surreal," Clara admitted, a soft smile playing on her lips. "Just a few months ago, this place was on the verge of being shuttered, forgotten. Now…" She gestured around the vibrant hall. "It's more alive than ever."

Jonah squeezed her hand, his eyes mirroring her own sense of wonder. "That's the power of community, Clara. When people come together, when they believe in something, they can move mountains. Or, in this case, restore a hall." He chuckled softly, a warm rumble that resonated deep within her. "And a pantry that will feed more than just stomachs, but souls too."

The afternoon unfolded like a cherished dream. There were speeches, heartfelt and brief, each one acknowledging the journey they had undertaken. Eleanor Vance, her voice clear and steady, spoke of the pantry's mission, not just to provide food, but to offer a hand up, a safe haven for those in need. Mr. Henderson, ever the pragmatist, provided a brief, reassuring overview of the hall's structural soundness, his words met with a chorus of relieved sighs. And then there was Clara, standing beside Jonah, her voice a little shaky at first, but gaining strength as she spoke.

She spoke not of architectural plans or engineering feats, but of the spirit of Cedar Ridge. She spoke of the quiet courage of those who had offered their skills, their time, their meager resources. She spoke of the children's artwork that now adorned the walls, a splash of vibrant color against the newly painted plaster, a testament to the future they were building. She spoke of the shared meals that would grace the tables, of the stories that would be told, of the connections that would be forged in this space. And she spoke, with a profound sense of gratitude, of the man standing beside her, the man who had believed in her vision, who had offered his strength when hers faltered, and whose quiet support had been a constant, unwavering source of encouragement.

"This hall," Clara said, her gaze meeting Jonah's, a silent acknowledgment of their shared journey passing between them, "is more than just wood and stone. It's a testament to what we can achieve when we work together, when we refuse to let fear or doubt dictate our future. It's a symbol of resilience, of hope, and of the enduring power of community. And it stands, stronger than ever, because of each and every one of you."

The applause that followed was thunderous, a wave of appreciation that washed over Clara, warming her to her very core. She felt a profound sense of belonging, a deep contentment that settled into her bones. This was it. This was what she had been searching for, a sense of purpose, a connection to something larger than herself. And she had found it here, in Cedar Ridge, with these people, and with the man who held her hand so securely.

As the afternoon wore on, Clara and Jonah found themselves drawn to a quiet corner, away from the main throng, but still able to observe the joyous scene. The sun, beginning its descent, cast long, golden shadows across the hall, bathing everything in a warm, nostalgic glow. They watched as a group of elderly residents shared stories, their voices soft with remembrance, their faces illuminated by the shared experience. They saw a young couple, hand in hand, admire the restored stained-glass windows, their whispers full of future dreams. They saw the pantry volunteers diligently restocking shelves, their movements efficient and practiced, a well-oiled machine fueled by compassion.

"It's beautiful, isn't it?" Clara whispered, leaning her head against Jonah's shoulder.

"More than beautiful," he replied, his voice a low murmur against her ear. "It's alive. It's breathing. It's everything you hoped it would be."

"And more," she added, a contented sigh escaping her lips. "I never dared to hope for this much. For this much... joy."

Jonah turned his head, his gaze soft as he looked at her. "You dared to believe, Clara. And that's where all of this started. Your belief, and your willingness to put in the work." He paused, his fingers gently tracing the line of her jaw. "And my belief in you."

Clara's heart fluttered at his words, a familiar warmth spreading through her chest. She had come to Cedar Ridge with a mission, a task to complete. She hadn't anticipated finding so much more. She hadn't anticipated finding a connection that ran deeper than a shared project, a bond that was forged in shared vulnerability and mutual respect. She hadn't anticipated finding Jonah.

"I couldn't have done any of this without you, Jonah," she said, her voice barely above a whisper. "You were my rock. My unwavering support."

"And you were mine," he countered, his eyes holding hers. "You showed me what it meant to truly invest, to pour your heart and soul into something. You reminded me of the importance of this town, of its people. You... you showed me what it's like to be part of something bigger than myself."

Their shared glances held a universe of unspoken emotions. The triumph of the day was undeniable, a tangible victory that resonated throughout the hall. But for Clara and Jonah, it was also a quiet celebration of a different kind of victory, a personal triumph that had unfolded in the hushed moments between meetings, in the shared cups of coffee, in the silent understanding that had grown between them.

The Grand Hall, meticulously restored, was a physical manifestation of their shared effort. The pantry, overflowing with provisions, was a symbol of their collective compassion. But the true foundation, Clara realized, was being laid in the quiet space between them, a foundation built on trust, on shared values, and on a burgeoning love that felt as strong and as enduring as the ancient oak beams that held the hall aloft.

As the sun dipped lower, casting a golden hue over the scene, the sounds of laughter and conversation continued to fill the air. The children, their energy seemingly boundless, had discovered a forgotten corner of the hall, their game of hide-and-seek adding to the lively atmosphere. The aroma of coffee and freshly baked cookies, courtesy of Mrs. Gable, wafted through the air, a sweet invitation to linger.

Clara felt a profound sense of peace settle over her. The weight that had burdened her for so long had been lifted, replaced by a lightness that made her feel as though she could float. This wasn't just an ending to a chapter; it was the exhilarating beginning of a new story. A story that would be written, not in blueprints and budgets, but in shared moments, in quiet conversations, in the gentle unfolding of a love that had been nurtured in the heart of this revitalized community.

She turned her face up to Jonah, a soft smile gracing her lips. "Thank you," she murmured, the words inadequate to express the depth of her gratitude. "For everything."

Jonah's gaze softened, his eyes crinkling at the corners as he met her smile. He gently cupped her cheek, his thumb stroking her skin with a tenderness that made her breath catch. "It's just the beginning, Clara," he said, his voice low and resonant. "We've built something solid here. Something real."

And in the warm glow of the setting sun, surrounded by the vibrant heart of Cedar Ridge, Clara knew he was right. They had built a hall, a pantry, and a community. But more importantly, they had built a future, brick by beautiful brick, together. The shared triumph of the Grand Hall and Pantry was a glorious testament to their collective spirit, but for Clara, it was also the silent, profound affirmation of a love that had taken root in fertile ground, ready to grow and flourish for years to come. The laughter of her neighbors, the scent of home-baked goods, the comforting presence of Jonah by her side – it was all a symphony of belonging, a melody of shared success that resonated deep within her soul. The foundation was laid, and it was strong, built on a shared victory and the quiet promise of a love that had found its home in the heart of Cedar Ridge.

The last echoes of joyful conversation began to soften, the vibrant energy of the Grand Hall gradually receding like the tide. Families, their faces flushed with warmth and contentment, started to gather their belongings, the lingering scent of Mrs. Gable's cookies and Eleanor Vance's meticulously prepared punch still perfuming the air. Clara watched them go, a bittersweet ache in her chest, a feeling of profound satisfaction mingled with a gentle melancholy that such a beautiful day was drawing to a close. She found herself standing a little apart from the remaining crowd, Jonah's hand a steady presence in hers.

"It's almost over," she murmured, the words barely a whisper.

Jonah squeezed her hand, his thumb stroking the back of it in a slow, reassuring rhythm. "And what a day it was," he replied, his gaze sweeping over the room, now less a bustling hub and more a testament to a community's enduring spirit. The remnants of their celebration – scattered confetti, a few forgotten wildflowers, the warm glow of the setting sun painting long shadows across the floor – seemed to hold a quiet magic.

Clara leaned her head against his shoulder, the familiar comfort of his presence a welcome anchor. "I never imagined it would be like this," she confessed, her voice laced with wonder. "So... much. So much joy, so much hope. It feels like we didn't just save the hall, we resurrected something in all of us."

He shifted, turning his body slightly to face her, his eyes, warm and earnest, met hers. "You did, Clara. You reminded them. You reminded all of us what Cedar Ridge is truly made of. And you... you reminded me."

The word "me" hung in the air between them, a subtle shift in its meaning. It wasn't just about his role in the town, but about her impact on him, a truth that had been growing steadily between them, unspoken yet undeniable. Clara felt a blush warm her cheeks, a shy, hopeful flutter in her chest. Their shared journey, which had begun with the daunting task of saving the Grand Hall, had unexpectedly blossomed into something far more profound.

"It's funny, isn't it?" she mused, her gaze drifting to the now-empty stage. "When I first arrived, I saw a town in need of saving. I saw a project. I saw a challenge." She turned back to Jonah, a soft smile gracing her lips. "I never saw... this. I never saw *us*."

Jonah's hand tightened around hers, his gaze unwavering. "And I never saw it coming either," he admitted, a quiet honesty in his tone. "My future was... planned. Or at least, I thought it was. This town, my responsibilities here... I accepted them. I embraced them. But you, Clara... you walked in with all the force of a whirlwind, and suddenly, the landscape of my life shifted. The lines I'd drawn for myself, they blurred, and then they disappeared, replaced by possibilities I hadn't even dared to consider."

He paused, his thumb caressing her knuckles. "I knew I had to help you, that this project was important. I saw your passion, your determination. But somewhere along the way, that respect, that admiration... it deepened. It became something more. Something I hadn't anticipated, something I hadn't planned for, but something I found myself wanting to protect, to nurture."

Clara's heart swelled. The carefully constructed walls she had built around herself, walls designed to shield her from disappointment and heartbreak, were crumbling, not with a violent crash, but with a gentle, loving erosion. Jonah's words were not a grand declaration of love, but a quiet acknowledgment of a shared reality, a tender confession of an unplanned, yet deeply cherished, connection.

"It was never a plan, was it?" she whispered, her voice thick with emotion. "For either of us. I came here to fix a building, and you were here, already invested in its soul. And somewhere in the midst of it all, we found each other. We found... this." She gestured vaguely between them, encompassing the hall, the town, and the undeniable current that flowed between them.

"This is the beautiful kind of unplanned," Jonah agreed, his voice low and resonant. "The kind that surprises you, that catches you off guard, and then makes you realize it's exactly what you've been waiting for, even if you didn't know it. You brought a spark, Clara, and it ignited something that was already simmering beneath the surface. And now..." He trailed off, his gaze searching hers, a silent question and a silent promise in his eyes.

Clara met his gaze, her own mirroring the anticipation. "Now?" she prompted softly.

He stepped closer, his arm sliding around her waist, drawing her gently against him. The warmth of his body seeped through her clothes, a comforting, grounding heat. "Now, we figure out what 'now' looks like," he said, his voice a low murmur against her ear. "For Cedar Ridge, yes. But also... for us."

The unspoken question hung between them, a delicate dance of hope and vulnerability. The future, which had once loomed like a dark, uncertain cloud over Clara, now felt like an open road, stretching out before them, bathed in the golden light of shared accomplishment and burgeoning love.

Jonah's presence beside her, his strength and his steady affection, made that road seem not just navigable, but exciting.

"I've spent so long trying to control every aspect of my life," Clara confessed, her voice barely audible. "Trying to build a future that was perfectly planned, perfectly safe. And then life, or perhaps fate, intervened. It threw me into Cedar Ridge, into this project, and into... you." She tilted her head back, meeting his gaze. "And it turned out that the unplanned moments, the unexpected detours, were the ones that held the most beauty, the most promise."

Jonah's fingers traced the line of her jaw, a gentle, almost reverent touch. "That's the magic of Cedar Ridge, I think," he said softly. "It has a way of revealing what's truly important. It strips away the unnecessary, the superficial, and leaves you with the core. And for me, Clara, the core has become... you."

Her breath hitched. His words, so simple yet so profound, resonated deep within her soul. She had come to Cedar Ridge seeking a sense of purpose, a place to belong. She had found it, not just in the revitalized community and the restored hall, but in the quiet strength of Jonah's gaze, in the steady beat of his heart against hers.

"And you, Jonah," she replied, her voice trembling slightly. "You are my core now, too. You've become the foundation on which I feel I can build anything." The anxiety that had once been a constant companion had receded, replaced by a profound sense of peace and a quiet thrill of anticipation. She no longer feared the unknown; she embraced it, especially with Jonah by her side.

"We've laid a strong foundation, haven't we?" he murmured, his lips brushing against her temple. "This hall, this pantry, this community... they're all tangible proofs of what we can build when we work together.

But I think... I think the strongest foundation we've built is the one between us."

Clara closed her eyes, savoring the feeling of his arms around her, the steady rhythm of his breathing. The cheers of the crowd had faded, the conversations had quieted, but the warmth and the hope of the day lingered, a promise of brighter days to come. The future, once a daunting unknown, now felt like a shared adventure, a path they would walk together, hand in hand, ready to face whatever came next, together.

"It's more than I ever dreamed of," she whispered, her voice filled with a deep contentment. "A future I didn't plan for, but one I wouldn't trade for anything."

Jonah's embrace tightened, a silent affirmation of her words. "Nor would I," he replied, his voice a warm rumble that resonated through her. "It's our unplanned future, Clara. And I wouldn't have it any other way." The last rays of the sun cast a warm, amber glow across the empty hall, a silent witness to the quiet, profound beginning of their shared story, a story written not in ink and paper, but in shared glances, gentle touches, and the unwavering certainty of a love that had found its unexpected, beautiful home.

The lingering warmth of the Grand Hall's celebration seeped into Clara's bones, a comforting counterpoint to the quiet hum of her heart. As the last guests departed, their happy murmurs fading into the twilight, she remained beside Jonah, their hands still linked, a silent promise exchanged in the gentle pressure of their grip. The events of the day, the whirlwind of activity, the shared triumphs, and the collective outpouring of community spirit had been more than just a success; they were a revelation. She had arrived in Cedar Ridge with a singular focus, a meticulously crafted plan to restore a building. She had seen herself as the sole architect of this endeavor, a solitary force destined to conquer the task at hand. The thought of needing assistance, of admitting she couldn't do it all alone, had felt like a concession, a sign of her own inadequacy.

But Cedar Ridge, and especially Jonah, had taught her otherwise. The very act of allowing others in, of accepting the outstretched hands and shared efforts, had not diminished her strength but amplified it. It had been in those moments of shared labor, in the collaborative problem-solving, and in the quiet camaraderie that true resilience had blossomed. She remembered the initial hesitation, the ingrained instinct to guard her independence, to prove her self-sufficiency. Yet, with each project she had allowed Jonah and the townspeople to be a part of, a new understanding had dawned. Vulnerability, she discovered, wasn't a chasm to be avoided, but a bridge to be crossed, a pathway leading to deeper connection and shared purpose.

She turned her head, her gaze finding Jonah's. His eyes, usually alight with a steady, reassuring presence, held a new depth tonight, a reflection of the shared journey they had navigated. He was more than just a partner in saving the Grand Hall; he had become her partner in a far more profound sense. The notion of interdependence, once a foreign concept, now resonated with an almost sacred truth. It wasn't about relying on someone else to carry your burden, but about the beautiful dance of two souls, each strong in their own right, choosing to weave their strengths together, creating a tapestry far richer and more resilient than any single thread could ever be.

"I used to think asking for help was a weakness," Clara confessed, her voice soft, barely disturbing the quiet of the almost-empty hall. "Like admitting defeat before the battle even began. I've spent so much of my life trying to be the one in control, the one who had all the answers, the one who didn't need anyone." A small, self-deprecating smile touched her lips. "I was so wrong."

Jonah's thumb began to trace slow, soothing circles on the back of her hand. "And what changed your mind?" he asked, his voice a low, gentle rumble that vibrated through her. He wasn't just asking about the hall; he was asking about her.

"You," she answered simply, her gaze unwavering. "And Cedar Ridge. This town, it's built on interdependence, isn't it? People here lean on each other, support each other. It's not a burden; it's a strength. And you, Jonah... you showed me that firsthand. You never made me feel like I was asking for too much, or that my contributions weren't enough. You saw my vision, and you helped me bring it to life, not by taking over, but by being there, by collaborating, by believing in me even when I doubted myself."

She squeezed his hand, a surge of gratitude washing over her. "When I first arrived, I was so focused on the 'doing,' on the task, that I missed the 'being.' I missed the opportunity to truly connect, to let down my guard. Saving the hall became my sole focus, a way to prove my worth, perhaps. But in the process, I found something so much more valuable. I found you. I found a connection that feels... vital. Like breathing."

The word "vital" hung in the air, a testament to the lifeblood that had begun to flow between them. It wasn't just an attraction, or a shared goal; it was a fundamental need, a recognition of a missing piece that had been seamlessly filled. Jonah's presence had become as essential as the air she breathed, a constant source of strength and a gentle reminder that she no longer had to navigate the world alone.

"It's not about admitting defeat, Clara," Jonah said, his voice laced with a profound understanding. "It's about recognizing that we're stronger together. It's about understanding that your own well-being is intrinsically linked to the well-being of those around you, and vice versa. When you allowed us to help, you weren't just making the project easier; you were creating space for a deeper bond to form. You were allowing for the possibility of something beautiful to grow out of shared effort."

He paused, his gaze sweeping over the now-quiet hall, the remnants of their successful endeavor scattered like memories. "You came here to rebuild a structure, Clara, but you ended up rebuilding so much more. You rebuilt trust, you rebuilt hope, and you rebuilt... us. You showed me that even the most meticulously planned life can be enriched by the unexpected, by the shared journey, by the simple act of walking side-by-side with someone you care about."

Clara felt a warmth spread through her, a deep sense of peace settling within her chest. The constant hum of anxiety that had been her companion for so long had finally quieted, replaced by a profound sense of belonging. She had always believed that strength lay in self-reliance, in a stoic independence. But true strength, she now understood, lay in the courage to be vulnerable, to open herself up to the possibility of connection, to accept the quiet power of interdependence.

"It's like... finding a missing piece of yourself you didn't even know was gone," she mused, her fingers tracing the subtle lines on Jonah's hand. "I felt so complete in my independence, or at least, I thought I did. But it was a brittle kind of completeness, easily shattered. Now, with you, with this town... it feels like a different kind of completeness. A more resilient, more vibrant kind. It's a completeness that comes from sharing, from trusting, from knowing that someone has your back, not because they have to, but because they choose to."

She looked at him, her heart overflowing. "You've become my anchor, Jonah. My safe harbor. And in return, I hope I've been that for you too." The vulnerability in her voice was not a weakness, but a testament to the depth of her feelings. It was an honest offering, a laying bare of her soul that felt both terrifying and exhilarating.

Jonah's eyes softened, a gentle smile playing on his lips. "You've been more than that, Clara," he said, his voice low and sincere. "You've been the catalyst. You've shaken up my well-ordered world in the best possible way.

I was content, yes, but you've shown me what it means to be truly alive. You've awakened a part of me I didn't realize was dormant. And that, my dear Clara, is a gift beyond measure."

He brought her hand to his lips, pressing a tender kiss to her knuckles. "Interdependence isn't about losing yourself," he continued, his gaze holding hers. "It's about finding a deeper, more expansive version of yourself through connection. It's about realizing that the love and support you offer are mirrored back to you, creating a cycle of growth and fulfillment. You helped me see that. You helped me embrace that."

The quiet intimacy of the moment was broken only by the distant chirp of crickets and the gentle rustle of leaves outside. The Grand Hall, once a symbol of a community's fading glory, now stood as a beacon of its enduring spirit, a testament to what could be achieved when hearts and hands worked in unison. And between Clara and Jonah, a new foundation had been laid, not of wood and stone, but of shared dreams, mutual respect, and an unwavering, unconditional love.

"I used to believe that love was about finding someone to complete you," Clara said, her voice barely a whisper, the realization dawning on her with profound clarity. "But that's a flawed idea, isn't it? We're not meant to be completed by someone else. We're meant to be strengthened. We're meant to grow, together. And that growth, that shared journey... that's where the real magic happens."

She leaned her head against his shoulder, the familiar comfort of his presence a soothing balm to her soul. "You didn't complete me, Jonah. You expanded me. You showed me the possibilities that lay beyond my carefully constructed walls. You made me realize that the most profound connections are born not from perfect independence, but from a willing, heartfelt interdependence."

Jonah wrapped an arm around her, drawing her closer. "And you, Clara," he murmured, his voice filled with a quiet reverence, "you've shown me the beauty of letting go of control, of embracing the unexpected. You've shown me that true strength lies not in standing alone, but in standing together, hand in hand, facing whatever the future may hold. We built this hall, brick by brick, board by board. But we built something far more significant, something that will endure long after the paint fades and the renovations are forgotten. We built a partnership, a love, a future."

The peace that settled over Clara was unlike anything she had ever known. It was the deep, abiding peace of a soul that had finally found its home, its purpose, its belonging. The journey had been arduous, filled with unexpected twists and turns, but it had led her here, to this moment, to this man, to this profound understanding of what it meant to truly live and love. She was no longer a solitary figure striving against the odds; she was part of something larger, something richer, something infinitely more beautiful – a shared life, built on the solid, unshakable foundation of interdependence and love. And as she looked up at Jonah, she knew, with a certainty that resonated through her very being, that this was just the beginning of their greatest masterpiece.

The doors of the Grand Hall, now lovingly restored, swung open not just to welcome back the townsfolk, but to usher in a new era for Cedar Ridge. The scent of fresh paint mingled with the subtle aroma of baked goods, a testament to the dual purpose the revitalized space was now embracing. It was no longer just a grand old building; it was a living, breathing testament to the town's resilience and Clara's transformation. The polished wood floors, once dusty and neglected, now gleamed under the warm glow of new lighting, reflecting the eager faces of residents who gathered for the inaugural town meeting in their newly christened Community Hall & Pantry.

Clara stood beside Jonah, her hand finding his as a familiar, comforting gesture. The nervousness that had once plagued her, the deep-seated fear of not being enough, had receded, replaced by a quiet confidence, a deep-seated joy in her role within this vibrant community. She was no longer the outsider, the lone architect of a restoration project. She was a partner, an integral thread woven into the very fabric of Cedar Ridge. The transformation had been as much internal as it had been external. The Grand Hall's renovation had been the catalyst, but the true rebuilding had happened within her heart, nurtured by the warmth and unwavering support of the people she had come to love.

The meeting began with Mayor Thompson's booming voice, filled with genuine pride as he lauded the collective effort that had brought the hall back to life. He spoke of Clara's vision and dedication, but more importantly, he highlighted the town's unified spirit, the countless hours of volunteer work, and the generous donations that had made the project a reality. Clara's cheeks flushed with a warmth that had nothing to do with the summer evening. She was no longer seeking validation through achievement; she found it in the shared sense of accomplishment, in the tangible proof that her efforts, combined with those of others, could create something truly meaningful.

"And now," Mayor Thompson continued, his gaze sweeping across the assembled crowd, "we have the pleasure of officially opening the Cedar Ridge Community Pantry, housed right here within our revitalized hall. This initiative, spearheaded by Clara and supported by so many of you, is more than just a place to receive assistance; it's a symbol of our commitment to looking after one another, ensuring that no one in our town goes without."

A ripple of applause went through the hall, a wave of approval that washed over Clara and solidified her sense of belonging. The pantry, a space that had been carved out of one of the hall's larger rooms, was stocked with donations from local farms, bakeries, and individual households. Shelves were lined with canned goods, fresh produce, and loaves of bread, all meticulously organized by a team of volunteers Clara had helped to train. It was a small but vital resource, a testament to the town's commitment to mutual support.

After the official proceedings, the hall buzzed with activity. The meeting transitioned into a lively social gathering, the air filled with laughter and conversation. Children chased each other across the dance floor, their joyous shouts echoing through the vast space. Adults mingled, catching up after the intense period of renovation, their faces alight with a renewed sense of community pride. Clara found herself drawn into conversations, not with the guarded reserve she once possessed, but with an open heart and a genuine smile. She spoke with Mrs. Gable about her prize-winning preserves, with young Timmy O'Malley about his aspirations of becoming a blacksmith, and with old Mr. Henderson about the best way to coax tomatoes from the soil.

Jonah, ever her steady presence, remained by her side, his hand occasionally brushing hers, a silent affirmation of their partnership. He had been instrumental in not only the physical restoration of the hall but in fostering her integration into the town. He had introduced her, vouched for her, and, most importantly, had shown her the deep well of kindness and generosity that characterized Cedar Ridge. He had a way of making her feel seen, understood, and cherished, a feeling that had once seemed an impossible dream.

Later that evening, as the crowds began to thin, Clara and Jonah found themselves alone in the hushed grandeur of the hall. Moonlight streamed through the tall, arched windows, casting long shadows across the floor. The lingering scent of cinnamon and wood polish filled the air. It was a moment of quiet intimacy, a stark contrast to the vibrant energy of earlier.

"It's... more than I ever imagined," Clara whispered, her gaze sweeping across the transformed space. The weight of her past anxieties seemed to lift with each breath she took in this place, a place she had helped to breathe new life into.

Jonah turned to her, his eyes reflecting the moonlight. "It's the heart of Cedar Ridge, Clara," he said, his voice a low, resonant melody. "And you've become its heartbeat."

The words settled over her like a warm embrace. She no longer felt like an outsider looking in. She was a part of it all. The skills she had honed, the determination that had driven her, had found a purpose far greater than she had ever conceived. It wasn't just about restoring a building; it was about restoring hope, about fostering connection, about creating a space where lives could be enriched and supported.

The Community Hall & Pantry quickly became a hub of activity. The following Saturday, a vibrant farmers' market sprang to life in the main hall. Local farmers, their stalls laden with colorful produce, artisanal cheeses, and handmade crafts, filled the space with a lively energy. Clara, with a newfound enthusiasm, found herself chatting with the vendors, sampling their wares, and enjoying the simple pleasure of being a part of this bustling marketplace. She even managed to secure a small corner to sell some of her own handcrafted pottery, a venture she had been hesitant to pursue before. The positive reception from her neighbors, the genuine appreciation for her creations, filled her with a quiet pride she hadn't anticipated.

Beyond the market, the hall became a venue for educational workshops. Clara, drawing on her expertise, offered a series of classes on home repair and renovation, sharing her knowledge with the eager residents. She taught basic plumbing, simple electrical fixes, and the art of restoring antique furniture. The workshops were always well-attended, filled with a mix of aspiring DIYers and seasoned handymen eager to share their own tips.

The collaborative spirit was infectious, with participants often forming impromptu study groups, helping each other tackle projects around their own homes. Clara reveled in this exchange of knowledge, realizing that teaching others also deepened her own understanding and appreciation for her craft.

Jonah, meanwhile, used the hall for community meetings related to local conservation efforts and town planning. He had a natural ability to facilitate discussions, to find common ground amongst diverse opinions. Clara often attended these meetings, not out of obligation, but out of a genuine interest in the future of the town she had come to call home. She found herself contributing ideas, her unique perspective often sparking new solutions to long-standing challenges. Her voice, once hesitant and unsure, now carried a quiet authority, a reflection of the confidence she had gained.

The pantry, under Clara's continued guidance, expanded its reach. She worked tirelessly with a dedicated team of volunteers, organizing donation drives, establishing partnerships with local food banks, and ensuring that the pantry remained a welcoming and dignified space for those in need. She understood that the pantry was more than just a distribution center; it was a lifeline, a tangible expression of the community's care and compassion. She often spent her afternoons there, sorting donations, chatting with recipients, and offering a listening ear. The gratitude she received, the stories of how the pantry had made a difference in their lives, fueled her commitment and reaffirmed the profound purpose of her work.

One afternoon, while organizing a shipment of donated books for the pantry's small lending library, Clara found herself reflecting on the remarkable journey she had undertaken. It had been a journey of restoration, not just for the Grand Hall, but for herself. The solitary, driven woman who had arrived in Cedar Ridge with a singular focus on a project had blossomed into an integrated, contributing member of a community.

The fear of vulnerability had been replaced by the strength of connection. The need for control had given way to the joy of collaboration.

Jonah entered the pantry, a gentle smile gracing his lips as he watched her. He carried a small box, his movements unhurried and familiar. "Still at it, I see," he said, his voice warm with affection.

Clara turned, her eyes sparkling. "Someone has to make sure these books find good homes," she replied, a playful lilt in her voice. "Besides, it's rewarding work."

He set the box down beside her, his gaze lingering on her. "You've done more than just organize books, Clara. You've organized hope. You've built a sanctuary."

She felt a familiar warmth spread through her at his words, the deep satisfaction of being seen and appreciated. "We've built it, Jonah," she corrected softly, emphasizing the 'we.' "Together. This whole place... it's a testament to what happens when we choose to build something more than just structures. We build relationships, we build trust, we build a future."

He reached out, his fingers gently brushing a stray strand of hair from her cheek. "And you, my dear Clara, have built something extraordinary within yourself. You've shown me the true meaning of strength, not in standing alone, but in the courage to stand together."

Their shared work had deepened their bond, forging a partnership that extended far beyond the walls of the Community Hall. They were a team, navigating the complexities of life and community with a shared vision and an unwavering love. The Grand Hall, once a symbol of a town's potential, now stood as a beacon of its thriving present and its promising future, a testament to the power of community, connection, and the quiet, profound strength found in interdependence. Clara, no longer defined by her solitary pursuits, had found her purpose, her place, and her love, all within the vibrant heart of Cedar Ridge. She was home.

The velvety cloak of night had settled over Cedar Ridge, a gentle embrace after a day filled with the vibrant hum of community life. Stars, like scattered diamonds, began to prick the inky canvas overhead, their soft luminescence mirroring the quiet glow that had settled within Clara's heart. She walked hand-in-hand with Jonah, their fingers intertwined, a silent language of comfort and connection passing between them. The worn leather of his hand was a familiar anchor, a grounding presence as they ambled along the familiar, tree-lined path leading away from the bustling Community Hall. The evening air, still carrying the faint scent of woodsmoke and blooming honeysuckle, was filled with a profound sense of peace, a quiet promise of the future that hung unspoken between them.

It wasn't a sudden, earth-shattering revelation that had brought them to this juncture. Their journey had been a more organic unfolding, a slow bloom nurtured by shared purpose, mutual respect, and the unwavering foundation of trust they had painstakingly built. Each shared success at the hall, each late-night conversation delving into dreams and vulnerabilities, each quiet moment of understanding had woven a stronger, more resilient thread into the tapestry of their relationship. It was a love that had not been sought, but rather discovered, like finding a hidden treasure in the most unexpected of places.

Clara's gaze drifted from the star-dusted sky to Jonah's profile, etched against the deepening twilight. His jawline was strong, his brow furrowed slightly in contemplation, a familiar expression that always stirred a tender ache within her. He hadn't showered her with grand pronouncements or sweeping romantic gestures. Instead, he had offered something far more precious: consistent, unwavering support, a willingness to listen without judgment, and the quiet strength of his presence. He had seen her at her most uncertain, her most flawed, and had loved her not in spite of those things, but perhaps, in part, because of them. He had embraced the entirety of her, the artist and the architect, the woman who had once felt adrift and the woman who was now firmly rooted.

"It's been a good day," Jonah said, his voice a low rumble that vibrated through her hand. He squeezed her fingers gently. "A really good day."

Clara nodded, her heart swelling. "It has. Seeing everyone so... connected. The pantry overflowing, the workshops buzzing. It feels like everything we hoped for, and more." She paused, her thumb tracing the back of his hand. "It feels like a new foundation."

The word hung in the air, resonating with a depth that transcended their shared project. The Community Hall and Pantry, their shared creation, was indeed a new foundation for Cedar Ridge, a tangible symbol of renewal and shared purpose. But it was also a foundation for *them*. The collaborative spirit, the trust, the deep understanding forged through shared challenges and triumphs had laid the groundwork for something equally profound in their personal lives.

"More than just for the town," Jonah murmured, as if he had plucked the thought directly from her mind. He turned his head, his eyes meeting hers, and in their depths, she saw a reflection of her own nascent hopes. "For us, too."

A soft smile curved Clara's lips. She didn't need grand declarations. The quiet assurance in his gaze, the gentle pressure of his hand, the shared rhythm of their steps – these were the promises that mattered. They were the silent affirmations of a love that had bloomed organically, a testament to the enduring strength of the human heart when it's open to connection and willing to build something beautiful together.

"I used to think," Clara began, her voice soft, almost a whisper, "that my purpose was tied to creating something lasting, something beautiful and functional. A building, a design, something tangible that could stand the test of time." She glanced at the hall, now a distant, warm glow behind them. "And this project... it was that, in so many ways. But it became more."

Jonah stopped walking, gently pulling her to a halt beside him beneath the shade of an old oak tree. He turned to face her fully, his hands framing her face, his thumbs brushing lightly against her cheekbones. The moonlight caught the silver streaks in his hair, lending him an almost ethereal quality.

"What did it become, Clara?" he asked, his gaze earnest.

"It became a testament," she breathed, her eyes searching his. "A testament to what happens when people come together. When they trust each other. When they believe in something bigger than themselves. And for me," she added, her voice catching slightly, "it became the place where I found... where I found you. And where I found myself, truly."

The vulnerability in her voice was met not with fear or hesitation, but with a profound understanding. Jonah leaned in, his forehead resting against hers, their breaths mingling. The world outside their small, intimate space seemed to fade away, leaving only the quiet thrum of their hearts beating in unison.

"You found yourself because you opened yourself up, Clara," he said softly. "You didn't just restore a building. You restored a part of yourself that was hidden. You let Cedar Ridge in, and you let yourself be seen. And that's where true strength lies, not in solitude, but in the courage to connect."

His words were a balm to her soul, a confirmation of the quiet shifts that had been happening within her. The fear of judgment, the ingrained habit of self-reliance, had begun to recede, replaced by a growing sense of belonging, of being cherished for who she was, not for what she achieved. Jonah had been instrumental in this transformation, his unwavering belief in her a constant source of encouragement. He had seen the spark of resilience within her, the quiet determination that had brought her to Cedar Ridge in the first place, and he had fanned it into a steady flame.

"I never imagined this," she confessed, her voice thick with emotion. "I came here with blueprints and a budget. I thought I was coming to build a hall. I had no idea I was also building... this. Us." She gestured vaguely between them, a soft, genuine smile gracing her lips.

Jonah's smile mirrored hers, a warmth that radiated from him, encompassing her. "Sometimes, the most important foundations are the ones we don't even realize we're laying. They're built with everyday moments, with shared laughter, with quiet acts of kindness. They're built with love." He gently brushed a stray curl from her temple, his touch sending a shiver down her spine. "And this love, Clara, it's not something I take lightly. It's been earned. By you. By us."

The word "earned" resonated deeply. Their love hadn't been a whirlwind romance, a passionate, impulsive connection. It had been a slow, steady climb, built on a bedrock of shared experiences and mutual respect. They had navigated the complexities of rebuilding a community, and in doing so, they had navigated the landscape of their own hearts. There were no lingering doubts, no unanswered questions, only a quiet, profound certainty that this was right. This was real. This was meant to be.

"It feels like the most beautiful kind of earned," Clara whispered, leaning into his touch. "It feels like coming home, not just to a town, but to a feeling. A feeling of being truly seen, truly accepted."

"And you are," Jonah promised, his voice low and sincere. "You are seen, Clara. And you are loved. More than you know."

The stars above seemed to shine a little brighter, as if in agreement. The gentle breeze rustling through the leaves of the old oak tree whispered a secret of enduring love, a promise of futures yet to be written. They stood there for a long moment, suspended in time, two souls who had found their anchor in each other, their shared purpose leading them to a love that was not only deeply needed but also beautifully, profoundly earned.

He lowered his hands from her face, but his gaze never left hers. He reached out again, taking her hand, and together, they continued their walk, their steps in perfect synchronicity. The path ahead was still uncertain, as all paths in life inevitably were, but they would face it together. With each step, they were not just walking away from the Community Hall; they were walking towards a shared future, a future built on the quiet promise of their love, a love that had taken root and blossomed in the heart of Cedar Ridge, a love that was as strong and as enduring as the very foundations they had helped to lay.

The night air, once just a gentle cloak, now felt like a silken embrace, a testament to the quiet beauty of a love that had been patiently, wonderfully earned. The stars overhead bore witness to their journey, to the quiet promise that hung in the gentle night air, a promise not of grand declarations, but of a deep, abiding understanding, a love that had grown organically from shared purpose and mutual respect, a love that had found its truest, most beautiful expression in the quiet heart of Cedar Ridge.

Glossary

Cedar Ridge: A small, tight-knit town known for its picturesque landscape and strong sense of community.

Community Hall: A central gathering place for the town, meticulously restored to serve as a hub for events and services.

Food Pantry: A crucial resource established within the Community Hall to support local families in need.

Honeysuckle: A fragrant vine, often associated with summer evenings and the charm of rural settings.